"In Memory of David J Andrews

11.4.56 – 24.2.17

Much loved and missed."

BEYOND NATIONS

A new novel from David J Andrews

Copyright 2018 © by David J Andrews

ISBN: 978-1-911124-77-1

*I know my fate, one day there will be associated with my name
something frightful, of a crisis like no other on earth*

Frederick Nietzsche - Philosopher

*Ambition leads me not only farther than any other man
has been before me, but as far as I think I can go*

James Cook – Explorer

To

my dear parents,
you taught me everything that was good

PRELUDE

Venice, 1432

The battered Chinese flagship made its way carefully towards the jetty, manoeuvring itself into a suitable position adjacent to the historic St Mark's Square. At over 137 metres long and over 55 metres wide it was nearly twice the size of the equivalent European ships of the day, and dwarfed all the other seagoing vessels as it slowly navigated its way to anchor. On the horizon other Chinese vessels stood at anchor lazily riding the lagoon waters as if in a slow motion dance. The locals had been informed that the ships came in peace but still stared in awe and fear at the sheer size, as the ship's crew returned appreciative stares at the ornate Doges Palace glistening in the early morning sun. They had never seen anything like it in their travels around the globe, a veritable floating city.

Orders rang out across the ship as the crew tethered large ropes to docks more accustomed to holding the ornate gondolas, and they slowly made preparations to embark. Venice in the early morning sun was at its best, with the water providing a uniform contrast to the rainbow colours of the buildings. It exuded the wealth that had derived from its two centuries rule as the most dominant sea power on earth. The Grand Canal to the sailors left led up to the Rialto, the heartland of the trading empire whilst to their right the gates of the forbidding Arsenal stood dominating the skyline, the most advanced shipbuilding dockyard in its time. Had they been allowed to enter through its gates they would have seen the engine room of the empire, production lines of wooden ships on a conveyor belt of fear, Venetian trade and wealth a direct result of the ships mass produced here. In front of the sailors were narrow canals, a myriad of water borne craft making their journeys oblivious to their important visitors. To the Chinese sailors it was akin to arriving on another planet, and they shook their heads in awe.

Their Admiral was a tall Muslim called Zheng He, who gloried in the title of the three jewelled eunuch. He was the pre-eminent navigator of his age, traversing the known world in his nations desire to achieve non-violent global domination. Each of his voyages had lasted around three years as carefully choreographed displays of power.

Zheng took in the scene with interest, seeing it as the epitome of how trade could transform a country, a demonstration of what was needed in his own homeland. Pragmatic trade was the answer, not the latest inward looking isolationism and militaristic behaviour his Emperor was increasingly showing and that had necessitated his recall home. He was already destined to his place in history as China's greatest naval commander, a man who imagined a new world of global trade and had set out consciously to fashion it. Strangely for an admiral he had been raised in China's hinterland, the mountainous heart several weeks' travel from the closest port. After being taken captive by the Mongols, ritually castrated, and trained at court as an imperial eunuch, he had grown in influence under the ambitious Emperor Zhu Di. He had been selected to lead one of the most powerful naval forces ever built and China's declaration to the foreign devils that it was they who were the subservient ones. After circumnavigating the globe he was on his way home for the last time, calling in the heartland of maritime Venice to meet the ancestor of a man revered in China for his friendship with the great Kublai Khan. Then he would take his final voyage before retirement, his work and his vision completed. The countries beyond the horizon and at the end of the earth have all become our subjects, he wrote in his journal. He had also developed his own ideas and agenda, however, a vision secret to him, a vision that he dared share with no one, a vision that involved the successful deliverance of three valuable artefacts, and artefacts that were in their own right his legacy to future generations. The final leg of his legacy was his chance to make a sustainable difference, something not associated with the new Chinese Emperors, who only thought in simple of terms of superiority. No, his vision was something for the good of humanity. As he travelled direct from the island of La Gomera in the Atlantic, his experiment had already started, now he needed help to transform it into reality. He signalled to his Captain and made ready to go ashore, making sure that his entourage was alert.

Niccolo Polo, the grandson of Marco Polo, watched as the ship completed its mooring before making his way down to the prearranged meeting point. He had been excited ever since the secret request had been delivered, his own chance to live history and make his illustrious ancestor proud. His childhood had been dominated by the many tales of how his grandfather Marco over 100 years earlier had travelled to Asia and met the great Khan during his wondrous adventures, including his attempt to facilitate a meeting for Kublai with the Pope. Now it was his turn to try and unify east and west, to surpass his grandfather's achievements. He smiled as the aged Chinese Admiral and his interpreter were carried forward in an ornate litter to the main reception room of the Doge's Palace. Niccolo was using the Doge's own rooms, which in itself was testament to the power of the Polo name in Venice. The room was covered in gold leaf, testament to the great wealth of the Empire and designed to impress visitors. Niccolo nodded in greeting as the aged Admiral was brought slowly into the room and gestured to his two aides to help. The Admiral looked up for the first time and smiled.

"An impressive room," he intoned in passable Latin.

"For an auspicious occasion," replied Niccolo, as his interpreter announced the translation from mandarin.

"Thank you for agreeing to meet me."

"You are a friend of Venice, you have travelled far."

"A short journey from La Gomera," replied Zheng through the interpreter. "The last stop before returning home."

"Your fleet on the horizon, over a hundred vessels, is very impressive and a demonstration of Chinese power and wealth."

"Many large ships for practical reasons, and resistance to the world's climates. I come in peace, not to demonstrate our power," continued Zheng. "You are a man I know I can trust. My travelling has given me a better perception of other races and human affairs outside the Chinese Emperor's court. I have become a citizen of the world and feel many are not so concerned."

"Concerned in what way?" asked Niccolo, grateful that the old man was keen to talk and so different from other taciturn Chinese.

"I have been fortunate to travel the world and have seen a great deal that makes me believe nation states and religion breed mistrust."

"Structure and faith bring great comfort," commented Niccolo, "particularly religion."

"Of course, but I am a pragmatist. You will be aware of the Khans' philosophy, the Mongols from Genghis' time practiced religious tolerance or shamanism where each is entitled to their own beliefs."

"There is merit in what you say. The Catholic Church is very rigid, but what else is there?"

"There are other ways, ways that can be engineered. I am not a man who believes in the chaos of our existence, it must have a purpose, an engineered purpose."

"How can I help?"

"I have a proposition for Venice, one that will be to its advantage and ensure your sustainable success, a great secret to share with you as the grandson of our greatest ally Marco Polo, a good friend of Kublai Khan."

"A great secret," repeated Niccolo fascinated. "You have my full attention," he said listening intently and with rising astonishment at the translated words until finally the old man sat back, exhausted. "It is true that travel broadens the mind and in your case you have provided great insight into men's affairs. I am sure I can speak for the Doge in saying we can reach a common understanding."

"What good is wealth if it is not used for good causes? We cannot take all the gold in the world with us to the next life," said Zheng quietly.

"True," acknowledged Niccolo, thinking the Doge would have to be persuaded on that, yet he was sure Zheng's story would be well received. "You are a visionary, a man who wants to make a difference, rise above the short term desires of others."

"As with your ancestor Marco," replied Zheng. "Our secret will underpin our nations long after we are gone; such a secret has of course to be protected from those who would misuse it."

"How do you propose to arrange such protection?" asked Niccolo, intrigued.

"La Gomera sits on the very western edge of our world, a stronghold where such defence can sit well away from any nation states direct influence, an island in the middle of nowhere, an island holding our secret safe."

"Protected?"

"Not by force, secret powers do not require such just like your Medici's and Calvi's. See, I have read my history," smiled Zheng through his interpreter.

"And you want the Doge's support for this arrangement to preserve this secret."

"It will make your empire truly sustainable led by a trusted few who when the time comes will rise to acknowledge the truth of what I tell you. In the short term your Venetian trading empire will grow supported by our pact spreading influence by trade, not force."

"And this body of wisdom in La Gomera will be called what?"

"A meritocracy called the Elders, a body of the smartest who are capable of managing the secret."

"This secret, is it a physical thing?"

"It's a secret to be treasured; one that I wish to bequeath to future generations, but unfortunately in the wrong hands it is as dangerous as it is beneficial."

"It brings tangible benefits?"

"Riches of the pocket and mind beyond the experience of anyone and guarded by these Elders."

"What do you want from me?"

"We must be alone, a different room please, it's not secret here."

"I have a confession," said Niccolo, rising, "the Doge has been listening to this conversation through our network of listening posts installed as a security precaution against Genoese spies."

"Does he not trust an old man," smiled Zheng, amused at the subterfuge.

"Precautions come with power and success; he has already indicated that he is in favour of your proposal," replied Niccolo, acknowledging the nodding head of an aide who had briefly appeared from the Doge's office, the prearranged signal that all was well.

"Then I can see my legacy is secure," replied Zheng, his old mind alive and excited. The artefacts had provided the tangible signs but now it was time for him to go home. He had carried out his instructions to the letter; granted, he had adapted them a little, but all for the good of humanity. Zheng was very wary of the gathering forces of darkness in his homeland, forces that could destroy all his hard work. He had his private meeting with Niccolo and then left, satisfied.

Unseen by both men as they made their respective ways was a small wiry Chinese man, a non-descript servant dressed in a sailor's outfit of the lowest order. On Zheng's ship for many months he had had his own agenda, and now took the opportunity to record what he had heard as carefully as he could. His name was Jainyu, which translated as building the universe'. His eyes gleamed as he went to the harbour front, his eyes intense and not those of a man dulled by being obsequious. This was a man of standing and a man on a mission; he had what he needed and would report back to the Chosen Ones. It had started.

Niccolo watched as the old man was carried down to his ship, and he reflected on the event. Zheng had achieved a great deal, but it was only the tip of the iceberg. He had always believed you needed to understand the full picture before making decisions of magnitude. No picture was bigger than the one he had discovered on the Silk Road as he travelled around Asia, a picture that in the wrong hands could spell doom. He talked briefly to his Doge then headed south on the road to Rome. Later, he heard that Zheng had perished at sea off the Indian coast. It had been a precipitous and fateful meeting.

Gibraltar, 1805

The famous limestone rock stood majestically against the skyline, a monument to the amazing strength of the millions of dead animals' remains bonded over centuries. It was a particularly welcome sight to the exhausted British sailors of Nelson's fleet as they made their way into the bay after the momentous sea battle at Cape Trafalgar. The Flagship Victory itself led the fleet limping into the docks carrying the body of its greatest hero, Horatio Nelson, encased in a large barrel of rum below deck. He had died a hero, stalking the decks in full uniform and encouraging his men to victory as their flagship had pierced the French and Spanish lines. The effect of his bold plan and his personal leadership had been dramatic, as the smaller English navy triumphed against the large combined Spanish and French fleet condemning Bonaparte's naval ambitions to ruins.

The two silhouetted figures surveyed the dramatic sight at the large dock under the shadow of Gibraltar's cliff. They watched from the Spanish port of Algeciras as the fleet slowly came around towards its moorings. One was Edward Tilley, a British banker, and the other was Carlos Vasquez, Spain's most senior state banker. They represented the most powerful economic forces on the continent and were well aware of how perilous their position would have been had the French won at Trafalgar. Both men now knew that the dictator's fleet had been sunk and Spain could successfully prosecute a land war against the French invaders by helping the Duke of Wellington on the Peninsular. They smiled in relief knowing that their huge gamble had paid off; if the French had won they would have been arrested and put to death as traitors. Now they would be seen as heroes, rescuing vast sums of gold bullion and gems from under the clutches of the French occupying regime. Such was the lottery of war.

"We did it Carlos, we did it."

"Close Edward, dammed close but a gamble that paid off, all thanks to the Battle of Cape Santa Maria last year and the treasure we appropriated at a time when our countries weren't even at war, a masterstroke of yours," smiled Carlos.

"Dear old Brigadier Don Jose de Bustamante and his frigates from Montevideo," murmured Edward, "treasure brought over here unloaded secretly, then the frigates sunk."

"Right under the French eyes," smiled Carlos thinking back to the frantic activity a year ago.

"All authorised secretly by our governments at our personal risk and one that will now pay dividends as the20 tonnes of gold on the frigates was a fraction of the real amount. The Mercedes frigate alone was carrying 30 tonnes of bullion when she went down, over 100 tonnes salvaged and hidden, to say nothing of the diamonds."

"Droits of the Crown," smiled Carlos, referring to the legalities of taking ownership of the gold when countries were not technically at war, in effect the British stealing the treasure. Their planning of the proceeds had been handled professionally to hide it as the French approached. A clever manoeuvre that had effectively ensured a hundred tonnes of gold and gems, along with four Spanish frigates, had disappeared as if they had never existed. The two men sat on a fortune hidden in the Spanish countryside, and the other men involved in hiding the treasure were killed, a necessary but sad precaution.

"We need to discuss the next steps over a celebration drink," smiled Edward, turning away and indicating the horse drawn coach as they headed back down to their carriages Edward outlining the next steps to Carlos. There was no time to lose if they were not to fall victim to the strong French spy network in the area to arrange for safe passage of the treasure back to Britain. It wouldn't be easy, as the vast treasure was much further to the east in the province of Almeria and spies were watching many unconvinced that the large amount of bullion had been lost. Rumours were rife that it had been spirited away into hiding.

"A drink, my friend," said Edward as they reached the old coaching inn sitting down in the corner with their backs to the wall from force of habit giving a good view of the other clientele, old habits dying hard. They relaxed for the first time in days and opened a bottle of the house's finest wine before becoming absorbed in a parchment in front of them, so much so that neither saw a large lady amble towards them. Edward and Carlos both looked up in unison as her shadow appeared, the last sight they saw before sharpened blades pierced their throats.

Paraguay – Present day

The heat was unbearable as the five men made their way carefully along the difficult narrow path through the jungle. The travellers were weary, having been walking for six days after a difficult sea journey, all kept going by the lure and promise of what awaited them. They shared a common faith and conviction that had led them to give up their previous lives. Each had told their families that they were going away for some time. Each knew that they may never return but that they were about to enter the most exciting time of their lives.

After trekking for another five hours from the river, trying to avoid the various insects and mosquitos, they finally entered a clearing and saw the iconic building they had spent much of their lives imagining. It was a building that was ingrained in their memories, a building that symbolised everything that their nation had alone represented. They broke into excited chatter as they reached the front door and an old man appeared.

"We have been expecting you."

"A long and difficult journey," said the leader of the men as they made their way inside and gratefully sipped the proffered drinks of water. "We are here now and ready to do our part."

"You will meet the great leader, protocol demands the correct greeting is '*the philosopher,*' and will only speak when spoken to and will not contradict," continued the man carefully leading them through. "The Philosopher is a direct descendant of Nietzsche so pay due homage."

"I can't believe we have finally arrived," exclaimed the smallest of the men as they were ushered into the grand room. "What a fantastic place, such ornaments."

"Welcome to you all," boomed a voice. "You are our disciples and shall have your rewards for the loyalty you have shown, men of the faith. Through your long journey you have demonstrated that you possess the necessary determination and strength, the journey was your test, you have passed by being here."

"We are honoured and have revered you all our lives, we are hear ready to begin the great fight," said the eldest man of the group.

"I am touched by your passion, gentlemen. The great adventure has started, an adventure that will turn you all into rich men and transform our world just as our ancestors intended it over a century ago. Tomorrow the great service starts, so now go and get some rest before dinner is served and we will arrange for some companionship."

As they filed out the Philosopher turned to the video screen to speak. "We are ready; our ancestors' dreams will be fulfilled."

"And what of the treasure you talked of, where is that?" asked the Germanic voice on the video link. "The Paraguay treasure, as I believe it is known?"

"The ancient treasure of President Lopez and his mistress stealing into the night in 1870 loaded with the entire treasury contents bankrupting his country."

"Yes the same, I am told 600 carts of gold from the vaults of the capital were dumped near Las Lomas, its location known only to you."

"Yes, it will finance Tutulus, shift the emphasis away from ZTW."

"Good to hear, the Teacher and the Professor were unwise. The world is about to change beyond recognition; we now have the necessary tools in place to ensure our new project, just as our forefathers predicted."

"Germania was more than just a dream," espoused the Philosopher grandly, "it was a great idea ahead of its time, the foundations of our new world."

"Absolutely. The Chosen Ones are ready; the loss of two of our group is of little consequence."

Chapter 1

Present Day

Bequia, Grenadines

The old lady went along the beach at dawn break, as she had done for every day she could remember. It was her favourite time of day because it felt like it was all hers, like the world was all hers. She loved the peace and tranquillity, and frowned when in the distance she saw something that looked like a dead seal, or a small whale. She made her way gingerly forwards, knowing that it was a foreign object to her beach. Five metres away from it she gasped in horror, fighting back the nausea as she saw that it was a human body, a young girl laid on her front at an unnatural angle, naked to the waist. She stifled a scream, feeling unsteady on her feet as she saw the girl's back was criss-crossed with what looked like whip marks.

Zelda Higuaín had been a top American journalist until it all went wrong. It was a combination of a disastrous personal life and alcohol, the perennial enemy of her job. She was freelance because no one would employ her, but she was good at her job and onto something big. She had heard of the body and flew straight down, her instincts telling her this was the missing girl for whom she had been searching for over a week. The poor girl had only being twenty, a native of

Antiqua where Zelda herself was based. Her name was Jolene Taylor, of that there was no doubt, as the distinctive birth mark on the right arm proved. Destined for university and extraordinarily pretty, it was a tragedy and no random killing, of that Zelda was sure. The poor girl had been repeatedly raped and strangled, and the inquest also said she'd been plied with copious quantities of heroin. Zelda cursed at the waste and determined she would find the killers.

North Queensland, Australia

Sergei heaved his not inconsiderable bulk into the helicopter after it had landed with a discernible thump onto the Sheraton hotel landing pad. He wasn't going to enjoy the next couple of hours but he had no choice. A rotund and overweight Russian, he had made his fortune in the remote north east of his country near Vladivostok before dedicating himself to the cause of the Elders. He grimaced as they jerked up into the air heading for the Danetree rainforest, and nodded curtly across to his colleague Anton. He hated flying in helicopters, but there was no option as time was of the essence, others were on the move and he had to act quickly before the enemy found his location. He studied the literature on his seat, seeing the Skyrail Rainforest cableway before the pilot pointed to it. That's what they were looking for and he grunted in satisfaction as they altered course. He noticed the Kuranda rail line in the distance as they came in, and recalled the lake below was replete with crocodiles before they swung in low over the treetops. At over twenty stones he couldn't move quickly, and struggled to get himself into the small seat, the seatbelt cutting into his shoulders his knuckles white as they soared up over the green dense mass below. The pilot gestured down to the trees below as they skimmed over tropical greenery that looked much the same as it would have been a thousand years earlier. It was said to be the world's oldest rainforest, and also its most deadly.

At 62 years old, and sporting a large white bushy beard, Sergei Rostov extolled an air of authority bolstered by years as owner of a Russian metals conglomerate. Following his support of the Elders during a terrifying Mongolian ordeal he was about to be confirmed as their new President, and yet all that would be worthless if he didn't act quickly. He was spurred on by the loss of his only son to the man called the Teacher, and was determined that his death wouldn't be in vain.

His goal was the Khans' Prophecy, an iconic document referred to in many ancient writings and said to offer secrets that had the power to change the world. It was said to have been buried in a deliberate and controlled nuclear explosion by the Mongolian government to discourage seekers, but Sergei now knew its real location; it wasn't in Mongolia, and what's more it hadn't been for 30 years. It grieved him to think his son's death could have been avoided, and the simple fact he had just discovered was the Prophecy was many miles away. His many contacts in the Russian government had alerted him to Bolshevik intrigue; Stalinist extremists in the Georgian heartland had seen the opportunity thirty years ago when Russian-supplied Sikorsky helicopters were contracted for a remote job here in Queensland lifting in place heavy pylons for the new sky rail, the first of its kind penetrating deep into the rain forest. He had found documents linking the same group involved in illegal mining in Mongolia at exactly the same place as the nuclear explosion; his contacts advised the old comrades were sending a new team out under new orders to find the Prophecy. The Stalinist rebels clearly saw their opportunity to strike against the new Russian regime, aided no doubt by the same dark forces Sergei had been helping the Elders to fight. He had no doubt they would use the Prophecy if they got their hands on it, but they had been betrayed by one of them, an old man called Anton Doskovitch. Anton was with him now, the only survivor from that group and over 80 years of age. Sergei reckoned he had a couple of weeks' lead over the Stalinists and whoever else was out there. The man called the Teacher had died, as had the man called the Professor, but unexplained deaths in Mongolia and a recent attempt to re-enter the buried cave meant the movement was active.

He hadn't told Guy Tresanton or the Elders his suspicions for the simple reason that he suspected a mole in that organisation, a suspicion that had been recently reinforced when some of the Elders left the organisation for no apparent reason. He was startled from his reverie as the helicopter jolted, changing direction to hover over the iconic Sky Train cable, its cars in winter storage. The pilot dipped down approaching pylon number nine, as specified by Anton flying low under radar detection to the fort where landing would be impossible as the forest was thick and impenetrable, the very reason that the Khans' Prophecy was here. Ahead were the large pylons put in place by the Russian Sikorsky helicopters and he saw Anton watch approvingly as the young pilot expertly manoeuvred and point downwards gesturing to the harness. Sergei gulped and looked down at the trees. This was the part he couldn't avoid, and he knew it was going to be torture. Anton swung out first, carrying his eighty-five years very well, and Sergei followed. He could almost visualise the tree tops as soft and welcoming, but knew they were lethal. He prayed that the pilot had full control of the machine as they swung frantically downwards carefully manoeuvring past sharp pine trees. He was beginning to berate himself for his foolish idea when with a sigh of relief his feet brushed the forest floor. With a light crunch the harness cushioned his impact, and then he was down at the foot of pylon number nine.

Anton made the drill equipment ready and marked the hiding place, starting to drill slowly and taking care not to underpin the foundations. Sergei watched intently, reflecting on the Prophecy; he'd always suspected that it had been removed from the grave of Genghis and Kublai Khan in Mongolia but had never dreamed it would be by fellow Russians. Anton had been the senior of the four pilots and had survived the Stalinist intrigues on their return to the motherland in the 1960's.

"This is it, Sergei," growled Anton, starting the heavy duty electric drill, "this is where I put it 20 years ago." The money Sergei was offering him would solve all his immediate and future financial problems in Moscow, and give him the chance to finish his days with deserved dignity and plenty of vodka.

"A last act of the old guard," said Sergei, feigning sympathy with the old man's position. He reflected on the strenuous efforts used by the Professor and Teacher two years ago to get the Prophecy from the Mongolian cave when all the time it had lain here. Why on earth Australia, in the middle of nowhere? He supposed the renegades would reckon it the least likely place anyone would look, and they did after all have a great opportunity. It made sense in many ways and must have delighted Joe Stalin, as there was no way anyone would think of looking down here.

"Why here, Anton?" he shouted above the drill noise.

"We were under orders," spat Anton, "I didn't ask I just did, that's how it was. We were told to put it somewhere safe, still we won because we killed the bastard."

"Who exactly?"

"The mastermind, he came with us down here, laughed a lot as if only he knew the secret but we were too smart for him, pushed him out the chopper on one of the runs, took all his money and told the commander it was an accident, pretty clever."

"Yes, pretty clever, Anton, and no one else knew about it?"

"Sure, it was easy, just some poxy rangers, and we took care of their bodies down here. They called us in because of the Sikorsky lifting power, we were the special ones. The most powerful lifting device in the world and they wanted us. Got more than they bargained for," he said, and grinned a toothless smile. "Just a stupid old box, never understood it myself." He smiled, wiping his brow and letting the drill bit cool.

"Keep going."

"You're paying, comrade," shrugged the old man, lifting the portable drill again and targeting a small area at the foot of the pylon. He was sweating in the humidity until finally the plate came away from the foot of the pylon. "Bloody battery is going flat, our chopper crashed after we planted the box, three of us survived because of these trees, cushioned the fall when the chopper hit the ground. Lived for days in this bloody place and never told a soul, my mates all died rather sudden, made my way back up through Asia to Archangel, now all I want to do is live with my daughter in Moscow."

"And you shall."

"A million dollars, you said," snapped Anton, starting to pull away wooden splinters, the batteries about done. "In cash."

"Agreed," Sergei grimaced, as Anton started attacking the metal pylon footing with a crowbar, then he saw the front plate move to expose a hiding place. No one would ever have found this, not in a million years. Sergei looked around shuddering to think what wildlife there was down there, the home of some of the world's deadliest spiders and snakes. He looked up briefly at the helicopter hovering oblivious above them as Anton stretched down and pulled out the ancient looking box.

"Told you so," he shouted as he showed the familiar script markings that Sergei had seen before, a combination of Mongolian and Chinese.

"Well done, old man," exclaimed Sergei as Anton lifted the box. "Put it over there in the chopper's net," he said, regretting what he had to do next. He swung the crowbar and connected it with the side of the old Russians head. The man collapsed with a grunt as Sergei radioed to the pilot to pull him up. He stepped back into the harness; the old man was a self-confessed killer and probably a cannibal. A snake had got him; tragic, but after all, they were in the world's most dangerous habitat.

Venice

At private residence Number 26 Rio Terra, S. Leonardo, Lucrezia Calvi looked around the familiar room, her usual stern demeanour and cold facial expressions easily mistaken for displeasure. She was as immaculate as her apartment's furnishings; in her late fifties, tall, slim, and dark, with neat short brown hair and brown eyes. She took pleasure in her Christian name being that of the infamous Lucrezia Borgia. Her usual retort to those that asked about any connection was simple: history had given her a bad name. In reality, Lucrezia Borgia's father Rodrigo Borgia had become Pope during the Renaissance and led a period of unknown calm in the church. Lucrezia Borgia, in her opinion, was the victim of bad publicity. Lucrezia smiled coldly, her demeanour commanding attention, a regal air that demanded respect. Extremely wealthy and influential, she was fascinated by the Venetian Republic's history and had devoted her life to it, alongside being one of the Chosen Ones, a secret group. Her philosophy was to influence behind the scenes so secrecy was her guide word unlike her recently deceased brother. Giuseppe, or the Professor, as was his chosen title, had been wrong to break the Calvi's golden rule drummed into them by their father: never lose your anonymity. Secrecy had ensured that their ancestors - starting with Cosimo Medici, the great and secretive manipulator - had run the northern states of Italy from his banking empire, controlling nations. Instead, Giuseppe had made mistakes in his quest to find the Khans' Prophecy and paid the ultimate penalty.

Many times he had chosen not to listen; now she would succeed where he had failed, and on a much grander scale. She would do it the Calvi way. Giuseppe had been associated with ZTW Corporation and she had to wrestle control of the same company from the other Chosen Ones. It was she who had set up Tutulus as the new trading entity and now the new corporation controlled all the funding. Time to flex her muscles and show them what she was capable of, particularly as ownership of a single block of shares equivalent to 40 percent had recently gone to another buyer. For decades she had mirrored her brother, decades in his shadow learning from his mistakes. Now was her time, true to the Calvi family roots unlike Giuseppe's high profile existence on Ascension Island in the Seychelles. She would achieve far more by being legal, she thought, and smiled across at her two cats, Genghis and Kublai. She mused on how she could wrest control of Tutulus and eventually had a breakthrough. Forming a group of advisers a Spanish banker had led to the breakthrough, a secret treasure.

She summoned her financial adviser Giuseppe Festo into the office, relishing the potential fortune from the Napoleonic era. All she had to do was find it and she would have the total control of Tutulus. For tha,t she needed the services of her most faithful companion and ally. Giuseppe was such a man, someone with his head buried in the minutia of running her empire, a crucial counter balance to her occasional impulsiveness.
"Have a seat, Giuseppe," she smiled as they sat in her office in the Doges Palace, hidden from the tourists and the ceremonial events. It had once been part of a huge prison complex with the condemned going across the Bridge of Sighs between the Palace and the prisons, but now it was her centre of operations. The man who ran the Council here was her puppet, a man called Fabrizio Grete, a man more concerned with looking good than running an office, which suited her. She was the government of the republic, the Doge in all but name and great preparation for her next step, to take full control of the small state, her grand plan to rescue Venice, and rescue was the right word.

"Lucrezia, we need to be very careful with this information, it exposes you to the overt sort of risks you warned Giuseppe about. It's clear that the Spanish authorities know nothing, and legally it's theirs."
"We aren't part of Spain Giuseppe."
"Perhaps not, but this will put you in a vulnerable position. We have always shied away from such stunts."
"It's not a stunt, Giuseppe, you more than anyone know we need the money. I will not have others taking control of Tutulus, there's a power struggle and our majority shareholding is lost."

"The Chosen Ones?"

"They are the problem, Giuseppe, I need you to check them out, make sure we know everything there is to know, look for weaknesses."

"Spain is dangerous, Lucrezia, exactly the sort of thing your brother would have done."

"It's legal, a respected banker of one of Spain's largest banks, manage him and get the secret, I want that treasure before, there will be no connection to me."

"We have everything we want here. Evolution not revolution, that's what you keep telling me."

"Giuseppe, you just manage the money and I'll worry about the rest, there are forces gathering and we must have control of the project."

"Mare Nostrum?"

"Yes exactly, you arrange Spain."

"Very well, as always I will trust your judgement, Lucrezia. Mare Nostrum is a great project."

"A previous Doge once took one of history's greatest ever risks, betting that the crusaders could repay a fortune he invested up front in building them sufficient ships to launch the crusades at the arsenale. When asked why he had put everything at such risk he replied that it was our destiny to protect our future and that is Mare Nostrum."

"He nearly lost everything."

"We either learn from the past, Giuseppe, or are destined to repeat it. The Doge will rise just as the Venetians managed for years to thrive as the underdog through cunning, stealth and wisdom," she summoned her Secretary Francisca to arrange her diary.

St Lucia

Jemima, or Jem for short, made her way down to the new Rodney Bay Marina, which gleamed with super yachts as she looked for her quarry. Jem Heston was in her late thirties, and the niece of retired

Chief Inspector Montgomery, or Monty, from Bermuda She had learned her investigation skills from Monty, but the relationship was a double edged sword as others thought her incapable in her own right. Of medium height with a slim figure, she was proficient in self-defence as part of her basic police training. In St Lucia on the trail of ZTW after they had recently and suddenly closed their headquarters in Bermuda, she knew they hadn't gone out of business and smelled a rat. After all, they had successfully bankrolled various criminal operations for a number of years and she was convinced that by tracking them down she would get to the heart of recent criminal events. Those events had brought her here following the claims of the journalist Zelda Higuaín. Unfortunately her current boss had taken a dim view, so she was here in an unofficial capacity, which didn't help her anxiety. She looked around and then saw who she was looking for, a statuesque blonde.

"Good to meet you, Zelda," smiled Jem, gesturing to a seat at the local café.

"I'm glad the police are at last taking my claims seriously," replied Zelda, taking a Diet Coke. "I've been suppressed by vested interests, both of which are powerful and dangerous," she said, looking nervous.

"Tell me what you have found."

"Five young girls have all disappeared from this island, all in their early twenties and all pretty. My contacts in the drug gangs claim not to know anything about it, then last week we had the murder."

"That's the reason I am here, was this the first?"

"First we know of but many are missing, the poor girl was molested and strangled."

"Do you believe the gangs know nothing?"

"Strangely, yes, as I have the same situation on other islands in the Caribbean. For instance, my colleagues in Antiqua and further field report similar occurrences, also there are other factors that make me believe this is more than a local gang and is coordinated."

"Such as?"

"The methods of disappearance are the same, always at night, and always the girls are intelligent, always in their early twenties, and always pretty."

"Anything else?"

"Usually in decent jobs lured by lucrative modelling contracts. The activity has ramped up significantly over the last few months so something big is coming off."

"Do you have any leads to substantiate this?"

"Just one who will meet with me tonight strictly on his terms, you can come along but it could be dangerous. It'll cost you a hundred dollars, name's Leroy."

It was a warm moonlit night as they arrived at the large warehouse. Jem shivered despite her long experience and took comfort in the small gun she carried courtesy of a local police colleague. Her nerves were on edge, which was good as it meant she was ready for anything. She nodded to Zelda from the shadows as a man stepped out in the light.

"I said to come alone," he snapped.

""She's a friend, Leroy," replied Zelda soothingly. "Just need to know what you can tell us about the girls disappearing. I will pay you."

"Said only you," repeated the man in a strong local accent and raising a wicked looking knife, "she's the dammed cops, I can smell it."

"Put the knife down," shouted Jem raising her gun.

"You are the dammed police."

"It doesn't matter who I am Leroy, we need to know more about what you know, these girls, where are they been taken."

"You don't want to get involved, really you don't, man, there's dangerous people out there, people who would think nothing of cutting you up and throwing you to the sharks."

"Where are they being taken?"

"Special camps here in the Caribbean, I don't know where, don't tell me nothing, say keep my dammed mouth shut and I'll live, threaten me plenty."

"What sort of camps?"

"Slavers," replied Leroy, "That's my guess. They tell me nothing but I am not stupid, the girls are pretty and good for use if you get my meaning."

"Keep talking," said Jem, looking around uneasily, her instincts on edge. She didn't like the area, too many opportunities for an ambush. "Need more for the money."

"Too dangerous, man," replied Leroy, looking around nervously.

"Talk," said Jem raising the gun.

"Big man, dangerous man, pirate man, he owns his own island, does what he likes, he runs the main camp, you need to get out of this before they get you, I mean it man, it's dangerous."

"Which island?"

"I can't tell you."

"Suggest you do," said Jem looking over at Zelda.

"It's called …"

The explosion was deafening and a glazed look came over Leroy's eyes as he fell forwards. Jem spun around then heard a piercing scream and saw Zelda being dragged away.

"Stop," she yelled, raising her gun and firing over their heads, and then she sensed something behind her and was plunged into darkness.

The early sun shone on her face as she lay there in the dirt. She struggled to pull herself up, realising she had been hit on the head. She sat up and groaned as she felt the bruises and dried blood. Her gun was gone and her police badge was laid in the dirt. Memories flooded back to her about the events. They hadn't killed her, because she was a policewoman and they didn't want that sort of publicity, but what of Zelda? She felt herself to make sure there were no other injuries, shuddering at what could have happened. She staggered back to the main marina, needing to get back to Bermuda and start the wheels turning. There was something major, something serious involving the young girls; the fear on Leroy's face had been palpable before he died and she dreaded to think what they would do with Zelda. First port of call was the local police station where her colleague, a man called Toby, shrugged off the loss of the gun and helped file the dead and missing person's reports. She then contacted the Herald, Zelda's paper.

"She called in this morning to say she was ill."

"You sure it was her?"

"Yes, but she did seem kind of strained, said she would be taking some overdue leave and would get back to us," continued the young female receptionist. "She's done it before so I paid it no attention."

"Thanks," replied Jem, thinking that Zelda was probably on her way to be a new recruit to the slavers. Her mobile vibrated.

"Jem, I'm in the Caribbean, thought we could catch up, there's something I want to discuss with you."

"Of course Lorna, where exactly are you?"

"Outside an island called St Bart's."

"I'll meet you there," replied Jem wondering if Lorna could help her, an acquaintance from the past she kept an interest in her cruiser that specialised in helping disadvantaged children, she hoped to God there wasn't a link.

Germania

They were all of a common heritage, born of a disaster many years ago in the cold North Sea, a disaster that had been man made. Bound together as dependents of a naval tragedy when their Battle Cruiser, the Scharnhorst, was sunk by HMS Belfast off Norway they were family in many ways, and they were now through interbreeding a very close knit community. Germania was their home and had been for nearly ten years since they had arrived at the homestead built at the turn of the 20th century by Elisabeth Nietzsche and her husband Bernhard Forster. Germania was to be a new way of life, free from the restrictions of the old Germany, where they could build a pure community. It was putting into practice what Elisabeth's famous brother Frederick Nietzsche had been writing about for some time. Ironically, he had thought the whole idea of a remote settlement mad and had refused to take part, talking about the theory of supremacy rather than practicing it. Elisabeth was different and wanted to see the reality, even attracting the attention of a rising orator in Munich named Adolf Hitler.

Her commune Nueva Germania had been built on the edge of the rainforest on the Aguarya River and the main house was built in a dramatic, gothic style and incongruent to the surrounding landscape. Beset by poor agriculture, mosquitos and fever, the commune had eventually failed at great cost to all who had taken part, including Elisabeth, who went home to Germany. This time was different, however, for they had a purpose and a leader, a leader who had sufficient funds and influence for them to achieve their original mission. The new ruler was one of the Chosen Ones, called the Philosopher, claiming direct ancestry with Nietzsche. Under the Philosopher's leadership they thrived again, keeping themselves to themselves and slowly building a strong and vibrant community.

Two men stood out from the crowd as the group grew. They were named Wolfgang and Helmut. Both had leadership qualities and were the archetypal blonde-haired, blue-eyed Germans. They were joined by a third leader, a dark haired man called Aitor who had arrived a year ago from Argentina. Aitor was one of the select few who exercised such power that even the Philosopher deferred. Aitor talked about his friend in reverential tones and would disappear to see her at regular intervals. Because of this powerful partner Wolfgang and Helmut handled him with care but he was not one of them, after all he wasn't pure German stock. The three of them ran the enterprise now of over fifty individuals, the Philosopher their spiritual leader.

"The time has come my friends, the time when we will lead."

"Can I ask when and how?" said Wolfgang, keen to take the lead over his rivals.

"You will be told all in good time. Just make sure you are ready, we have a large meeting imminently in the Caribbean, here's what you must do."

La Gomera

His beloved Hidalgo sailing yacht had handled beautifully during the long crossing from St Lucia. Guy Tresanton and his new wife Rose had taken the trip as their delayed honeymoon as they prepared for their new life leading the group called the Elders from its monastery in La Gomera. Together they had fought and defeated both the Teacher and the Professor and hoped the whole evil enterprise underpinned by the company ZTW was consigned to history. Over six foot high with sandy hair, Guy had chosen a life running a yacht charter business in the Caribbean until dragged with Rose through a combination of circumstances into leading the fight against the Teacher and ZTW. The secret organisation had been at the forefront of that fight, and now its Chair, an older lady called Victoria, was retiring, having chosen Guy as her successor. Accompanying them was an old friend Padraig Reilly, an itinerant Irishman who looked after the Hidalgo.

At 36 feet in length, she needed full time care, and Padraig had no other attachments or interest; at over 60 years of age was happy to spend his years sailing the seas. They left Padraig to moor the Hidalgo at the main harbour on the island where he would live on board. Guy and Rose made their way across the island to the monastery hidden in the mountains, the ideal secret hideaway. For over a century it had served the secretive Elders well as they gathered. Comprised of senior industrialists and other influential people carefully chosen for their ability, it existed to fight evil wherever and whenever it was constituted. In addition, through its foundation by the Chinese sailor Zheng He it had a mission to resolve his great puzzle, a puzzle that had involved a quest for long lost artefacts and now for the Khans' Prophecy.

They were welcomed at the door by their respective mothers, who lived out on the edge of the large estate with Victoria. Both widowed during the fight with the Teacher, they were happy to live their lives quietly. Guy and Rose were also welcomed by the head monk Hernandez as it was a working monastery in order to provide a cover. It was an arrangement that worked well, as for the monks it was a quiet and contemplative retreat free of charge whilst for the staff of the Elders it gave them cover from prying local eyes. Guy and Rose would live upstairs with support staff whilst the monks occupied the ground floor. Down in the basement were the Elders' own vaults, containing riches of knowledge heavily protected by an advanced security system.

"Our new home, my dear," smiled Guy as he looked down from the panoramic main lounge window across the valley.

"Different from the deck of the Hidalgo," smiled Rose as she settled into one of the chairs. "Do you think we can have a little period of peace now?"

"I hope so, though Victoria has asked to see me tomorrow about the vaults."

"Well that's not dangerous."

"I would hope not," smiled Guy as he reached for a drink, surprised to see Victoria at the door.

"Afraid we have a problem, Guy."

Chapter 2

Gibraltar

The nightmare often returned at the strangest times, each more vivid and shocking than the last, and even for such a strong willed person it was almost unbearable. It had been a long dark tunnel until light came in the shape of a mysterious benefactor responsible for saving her in the Seychelles and then taking her to safety in the tunnel, her home nearly a year. A year of slow recovery from horrendous wounds suffered when she had escaped from Ascension Island after being shot in the stomach and stabbed twice in the chest. Attended to by mysterious servants and at times convinced she was being taken on a train journey through to a different country she slowly grew stronger. She had certainly used up her nine lives.

Her benefactor had brought her here, though everything had been a blur of pain before consciousness returned as her body slowly recovered from the loss of blood. She was looked after by two skilled nurses, and was amazed that someone had gone to such lengths to save her, so much so that she resolved to recover, which was to be a long, arduous, and difficult process. Finally her recuperation was complete; she was ready for revenge. She had become curiously attached to the underground network of tunnels in limestone caves that the British had utilised during World War Two. It was her private world, a secret tunnel complex beyond the tourist tracks and below the large cavern often used for concerts. Slowly and methodically she regained her health and fitness, working hard in a superb gym. In time she also met with some other inmates, all young females but all, unlike her, looking cowed and afraid to talk. They had a different purpose, she was told by the only person to speak, a burly looking Spaniard woman called Hortense. Slowly Hortense told her why they were there and then finally she met her mysterious Arab benefactor, who explained to her the reason she was here and her chance for revenge.

He talked to her brusquely as if she was second in importance; he was called El Hamill and a man of few words, telling her that she would be taking her orders direct from Venice, from a woman. Sabine had unique skills, so had been saved for no other reason than she would help them fight back, start repaying the debt, begin to re-enter the world. The views were breath-taking from the top of Gibraltar rock, but she didn't see anything other than the potential for revenge.

Qatar

Rashid El Hamill was a tall, bearded Arab with a neatly cropped beard and a strident voice, a man used to giving, not receiving, orders. Upon returning from seeing the redheaded woman in Gibraltar he surveyed the scene in front of him and walked purposefully to the window of his air conditioned office at his headquarters building. He was a Qatari nobleman with a burning ambition; born to his noble father's mistress he had been condemned to working his way up outside the normal patronage routes to power. Unlike those of more noble birth he had to work hard, going into the world of commerce and showing a ruthless ambition that made many enemies. His father, a Prince from the Royal family, had long since disowned his wayward son as he fought for his own influence in the rigid Qatari hierarchy. El

Hamill didn't care, as he was soon on his way to success in business. Schooled in England, he had an aptitude for computer programming and quickly realised its vast potential. He graduated with a science degree from Cambridge before forming his own company and employing cheap labour for the consumer revolution. He had quickly seen opportunities in the digital world and funded a number of start-up companies, one of which had hit the rich seam of advanced sensor controls in the natural gas industry. It had made him a wealthy man in his Qatari homeland, and allowed him to indulge in his own fantasies, which included fast cars and loose women.

That indulgence led to problems, as he started taking drugs and had been caught with large amounts of heroin at the wrong place, one of the Qatari Palaces with a minor female Royal. His downfall was quick and immediate until at the last minute he was spared from a jail sentence by the patronage of an anonymous person in Venice. Indebted to Lucrezia Calvi, he had undertaken a number of jobs for her, including nursing Sabine back to health, a distraction he had disliked as the redhead was certainly not subservient. He was the technical genius behind the project of a lifetime, a project that was costing billions of dollars and his chance to design unbound by the usual moral codes. Lucrezia let him do things his way providing he delivered, and he had been given control of the Mare Nostrum, the project that would define his life. He was on the most exciting journey.

The minions bowed as he swept into the main office, his white dish dash flowing as he gestured to his second in command Waleed. He was master of all he surveyed at Hamill Electronics, and even believed that an act of God underwrote why he had to now change the world. Qatari Royalty were lazy and too rich for their own good, with no ambition, and he would show them as the sheer scale of the Mare Nostrum project gripped him. He called to Waleed to bring the plans and surveyed the four sets of drawings. They looked like outsized oil rigs, but their purpose was very different. They would revolutionise the way the rich lived and ensure the survival of the best, providing the most luxurious living space that money could buy. Four had been built, three here and one in the Asian region, and all bristled with technology. He had designed systems of intelligence that would create a unique experience, whilst extensive use of robots would provide the running of the platforms all the way down to room cleaners and even sex robots. More importantly, the robots would provide the latest security and would all be programmed to take only his orders. That was what really excited him. In addition, he was hiring the top talent available to him on his huge budget as the timescales were getting ever tighter. He couldn't wait for them all to be installed; he was the technician, the genius on the brink of turning the world on its head.

"Progress?"

"Ready for the trial runs on the rig," replied Waleed.

"You have a week to meet the timetable, no excuses," he smiled coldly, looking at the detail of the rig. He was particularly proud that two of the rigs were being built in Abu Dhabi and one here in Qatar, the one that had to be right from day one. It would be ready on time, whatever the cost.

Venice

Lucrezia looked across at the familiar sights as she walked down the canal side, keeping to the shadows, as she habitually did, and reflecting that her life was about to change significantly. Mare Nostrum, a name she had chosen as it translated literally as 'our sea', the Roman words for the Mediterranean, though what they really meant was the entire world. In her case it meant a new world outside the conventional nation states, a world at sea beyond nations. The concept was hers borne out of the fanciful idea of Venice being a floating island. To her it would be 'Beyond Nations', an idea ten years in the making and why she had been christened the Architect by the Chosen Ones. The concept was beautiful in design and easily self-perpetuating, a self-sustaining life on platforms away from national waters for those wealthy enough, only she would take it one step further, it had to be self-sustaining in the long term. The whole concept was costing billions of dollars, all funded by the holding organisation Tutulus and the fact that it was outside national waters meant it was free from democratic or national interference, and indeed taxes, which had attracted many wealthy donors. Subscriptions on the four rigs, as they were colloquially known, were well advanced and nearing the point where all four were operational financially.

Operational physically was another matter, but they would be a going concern soon. The second significant reason her world was changing was that she was bringing a controlling management group together, investors who would lesson her share of the burden in the hugely expensive platforms. This group, the Doge Council, would also give her an edge with the Chosen Ones. The original Doge Council of 1340 had over 1200 members; this one would be ten plus her with the casting vote as Chair. She needed that element of authority as she reflected on the Chosen Ones, a concept she had liked but now felt was a risk. She needed that edge as she reflected on recent developments, needing cash to ensure she gained control, and the donors would fund the majority of the rigs operational costs, including future investment. She saw a time when anyone over a certain wealth would be registered to live on the platforms living a daily life under her control. She needed a council of senior sponsors, and had even settled on the name Doge for this council of sponsors, though in reality the Doge was the name of Venice's leader from historical times, which was particularly apt for her because the Doge had ruled often by guile with influence far beyond reasonable for a small island republic. From convening the council she had heard of the reputed treasure in Spain and she had just the person to find it: Sabine.

She climbed aboard her private gondola and watched the waters ripple as she was conveyed through the back canals by expert hands towards St Mark's Square. They arrived at a secret side entrance and she was helped through the old wooden doors into the Doge's Palace. She had an early appointment first, a very important one, before she met her new council. "Show him in," she told her secretary, a severe looking lady called Francesca.

Welcome," she smiled at the tall man who was ushered into her private office, an important banker from Madrid named Jose Barr. His countenance was severe and his mood was sombre.

"Time to deliver, Jose."

"You have to understand it is totally against the bank's policy to give out client confidentiality."

"You know the deal," snapped Lucrezia impatiently.

"It is important you maintain my total confidentiality in this matter."

"You will arrange the meeting now," replied Lucrezia coldly, "or I will need to talk to Madrid."

"I am in a position of trust, helping you in this endeavour of yours is not right."

"Prison if you don't," replied Lucrezia coldly.

"What protection do I have?"

"The name of your bank is very apt; so apt I'm using its name for my own operations; after all, you will be funding a sizeable part of it."

"Bank Mare Nostrum is a respected name," replied Jose stiffly."

"The Romans used it to describe their world. The name of this man, please."

"He is a wealthy client in the south of Spain, to be handled carefully. There is, shall we say, a certain amount of risk here: we have turned a blind eye to this situation for many years."

"Come on, Jose," said Lucrezia.

"I inherited this situation and my superiors want it to disappear."

"You were chosen for your own discretion in these matters," replied Lucrezia. The man was really the most frightful bore.

"That is good to hear, this situation is complicated by the fact that this fortune could be a national asset, technically government treasure from both Spain and Britain."

"Names and location, Jose."

"Almeria province, that's all I know, we have preserved the secrecy of this client for many years; he does not let us near the so-called treasure."

"And yet he's been bringing you gold and diamonds all this time."

"It is a little irregular."

"The client's name if you want to avoid a jail sentence."

"It's an unconventional arrangement where he agrees to meet our people in a certain place at a certain time four times a year. Here are his details," said the man stiffly, passing over a piece of paper.

"It is time," she announced to Giuseppe as she reached the main ante room pondering over the conversation with Jose. The man was desperate to avoid prison, giving her huge leverage. He would stay on the Doge until she had the treasure then he could rot, she signalled to Francesca to take the minutes. The ornate conference room was covered by the largest unsupported ceiling in Europe and was cold and cavernous. She saw the small select group ahead of her.

"Ladies and gentlemen, please be seated," she said, turning to the audience of ten men and women. "You are seated in the very place where the original Council of Venice sat under this very roof, which incidentally is all held together above us with an intricate web of steel wires, let's hope it lasts a little longer," she smiled. "The last the Doge of the independent republic met was to accept Napoleon's terms of surrender and let him occupy the city in this very room, but now we are reassembled for a very different reason. They used to say Venice was the most serene and Genoa the most proud," she continued, recalling the ancient words about the two leading super powers of their time, the fiercest of rivals. "Genoa had Columbus and we had Marco Polo, the Stato de Mar, the first ever sea empire, long before Britain, and all relevant to what I am about to tell you at the dawn of a new age."

"I fail to see what this has to do with being dragged halfway around the world," said Dirk Benedict, a South African Boer billionaire. "I am a busy man with no time for history lessons and I don't take kindly to having my mobile confiscated at the door."

"All necessary," replied Lucrezia, who had been pre-warned about the South African. "Modern communication devices can be used as microphones in any meeting, which is very dangerous to security, so we cannot take that chance, as what I am about to tell you is very confidential."

"Interestingly, Genoa came within a hairs breadth of destroying Venice," said Hatari a Japanese billionaire, "Commander Pisano saved the day with the support of the Venetian leaders."

"Ah, another historian," smiled Lucrezia, turning her attention to the diminutive Japanese. "Venice survived to control the whole of the Mediterranean, which in those days was the whole known world. It all went wrong when the corrupt and ineffectual Italian state took over."

"So why are we assembled here today?" asked Jose Barr, still smarting from his earlier meeting.

"This is a tourist site not an industrial powerhouse," sneered the Russian delegate Antonin.

"Perhaps now but the world's first mass production line for assembling sea war craft started here in the arsenale, a 60 acre site enclosed by 50 foot high brick walls topped with battlements and in its time the largest industrial complex in the world."

"And now defunct," muttered Contessa Gebaud from Italy. "More interestingly Casanova was imprisoned right here in this very building until he escaped."

"Ladies and gentlemen," continued Lucrezia, reminding herself that they had been selected because they were high achievers in their own fields. "I am about to take you on the most exciting journey of your lives. You have all been successful but wealth has no meaning if you can't use it to make a difference, or if you have to give it to some undeserving government. We are surrounded by inadequate democracies and have to submit to the so-called will of the people and see ridiculous laws finding new ways to reward the have-nots and penalise those who have succeeded in life. I think you will all agree that is not a satisfactory set of circumstances and we have the answer to make us all masters of our own destinies, 'Mare Nostrum'.

"Mare Nostrum," repeated the Contessa, "that's the old Roman word for the Mediterranean Sea."

"Their seas because they owned it and saw it as their total world and knew no better, a good name don't you think for a life changing experience."

"You have my attention," said Benedict grudgingly.

"Beyond Nations is the subtitle for luxurious living platforms by invite only, for an investment they pay no taxes, get to have the best security money can buy and other special privileges I cannot yet disclose. All this will only be open to select people and we already have huge demand."

"Why a secret?" asked Benedict, intrigued.

"Because you will be the rulers and some governments may react badly, we need to be careful with the world's media. Ladies and gentlemen, this plan has been put together over four years, you have all been carefully selected for your unique abilities to be part of this exciting adventure and for your investment you will all get reserved places on one of the MN platforms, including of course private jets and helicopters, powerboats, the latest in artificial intelligence and robotics, and many other pleasures."

"I can get all this and more elsewhere," said Benedict. "What you talk of is available on other such creations like the cruiser called Sea World."

"They don't get Project Valkyrie."

"Valkyrie, what the hell is that?"

"Afraid I can't reveal that until you are all fully signed up and paid," said Lucrezia firmly. "All I can say is that Valkyrie will make everything you do sustainable."

"Meaning?"

"After the formalities are completed."

"What about security?" asked Benedict

"Special Forces, who will be stationed on site, the best in entertainment systems and many more, all detailed extensively in the brochures you are about to receive."

"Why do you need us if you are already fully subscribed?" asked Benedict

"We need a fund for the future, investment funds so we can continually create more MN platforms."

"An elite that self-perpetuates," asked Benedict.

"Precisely."

"Quality control?"

"The careful selection of all members by our teams."

"The next generation."

"As I said a question for another day," smiled Lucrezia.

"What makes you suitable to lead all this?" intoned the Contessa.

"I designed the rigs."

"What about the Elders, where do they fit into this?" asked Benedict. "I believe you have history with them."

"Congratulations, you've done your research, they are a problem, however I can tell you that in your group is one of the former Elders, former because he left last week and joined us today. Welcome, Mr Stanton."

"My pleasure," said Stanton smiling as he looked around. "The Elders have had their day, my being here is proof of that. They are badly managed and will not be a threat."

"The big difference is we will take a pragmatic approach led by actually doing something, not trying to act as some glorified referee."

"All sounds great in theory," said Benedict.

"Not far from here was one of the most powerful dynasties, the Medici bankers, who for centuries funded the Italian states and can be credited with fuelling the Renaissance itself in secret. Many things are possible if well organised and circumspect, that is how I operate. As I said you have all been carefully selected for your great knowledge and passion, and of course your money, which I can promise to return tenfold."

"The demise of your brother, what happened?" asked a man called Pissarro.

"He didn't accept the need for planning and committees. No one will get hurt my way, what you are about to hear from my colleague is the culmination of four years of planning and learning what went wrong with my brother's scheme. Before we proceed I require that you all commit to the future vision by signing non-disclosure agreements. After that you will be taken on a fascinating journey. What you are about to see will I am sure convince you of the opportunity for your own lifestyles in a world of meritocracy. Ladies and gentlemen, congratulations, and now I will leave you."

She went back to her own office glancing across at the darkening sky. As she reflected on the day's events, her private line buzzed.

"Architect, we are on the verge of exciting times."

"Philosopher, I agree, but we must be prudent."

"We are part of a great cause; there must be no slowing down."

"I have a problem with aspects of the Valkyrie plan."

"Morals don't come into this," snapped the voice, hardening. "We have to accelerate our plans, and that means the full impact of Valkyrie whilst you take care of the Elders; they're starting to prove to be a nuisance, poking their noses into the affairs of ZTW."

"ZTW doesn't exist anymore."

"They will find a route back to Tutulus so we need to take steps, I don't need to remind you, Architect, of the billions of dollars we have put into this enterprise relying on your designs to work."

"They will work and we will take care of the Elders, plans have been put in place with Valkyrie, there are ways of achieving the same result without the moral issues."

"Valkyrie doesn't allow for that and you well know it, we must have full commitment or I will be obliged to call an extraordinary meeting."

"You have my commitment," said Lucrezia.

La Gomera

"Victoria, it's good to see you after all this time, what's so urgent?" asked Guy as he ushered her in.

"We have a significant increase in traffic around the financial entity we knew as ZTW, now called Tutulus."

"Tell me a little more about the Elders organisation and its goals," asked Rose.

"The purpose of the Elders is to act as a referee or governor, a trusted advisor seeing any disproportionate abuse of power as a reason to act. It was created centuries ago by the great Chinese Admiral Zheng He," explained Victoria, already missing the direct action of being involved as Chair. In her eighties, and weary of the constant responsibilities of running such an organisation, she had made the decision to appoint Guy Tresanton.

"I know that, Victoria," said Guy turning from the window. "What I really need to know is the relevance of the Teacher, the Professor and this Tutulus to the archives here. We went through hell defeating them and yet it doesn't seem to have had any effect whatsoever on the continual surge."

"I'm going to share with you one of the Elders' biggest secrets," continued Victoria. "We have always seen our role as defending against tyranny and ideally killing it at birth so to speak. That was what Zheng He originally intended when he arranged the establishment of the organisation. But he also intended for a greater secret to be held.

You have to remember that at this time the world was suffering from isolationism. After the global nature of the Romans and indeed the growth of the Silk Road added to Zheng He's own global voyages it was the start of international trade. Zheng himself was a huge advocate of this, seeing first-hand how travel broadened the mind. He decided to set a puzzle for future generations as he knew how temporary his own existence was, and by doing so he intended that tyrannies of the past like the Mongol empire for instance and its legacies were contained. To do that he hid artefacts on his travels, as you well know, but there was more."

"He couldn't trust the Elders themselves."

"That was his problem; he had the view that someone was spying on him, that he had been compromised and that he was going out of favour with the Chinese Yongle court. He had already been told that his voyage would be his last one and that all future voyages would be stopped. However, what really worried him was a spy in the camp, someone on his own ship who was spying on his every move. He began to suspect everyone and knew he had to do something. It may be in the end that this spy actually killed Zheng, as he died on that last voyage. What we do know is that spy was part of the ancestry of the man you knew as the Teacher and probably others are arraigned against us. They have as their ultimate goals the destroying of the Elders organisation in all its forms and finding the secret left by Zheng, which related to the Mongols and indeed to the Chinese empires who you must remember at that time ruled the world. The company you know as Tutulus is at the forefront of all this, or whatever it becomes next, as after all it's the funding mechanism."

"So all along the Teacher and the Professor were parts of some larger conspiracy?"

"I fear so, yes," replied Victoria. " I have been doing a great deal of research now I have much spare time, and I am finding things in the archives all the time, mostly in the Chinese section, and have even taught, myself with the help of Rose's mother to learn to read Chinese.

I am afraid that we are engaged in a generational fight to the death, and I fear the worst is yet to come."

"Thanks Victoria, that has helped a great deal, what do we do next?"

"The answers lie down in the great vault, I am convinced of it, there's something down there that has huge power and something that others are desperate we don't unveil."

"We must increase security on the vaults."

"Already done, the best system I could find and afford. Knowledge is everything and we must keep ahead of the forces arraigned against us."

"Are you saying that the Teacher in particular had descendants who are engaged in this?"

"The Teacher but also the Professor, they both had well organised activities but somehow I think there is something even bigger that has overseen all their activities, and as I said it all goes back to the vaults."

"Why now Victoria, what's suddenly become more urgent?" asked Rose.

"We have seen a significant increase in traffic we monitor through the Elders, in South East Asia but also in the Caribbean. The financial trial left by ZTW is ever more active and reputed to be funding many nefarious activities. Worst of all, we are picking up direct threats on social media to the institution itself."

"What else can we do?

"We need to be vigilant but unfortunately without any direct threat we can't take direct action."

"I only hope I am up to the task. It already feels like a massive one."

"I wouldn't have recommended you for the role, Guy, if I didn't believe you could do it, besides we cannot just give up and wait. That would be disastrous."

Germania

"We are indeed honoured to have you visit us."

"I am here on disagreeable business, Philosopher. We need to move faster. I don't care for all this evangelising, and it's getting in the way of progress towards Valkyrie."

"I have no idea what you mean."

"Too many philosophical debates about the ascent of humanity and not enough practical work. We are behind on the recruitment programme to the camps."

"The biggest issue we face here involves your friend."

"My friend?"

"Aitor is not one of us, no matter how much you may wish it."

"He is core to this movement."

"Interesting, when he has been making disparaging remarks about you."

"That's my business. In the meantime, you will ramp up the recruitment activities. After all, there are over 300,000 German living in this country, I want to see more of your foot soldiers out recruiting, and want them to be more varied in their approach. We are picking up reports of suspicious journalists on the trail of the girls disappearing in the Caribbean. Focus your efforts down here; after all, I am sure the girls here are as clever and suitable."

"Don't tell me how to run my business; I have met every goal so far and fully intent to deliver on my side of the bargain."

"Then I am pleased. We have sunk billions into this project, it must not fail."

"I suggest you turn your attention more to the Architect. She's the one taking all the money, and she has expressed doubts about the Valkyrie project. You should watch her more closely. Trust me."

Chapter 3

La Gomera

It was his first board meeting, and they had already lost two key members who had inexplicably resigned last week, one of whom, the American Stanton, would be sorely missed. Guy stared purposefully around the boardroom as he started his first Elders meeting as Chair, and he wondered how Victoria would have handled the situation. He was indebted to her advice and would never have taken the role without her full support. It was disappointing that Sergei had not made an appearance but he intended to progress the Russians appointment as President. He turned to Rose, who was now acting as Secretary, and smiled briefly as he counted the seats that were activated. It took some getting used to, as blank faces stared out of the gloom: the recessed lighting precluded facial recognition. It had always been a key principle of the Elders that all would have total anonymity, with only the Chair and Secretary in possession of all the names. Anonymity was essential for ensuring their full participation as they came together to share their ideas and thoughts. He frowned as he noticed that the Italian member Enrico Mazzola was also missing.

"No sign of him, nothing, not even an apology," said Rose, checking her list. "Gone after Stanton announced he was going. Sergei should have been here, he's usually so reliable."

"It doesn't feel right," agreed Guy. "It must be something serious. Sergei was delighted to be asked."

"I suggest you leave the role open until the next meeting to avoid unnecessary debate. It's largely ceremonial anyway. I was even wondering whether we needed it."

"Know I can rely on you to handle the rough stuff," smiled Guy.

"Of course," admonished Rose as she focussed on the copious notes left by Victoria and her Secretary.

"Ladies and Gentlemen, I would like to call the meeting to order," said Guy, looking out into the black space. It had been some time since he'd run a formal business meeting and his heart was pounding. He would have gladly given it all up to return to his yacht chartering business, but had agreed with Rose that they needed a more stable lifestyle. Still, it was a shock to the system returning to such responsibilities; his success in the running saga fighting the Teacher and Professor had given him little choice: he was the natural candidate. It was disconcerting to sense old habits return. His enforced rest on the sea journey after the horrors of destroying the Professor had revitalised him, and he was ready for action.

As he went through the previous minutes he looked around the room and sensed that the meeting felt forced and rigid, thinking that perhaps it was him and his lack of confidence was showing. They were a robust group who didn't hide from hard decisions, though their activities were never publicised. The affairs of nation states were a constant source of concern for the group but their mandate for centuries had been crystal clear, self-imposed and rarely appreciated. Working within the parameters of the international and national legal systems was a constant difficulty, and the reason Guy and Rose had formed a close operational attachment to Chief Inspector Montgomery of the Bermuda police. Unfortunately, he had retired after they had hunted down and destroyed the two master criminals, only it wasn't over specifically he suspected because of the Khans' Prophecy. The Teacher and Professor had both perished, but the fight was still going on, and Guy was increasingly getting the uneasy feeling that there was something much bigger developing than they had ever faced. He prided himself on sensing trouble before it hit; that was what had kept him alive so far, and he had no proof of anything, only his gut instincts.

All these things flashed through his mind as he looked around the room, knowing that these were people who had made a major success of their lives; they were business leaders, philanthropists, scientists, people who made things happen. They were very carefully selected and would have to find new members quickly. That's what happened with a leadership change, and Guy had already lined up an American replacement from his long list, a Texan called Harry Jackson, along with a woman from Africa named Madam Ramping, and an American Senator named Charlotte. It was his first major crisis, the kind of thing that his predecessor Victoria had been a master at handling. He finished the review of outstanding business from the last minutes then reached the key issue raised by the new and clearly strong-willed Jackson. Like his predecessor Stanton, he shunned the anonymity and looked like he could also quietly alienate people.

"My congratulations to the Chair on his appointment. I have the feeling that we are under siege and no one is admitting it," he barked. "It seems to me we have our heads in the sands. We are losing members and we don't know why."

"It's only just happened," replied Guy

"What of this outfit ZTW, why aren't we targeting them? The business world is abuzz with rumours that they are flexing their muscles, albeit under a different name, that it intends to announce a number of public good initiatives and is publically questioning the role of this group, the Elders."

"Who is their new management team?"

"That's for you to find out, Chair," intoned the Texan, a larger than life billionaire from the cattle trade. "They certainly have a good public relations team behind them."

"I will find out more," asserted Guy, "I have already initiated a search in the Caribbean."

"Perhaps I can help a little," came a voice from the darkness, "their assets have been acquired by a company in the Caribbean who are promoting themselves there. At least, it's one of their companies." It was the new African member, Madam Ramping.

"Do you have more details?" asked Guy.

"They are pioneering an investment fund for the education of young girls in the region and in my own country of Nigeria working with respected universities to get free education for girls in the region," Ramping continued. "I can give you their contact details. It's a well-known initiative, but unfortunately there are also bad rumours."

"What sort of rumours?" asked Guy, painfully aware that they didn't know this and wondering why Jem or Monty hadn't told him.

"That they only choose the prettiest girls, and that some of those are sent away for so called 'special education'. Recently there was a death on one of the islands, a Jolen Taylor, promising student."

"Prostitution, you mean," snapped Jackson.

"Slavery where their liberty is taken away. I am a member of the Freedom Foundation that is fighting modern day slavery and they are well and truly in our sights, which is why I know so much about them."

"We will investigate and have a full report for the next meeting," replied Guy.

"I have one other item," said Jackson as the meeting drew to a close. "We have reason to suspect that there is a rival organisation out there who intends to take our place."

"How do you know this?"

"Through various avenues."

"Of course," said Guy, sensing the unease in those around him hidden in the darkness.

"There's a call for you Guy," said Gisele, a Chinese friend of Rose's family who was now working at the monastery.

"Thanks," said Guy, gulping down the much needed malt whisky and staring down at the panoramic view of the valley as he took the handset.

"Monty, it's good to hear from you, how's the fishing?"

"Excellent. Only disturbed by humans."

"ZTW you mean?"

"Jem got assaulted in St Lucia and a female journalist with her disappeared. She is convinced that it's ZTW or Tutulus."

"What happened to the journalist?"

"Called Zelda and just disappeared. Apparently this Tutulus have launched a charm offensive with coverage in the press, with anonymous interviews proclaiming themselves as an investor in diversity for females in the region. Massive coverage in the press with the free education for the underprivileged girls, they roped in some celebrities to endorse them."

"Any more?"

"Seems that they have a named front company in the Caribbean in Grenada with a sub branch in St Bart's. They closed their headquarters here in Bermuda with Grenada as their operating centre but it's impossible to tie down what they are, there are some fund transfers from Latin America, Paraguay to be precise. The rest is restricted."

"The Elders meeting today wasn't a great success. I'd much rather be out in the field."

"Stick with it my boy, you'll get used to it. It's less dangerous than field work; leave that to the youngsters."

"You mean Jem."

"She's like a bloodhound."

"Dangerous."

"Can't stop her, my boy, she's determined that one, a chip off the old block."

"According to Jackson, we are about to be made irrelevant."

"There is something going on in the Caribbean, a loud and obnoxious Dutchman behaving like a modern day pirate, we will check him out."

Victoria smiled as she raised her head from the small kitchen garden. "Problems."

"You were right," said Guy explaining about the missing journalist and the Elders meeting. Victoria lived in a cottage with their respective mothers well hidden from the Monastery in the next valley, small and innocuous yet not too far away.

"You need more facts," replied Victoria as they sat in her kitchen. "Give some thought to what has happened before. What we are dealing with is a continuation of the threat started by the Teacher. Follow the money through this trading company, I need to do more research into the documents in the vaults, I am convinced there is a link to the Chinese somewhere. We need to try and find the head of the serpent; sometimes what looks like the head is only camouflage. That's what the Teacher was good at, the rumours about the Elders are concerning, be on your guard for the worst possible things imaginable."

"You should be left in peace just like Monty."

"Nonsense, it's a lonely place when you get to the top, I should know that, and I found quiet contemplation was often the answer, whether by taking a walk or just shutting the door. Incidentally there was one other thing."

"What?"

"There is a secret way out of the monastery should anything happen, a route all the way down to the northern coast. As for me, below here is a nuclear proof cellar I had built years ago. That's why the cottages exist."

Qatar

"So this is the security gadget," queried El Hamill, looking at his technical officer Habib, a tousled and nervous looking computer whiz-kid.

"Designed exactly as you specified, a totally integrated platform for security and communications all controlled from here with secure access."

"For all four rigs?"

"Yes all four, this is the master console."

"Excellent, these will ensure we have the communications to make the platforms unassailable. Let me see the functionality."

"System X here is the heart behind the operation, triple tested to our satisfaction," beamed Habib.

"Always thought you could do it," said El Hamill, smiling to himself at the thought of the power he would have at his fingertips.

"We still need to complete all the functionality tests," continued Habib, knowing the dangers of raising his master's expectations too greatly. "It may yet fail."

"I'm sure it won't," replied El Hamill quietly.

"Time to start getting serious, you must say nothing of this to anyone on the pain of death, understand?"

"Of course," replied Habib. He was a refugee from Syria; his parents depended on his money, and his choice was stark: either join El Hamill or the Islamic State. "Only you and I will ever know the System X's true functionality," he explained as they walked through to the control room with his boss.

"Time to try it out then," stated El Hamill as he heard the computer reply to him.

"I trust you here, Habib. Make sure you deliver and you and your parents will be rich." El Hamill walked away deep in thought; he was bound to others, and had debts to service, but there was no reason why he couldn't ensure that he made a great deal of money out of the huge enterprise. After all, the rigs were costing billions and he would have control. It was always good to plan ahead for number one and it was too lucrative a world to have qualms, moral or otherwise, about doing so.

Venice

"This is very ambitious, Lucretia," gasped Giuseppe as they sat at the small coffee shop in St Mark's Square, the one place Lucretia would go in public satisfied that no one would see her amongst the crowds. She sat in her favoured chair in the corner so that she could see everything and be seen by no one. Giuseppe, a balding rotund individual with a permanent frown on his face, was finding the sheer scale of his boss's plans difficult to comprehend. All he wanted was to make a lot of money and then retire to his beloved mountains.

"My brother went on a fool's errand; my way is legal, Giuseppe, providing I can keep hot heads like Sabine in their place." She privately wondered whether she had made a big mistake with the red head, but the girl had been strongly recommended. Their calls so far had been awkward and she had wondered where the woman's real motivations lay.

"I feel very uncomfortable," replied Giuseppe.

"Leave that side to me; you look after the numbers."

"Just remember, history has a nasty habit of repeating itself. Centuries ago, the Doge took its greatest ever gamble with the crusaders without any payment guarantees, and their debt default nearly finished Venice."

"I am not borrowing huge amounts, and besides, we now have an opportunity to self-fund."

"You mean this possible treasure, I don't understand why with all your great plans for the city you would want to risk so much."

"You don't understand because you don't have all the facts, Giuseppe. Don't worry, I shall not expose you, but this is about far more than making money and running Venice."

"You are right. I don't understand, but my job is to look after you."

"My dear man, that is very sweet. Trust me, this is going to be an incredible journey."

"This group of investors you call the Doge Council, they will demand good returns?"

"They will have nominal control of the holding company with their investments but what they won't know if you and I have the controlling stake, that will be kept secret and that's one of the reasons we need the Spanish treasure. It's real, Giuseppe, and it lies within our grasp. Now let's get ready for our meeting."

She looked around the room at the gathering. "Firstly, let me thank you all for your commitments. All but two of you have signed up and I can now reveal more details of the Mare Nostrum project. Firstly though, please indulge me as I talk of my own country. Nearly two and half centuries ago to this very day the Doge Council has returned. At one time the Doge was the most powerful person in the world leading a small trading republic that controlled global trade and stood as a bulwark against the strength of the Ottoman Empire under Suleiman. It is time for it to be established outside of a corrupt and bankrupt Italian state that cannot hope to get itself out of debt and a state that takes all the money from successful provinces such as ours and squanders it in the south."

"I assume you haven't brought us here to listen to a diatribe on your Italian ambitions," said Benedict.

"You have each been selected for your vast fortunes but also for your influence, because change does need to happen. You are meritocrats in every sense of the word. Modern democracy is suffocating us all, pulling the best down to the lowest common denominator instead of pulling the lowest up with the best."

"Yes we heard all that, but now tell us what sustainability and Project Valkyrie really mean," said Benedict. "What are you going to do about the Elders?"

"As we speak activities are already underway to contain the Elders."

"They will try and stop us, what I have picked up that they are concerned about developments."

"Stanton here is helping us make a substantive response to them."

"Very well then, tell us what we all really want to hear about, Project Valkyrie."

"We all live on this planet for a short while, we all hope and wish that our offspring can continue our good work but never really know. We don't even know if they will be capable of doing so and eventually we all must die. The exception to that rule is the rise of robotics and of course artificial intelligence."

"What this got to do with Valkyrie?"

"A mythical tale made famous by Richard Wagner, it tells of the quest for eternal life, what if we can give you that eternal life through guaranteeing the quality of your offspring?"

"You mean through artificial controls?"

"Selective breeding."

"Like the Nazis," sneered Benedict.

"We are far more sophisticated than that, with scientifically monitored programmes that ensure that the smartest and the strongest thrive. No one is hurt in these programmes but clearly they do involve overriding the natural selection processes we have all been familiar with. With the rise of artificial intelligence we must ensure the human species stays ahead of the ability of computers, and this is a way of doing that."

"There are huge ethical and moral challenges," replied Benedict.

"Of course there are, and that's where you have to trust us. It goes without saying that you have all been selected here today as suitable specimens and will be given the ability to control your own reproduction in a closed environment away from the judgements of other societies."

"When do these programmes start?" asked Benedict, intrigued.

"For ethical and moral reasons I cannot tell you more as a group: this will now be a series of private consultations where you will all get to decide."

"And what of our current offspring?"

"They also will be assessed and improvements made if necessary."

"What on earth does that mean?" asked Benedict.

"As I said it's a matter of private consultations, and you all have my word that no individuals here will lose out; after all, as rulers of new independent nations the only rules are the ones that we as a group will make."

"Beyond national boundaries is surely illegal," said Hatari. "You are trying to put yourself outside the jurisdiction of the authorities. Even Swiss bankers no longer have absolute discretion from national sanctions."

"It's all perfectly legal, I am not yet ready to give you all the finite details of our new world but Beyond Nations will be reality."

"Sounds too good to be true," said Antonio. "How much will it cost to take us outside national borders?"

"It will be expensive for you, but think of the ramifications of zero taxes; an investment of fifty million dollars would be a bargain for people like yourselves."

"What exactly do we get?"

"The chance to set our own rules. The top 1% of the world's population own over 15% of its wealth but are increasingly restricted by democratic foibles. As it is, we get leaders who you wouldn't employ as janitors, no hopers who make it to the top on the back of the uneducated. There are no rulers that any one of you can name who are worthy of the respect that would come from a meritocracy. That is what I am offering you."

"And the Elders will be taken care of?" asked the Contessa.

"We will take their best parts and leave the worst, like their lofty ideals to help nations, and will deliver a new and safe lifestyle for your families and yourselves."

"And what else do you want," asked a no-nonsense Taiwanese delegate named Zia Cheng, who had made her fortune in the gambling mecca of Macau.

"Your full commitment to the process. As I said, you will get the chance to live your lives without interference, your investments safe, and safe in the knowledge that all your time will be spent on doing the right thing. You will have the security of knowing that your inheritances will be safe and that you will have sustainability, there is no greater thing I can offer you, plus of course the best security systems and access to the latest robotic technologies to make your lives as productive as possible. It will no longer be necessary to read the world newspapers and wonder where the next disaster will strike, and you will be comfortable in the knowledge that you are one of the privileged few with ultimate control of the world's human affairs."

St Petersburg

Sergei smiled across to his secretary Tatyana, a leggy six foot Russian blonde with an athletic figure. She had been born in poverty in Moscow and had made her way through life by utilising her assets: a first class brain and a determination to be able to fight for what she believed was right. She had joined the elite Russian Spetnaz division as soon as she was able and before she could be taken advantage of by others stronger than her. The training had seen to that, and ensured no one came near her with intentions that were other than honourable. She had served in combat and learned the hard way with hand to hand combat. From there she had finished her service and signed up for security work, meeting Sergei in the course of applying for jobs and now in a place where she was happy and valued. Sergei for his part had been delighted when she had agreed to be his private assistant, though he knew his money had helped. She had been honest on that score so they knew where each other stood. They had grown to respect and like each other to the point where he now trusted her fully, which was why she alone was with him as they entered the secure apartment he rented on the outskirts of Moscow. The Genghis Prophecy preyed heavily on Sergei's mind after his return from Australia, it was a huge responsibility and the fact he had killed another man weighed heavily on his mind. It was far too dangerous and had to be well hidden.

Something is wrong Sergei," breathed Tatyana as they passed through the security system. "I'm sure we are being followed; it's a gut feeling but my gut doesn't often let me down."

"Surely not here."

"That's what you pay me for." Tatyana smiled back at him, she had an immense fondness for the old man as he valued her for her brains rather than her body, respected for who she was not what she looked like. "You want my professional opinion on where to hide the Prophecy."

"Of course."

"Buildings are manmade objects and can be destroyed. We need to trust Mother Nature."

"What do you mean?"

"The Prophecy was hidden before in a cave, it can be again."

"There are no caves near here."

"You're just not thinking in the right way," she smiled as she told him her thinking.

"Brilliant Tatyana, why didn't I think of that?"

"Because that's why you employ me," she smiled.

"You're right, that's why I employ you. Do it immediately and then we get away from here. There are forces out there I have sensed shadowing us since Australia."

"If that's the case Sergei don't we need help, the weight of the world is on your shoulders ever since you lost your son."

"I need to work with the Elders. They are facing a multi-faceted challenge far greater than ever before and I thank God that I have you and Rostov to support me."

"Only the best Sergei, only the best," smiled Tatyana thinking of her fellow ex Spetnaz soldier Rostov, who had also joined Sergei's team on her recommendation. She turned away so Sergei couldn't see her face. He had good reason to be worried; she now knew things that made her wary of the future, and was going to need all of her skills to survive. They were facing a dangerous enemy.

Chapter 4

St Petersburg

It was ten degrees below freezing. Sergei had long forgotten how cold it could be in the Baltic chill wind. He pulled his collar higher and climbed into the back seat of his S class Mercedes and gestured to the driver as Tatyana joined him in the back. The car was a luxury, but Russians expected you to flaunt your wealth, and he was wealthy, at least he had been the last time he looked. His oil and mining enterprise in Vladivostok had weathered the economic downturn and seemingly thrived in his absence, hence his decision to leave the running of it to others and concentrate on his philanthropic work. The search for the Khans' Prophecy was all consuming, but it was his decision; he'd sometimes wondered why he was so engaged with the Elders, but the more he thought about it the more convinced he became that what he was doing was essential.

"Ilich, drive slowly, we don't want to draw attention to ourselves. They say our fair city is the Venice of the north, but today I'm not so sure."

"Very well," replied the older man, a fully trained bodyguard and someone Sergei trusted implicitly.

It was early morning, and the cold mist hung over St Petersburg, creating a foreboding atmosphere to match Sergei's mood as they made their way to the waterfront. The stunning harbour lay ahead of him sparkling in the morning sun, and he thanked his lucky stars again for Tatyana, who seemed to have the knack of thinking ahead. This water front had been the cradle of the Russian revolution and it still inspired him when he looked across and thought of the impoverished seaman taking on the might of the Czar. Not that he would have any sympathy if such an event happened now, but he had been brought up on stories of the glorious revolution.

"Is everything set for our quick departure?"

"Everything is organised," smiled Tatyana, looking across at the Peter and Paul fortress as they approached the harbour area.

"I trust no one on this Tatyana, only you; even my Uncle Georgiou needs watching as he's one of the old Bolsheviks."

"Blood is thicker than water."

"I hope so, he knows his stuff in this water, it's in his hands. I have much to do, and little time." Sergei hadn't attempted to look inside the heavy black sealed trunk in front of them. He had been tempted, but genuinely feared what he would find; after all, enough people had already lost their lives over it, including the Teacher and Professor. Also it was hermetically sealed, and it would be a specialist job to open it properly, something he would need an expert for, and he couldn't risk that, certainly not in Russia. His concerns grew as they neared the power boat. Tatyana sensed trouble on the horizon, and every moment they were there felt as if it brought greater risk and potentially drew attention to the Prophecy. It was known to the Stalinists, so it would be known to the current authorities; a real Pandora's Box. "The team is waiting down there," he gestured as the bulletproof car was driven fast and expertly by his driver.

"Good driving," said Tatyana, keeping her eyes peeled as they drove down along to the rendezvous as Sergei busied himself with the box. She had no interest in what was in there and concentrated on the next step checking their location carefully and relaxing slightly when she saw the familiar men ahead.

"Rostov," she smiled to a burly Russian who stepped forwards. They had known each other since their days together in the spetnaz, a burly man with crew cut and infectious sense of humour.

"Good to see you again Tatyana, Sergei acknowledged the tall Russian commando pointing to his three men. "We have the full team here, Kirov and the Spassky twins."

"Good then make sure that reprobate over there is watched," smiled Sergei as an old man came hobbling into view.

"Sergei you old rake, that girl could be your granddaughter," hissed Georgiou in heavily accented Russian.

"Perhaps she is."

"Pretty girl Sergei, too pretty for you and too pretty for here."

"Let me worry about that, Georgiou."

"Aren't you going to introduce me?"

"Tatyana, meet my Uncle Georgiou, and watch him: he's a letch."

"Think I can take care of myself," smiled Tatyana shaking the old man's hand.

"If only I was forty years younger," smiled Georgiou. "Now where is this item you want disposing?"

"Here Georgiou," said Rostov, carrying the box.

"You must record where you place it."

"You will know Sergei, but we do this my way, like the old days; you have to trust me, it's out of your hands now."

"It's been some time since I could relax," replied Sergei, smiling at Tatyana.

"Any news on the Prophecy?" asked Tatyana.

"The social networks are full of speculation on whether it existed or not. The word is vague, which is how I like it."

"It's a great thing you have done, but it's taken a toll on your health."

"A little holiday then," smiled Sergei. "This place called La Gomera is nice and hot: just what we need."

"Tatyana, are you going down with Georgiou and Rostov? I need reliable witnesses."

"Of course," replied Tatyana, "it will give the old man plenty of chance to see me in a wet suit." The three of them prepared their equipment and boarded an inflatable whilst the others guarded the boat. They headed out into the waterfront and then upriver for a while. "This is it," said Georgiou, suddenly stopping the boat and appreciating how well Tatyana and Rostov worked as a team.

The river was opaque so Tatyana relied on her equipment. It was hard enough to see the old man ahead as she and Rostov carried the heavy box. She marvelled at Georgiou's knowledge of the murky depths, and a shiver went down her spine as she thought of the deaths in this area. It took them an hour down there and old Georgiou whispered with a twinkle in his eye.

"The cave is good, there's plenty of space down there. We can manage this now."

"Job done Sergei, you can relax now," said Tatyana as they surfaced, and Georgiou winked at her on their shared secret.

"What now?" she asked, stripping off the wetsuit to her bikini, Georgiou's eyes bulging.

"To La Gomera," said Sergei, as they were whisked to the apartment, he switched on his mobile and saw missed messages.

"Sergei, switch the dammed thing off," said Tatyana, "we're not out of here yet, they will track you on that."

"Sorry Tatyana," he replied as he heard the voice message from Guy and frowned. Guy suggested the package should have been brought down to the monasteries vaults. Sergei snapped the phone shut and Tatyana took it from him, taking the SIM card out and throwing it out of the window.

"It's like giving them a map of where we are," she said, looking around and stopping at the door to the apartment before suddenly flinging herself to the floor. "Get down," she screamed, as the front door disintegrated in a mixture of metal and glass. She grabbed Sergei, slammed him into the car, and they sped back to the city.

"What the hell was that," asked Sergei. Tatyana called for Rostov and made sure Sergei was alright.

"They've found us," said Tatyana. "The dammed phone signal."

"I'm sorry, it was stupid," replied Sergei calmly. "Seems like we'll be spending a little more time in Russia."

La Gomera

"Trouble," said Rose, entering the main room. She had quickly revamped the old living quarters, modernising the furnishings in front of the panoramic glass window that reached from floor to ceiling. The views were outstanding across the valley and Guys only regret was that he couldn't see Hidalgo anchored on the shoreline. Guy trusted Padraig implicitly ever since he had overseen the major repairs required after an explosion nearly wrecked it.

"Sergei hasn't replied to my message."

"Hernandez the head monk wants to speak to you. Says it's urgent." The monks provided the ideal cover for the activities upstairs. If Hernandez wanted a meeting, it meant there was a problem.

"Hernandez, how are you?" asked Guy, sitting at the huge desk as the head monk entered and stood in front of him, he'd had the desk moved to the centre of the room to dominate the space. "Are you enjoying your new responsibility?" he asked of the middle aged man in front of him.

"It's good," replied the ex-Spanish policeman.

"You want to speak to me, a problem."

"Security, this old building is decaying and needs to be rebuilt in parts with better security systems, the geography is not enough."

"I guess Victoria had other priorities from a different age."

"It's not fit for the digital age; we need cyber protection and have to protect the building and its contents."

"The vaults have an advanced timing and locking system."

"The real problem is the physical security here and the cyber security; I ran a division fighting it in Seville for three years."

"What do you want to do?"

"A complete security overhaul, I can do the specifications, just need experts to fit it, we need an expert."

"Consider it done," replied Guy as he walked over to the window and began to read past minutes of the Elders meetings. The rest of the day passed quickly as he tried to come to grips with the many nuances of the group. He paid a brief visit to the vaults below and was amazed at the degree of security. Touch sensitive pads and a complex coding system had all been installed on Victoria's insistence. In the vaults he saw rows upon rows of old manuscripts going back centuries. As the sun was setting he made his way back to the lounge area heartened at least by the security down there and looked up in surprise as Rose burst in red in the face, "there are people moving around in the valley, a group."

"Who are they?"

"Not normal tourists and certainly not locals; our cameras can't get the range yet."

"I have a long distance telescope," replied Hernandez entering, "if you follow me to the control room you can see more."

"They look harmless enough," said Guy looking at the line of figures walking along the mountain path towards the monastery. "They don't look particularly threatening."

"They are trouble," said Hernandez. "See the way they are walking with purpose, and those large bags on their shoulders aren't fishing rods."

"Can't be sure," replied Guy, "to be safe we need to get arms from the storeroom."

"I'll send out a couple of my younger monks to greet them wired; after all, we are men of peace."

"Very well, but be careful," replied Guy, now concerned as he watched the monks make their way down to the group edging carefully along the difficult terrain. It was normal to approach the monastery by road on the other side of the valley. He looked closer through Hernandez's telescope as the figures came slowly into vision.

Something bothered him about the second figure; the mannerisms in the stride looked familiar.

Suddenly it hit him like a thunderbolt, "Oh my God, get your men back, Hernandez, it's a trap." It was too late, and the ominous thud of helicopter rotors filled the sky. "Emergency," he bellowed into the intercom, "lockdown the vaults, we are under attack."

"What's happening?" shouted Rose in alarm.

"Activate the locking mechanisms and protect the vault at all costs. It's bloody Sabine, I'm sure of it. You and I have to get out fast, the monks will be safe and our mothers are on the other side of the valley, Victoria showed me the escape route yesterday."

"It's impossible, I saw her die," murmured Rose, ashen-faced. "It's impossible."

"I'm sure it's her," said Guy, staring out of the window. "Come on, we will be targets after the vaults, where is your friend?"

"Sent her over to our mothers on an errand earlier, she will be safe."

"We need to get to the Hidalgo," shouted Guy, barely believing what was happening as they were hustled out by the two bodyguards, local Spaniards named Monterey and Horte. They were ushered down into the basement as Guy's mobile rang. It was Hernandez. "Go with Monterey; I will contain them, we are men of peace."

"Do nothing, Hernandez; she will kill you if you fight, it's us they want."

"This way," said Monterey. "The vaults and basement are locked down but they are breaching the main gates so the place won't hold long. They are abseiling down from a helicopter," said Monterey. "This area isn't secure so we need to get you both out of here fast," he added, leading them across to the entrance to the emergency tunnel. He heard sporadic gunfire above them as Monterey pushed open a heavy old wooden door to reveal an old tunnel. They ran down a set of steep steps before merging in a small back area next to a large wooden door.

"Secure these areas Horte, stay here, you two follow me," barked Monterey leading the way. They ran on downwards in the dark using their mobile phone lights to avoid injury. After twenty minutes Monterey finally started to climb before they emerged in a forest.

"There's a shelter on the side of the cliff over there, we are on the north side of the island so should be safe," gasped Monterey, looking around. "I have to get back; you should stay here until dark." Guy nodded breathlessly as the burly man headed back; he had to concentrate on getting them out.

"I thought this place was impenetrable, I can't believe what has happened," gasped Rose, catching up.

"It's either the vaults or us, Sabine won't spare us that's for sure, I was just discussing the dammed security."

"What's done is done," replied Rose as they reached an old wooden shack.

"There's a hidden path that takes us down to the sea front, we'll be in the open but they're focussed on the monastery at the moment, hopefully no one will spot us," shouted Guy as he led the way weaving across the open ground trying to avoid slipping in the shale. He breathed a sigh of relief as he made it and then cursed as he heard a shout. "Run Rose," he yelled going back into the open and seeing a figure high up on the cliff top. He ran to one side to draw them away from Rose, swerving and reaching the hut realising he had been nicked. "Are you all right?"

"Yes, there's blood on your sleeve."

"Nothing but a nick, possibly a stone hit by a bullet, nothing serious," he winced. The shed was dark and musty; he switched on his mobile phone light to see where the old path lay and spotted an old curtain that revealed a path heading straight down. "We have to keep moving, they'll be down in minutes." They made their way slowly down a slippery path, praying that they didn't lose their balance. It dropped steeply and after what seemed like an age levelled out a little. After another fifteen minutes they both gasped with relief as they reached the coastline and Guy looked around relieved to see the familiar sight of Hidalgo.

"Padraig you're a star," he exclaimed grabbing his mobile and calling the familiar number.

"Sounds like a bad day on the Falls Road Belfast," boomed the familiar Irish brogue.

"We need to get away fast, Padraig."

"Ditch the mobile they'll be monitoring calls if they have any sense."

"Thanks," exclaimed Guy helping Rose to the water's edge and looking around nervously, watching as Padraig got into the inflatable and started the engine. He was fifty metres from them when a dark shadow appeared above. "For God's sake Padraig, get back to the Hidalgo," yelled Guy into his mobile as the bullets struck the nose of the inflatable, which deflated rapidly.

"Bit hot here," shouted Padraig, turning back.

"Take the Hidalgo out to sea; they won't let you get here, save yourself."

"I'll wait further out," shouted Padraig, desperately trying to reach the Hidalgo and having to swim the last few metres.

"We need to head back to the shed, the bastards are playing with us," snapped Guy in frustration as he saw the Hidalgo lift its anchor.

"We need to get to safety before the chopper comes round again," said Rose.

"Padraig will take her over to St Lucia, how the hell has Sabine survived, and now we're stranded at her mercy."

"So this is the Elders' headquarters," intoned Lucrezia's voice on the video screen as Sabine activated the connection. "Very quaint."

"Not much, is it," replied Sabine, seeing Lucrezia's face in clear detail. "We have full control of the monastery, Tresanton and his wife are trying to flee but we will find them," she smiled. It was good to be back in the hot seat and at the centre of the action.

"Well done, a smooth operation, but I don't want any more violence; the objective has been achieved, when you capture these individuals they have to be kept alive."

"It's a mistake, Lucrezia, they are ruthless."

"That's not how I work."

"You're the boss," replied Sabine, determined to make the most of the situation. Her only frustration was that Tresanton had evaded her despite being in the frontal attack deliberately to draw him out. Still, it was sweet revenge taking the headquarters of the Elders and the attack had been a masterpiece. Quickly they had taken control and left her with one thing to do, she turned to her new aide, a dark haired and close cropped woman called Danielle.

"All the areas secured?"

"Yes, but we can't access the vaults, it's protected by lock down codes."

"Then call El Hamill to help with the electronics, they're supposed to be experts," snapped Sabine, looking down the valley.

"That was too easy," said Danielle as she helped herself to a drink. Sabine had found her in a massage parlour in Prague, a girl who was ruthless and hard but also one who would take orders without question. "What do we do with the monks?"

"They're harmless, though I'm not sure about the head one, check him out. As for the two bruisers, toss them over the wall. It'll give the locals something to think about and send out the right message."

"Lucrezia said she didn't want bloodshed," replied the man called Matarife, a sombre-looking, bull-shaped man who had been drafted in to run the site.

"They died in combat, do I make myself clear?" asked Sabine menacingly.

"I shall enjoy that," smiled Danielle coldly. "Tresanton and the bitch… should I go and get them?"

"They're mine," snapped Sabine, "find them and let me know their location, they've being spotted in the north of the island."

"Yes boss," replied Danielle, she had no intention of getting on Sabine's wrong side. Her radio sprang to life and she smiled, "Tresanton's yacht is heading out to sea, we have them."

"Too obvious, it's a decoy, I know him well enough," she said, cursing as the video screen sprang into life again.

"Access to the vaults?" asked Lucrezia.

"Not yet; they have an elaborate coding system, we have our best people working on it," replied Sabine patiently.

"You must breach the vaults, there's going to be a lot of worried people linked to that invidious organisation. I will send you an expert, and no killing," said Lucrezia, terminating the connection and calling Giuseppe into the room.

Guy and Rose struggled up the steep slope as darkness slowly arrived. There was no sign of Monterey so he assumed the worst: they were on their own. He saw twinkling lights down below and a fisherman getting ready to go out for his nights catch.

"Come on Rose, our one chance is down there, we can still get away as they won't spot us so easily now. Hopefully they are following the Hidalgo, giving us enough time to get to Tenerife. They made their way down the slope and hailed the man, who looked around, puzzled. "My wife is pregnant," improvised Guy as they reached him. "We must get to Tenerife urgently. We will pay you well," he improvised in pidgin Spanish, belatedly realising the man didn't speak that language either. There was little else for it and he raised a knife. "We have to go now," he shouted. The man nodded dumbly and pointed to his fishing boat, bobbing at anchor out in the bay.

"What of our mothers, they're old and vulnerable."

"They have a safe refuge and are not targets," replied Guy as they made their way down to the boathouse. They clambered aboard the small rowing boat and the fisherman pushed them away from the shoreline, rowing hard to get through the prevailing current towards his fishing boat. Guy tried to relax and smiled at Rose as they bobbed up and down across the dark foreboding water. They had reached the larger boat when they heard the horrible familiar noise of a helicopter in the distance. It flew in suddenly from the north then it spotted them, and all hell broke loose as it swooped down the downdraft, nearly capsizing the boat. Guy looked around in despair as a figure with a machine gun and familiar red hair looked down demonically.

Abu Dhabi

El Hamill grimaced as he entered the sterile room, his dark beard bristling with anger. "I thought we had the problems fixed."

"Glitches with the software," replied Habib nervously, "nothing too serious but it won't be ready fully for the launch. We need to reprogram and get some new units, it means that the security system won't be hundred percent for a month or so but we want to get it right, the Turkish company are sending out engineers."

"Then we proceed as planned and no one knows about this, okay?" said El Hamill. "I assume the hydraulics and electrics are working," he said to no one in particular, his humourless eyes looking around the room.

"Yes, they are designed to withstand all that the weather systems can throw at them," said his Chief Designer Doreil quietly. "Stress tested to withstand a hurricane."

"I meant humans, terrorists," snapped EL Hamill, "they are the real problem in this region."

"We have built prevention measures to counter such events," replied Doreil pointing to a separate room that was sealed off. "The electronic security system is in there." He led the way through with only El Hamill allowed into the secure area. "I will take you through all the measures that are designed to stop any attack including missiles."

"I don't need all the details but I do need to see how they work," said El Hamill looking closely at the plans impressed with what he saw despite his mood.

"The most advanced electronics in the world capable of predicting attacks so preventative as well as corrective," said Habib nervously.

"Interesting," said El Hamill, "so with this I will be totally in control of the four Nostrums."

"Totally," replied Habib pleased his boss's mood was improving. "All aspects will be managed from here including of course monitors in every room."

"No one else will know this, and I mean no one," said El Hamill, immediately seeing the possibilities, his own little insurance policy. "Who else knows about these systems?"

"Myself and Waleed," said the designer nervously.

"Keep it that way," thought El Hamill. "What are they called?"

"The control units are LSU12 life sustaining units," replied Habib. He had been a top graduate from Harvard in computer sciences and had taken this job because it had no moral imperatives unencumbered by restrictions. He could have gone to Masdar, the environmentally friendly complex in Abu Dhabi, but to his mind that would have been boring. Electronics and robots were cutting edge and he wanted to be part of that. The problem with pushing boundaries was societal restrictions. El Hamill had offered him a blank cheque. He would have artificial intelligence ruling the world because humans made such a mess of it, and knew that El Hamill shared his view.

El Hamill sat down at his desk to reflect on progress. The first Mare Nostrum was now being finished in Gallipoli ready for launch. The two Abu Dhabi MN's were for the American and African markets respectively and the one being built in Singapore was for Asia. The programme schedule was broadly on course and the experts had done a very good job the entire artificial island building programme. The large Gallipoli shipyard was working around the clock now under strict secrecy to get the first Nostrum ready on time, hidden between two huge liquid natural gas ships, monsters that were slowly being assembled either side. Even better, the two in Abu Dhabi were ahead of schedule; it was all his train set, the chance to make his own mark far beyond that of his pampered brothers in the Qatari elite. The whole programme was revolutionary, particularly with the final ingredient and the one that he would take a particular interest in, Project Valkyrie. That would be his favourite moment, and he had already chosen suitable candidates to ensure his legacy was permanent.

Chapter 5

La Gomera

"You," gasped Guy as Sabine stared down at them, pointing to the harness and raising her gun. "Take the boat away," she snapped at the petrified fisherman. She stood there suspended like a demon in their worst nightmare and gesturing. "Get in the harness," she yelled through a loud hailer, "and please give me reason to shoot you."

"We have no choice, Guy," said Rose resignedly as she stepped forwards, fighting the air blast from the chopper. In the chopper they were roughly bound and tied to a stanchion by Danielle. "You don't seem over the moon to see me, Tresanton," smiled Sabine demonically.

"Go to hell."

"I'm indestructible," she grinned, relishing their discomfort. "You've no idea how long I have dreamt of this moment," she said, raising her gun, aiming at Guys forehead and releasing the safety latch. She pulled the trigger and Guy closed his eyes before hearing the click. "Unfortunately I can't kill you yet, much against my better judgement, but I wanted you to feel death." She slammed the butt of her gun against Guys head and he collapsed backwards unconscious, his body jammed against the stanchion. "I seem to recall you tried to kill me also," she said, and hit Rose hard on the head with the gun then sat down. "See to them Danielle, what a waste," she muttered to herself as she sat up front with the pilot. An idea struck her. "Get the private jet ready, these two will wish they were dead before I've finished with them."

Lochiel, Scotland

Shaw Farquharson, the Chief of the Mackintosh clan, was a proud and determined man. His ancestral home, Moy Hall, had fallen on hard times, so he found himself hiring out his particular skills to whoever paid the most. It was usually outside the law and he had debt to repay to Guy Tresanton for what had happened at Culloden, an experience that had severely embarrassed him. He was a large burly man who liked to demonstrate his strength with ridiculous feats of endurance. He was quite capable of walking for days in the mountains without food. His strength, however, was at the expense of his brains, which were limited, especially regarding the perfidious English who he saw behind every misfortune he encountered.

He was a passionate Scottish nationalist who needed leadership and that came from his fellow agitator Kenneth Macquarie, the leader of Clan Chatten and a small ferocious but weedy looking man who had the brains. Now was the time for revenge and Shaw was a man whose memory of his great ancestor Cameron of Lochiel, who had been ruined at Culloden, burned into his consciousness. Both men were in their late sixties and their respective wives had long ago given up on them, leaving them to whatever it was they did. Some would call it kidnapping, but Kenneth preferred to think of it as providing a temporary holiday in the lovely glens of north Scotland. There was nowhere to hide up there, nowhere at all, and this could lead to other work. The drugged couple had been brought to them last night from a remote airfield near Culloden, arriving at two in the morning.

"Safely locked up?" asked Kenneth, shivering and stirring the fire.

"Sleeping like bairns," smiled Shaw, "one of them is the English bastard from Culloden, we owe him."

"Stick to the instructions, we need to deliver on this one, I don't want any more problems. The wife is giving me a hard time as it is about the money situation. We keep it simple and deliver, understand?"

"Aye, guess I do, but I'd love to beat the bastard up."

Guy was in a long, never-ending tunnel and felt increasingly dizzy until finally his senses returned in the darkness. His head hurt like hell and he groaned as he tried to sit up before sensing movement next to him. He rolled across hitting his shoulder against a hard wall. "Rose is that you?"

"Yes," came a mumbled reply.

"Are you alright?"

"My head is killing me, the bitch hit me on the jaw, where are we?"

"I would guess down in the cellars below the monastery," replied Guy, trying to stand up and failing. "It's bloody cold."

"Feel like I've being drugged."

"The dammed door is locked," snapped Guy, looking around as his eyes adjusted to the dark.

"It's so cold," said Rose staggering over.

"Solid and barred," said Guy ramming his shoulder against it and feeling it move a little.

"I don't think we're in the monastery."

"Why?"

"It's freezing and there's a cold biting wind, I dreamed I was on an aeroplane and perhaps I was."

"Stand back," rapped an accented voice. The door slammed open and a large man came in carrying a rifle.

"Where are we?"

"All in good time," said Shaw, "down on the floor, now."

"Who are you?" demanded Rose.

"I ask the damned questions. Behave and do as you're told and all will be well. Eat this food, I will be back soon so don't try anything."

"Porridge," exclaimed Guy as he replayed recent events over in his mind. The voice evoked memories of a time past, Culloden Battlefield and the fight to find the Prophecy. "We're in bloody Scotland, that's why it's so cold, well out of the way whilst the Elders are finished off. You were on a plane, and so was I."

"Are you sure?"

"Must have been unconscious for hours," said Guy shivering. "We have to get back to La Gomera."

"Why didn't they just kill us?" asked Rose, "that bitch certainly wanted to."

"Orders from someone higher than Sabine, the mercenary bitch. We are no harm to them up here in the middle of nowhere with sheep and stags for company. Suggest we best get some rest and eat this stuff, it's indigestible but at least it'll warm us, we need to figure out how to get out of here."

Sleep was impossible, as their light clothes were little protection from the cold. The door swung open again, revealing light as more porridge was slammed down. "This is kidnapping," snapped Guy.

"An enforced holiday," smiled Shaw coldly.

"Where exactly are we?"

"In the middle of the highlands, about ten miles from Fort Augustus and nowhere near any help, not that a lily livered Sassenach like you would survive long up here. Either the wild animals or weather would get you. You and I have history, remember?"

"How did we get here?" asked Rose, staring at the large man.

"Flown in all trussed up like turkeys."

"So we've being unconscious for days."

"Enough talk, our instructions are to keep you here until further notice, so don't try anything, see us as your friends and the time will pass a lot better."

"I do remember you from Culloden," said Guy, "shooting at us, you bastard, you're with the bitch Sabine, she brought us here."

"Too many dammed questions," snapped Kenneth, entering behind Shaw. "You're stuck here so cause us no trouble or we will have to restrain you."

"You helped that assassin who was trying to kill me."

"Getting me confused with someone else, boy," said Shaw. He grabbed some rope and roughly tied them to the two chairs, their hands behind their backs. "A day tied will soften you up, and there's a hard frost tonight."

"Sorry Rose, I made things worse, but those bastards were at Culloden. God knows what is happening back in La Gomera," gasped Guy as the door slammed shut and something was wedged against it. "Sabine has taken over the Monastery, I could go down as the shortest serving Chair in history, and God knows what has happened to Victoria and our mothers."

"Get some rest Guy; it's not your fault."

"Perhaps, perhaps not: either way we are in severe trouble."

Despite his worries Guy fell asleep intermittently as the long day stretched on into evening. Both of them were woken periodically by something being pushed inside the door and it slamming shut. Light was fading as Guy finally managed to free himself from the ropes he had been working on during the day.

"Bingo," he said excitedly as he searched the building, "I think there's a way we can get out of here."

"How?"

"At the back I felt a loose board; if I only had a sharp blade I could loosen it, see there where the light strikes there's a small space."

"Yes I see it, we need a knife and they didn't search me," smiled Rose. "In my shoe, it's still there, I can feel it."

"Now you're talking," said Guy, who freed Rose and started to work the blade on the wood. He grunted in pain, as his shoulder still smarted from the bullet nick on La Gomera. With agonising slowness, he managed to loosen the plank, and cursed as part of the blade snapped off. Starting again, he managed to insert the knife in a leverage point and grunted in satisfaction as the board came free. He went to work on others and finally created a space large enough for them to get through. Just as he was removing the last piece of wood he heard the noise of someone approaching. Panicking, he just managed to replace the boards and scamper back to his seat as the door opened. Fortunately for him, Shaw didn't come in, and simply pushed a bowl through.

"Come on Rose, we have time now as he won't be back for at least an hour."

"Well done Guy," she whispered as he pushed hard and the wood came away. The hole was large enough.

"He's not going to like what we've done to his precious shed. Shaw doesn't bother me, the oaf, but Kenneth looks a nasty piece of work"

They both emerged from the hut into the darkness, their eyes slowly adjusting to the moonlight. They still had their watches and indeed all their possessions, except for the mobiles. "Amazing, we still have our passports," said Guy, "though little in cash and the credit cards have gone." It was just past midnight as he looked over to the house in the gloom and saw shadowy figures in the front room. A half-moon gave a ghostly glow to the scene as he looked around, seeing little but forests on all sides. The house was twenty metres away so they needed to head the other way fast, and Guy groaned as he saw Shaw emerge from the back door with blankets. "Bugger, he's coming down, we need to move, and fast," Guy hissed. "To the trees, we need to get a head start as they know the terrain."

Silently they made their way down to the forest near to the canal. Guy saw a sign in the moonlight, reading 'The Great Glen Way', accompanied by the Gaelic words 'Slighean a' Ghlinn Mhoir' with a plaque underneath it displaying an image of a green locomotive.

"What's that say?" asked Rose, panting as they stropped to catch their breath.

"A train line was planned to run along here from Fort William to Inverness but the company couldn't agree on funding," replied Guy reading by the moonlight, "what a waste, that's a huge viaduct."

"So where are we exactly?"

"The Caledonian Canal," replied Guy, "about 80 miles from one end to the other and the Great Glen Way runs alongside and over the top of the mountains, not for the faint hearted. We're about equidistant between the east and west coasts, but slightly nearer the west so I suggest we head to Fort William; all we have to do is follow the canal."

"Reminds me of Norway," muttered Rose as she fell in behind Guy, "it's certainly as cold." She had the two blankets wrapped around herself like a cloak for warmth.

"Marina ahead, I can see boats," whispered Guy after forty minutes walking.

"For a ride?" asked Rose marvelling at how extraordinarily beautiful everything was in the moon light.

"We must be at the head of Loch Lochie, the main loch leading down into Fort William. It'd be a hell of a walk around it, we need a boat."

"Over there Guy, that small cruiser, it's got an open cockpit."

"Worth a try."

Guy approached the old cruiser with peeling paint and saw that there was an outboard motor under a tarpaulin. "I know how to start these. Let's get the cover off, we don't need keys," said Guy, clambering aboard. He cut the two holding ropes and they quietly slipped the moorings and floated out into the loch, before Guy got the engine primed and grinned as it roared into life. Power and warmth were a wonderful combination and for the first time they both smiled. They made good time, and after an hour Guy saw a faint light in the east as the early sun started to rise, the head of the loch still some way in the distance.

"Dammit, thought it was too easy," groaned Guy suddenly as he looked behind. "A boat is heading towards us at speed." He cursed as powerful lights scoured the loch. With their aged Yamaha they would soon be caught.

"What do we do?" asked Rose seeing the powerful lights come inexorably closer.

"It's them, we have to abandon ship. Unless…"

He looked down in the locker and saw flares next to something even more interesting: a full oil drum. "Take the engine, I have an idea. It's a long shot, but they mean business, look at the rifles." He bent down and struggled to lift the heavy drum, slowly manoeuvring it to the side. With a huge heave he pushed it over, removing its cap as he did so, and then he heard the horribly familiar sound of gunfire. "Floor the throttle," he yelled, waiting until the drum was equidistant between them and the fast-approaching boat then firing the flare gun. It arched in the sky before falling short into the water. Three flares left. He tried again and cursed as it too fell short, as did the next: it was all down to the final one. He took extra care, trying to compensate for the rocking boat, and fired carefully, grinning with relief as he saw it strike the oil slick and catch fire. An enormous blinding light filled the sky as the approaching vessel erupted into a ball of fire.

"My God, what have you done?" screamed Rose as the back flash seared in front of them.

"Get down and cover your face," yelled Guy, and they fell to the floor of the boat, feeling the intense heat wash over them. Guy looked up in awe at the carnage he had created; he thought he saw someone jump into the water. "Must admit it worked better than I thought possible," he muttered as he checked if Rose was alright.

Fort William

It was just before nine in the morning and they were both exhausted as they reached the old fortress town and made their way down to the harbour area, the Ben Nevis mountain range towered over them. They had left the cruiser at the head of Neptune's lock then walked down the impressive staircase to sea level.

"An amazing discrepancy in water levels," said Rose as they reached the bottom.

"The Atlantic and North Sea are the same height, obviously, but Loch Lochie in the middle is a great deal higher, amazing engineering considering it's over a hundred years old and still going strong, come on we need to find transport." The watery dawn promised a dull, cold day, and Guy knew it was only a matter of time before they were caught, they were hugely vulnerable in their current state and he wondered what influence their captors had in the town.

"Hire a car?"

"They'll be watching for that and the trains. I was thinking a boat would be the best option; we should get a ride on a fishing vessel, something that wouldn't attract suspicion." They reached the harbour area and saw some early morning activity as fishermen came in from a night at sea with others preparing to leave. He looked down to the sea front. "We need to find a trawler just about to leave; it's likely the police will be alerted by the explosion up at the loch. You take one side of the harbour and I the other," said Guy. He knew it was going to be risky and difficult, and it suddenly got worse as he saw movement in the far distance up on the high road. To his dismay, he made out Shaw's profile. Then he saw something that gave him hope: a Spanish fisherman registered in Cartagena making ready to leave. "Rose," he yelled, gesturing to her and then running up to a bewildered looking crewman. "Your Captain please, I need to see him urgently," gasped Guy.

"Over there," mumbled the man, pointing to a grizzled-looking man in the wheel house. Guy shouted at Rose to jump aboard and groaned as he saw the Land Rover scream down the other side of the dock. He could see Kenneth at the wheel, and the brakes screeched as he was spotted. He was relieved to see Rose aboard as in his peripheral vision he saw the Land Rover turn and accelerate just as the trawler cast off its remaining lines.

"What are you doing on my ship?" growled the Captain, a large bearded man called Alfonso staring hard.

"We need help and will pay," gasped Guy, "a man is chasing us; he tried to rape my wife."

"A police matter."

"It's not that straightforward," pleaded Rose.

"The authorities will not like this."

"Please help us," repeated Rose, in Spanish this time, as the boat pulled away. "He attacked me."

"Very well," said the Captain warily as he saw the Land Rover screech to a halt, "five hundred Euros."

"Done," replied Guy, reaching in his pockets and realising they hadn't enough. "I will wire it to you when we land."

"Then you work your passage," snapped Alfonso, drawing himself up, "I will help you but you work hard."

"Agreed," said Guy, "two hundred Euros as a gesture of goodwill."

"Two hundred euros and you work a passage to Santander."

To Guy's relief they quickly made distance from the harbour, and watched the irate figures of Kenneth and Shaw disappear into the distance. He felt dreadfully tired and weary. The both looked at each other and nodded, slinking away to a small cabin where they slept heavily until awakening in late afternoon to nothing but sea. The boat was wallowing badly as they reached the Atlantic waters.

"That was a close escape," said Rose, sitting up as Alfonso opened the door to their small cabin.

"Dinner, ma'am, "he gestured to Rose, "and you the net repairs," he snapped, making his way to the bow.

"Oh my God," gasped Rose as she saw the state of the galley. The smell made her want to retch, which was not helped by the lurching of the old trawler.

"You'll manage," whispered Guy as he made his way to the nets, "better than being a prisoner. We need to find a way to communicate once we're out into the ocean and not being followed."

"Where are we heading?" asked Rose.

"Spain, via the fishing grounds off Brittany," replied Alfonse gesturing to the kitchen, "clean it up, it's a health risk as it is."

"You bloody idiot," screamed Sabine down the phone at Kenneth and kicking an old table at the monastery in frustration. "I trusted you to handle a relatively simple task and you let them escape, I can't believe you could be so incompetent."

"They won't get far," replied Kenneth, squirming at the verbal onslaught. He had just left the hospital after getting Shaw checked for concussion after the explosion.

"They'd better not or you will pay."

"They blew up my boat."

"That's your problem," snapped Sabine. "You were lucky to escape unscathed from the debacle at Culloden and I can't think why I decided to give you another chance, God knows you don't deserve it."

"I know where they are heading," said Kenneth.

"Then make sure you catch them and don't bloody fail or I suggest you disappear from the face of this earth because I will come looking for you."

"I don't report to you, lassie, and I don't take kindly ..."

"You'll do what you're bloody told, you idiot. Now get on with it."

Kenneth cursed as the line went dead and drove north along Loch Lochy turning alongside Neptune's Staircase. "I'll not have that woman talking to me like that," he snapped at Shaw.

"Perhaps it's time to take our own road," replied Shaw, shaken by the explosion and wishing he was back up in the glen shooting stags.

"I blame you for this bloody mess," shouted Kenneth as he screamed to a halt, "you didn't fasten them properly."

Sabine slammed down the phone and cursed long and hard. Why the hell had she listened to Lucrezia and let Tresanton escape; she'd had him in her power and could easily have finished them both off. Now because of the incompetent Scotsmen they were back to square one. She turned to the video monitor as she saw the caller's name. "They got away, but we will catch them."

"Careless, Sabine, but I don't want anyone hurt," replied Lucrezia sternly.

"You're the boss."

"That's right, I am the boss and saved your life, now things are moving faster than we anticipated. I've got a job for you, a lucrative one in fact, after you run a little errand up north." Sabine listened intently, her interest growing, before the line went dead. She looked across the valley from the monastery reflecting on what Lucrezia had just told her. A real treasure, and a chance to appropriate a fortune for herself, unlike this pile of old stones symptomatic of the archaic institution she had finally eradicated. The chance to be a rich woman; she smiled at the thought as she placed a call through to the private jet reflecting on the phone call at what a fickle creature fate was. She had always missed out on financial reward, all her work for the Teacher and Professor had earned her nothing, and it was only right and proper. "Next time, Tresanton, next time. I will get you, make no mistake on that. Matarife, you are in charge here now so don't screw up," she snapped at her assistant Danielle and they headed for the helicopter.

St Petersburg

Rostov completed his surveillance check for the sixth time and could see nothing wrong. It was time to make a move. They had been holed up in the luxury dacha near Petergof for three days now as they tried to work out whom they faced after the explosion at Sergei's apartment. Nothing, it was as if there was some invisible force keeping them here, he had used all his old contacts and still nothing. Time to take a chance; the inactivity was haunting him as he was a man of action. Years of fighting in Afghanistan and Georgia had hardened him, now he fought for what he believed in and not the state. What he believed in was Tatyana, she was his inspiration and someone he wished could return his infatuation. Instead they were comrades in arms and he had always acted professionally with her. He tried to clear his head and looked around at his men, thinking that it was time to make a decision. Instinct made him glance up at the sky and the decision was made for him. Maybe it was nothing but his gut told him otherwise, something was coming in and coming in fast.

"Action stations," he bellowed cursing as the spot in the sky became a helicopter moving quickly, too quickly. One of his men ran forwards but was gunned down as he did so and Rostov cursed at his unpreparedness. The helicopter landed and four heavily armed men climbed out before running towards him. He grabbed his radio but a black clad figure knocked him sprawling to the ground. "What the hell are you doing here, this is trespassing," he snapped at the black clad figure.

"The fat man, where is he?" came a gruff voice.

"Go to hell."

"After you," said the man, gesturing to the figure behind him. "Don't kill him, we don't want to draw too much attention. The old man is in the main room."

"This is private property," shouted Sergei as the door slammed open.

"You should be grateful I've taken time out my very busy diary for this little excursion when I have much more lucrative things to do," snapped Sabine. "You have something I want."

"I have no idea what you are talking about," said Sergei, looking desperately around the room.

"Nice company you keep," smiled Sabine. "Against the wall, and hands high or I'll have to shoot holes in that beautiful figure. I'm waiting, old man," she snapped, gesturing to her men. "Use the knife on the girl, the prophecy Sergei or she dies a slow and painful death."

"Ignore the bitch," snapped Tatyana, steeling herself as one of the two men approached drawing a wicked looking knife.

"I suggest you stop now, you see we have a problem," said Sergei calmly. "Russian billionaires like me always take extra precautions with security, hidden groups of special services men, and my own personal bodyguard and as I haven't given them a coded signal that goes out every ten minutes, I suggest you surrender before it's too late."

"Nice try," snapped Sabine, gesturing to the man with Tatyana. "The breasts first, that will get him singing like a canary then I will finish her off, which will be a great pleasure, you watch the old man," she said as she stepped forwards, ripping at Tatyana's clothing and proceeding to grab her, then cursing as she saw two of her men crumple to the floor in front of her, blood spurting from their necks.

"You were warned," snapped Sergei as all four invaders went down. "Now there's a few thing I would like to learn from you."

"Go to hell," cursed Sabine disbelieving what had happened as it had been so fast, she was in serious trouble, made worse as Rostov staggered into the room.

"Sorry boss, they got the drop on me out there but I managed to get the backup crew activated."

"What's happened at La Gomera?" asked Sergei, advancing. "We've lost all contact."

"You'll find out," replied Sabine, cursing as Tatyana hit her in the stomach and doubling up in agony.

"You can imagine my men here have many things they will do to you in the next few hours that will make you wish you were dead, I repeat the question."

"Answer him," snapped Tatyana, raising her fallen knife, "or I'll do some carving of my own. Who's behind all this? It's certainly not you, and you're well-funded judging by the equipment, perhaps you are still working for the Teacher and Professor's group?"

"Do you really think the Teacher and Professor are what this is all about? You haven't got a clue, this goes way beyond the so-called Prophecy, that's just a means to an end?"

"So we have plenty of time now, I'm listening," replied Sergei.

"You really don't want to know, believe me," Sabine swore as Rostov jerked her shoulder nearly out of its socket. Her arm was badly twisted and she screamed in agony as her teeth bit hard. "Alright, but we operate in cells on a need to know basis."

"Let's start with the Elders."

"La Gomera had been taken, the Elders are finished and Tresanton taken care of, the island monastery is in our care along with all its secrets."

"Who are you?" asked Sergei, astounded.

"Lucrezia and her Doge Council," screamed Sabine as Tatyana pricked her neck with the knife

"What organisation?" asked Sergei. "There's more behind this, has to be."

"Told you all I know, they're led by a woman who will eat you alive, old man."

"Who is she?"

"Told you, Lucrezia as in Borgia based in Venice," spat Sabine, the pain in her shoulder intense as Tatyana raised the knife.

"You're not trying hard enough," she hissed, ripping Sabine's blouse and drawing blood.

"Might have known you'd be braless, slut," she sneered.

"You'll pay for this," hissed Sabine under her breath.

"Talk or I cut, where do you go next?"

"There will be a meeting in Southern Spain in the next couple of days," gasped Sabine desperately moving her body away from the Russian and getting worried as her old scars started to ache. She had her limits after previous attacks. She only had one chance left and gritted her teeth. "Place called Alhambra, something important, I'm to meet an old man there in two days, something to do with a bank scandal, I swear that's all I know, stop the bitch."

"A meeting with whom?" asked Sergei.

"Cells within cells, you can torture me all you want but I know nothing more."

"I think you do and you're going to tell us," replied Sergei coldly. "For instance who saved you, and where have you being hiding?"

"Think you have it covered, do you?" said Sabine, suddenly slumping as Tatyana raised the knife. Suddenly there was a muffled bang, and smoke filled the room. When it cleared, Sabine was gone.

Chapter 6

Atlantic

They had been out on the rough Atlantic for four days, and were sick of the smell of fish, but at least they were making progress south through the main fishing areas. There had been no sign of any one chasing them so they were safe for now though both constantly on their guard. To the south-west of Ireland Alfonse had announced they were heading down to Santander much to the relief of everyone and particularly Rose. All attempts to get to the communications room had failed as it was guarded at all times. Their mobiles were long gone, as Alfonso had a peculiar aversion to any of the crew using them. Without communication Guy was worried that Sabine would track them down again without warning, as they were sitting ducks, and he began to plot to get access to the radio room. The all-male crew stank even worse than the fish and Rose was getting uneasy at the increasingly lustful looks of two of the younger lads. Her cooking skills had long being exhausted, and she was sick of the whole experience. There was an increasing sense of tension amongst the crew; the Captain was increasingly uncommunicative, and Javier, the radio operator, was forever staring at Rose. Guy outlined his plan to get Javier out of the radio room. Only one obvious way presented itself and Rose gritted her teeth as she approached the task. She opened the door smiling at

Javier, who initially looked puzzled and then delighted when Rose smiled suggestively at him.

"I was thinking we could take a little walk up to the bow, someone saw dolphins earlier and I'd like to get to know you better," she said in her most suggestive voice.

"I can't leave the room, my job."

"Only a few minutes, it must get very boring here."

"Very well, five minutes."

"You won't regret it," smiled Rose, grimacing at the smell of body odour as they walked down to the bow and hoping to God Guy wouldn't take long. Guy looked at the various controls on the radio panel. He was familiar with ship to shore sets from the Hidalgo and soon found the emergency wave length he needed. He worked quickly and efficiently, sending a stream of messages before jumping up as he heard footsteps.

"This is off limits," shouted Alfonse.

"Heard the radio and thought it was a mayday call," improvised Guy, "there's no one here, I thought it might be important. The place was empty."

"The hell you say."

"Yes empty, your operator and my wife, I'm angry," frowned Guy, turning to Rose, who was trying to extricate herself from the youth's clumsy fumbling. "What the hell are you doing with my wife?" yelled Guy. "Got a message to Monty along with our coordinates," he hissed to Rose as they walked away from an angry Alfonse.

The next day passed agreeably as the weather became warmer and the sea calmer. They were watched ever more closely by an increasingly suspicious Alfonse, so tried to behave normally. Rose even risked a little sunbathing on the deck, although she took care that she was alone and kept her clothes on. By the second day, Guy was restless, and wondered what on earth was happening back in La Gomera. He calculated they were now off the west coast of Brittany as he surveyed the horizon for the umpteenth time before stiffening. "Here comes salvation," he shouted, as in the distance a powerful craft came into view with markings. "It's a police launch, has to be Monty."

"Prepare for boarding," boomed a French voice as Alfonse looked angrily around and glared at Guy, "I blame you for this."

"You're not in trouble, just let us go, you have the cash, and I suggest if you don't want to lose your licence you stop."

"Thank goodness," smiled Rose as she saw the police launch get closer, "I don't think I'll ever eat fish again."

"You two look a little rough but at least alive, we were concerned you were dead, dropped everything to look for you," smiled Monty as he helped them aboard, "just in the nick of time, we need to get across to Spain post haste."

"Good to see you Monty, your retirement," asked Rose.

"Sergei has a lead, our first breakthrough, as soon as I retire everything falls apart all hell breaks loose but I was getting bored with the fishing." Monty looked exactly the same as when they'd last met him a year ago.

"What sort of lead?"

"He had a run in with our old friend Sabine in Russia, she let slip there's a meeting at the Alhambra in southern Spain tomorrow, I have a private police jet waiting at Cherbourg."

They basked in the warmth as they landed at the small Almeria airport. "I remember this place from the fight with the Nasrid two years ago," said Guy stepping down.

"Sergei has called, he says to move fast," shouted Monty as they jumped into a waiting police car. "For the first time since the attack, we are fighting back.Now tell me whilst we are driving, who do you think is behind all this?"

"Wish I knew, Monty, it came out of the blue. First we suspected something was losing two Elders members, and then the attack, we also heard from your niece Jem mentioning Tutulus, a strange name."

"I'm worried about her; she's gone solo and I've a horrible feeling that the Elders are being targeted for extinction. Tell me about the attack."

Bermuda

Jem was in a hurry as she boarded the small jet to the British Virgin Islands, squirming as she saw a fat American in the window seat next to her, one of the hazards of flying in the region. She was well versed in fighting her way around the macho police world of the Caribbean, however at this very moment she was annoyed and worried. Annoyed because for too long she had lived under the shadow of her illustrious Uncle Monty, and hadn't got the credit she deserved. She had played a key role in the Elders' victory over the Professor and was ready to strike out alone. She had been dissatisfied with the way the fight with the Professor had ended and had followed through to the holding company ZTW. Its headquarters were in Hamilton, Bermuda, and her instinct that not only had ZTW survived the demise of the Teacher and Professor but was actually thriving. Speaking to a Police Sergeant in St Bart's he confirmed they were trading under a different name. That had been her breakthrough: 'Tutulus' was the listed holding company registered in Grenada in the Caribbean with all ZTW assets absorbed.

The name Tutulus didn't translate into any well-known language but she was told it meant broadly 'keeping your spirits up'. It made little sense and nor did the German names of the owners Schmidt and Hofstadter. The attack in St Lucia had shocked her and convinced her that this Tutulus was behind the trade in young girls, whatever that meant. The registered headquarters were nothing more than a shell holding company: intriguingly, the trading records showed that most of the activity came from Latin America, from Peru, Bolivia and Paraguay. There was nothing more she could find through desk research; she would have to get on the ground, and that was risky, doubly so because her uncle's replacement in Bermuda, Chief Inspector Coates, had told her plainly to do some real work as there were two unsolved crimes on the island. She no longer had the protection of her uncle, which was dangerous, as the disappearance of Zelda had confirmed. Her enquiries had gone nowhere and she couldn't get the police on the island interested in Zelda's disappearance. She had come to a decision; she had to do something and this was the time as she couldn't get Tutulus out of her mind even more so when Monty called to tell her the Elders' monastery had been invaded. Her mind was made up; she had taken an unplanned holiday. One lead had led her to a bar in Bermuda and an encounter with a large grizzled sailor who had told her of a self-styled pirate who was terrorising people. The two had to be linked which was confirmed when he mentioned the word 'Tutulus. Pushed further, he had told her of inordinate quantities of drugs being shipped around St Bart's and a rumoured flourishing trade in young girls and the recent murder.

The flight was painful but mercifully short and she was thankful when the fat American waddled to the exit. She had called ahead to notify the local police she was coming and was grateful when she was met by a uniformed officer and driven quickly down to the main police station. The ostentatiousness of the island was astonishing, putting Bermuda into the shade; more surprisingly the police station itself was decked out in the latest furniture and expensive looking paintings, complementing the latest Ferraris and Lamborghinis outside, far too expensive for someone on a policeman's salary.

"Welcome," boomed the large and rotund Inspector Montalban, motioning for her to sit down. "Peaceful here and we aim to keep it that way, small and perfectly formed," he smiled, looking suggestively at Jem.

"I'm sure," replied Jem, ignoring the innuendo. "Thank you for seeing me." Judging by the luxurious furniture, his was more like a successful banker's office.

"As I said we have a very low crime rate and will keep it that way. These tales you tell of a modern day pirate are ridiculous, I'm afraid you've had a wasted journey, however I am prepared to offer you a nice meal out at my expense."

"I have reports that have been substantiated," replied Jem coldly, ignoring the man's patronising tone.

"What sort of reports?"

"Many, including your own Sargent Murat told me that there had been strange financial activities here linked to a company I am investigating, name of Tutulus, have you heard of them?"

"He was overzealous, I know nothing of this."

"Can I speak to him in person?"

"I must ask you, Detective Sergeant, to proceed with caution. We have a rich clientele here who come for the simple reason that it's safe, the last thing we want is unnecessary scandal, do you understand me?"

"I work to the letter of the law," replied Jem coldly as the inspector beckoned her through to a side room where a nervous little man sat.

"Sergeant Murat?" asked Jem

"I may have been mistaken about what I said," he mumbled.

"You told me there were links to Tutulus," coaxed Jem, trying to encourage the nervous man, "it's an unusual name."

"Well the name did catch my eye. They may have been trading here on the island, and they do have substantial amounts, but that's not unusual here, and it's not illegal."

"Any assets registered?"

"A yacht registered as an asset."

"Located here?"

"Yes, down at the Marina, name of Fireball, been here for a week or so."

"Excellent," smiled Jem, "then we'll pay them a little visit later."

"We?"

"I would appreciate the help, I'm sure it's perfectly safe and I only want to make a few enquiries. I have no jurisdiction but can get it if necessary," she bluffed.

"I'll need to check with the boss."

Jem was pleasantly surprised when Murat met her on the main street later that day. They made their way by foot to the gangway of a large Sunseeker yacht, a veritable floating palace that certainly didn't look out of place on a marina full of such palaces. Jem gestured to a man lounging at the top of the gangway and walked over with a nervous Murat behind her. "I would like to see the owner," she said raising her police badge.

"Private property."

"Not to the police."

"Still private."

"Do I need a warrant?" she snapped, irritated by the man's condescending manner.

Wait here," he said, and sauntered off before returning two minutes later. "Follow me, the little man stays here."

"He comes," said Jem, angered by the man's sense of superiority.

"Your decision," said the man, opening a door to a state room. "The owner will be along soon."

"My God, the money these people have, it's obscene," said Jem looking around at the sheer opulence of the teak wood and white leather seating.

She whistled in awe at some of the antiques on display, and looked out of the front panoramic window seeing the island shimmering in the evening heat. She sensed danger, and heard a faint thud and then saw Murat fall to the ground. She grabbed for her gun, realising it wasn't there as the room began to spin and she smelled gas. She desperately wrapped her light cardigan around her mouth and struggled to the couch before the world turned black.

Venice

It was one of those precious moments when she knew she was going to succeed, the terrified old man Jose Barr's weakness had been gambling and she had him exactly where she needed him. He had crumbled and spilled the beans on what was an amazing secret, a secret going back centuries and covering a hidden fortune buried in Spain. The man had arrogantly sought to justify why his veritable old bank BMN had sat on treasure that clearly belonged to the state. The Banco Mare Nostrum malpractice was about to fund the Mare Nostrum rigs.

"This is not the sort of thing I can put on the balance sheet," said Giuseppe, "it's not legitimate."

"The bank is well respected and we will transfer the value of this treasure through them, Banco Marie Nostrum or Mediterranean Bank, we have their Chairman Jose Barr and a key customer who has banked with them for decades, he brings gold and jewels once or twice a year to generate cash, now it can be ours perfectly legitimately."

"It's still illegal if traced to us, handling stolen goods, it's officially a treasure trove and there are strict rules around it."

"That's why Jose is singing like a canary."

"It's government treasure trove," repeated Giuseppe.

"Told you, it's totally safe for us," smiled Lucrezia. "Think of it as an endless supply of petty cash; that's all you need to know."

"Two failures now Sabine, this is becoming a habit," rasped Lucrezia into the phone in her private study.

"I told you we shouldn't have let Tresanton live," snapped Sabine angrily. "Way I see it I was lucky to escape with my life in Russia; your so called expert fighters from Arabia let me down, it's time to do things my way if you want results."

"I don't want violence, Sabine; we will achieve our ends without the need for that."

"Hard to avoid sometimes," replied Sabine, nursing her mouth having spent the morning in a dentist's chair having four caps on damaged teeth, "this treasure, is it real?"

"Of course, El Hamill will assist you in finding and recovering it, I'm assuming you didn't tell the Russians."

"Absolutely not, I've got four busted teeth and damaged shoulder as a result."

"Tresanton has been seen heading towards the Alhambra, how did he know?"

"I was tortured, Lucrezia, I don't suppose you know what that is like. I may have implied the Alhambra was a meeting venue but so much the better, he won't escape this time."

"Don't fail, Sabine, and don't think about playing games with me. I assume we understand each other?"

Saba - Dutch West Indies

"Dirk, you little turd," yelled Kobus from the top of the staircase, "where the hell are you?"

"Next door and with you, sir," replied Dirk.

"Well get in here fast," Kobus scowled down the landing, looking beyond to the island's capital town, ironically named 'The Bottom' sitting as it did resplendent with white houses and red roofs in the only valley on the rock. He looked like a pirate and behaved like a pirate, taking as his role model Captain Blackbeard who had terrorised the Spanish and English navies two centuries ago. His lair was a large barren volcanic rock of a potentially active volcano, Mount Scenery, that towered over the very small island, which itself consisted of little more than a sheer cliff rising almost vertically out of the sea, an imposing sight for anyone approaching by sea. Aside from a very small landing stage and a perilously small airport landing strip there was no other access to the island, precisely the reason he was based there. He stared down through his binoculars trying to find his secretary. Master of all he surveyed and servant to none he sat back in his luxurious villa, a former hotel and did indeed feel like he ruled the world. He idly watched a large craft manoeuvre carefully as it entered into the landing area and smiled to himself. Kobus Bergdorf was larger than life in every sense of the word with a large grey bushy beard covering an ample stomach. He had damaged the knee of his left leg in a boating accident which had given him the inevitable nickname of Long John Silver as he walked with a limp, although he preferred the 'Flying Dutchman'. For years he had planned and schemed building his empire on extortion and drugs, and he wasn't going to lose it for anyone.

Tutulus and what it represented was his master, but only on paper as he didn't report to anyone, there was little they could do to him, and they needed him. He had to admit, though, that their plans were bold and audacious far beyond the scale of his own private fiefdom of fifteen hundred odd souls who lived there unaware of the extent of his control. The local police force was on his payroll; it was impossible to hide from him as he knew everyone and their weaknesses. He also had an informal understanding with the Dutch Government in the shape of a local Governor, a career civil servant who was more interested in his plants than governing and would do anything for the quiet life in what was the smallest municipality of the Netherlands. The rock made seaborne assault all but impossible, and he made sure the grass landing strip at the north east of the island was well protected. Tutulus could well think they owned him, but he was his own master. Project Valkyrie, however, was breath-taking, and he was more than happy to carry it out here on his soil; it was for Valkyrie that he had appropriated the old university research building, adapting it for his own needs. It was now performing a very different type of research.

"Dirk," he yelled down the stairs, "get the maps over here for God's sake you lazy good for nothing, I have an important call."

"We have a problem," replied Dirk, a small mild mannered man with a hangdog expression.

"I pay you to deal with such things."

"The police are nosing around on St Bart's."

"I pay that idiot Montalban, kill them and make it look like an accident."

"We have a more constructive approach, "replied Dirk.

"She's good looking you say, all the bloody police I ever came across were fat, male and bald."

Alhambra Palace Granada Spain

Guy walked into the main courtyard and squinted in the unrelenting midday sun, his stomach churning at the horrific memories of couple of years previously when his then-girlfriend Leila, who was Lorna's sister, had died after being pushed from a helicopter in the palace grounds. He shuddered at the memory and turned to Monty and Rose. In the distance he saw Sergei and Tatyana approaching the palace from the other end, and Monty's mobile rang.

"I have a problem, Guy."

"What's happened?"

"Jem has disappeared off the face of the earth."

"Where was she when she disappeared?"

"Place called St Bart's, they say she went off investigating a drugs ring without any support. I'm worried and her mother is frantic."

"Very well. We can manage here, you must go."

"What is it Sergei?" asked Guy arriving and hugging his old friend. "Where's Tatyana, I thought she was with you?"

"She got a call, something about family business."

"What did Sabine tell you?"

"Only that the meeting was here, she didn't give the information voluntarily."

"Was that all?"

"I noticed a name on her mobile as she was held. Perseus."

"So?"

"The name of the room there," he pointed.

"We should go down then, what about the rest of the area, have we any idea who she is meeting?"

"None, Tatyana will reconnoitre the area, Sabine may have deliberately misled us but I doubt it. I have Rostov on the perimeter checking all visitors but there are a lot of them, it's a popular place."

"Not with me it isn't," replied Guy with feeling, "it's a place of bitter memories."

"She was pretty desperate, my men normally get what they want," smiled Sergei as Rostov came over.

"Old man is approaching, looks shifty, reckon he's our man."

"Where is he now?" asked Sergei.

"On his way down the steps."

"So Perseus it is then," replied Sergei

"He's very nervous, a typical bank clerk type," cautioned Rostov.

The old Spaniard man walked slowly across the room and looked at the sign carefully before entering. He sat down and nervously glanced at his watch.

"Woman named Sabine mean anything to you?" rasped Sergei in broken Spanish.

"I'm only a humble bank clerk, I have done nothing wrong, I come to the bank once or twice a year, do my business, and then go."

"I'm sure you are honest, I'm not here to pass judgement, just to warn you. Who are you meeting?"

"A red haired woman, she told me to talk to no one, why should I trust you?"

"You have your hands on items that have come to the attention of others and you are naive if you think that could go on, why didn't you report what you found?"

"Why should I report it? It's on our land."

"You are in serious trouble friend and worse if you don't let us look after you, I can help you get the police involved."

"The red haired woman, she told me to stand in this courtyard every day at noon, she hasn't showed so far."

"I have the Police Inspector Columba of the Almeria region here ready to meet you, there will be a finder's fee for the treasure though it may be you've already taken your share but we will do our best, I want you to wait here whilst I get the police, there is no signal here."

"Very well, but just you."

"I have other people here, dam the door is locked." Sergei looked around urgently, his heart sinking; he couldn't see anyone lurking in the shadows, he shivered involuntarily in the damp cold and hoped to God Tatyana and Rostov were on their way. "What's your name, I need a name," he snapped.

"Enrico."

"Enrico, help me with this door, we have to break it down," he said, but he got no further as something hit him from behind and he collapsed to the ground.

Venice

Lucrezia knew that they were no closer to the dammed Khans' Prophecy; the bloody thing was still missing, and probably in Russia, or locked in the impenetrable vaults at La Gomera. Lucrezia looked down on Saint Mark's Square from her private office in the Doges Palace, an office that had once housed the most powerful man, the Venetian Doge. It's time had come again, a new Venetian Republic and she would be the secret ruler the power behind the throne, just as the Calvi's had been long ago in the Renaissance. That was where her brother had got it wrong; all consumed by the Khans' Prophecy he had forgotten the first role of the Medici's and the Calvi's - never be seen or known. The tourists outside would be amazed if they knew what was going on inside the historical building, new history in the making, and years of planning were coming to fruition under Mare Nostrum.

She put down the book she had been reading by Lee Kwan Yew, the father of Singapore, a man who had led under a benevolent dictatorship just like the Roman and Venetian Empires and one she meant to replicate. Her empire would be invisible, a real meritocracy.

"Good to see you," said El Hamill, entering the room.

"Progress with Mare Nostrum?"

"On schedule for the first launch."

"And the others?"

"On target; there is huge demand, we will fill the quotas and make sure we select the best."

"Leaving ten percent for Project Valkyrie."

"Of course," smiled El Hamill.

She looked around the Council room, smiling. "Ladies and gentlemen, it is my great pleasure to invite you all here today, and a particular welcome to the most senior of the Elders, Jack Stanton and Jose Barr, the head of the Banco Mare Nostrum."

"Was it necessary to attack their headquarters?" asked Stanton.

"It was in self-defence, they were threatening to expose Mare Nostrum in the wrong light and I had the support of the local police as subjugation of monks was involved. So in collaboration with the Spanish police we rescued monks being held illegally at the Elders stronghold. The head of La Gomera police assisted us in our freeing them."

"So they are gone?" asked Benedict.

"Now let me tell you about Project Valkyrie and Tutulus."

Chapter 7

Alhambra Palace

"I don't understand, they've just disappeared," yelled Rose staring at a puzzled Rostov and wondering how the hell it had happened. They were down in the Perseus room having waited ten minutes as instructed by Sergei; it was clear there had been a scuffle and the door's lock had been tampered with. "Sergei's a big man, he couldn't just disappear. This corridor doesn't lead anywhere; it's as if they have vanished into thin air."

"The old grate is loose," shouted Rostov, trying to move it. "I'm going down, my men have the boundaries covered so they can't escape." He slammed the grate up and started to crawl, squeezing his large muscular bulk into the hole and cursing as he did so.

"They're both gone?" yelled Guy in disbelief as Rose told him the news. "The bitch Sabine must be here I can sense her at work, where's Rostov?"

"Down the drain, the whole area is cordoned off, they can't get away."

"It's impossible to check all of the exits. We need to think where they would take him," said Rose.

"I wish Monty was still here, he could authorise an immediate police shut down."

"Come on Guy, it's not too late, I'll try and persuade Inspector Columba."

"The bitch always seems to be one step ahead of us," replied Guy. "It's hard to know where to turn next, our only lead gone, and Sergei too."

"We've been in worse circumstances before, we'll find a way."

Three hours later and there was still no sign of Sergei. Guy sat with Rose explaining what had happened to the local Police Inspector Columba, who looked quizzically at them both as they tried to get him to search the drainage system.

"You have no proof of any wrongdoing, for all I know your man left of his own accord. As you will appreciate I have many things to do and only came here at the direct request of the retired Chief Inspector from Bermuda, but please don't bother me again unless you have real facts."

"Well that's that," reflected Guy as the man left, and he thought over what had happened. "Always seems to bring me bad luck, this place, and there's no sign of Tatyana either, just disappeared into the ether."

"Unless she was part of the conspiracy," replied Rose thoughtfully.

"What do you mean?"

"She could have been turned by Sabine for all we know and lured Sergei away. It's possible she could have engineered the whole thing to make sure we were heading in the wrong direction."

"Creating false leads."

"Quite possibly implanted to gain our trust."

"We have nothing, then; the old man has been taken to find the treasure and we are back to square one. I need to speak to Victoria."

"It's a real dilemma. We now have a war on two fronts. Monty is distracted by the loss of Jem, and we have to find this man," continued Victoria.

"What about at La Gomera?"

"All quiet here, someone called Matarife is in charge, seems a low level sort of person from what I can discern, I presume they have lost interest in it as they can't get into the vaults."

"How do you know they can't?"

"Trust me, I know, it's all linked electronically to me. they are much better protected than the monastery, all our history is down there, you should focus on the two other dilemmas."

"What do you suggest?"

"We mustn't fall into the error of thinking its personal and about Sabine or the monastery. My view is that it's much larger than that; someone is out to destroy the Elders, and we need to grasp at what leads we have."

"Thanks Victoria, we will talk soon."

"A war on two fronts," related Guy to Rose, "the problem is we have lost the local lead on Enrico."

"Call it woman's intuition," smiled Rose, surprising Guy.

"What do you mean?"

"I thought there was something about Tatyana couldn't put my finger on, so I took a precaution."

"What sort of precaution?"

"Our new head monk Hernandez showed me some tracking devices he had when he was in the police. I took the liberty of attaching one."

"Attaching one?"

"Inserted it in her shoe last night when we were travelling, tried to get one in Sergei's shoe also but he never took them off."

"You're a genius Rose."

"I try to be," she smiled as she lifted the small hand held receiver. A red light was blinking. "Come on."

Venice

"So, ladies and gentlemen, I have talked to you about the significance of the Project Valkyrie and Tutulus, I take it now that you are all comfortable."

"Not sure comfortable is the right word but it's certainly breath-taking," admitted Benedict, "and I'm not easily impressed. I take my hat off to you and your colleagues, providing of course you can deliver what you say. I do, of course, have certain reservations around the ethics of the whole thing and assume that you can deliver it in a proper manner."

"I share some of the moral and ethical concerns but providing it is done to certain rules and regulations it will work and will provide the security we are all looking for. I will personally ensure there are assurances on the ethics before we go live, I will promise you that. As you can see from the screen in front of you we have now got MN1 in place and ready to go live. Each of you will be divided as much as possible between the four rigs to ensure a correct spread of control."

"Remind us of what MN means?" queried Benedict.

"A delicious irony naming ourselves after a bank, don't you think? Gives it all the air of respectability," smiled Lucrezia seeing the banker squirm in his seat. The meeting had gone according to her expectations; the wealthy backers were on side and would be their allies in the weeks ahead as everything went live, all lending legitimacy to her venture. After all, she had no intention of following in her brother's footsteps. She glanced down at publicity on the glossy brochure in front of her as she made her way into her office, leaving them to talk amongst themselves.

Marie Nostrum, a world beyond the boundaries of nations, protecting from national politics, a meritocracy at the forefront of human endeavour sustaining and growing humanity's intelligence.

"I hope for a change it's good news after your past failings," she said as Sabine appeared on the video link.

"We've got Sergei; he will be with you in a couple of hours, courtesy of the private jet."

"And the location to the treasure?"

"The old man Enrico will start singing soon. There is considerable risk, as this treasure, if it exists, belongs to the Spanish nation."

"You have your instructions."

"The Russian will be with you in two hours. I have an insurance policy if he is obstinate."

"What sort of insurance?"

"His pretty assistant, she will make him talk and she will have other uses, she's very concerned about her family."

"Segovia, the girl in Giuseppe's department, so they are linked?"

"Yes," replied Sabine smiling to herself: her prior knowledge of the Alhambra's sewage systems had bamboozled the police and Tresanton.

"I want a team effort."

The next morning she made her way across the 'Bridge of Sighs' and into the prison complex, to be shown upstairs to a single cell, where a large man dishevelled and bruised turned to face her.

"What the hell is all this about?" snapped Sergei. "This is kidnapping."

"You attacked my people in St Petersburg," replied Lucrezia coldly. "The Khans' Prophecy, I'm told you are the expert."

"Don't know what you are talking about."

"Your lovely assistant betrayed you, did you know that? Told us all about your quest to Australia and the Prophecy. The trouble with you men is you always fall for a pretty girl. You don't think with your heads. You should never trust someone who is young and beautiful, particularly if they're blonde."

"Tatyana would never betray me."

"She's doing a good job of it as we speak," smiled Lucrezia, sensing the man's discomfort and uncertainty. "You were responsible for my brother's demise," she hissed.

"Ah now I get it, the mad professor, you're his sister, you are as mad as him."

"You are in no position to insult or negotiate, you are in a prison and no one knows you are here. You will remain here until you are ready to talk. Incidentally, this was the cell where they kept Casanova. Very apt, as, like you, his downfall was women, though I suspect he was a lot more energetic in that department than you judging by your size. Tunnelled his way beneath the cell and then the night before he was going to escape they moved him. Amusing, don't you think?"

"Forgive me if I don't laugh," said Sergei.

"He was the only person to ever escape from here, don't think you will be the second."

Saba - Caribbean

The smell made her wince and she woke with a start, feeling nauseous and disorientated. It was cold and gloomy, and she shivered involuntarily as she looked around. As a trained police officer she tried to put her personal feelings to one side and rationalise where she was and what had happened after being gassed. She stood up and looked around, seeing that she was in a cell of some sort with thick walls. She tried the door, and to her surprise it opened, so she made her way along a small corridor to stairs that led her to look out across a vista of red and white painted houses.

"You like the view," came a gruff voice.

"I am a police officer, this is kidnapping."

"You are here unofficially without the knowledge of your superiors so no one will miss you. Inconvenient of you to arrive yesterday, a most awkward time, means we will have to involve you directly in our plans."

"Who are you?"

"Someone you really don't want to upset," snapped Kobus. "The absolute ruler of all I survey, and your destiny, young lady, is entirely in my hands."

"That's obscene," cried Jem. "Where is this place?"

"No more questions."

"The mad Dutchman," guessed Jem looking around, "the man behind the kidnappings."

"An awful accusation my dear, I am saddened by such thinking, particularly as I've got something useful for you."

"I'm not your dammed property," said Jem angrily.

"You're a most pretty one, which is why you have an opportunity."

"What on earth are you talking about?"

"Why don't you have a good rest? They work you so hard these days in the police, look after yourself." Kobus smiled, turned, and locked the door.

Alhambra Palace

"Tatyana has gone," shouted Guy angrily as they drove towards Almeria. "You're sure about splitting, Rose?"

"You heard Victoria, we are fighting for our lives and need to split our resources. Both Sergei and Jem are important to us, so we must pursue both. The tracking device shows her still heading south-east at speed, she's in a car."

"How far ahead are they?"

"About three hours; as far as I can tell they are near Almeria city already, we have to split there, I have a feeling Jem has made progress, and I need to help her whilst you track down Sergei and the treasure."

"Guess it doubles our efforts, though I don't like it," replied Guy. "I will follow you as soon as I can. There is more developing in the Caribbean."

"At least this way we are taking every advantage," smiled Rose, looking at the gadget in her hand then frowning. "That's odd, it appears to be heading out to sea, must be on a boat."

"Give me the device," said Guy as they approached the small provincial airport of Almeria.

Abu Dhabi

The sun bore down mercilessly on the shimmering sea as the shipyard slowly arose from its slumber. This rig was no exception, although the secrecy surrounding its construction was different. As the second of the new ground breaking platforms called MN, it had huge security presence, with huge Perspex screens surrounding the site disturbing views and keeping snoopers away. Its top was covered with large opaque sheets: fake buildings to hide the real building work beneath. Its predecessor had been pre-fabricated at Doha Qatar before being towed through the Suez Canal in pieces to be assembled in Gallipoli shipyard for the European theatre. Like all four rigs being built, this second rig's completion date was coming up fast and two tug ships were already making their way to the site to take it on its journey down around the tip of Africa and across to the Americas. The man in charge, El Hammill, looked around with a practised eye, reasonably pleased with progress. His mobile bleeped, and he took the call in the control room. "Ah, my redheaded friend who I saved from certain death and who has never thanked me," replied El Hammill, "where have you been?"

"Reporting to Lucrezia."
"Well now you report to me," said EL Hammill staring at the phone screen, "in my country, respect is given to one's superiors."
"In my country it has to be earned," replied Sabine, "I have instructions for you."
"I take orders from Lucrezia only," said the Arab, his good mood evaporating. "Should have left the bitch to die in the Seychelles," he murmured to himself.

St Bart's, Caribbean

Lorna stared down from the familiar bridge of her cruise ship as it slowly made its way north-west in the harsh sunlight. She had to keep pinching herself that the ship was hers; the tangible result of her late unlamented father's estate, which she had inherited when he died. It had more than sufficient space to accommodate up to three hundred deprived children and was always oversubscribed, her way of easing her conscience over her father's misdemeanours.

Captain Jellico approached her from the bridge. "Morning ma'am, I hear you want to go ashore."

"Someone has requested to see me urgently ashore about rescuing children on the island so we may have more little people. Diane will be in charge, I assume you are taking on supplies."

"We need to be here for about four hours for fuel and supplies. You should have someone with you for safety."

"Nonsense Captain, this place is safe and we have much to do to get away on time. "I've heard this place is the San Tropez of the Caribbean, looking over there at the floating gin palaces I can see why," she exclaimed as they slowly edged their way in.

"Not my sort of place either, ma'am," replied Jellico, a grizzled bachelor set in his ways.

"Nor mine," replied Lorna, staring down at the main deck where children were milling. This was her life's quest, looking after disadvantaged kids, having inherited the cruiser from her father, who had used it as a mobile breeding camp. This was her penance, blonde and pretty in her late thirties; she had been linked with Guy Tresanton but it wasn't to be particularly as his real first love had been her sister Leila. She then had made the cruiser her life, along with the children and her stepmother Diane. Sometimes she regretted it but today when she saw the happy faces of the deprived children she knew she had done the right thing. This trip had been a month long cruise of the Caribbean with different children every week under the auspices of her 'Oleson Foundation', a charity dedicated to supporting children of all nationalities.

"I'm going ashore for an hour," she said to Diane, who had joined her on the bridge.

"Get yourself some nice clothes my dear, you deserve a break, it's been non-stop for three weeks."

"I will be back by nightfall," she said, and made her way to the small tender, who had been slightly puzzled by the short message saying that there were children in trouble who were very nervous and would only meet her. She had been directed to meet their guardian at St Bart's Marina, and she was intrigued yet cautious as she stepped ashore, marvelling at the rows of designer shops.

"Names Dirk, ma'am, I have transport here."

"Who do you represent?"

"Guardian of the children, they escaped from an orphanage on the other side of the island, we heard your cruiser was in town, the ideal opportunity to get them away, three little girls, you'll love them."

"I don't know you from Adam."

"Guy Tresanton, I sailed with him in the Caribbean, he mentioned your name to me. Here's my card; time is of the essence if we are to get them and they won't move without seeing you face to face."

"This is taking forever," said Lorna half an hour later as they crested yet another hill.

"Slow roads," replied Dirk, turning off the main road and down towards a little hamlet by the sea.

"Why are you stopping down here? I don't like this," said Lorna.

"Something wrong with the engine," said Dirk, "just take a minute."

"I don't like this," repeated Lorna, who gasped as something was held across her face.

Almeria

"Welcome, I was beginning to wonder," said Sabine as she welcomed Tatyana aboard the large yacht anchored in Almeria harbour directly down from the magnificent old castle, the Alcazabar. She had travelled with Danielle and Enrico after they had deposited Sergei at Gibraltar airport for onward dispatch.

"I didn't have much choice, did I?" replied Tatyana coldly.

"The world is full of choices, my dear."

"My family, where are they?"

"They're just fine, my dear. Now relax, we need you focussed. Oh, and by the way, this is for Russia," snapped Sabine, swinging her fist and knocking Tatyana to the ground. "I always pay my debts, now we can get our relationship off to a new start."

"You will regret that," said Tatyana, dragging herself up.

"I'm the sole reason you are still alive, now I am sure we will get on like a house on fire providing you do not argue and don't try to escape. Well done for helping us get Sergei but that's doesn't mean I trust you, understand?"

"My parents?"

"Here a picture of them with yesterday's paper, they are safe and Sergei is in Venice; he will never know you betrayed him."

"I didn't betray him."

"Whatever you want to call it is fine by me. Cast off," she yelled to Danielle, "should get fifty knots out of this."

"Where are we going?"

"On a treasure hunt, do well and you will find it extremely rewarding, now let's go below and meet our colleague."

"I don't know any more," pleaded Enrico, handcuffed to a chair. "I told you everything I know."

"The gold, Enrico, I want the exact coordinates and fast before I take away your manhood, such as it is," spat Sabine. Danielle grinned wickedly.

"It's in San Juan de los Terroros," shouted Enrico as he saw the wicked looking knife in Danielle's hand, "in a crystal mine outside the town."

"Now why couldn't you have said that at the start?" smiled Sabine. "Where exactly is this crystal mine?"

"An hour north of here on the side of the mountains."

"We can sail up the coast as close as possible then we hire transport," replied Sabine. "Organise that, Danielle. Now Enrico, tell me all about Signor Jose Barr."

"I have only met him once. He came down to see me; he seemed nervous, and wanted to get the meeting over as quickly as possible. He said that they would have to do something about the treasure."

"So the bank is in it up to their pretty necks. Interesting. He will go to prison if the Spanish find he was complicit in hiding it."

"What do we do with the Russian?" whispered Danielle as she caught Sabine alone.

"She's on our side for now, but keep an eye on her. If she misbehaves then you get first go."

"I would enjoy that."

"I know you would."

"I suggest you keep your distance," said Tatyana, and the Czech girl came over gasping as she slammed the throttles open.

"Keep her steady," said Sabine as she busied herself with her smartphone working out the exact location, "get the hire car brought to a place called La Garrucha."

"Sounds like a Mexican band," said Danielle sardonically as she raised her mobile.

"It's the nearest deep-water port to this mine which is called Giant Geode Cave Pulpi," replied Sabine examining the map. "Tell me more about this cave, Enrico."

"Before the treasure came it was well known as the home of spectacular underground crystals that shine white in artificial light. Only the locals know of the cave and they hid the treasure in the early eighteenth century."

"So how did you find it?"

"My family acquired it after the Napoleonic war and brought it here as a good place to hide it as no one else knew of the caves. Then in 2000, the caves were discovered by scientists and became well known in Spain, which was very worrying, but the scientists were so taken by the crystals they never thought to explore a parallel mine shaft that we built containing the treasure. We made sure it was better hidden than ever."

"So the treasure is safe?"

"At the moment, yes."

"Good, then you will be suitably rewarded when we find it," said Sabine. They docked at La Garrucha and made their way to a Toyota Land Cruiser that Danielle had specified. The three women plus Enrico drove northwards along a rugged coast road cleaved into the cliffs. They reached San Juan de los Terroros and then headed upwards away from the sea. He concentrated intently and then gave a grunt of satisfaction as he found a recognisable marker.

"Drive over that mound there, then go through the cactus, they are harmless to a high vehicle."

"Well hidden, we wouldn't have found it without you Enrico," acknowledged Sabine as the Spaniard led them inside, taking care they weren't spotted. The tourist season was long over so there was little danger, but they knew that it was best not to take chances. Enrico led them down a maze of dark corridors, shining powerful torches to see the way until finally they emerged into a larger space where they could see the stunning geode crystals.

"There's far more in the main cave which we are behind, only a narrow wall separates them. I come here once a year to get enough to meet my living expenses, it has served me well for many years," said Enrico.

"Wow, they are spectacular," gasped Danielle.

"Who else knows about this?" asked Sabine.

"No one, it's best that way."

"Which way now Enrico?" she added as they reached a fork in the tunnel.

"This way, replied the old man, stumbling as he led them through into the larger cave, where it was Sabine's turn to whistle at what lay before them.

"You have done well, and what better reward than to give you this as your home for eternity?"

"What do you mean?"

"End of the road, I am afraid," replied Sabine, who drew her gun and shot Enrico in the chest.

"Why did you do that?" gasped Tatyana.

"We are the only ones who know now, trust that makes you feel more secure," she grinned as she busied herself with messages that would have to be sent outside the thick walls. "Time to get organised."

Saba

"A police officer, not really my type," boomed Kobus as Jem was dragged into his office. She had been driven up the hill to Kobus's lair by a large matronly Dutch woman. Despite her predicament she had to admit the views were stunning. "She's a bit scrawny also, I like my girls well built."

"I'm a police officer and kidnapping is a custodial sentence," said Jem angrily trying to draw herself up but feeling wretched after enduring a miserable night in the cell.

"Ja, it's terrible, but don't hold a lot of faith in the police here, they are mine," he smiled.

"Just who the hell are you?"

"I'm asking the questions, this is my island, which means you do what I say; it's well beyond the jurisdiction of jumped up little officers like you and answerable to no one, in fact a blue print for our future world. Now I can see that you are lonely, so we are bringing you a friend, someone who has good reason to be part of this experiment."

"Who?"

"Wait and see. I believe she is on her way now, thanks to my smart assistant Dirk. Don't think you can escape, it's virtually impossible. Take her away and clean her up, she's no good as she is," he snapped to a matron called Juanita. "I want her ready and in good condition in two days."

"Like a piece of meat in a butcher shop."

"Exactly," smiled Kobus for the first time, "I can tell you are an intelligent cop, best stay one, eh?" He stared thoughtfully across the Caribbean i as Jem was led away, and then he heard his secure line buzz.

"My Roman Empress, to what do I owe the pleasure?"

"Not remotely funny, Kobus," replied Lucrezia as the man's large form materialised. "The organisation is pressuring for faster results, we need to double the quantity of merchandise but it has to be done ethically."

"Ethically? I don't see how ethics comes into this," boomed Kobus, "however, I know you are a sensitive soul, so yes it's just as well I planned accordingly then, despite all the grand plans and ideas it all comes down to the sloggers like me who get their hands dirty."

"I would hardly say it's getting your hands dirty, Kobus. I don't hold with aspects of Project Valkyrie, it goes against my moral code."

"Come on Empress, you want the results as well as anyone else. Don't worry dear, you shall have what you want no questions asked, just put in a word for old Kobus when the time comes."

"Mare Nostrum is ready."

"Good, then I will commence shipments as you request. Project Valkyrie has started," boomed Kobus.

Venice

Sergei shivered as he surveyed the old cell, wondering how the hell he was going to get out. He still couldn't believe that Tatyana had betrayed him; if she had it must have been for a good reason, but what was it? As far as he could tell he was up in the rafters of the large building, and he occasionally heard what he assumed were tourist groups far below. A small tourist pamphlet did indeed explain that it had taken Casanova years of tunnelling to be ready to escape when they had moved him to another cell on the day before his big escape. That's what he was up against though he didn't expect to be kept there long; it would only be a matter of time before he was being taken north, of that he was sure. Lucrezia was the Professors sister, effectively their enemy, at least he knew that now and they still they hadn't got the secret of the prophecy from him. Somehow he had to escape before they did.

It was just after midnight and he was in a troubled sleep when a noise alerted him, a thump followed by the rustle of keys. He heard someone approach, then another thump, and someone tried to open the door. He tried to get behind the door but was too late. It swung open, and to his astonishment he was confronted by a blonde girl not dissimilar to Tatyana.

"Come on, quick," she hissed, "we have to go."

"Who are you?"

"Tatyana's friend, Segovia, she told me where you were, she wanted you to know she had no choice."

"What do you mean?"

"They have her mother and father captive; I've been here for two months now, her secret insurance."

"I thought she wouldn't betray me easily. How do I know you are genuine? This could be a trick."

"I was with her in the army; do you want our regiment and registration numbers?"

"No, that's good enough for me. I'm hardly in a position to argue. Where are we going?"

"I knocked the guard out when he was preoccupied."

"Preoccupied with what?"

"My body of course," smiled Segovia, "works every time, also I had some inside help."

"You mean there is someone else here on our side."

"Without him I wouldn't have got this far as the palace is crawling with guards, I had to use my assets on the last one as we didn't expect to meet him."

"Who is this implant and where are we going?"

"Can't tell you, as I don't know his name either. You are going back to Spain. Guy Tresanton has managed to put a transmitter on Tatyana so they are following her. He needs help, and fast. My job is to get you there."

"And you, this will get dangerous for you?"

"No, I have to stay here, I am of more use here and they may need me again," smiled Segovia. "Come on, we need to move fast before the new guard arrives." They ran down through the old corridors and out to the canal side. "Your best bet is the water, it's hard to patrol but it will mean getting wet, at the other end you will be escorted from here by Manuel down there." She pointed to a small Venetian gondola moving quietly with muffled oars. The rest was a blur for Sergei as he was whisked through the night from Venice in a darkened boat to the airport and from there in a private jet to Almeria, where he was greeted on the tarmac.

"A sight for sore eyes," smiled Guy as he emerged from the small café in San Juan centre next to a large fountain. "Sergei, how are you?"

"How on earth did you get Segovia in there, she was brilliant?"

"All Tatyana's work and news to me, first I knew was when Rostov here arrived smiling. We need to get Tatyana out from Sabine's clutches now and have a coordinate for the treasure."

"Excellent. And thanks, Rostov."

"Don't thank me; thank Tatyana and her for their advance planning."

"Wasn't sure it would work so kept it to ourselves, old Spetnaz training," acknowledged Rostov. "We arranged it between us when we identified the Venice location, it's standard practice."

"I should have known," smiled Sergei.

"Sorry for losing you at the Alhambra, it was unforgivable."

"We all make mistakes Rostov, the bitch Sabine is resourceful, they used a network of sewers that came right into the room we were in, now how do we rescue Tatyana and how on earth do you know where she is?"

"We have a tracker on her, that's how, all thank to my dear wife and her intuition."

"Fantastic, so we have time."

"No. The signal is fading but we do have the last coordinates. It's good to see you again old friend, I thought you were done for this time."

"A bad experience all round, but at least we now know who we are faced with," replied Sergei.

"So she is behind everything?"

"She's certainly behind a great deal. Her organisation from what I can gather is called the Doge, people who are planning a new society called Mare Nostrum, basically an elite community of investors who want to do what they like, hence the reason they want the Elders out the way."

"The tracker light's about gone, come on Sergei, we have to rush."

Chapter 8

La Piazza, Venice

Giuseppe Hyannis was a worried man as he walked into the Caffe Florian which claimed to be the oldest café in the world. He felt like the oldest man in the world as he contemplated what was happening. There were too many unexplained events. As an accountant, he liked certainty; he found comfort in numbers, not in ideas, and there were too many of the latter in Lucrezia's world right now. He had known her for a long time and her judgement had always been sound, but now he wasn't so sure. She looked after him and she was an icon in Venice society, the real power behind the throne. The puppet ruler of Venice council was a shallow man who Lucrezia manipulated to her own ends, as he was far more interested in his appearance.

All in all, he was ideal for Lucrezia's purpose for now, but that would change. Her family had always looked after his family; it was the natural way of things, and he respected it. Lucrezia had always shared her plans with him in the early days, but now she wanted more much more and outside the City state and that made him nervous. Her grand plan and extortionate amounts of money coming from a strange organisation worried him even more. He had to try and counsel her to be prudent and stick to what made sense, to be the secret ruler of Venice as an independent state.

"You sure this is a good idea Lucrezia, it will expose you to the sort of risks that you warned your brother about," he exclaimed as she joined him in the café, sitting in her favourite seat."

"This is not some fool's errand into Mongolia. Don't worry, Giuseppe, it's all above board."

"This treasure legally belongs to the Spanish government," said Giuseppe taking comfort from the café's luxurious surroundings as they sat down in their especially reserved seats hidden from the outside world. The Caffe Florian was their little secret; only he knew she spent time here, and only he knew that she owned it.

"The Banco Mare Nostrum will take the hit."

"Ever since the Doge bankrolled the Crusaders without any guarantees risk financial safeguards have been a dirty word."

"He won the gamble, a calculated risk."

"He nearly didn't, and that's the point. Risks are only worth taking if they are based on logic and intelligence."

"I have done that," said Lucrezia, looking around the café irritated.

"You have everything you need here, Lucrezia, don't make the same mistakes as your brother."

"It's only a matter of time before someone connects my foolish brother's affairs and then I'm exposed anyway. The grand plan is set, Giuseppe, stick to what you are good at."

"There is something you are not telling me."

"Best you don't know everything, just trust me," replied Lucrezia, sipping her cappuccino and looking across at the early tourists in St Mark's Square. She scowled as she was interrupted by Margo, her highly strung assistant who had seen it all. "What is it?"

"The Russian has escaped."

"Then find him," she snapped, "and get me the Russian girl, Sergovia. Giuseppe, I want you to discuss the financing plans for Mare Nostrum and make sure we get a controlling interest: that is essential."

"Very difficult when Tutulus is putting up most of the money."

"Yes, but under a number of different shareholdings."

"It will take money, Lucrezia."

"Or an alliance," thought Lucrezia, "or an alliance."

San Juan Almeria

"Why did you kill him, we need his help to get out of here," gasped Tatyana staring down at Enrico, the Spaniard lying in the dirt.

"Do not question my actions," said Sabine, "now make sure the body is hidden in the cave whilst I signal the trucks to come to these coordinates, we're heading out as fast as possible by sea." She looked at her phone and cursed. "I don't believe it."

"What is it?" asked Danielle.

"Tresanton has been seen in Almeria, I thought I could smell the bastard, how the hell has he managed to follow us? No matter, this might be my chance to draw him in and finish it once and for all whilst my squeamish boss is out of the way. Now both of you get counting; most of this is gold but over there's a hoard of diamonds, they're easier to move and more valuable so count them first. It's going to be a long night but a chance to make some serious money."

"You don't mean all of it," replied Danielle, looking at the piles of gold.

"As I said, diamonds and gem stones first. We can't take it all but muscle is on the way."

Forty minutes later there was a commotion at the other end of the tunnel and six men arrived. "Where are they from?" Danielle asked.

"Morocco, trusted servants from the tunnel," smiled Sabine meaningfully.

"What do you mean the tunnel?"

"Never mind Danielle, get them working, and remember they are expendable so don't get too friendly."

"You don't mean…"

"No, of course not, but this cave must remain secret at all costs until we are done. Tatyana come here, your shoes."

"What do you mean?"

"Take them off. Thought so, a tracker."

"I didn't know," exclaimed Tatyana as Sabine broke the tracking device out of her heel where it was embedded under the heel.

"Didn't you now, no wonder bloody Tresanton is on our backs." Sabine kicked out at her, knocking her to the ground. Blood poured down Tatyana's face.

"Bitch," cursed Tatyana, staggering to her feet before being restrained by a grinning Danielle.

"It's the only way I work my dear, my rules or no rules, your call."

"Try this then," snapped Tatyana, breaking free of Danielle and flinging a rock at Sabine's face before turning and running as fast as she could. She ran down the tunnels, desperately looking for a way out, under no illusions as to what lay in store for her if she was caught. Finally she emerged into the early evening gloom, and she ran across scrubland to the car they had arrived in, cursing as she saw there were no keys in the ignition. She heard a commotion at the cave entrance and the car window shattered into fragment. Ducking, she ran across the wasteland, praying that they didn't have night sights as the darkness enveloped her. She ran on for all she was worth, covering about a kilometre before slowing down gasping for breath. She had deliberately run into the hills, knowing Sabine would have to follow her on foot or not at all. She listened hard for pursuit then set off again, going more carefully now. She was very worried about her family but hoped to God they would be obsessed with the treasure and leave them alone. The world was deafeningly quiet, a star lit night where she felt entirely alone in the universe. She heard a noise and cursed. Someone was following. They were more determined than she had assumed.

Venice

"Good morning everyone, and thank you for your contributions. With your confirmed support we have made Mare Nostrum a reality and your own places on the platforms are secure. You are all now officially owners of the shareholding in MN Enterprises with appropriate governing rights in the 'Beyond Nations' living experience. You all have in front of you the full brochures explaining your assigned MN platform and living quarters plus voting rights."

"Very expensive for a high grade apartment," replied Benedict.

"You know it's more than that, a life changing experience, as it says in the brochure, Islands that owe no allegiance to any nation state, their own legal entity outside national boundaries."

"No different to sea-steaders if I Google that name."

"Told you that's no more than a glorified cruise liner; this is a real state in its own right. As a human race we have for thousands of years been constrained by either by religion or nationality and uncontrolled reproduction. That labels you from the day you are born to a particular nation, religion or family. This is different; we will give you the chance to label as you see fit, a different society."

"Sounds utopian, good in principle but impossible in practice," said Benedict from the back of the room, "nothing more than a new way of building an empire, the national bit I get but not the religious stuff and this implication of a master race; previous megalomaniacs that have tried that."

"This is very different," said Lucrezia stiffly. "You have the choice here to ensure the best are not constrained by the weak, our island man made states will be governed by their own laws without allegiance to historical religious or political ties."

"Sounds idyllic and impractical," continued the Contessa. "Are the platforms safe?"

"Islands are anchored to the sea bed; they are floated into position and then fixed, the technology is proven and working."

"Really? Where?"

"All in due course, you will have a direct say in the running of the enterprise."

"How do we know that we aren't simply swapping one tyranny for another?"

"Humans are created unequal and will always be so; we are recognising that you are all part owners in the elite."

"Sounds to me like you want to play God," said Benedict.

"We are all unequal and it will ever be that way, Marxism and the liberal do-gooders only ensure only the lowest common denominator wins out and the best are pulled down. You all have equity ownership in perpetuity, for that you get the best security money can buy. For most of you here the savings on tax will more than cover the cost."

"Again what's different?"

"In perpetuity."

"Plenty of schemes like that," said Benedict.

"For generations?"

"What do you mean generations?"

"The final stage of Project Valkyrie, the part we haven't fully explained to you yet."

"I thought it was a breeding programme where we could insert our own genes into the medical gene pool."

"I guess the part we haven't shared is how we do that. You see, we preselect the girls that carry the next generation's genes by finding the most intelligent and physically perfect."

"That is playing God, and what about the poor girls, how are they found?"

"That's the part I can't explain to you," said Lucrezia, wearily knowing that her own morals were conflicted.

"I must admit it's attractive," mused Benedict, and others nodded. "You mentioned that the security arrangements were exceptional, in what way?"

"Alas, I have to be elsewhere, but you won't regret what you have just committed to, a life changing experience, a meritocracy, the smartest not the richest ruling."

"The locations."

"Precise locations will always change, but initially the four Mare Nostrums are one per continent in Europe, Africa, Asia and the Americas with the European one ready now and the others later this year. You have been allocated your individual platforms based on your primary locations but can move around, subject to the goodwill of the communities."

"Are you sure we avoid paying taxes?" asked Gerhardt suspiciously.

"Yes, providing you observe your respective countries' residency tax laws, but you know all that by now. My financial team led by Giuseppe here will make your arrangements with a time limit of tomorrow noon, as, as you can imagine, there is a waiting list."

Stanton left the meeting early, pleading an urgent appointment and wondering whether he had done the right thing in leaving the Elders. He had become wealthy through a banking empire in America, and had served years with the Elders until recently he had made the decision to leave. He had to confess Project Valkyrie was amazing; he reached for his mobile and then remembered he'd had to check it in.

"My phone, please."

"It will not be available to you until the meeting finishes, sir."

"I am a senior American business man, you have no right," he snapped at the security guard.

"When the boss says I can release it you will get it, her rules," smiled the man.

Saba

"This is monstrous," yelled Lorna in disbelief as the powerboat roared forwards. The door was locked, the windows barred, and she was feeling sea sick. She looked around and groaned wishing she'd stayed on her cruiser instead of going off on a fool's errand. She should have known that her past would return to haunt her and it undoubtedly had. Why else would someone go to all the trouble to kidnap her unless it had to do with her dammed father like always? She had been instrumental in bringing him to justice and to his death but his name hadn't died, it had returned to haunt her time and again. To her disgust she had discovered he had set up breeding camps in the north of Norway, and, even worse, that she had been the product of one. It was that background that made her feel that she had to continually atone by helping the disadvantaged. She still hoped it had all being a ghastly mistake with her father but in reality she knew it wasn't. The evidence was overwhelming. With these uncomfortable thoughts spilling around in her head she drifted into a fitful sleep as waves rocked the craft in a steady rhythm. Once she heard a slight noise in the next cabin and yelled out, but to no avail. Finally, the craft came to a halt and a hooded figure opened the door. "What the hell do you think you are doing?" she yelled as the figure to her horror drew a hypodermic syringe.

It was dark when she awoke to find herself in a cell, her arms aching and feeling like someone had thrown her into the room. Her legs were sore and her arms stiff. She staggered to her feet and looked around; it was literally a cell no more than eight feet square with a single small window high up no more than thirty centimetres in diameter. She cursed and banged on the door to no avail, until she heard a faint voice, and strained to hear it.

"Is that you, Lorna?"

"Who is that?"

"It's Jem, thank goodness; I was going mad in here."

"I can't see you?"

"I'm a prisoner in the next cell, no idea where we are."

"What are they holding us for?"

"No idea," replied Jem, sinking down exhausted as she also tried to make sense of things. An hour later her door opened and she was blinded by a light.

"Who the hell are you?" she snapped, blinking hard into the brightness.

"No questions, eat this." She crammed the hard bread and mouldy cheese into her mouth, which made her gag. The door slammed shut, and she cursed and banged on it to no avail. She couldn't hear Lorna anymore, which was worrying, though a diesel generator was now humming away in the background. She thought she heard sobbing, and desperately looked around for a way out.

Lorna cursed again as she heard Jem's door slam shut, and shouted, but there was no reply. She sat down and tried to think through what was happening. The door suddenly sprang open and a red dress was thrown inside.

"I'm not putting that on."

"Voluntary or involuntary, it's all the same to me."

She was pushed out and along a narrow corridor feeling like a tart; it had been a long time since she had worn such a dress preferring shorts and blouse on the cruise ship. She felt awkward and vulnerable as a door ahead opened and a hooded figure pushed her into a large room with sun streaming through its windows. She blinked hard and stumbled to the floor, giving a small cry as she banged her knee on the hard floor. She looked around to see a large man sat at a chair in the window with Jem in a similar red dress to his left.

"Welcome, ladies," boomed his accented voice as he stared at them. "I trust you both have had a good rest."

"This is kidnapping," objected Jem, "I demand to speak to the police."

"You won't be speaking to anyone for a little while," replied Kobus, grinning. "You are both here as my personal guests, and as long as you behave you will be well treated."

"Why the hell are we here?" asked Lorna.

"All in good time: let's just say you have been carefully selected. You will both need to get some rest before the activities commence. My, you do look fetching in the dresses: I think we will have a successful arrangement."

"What do you mean 'successful'?"

"Patience," smiled Kobus. "First, photographs, and make sure you smile or there will be no food tonight."

They were bundled unceremoniously into a smaller room by a fierce looking man and woman against a backdrop that looked like an eighteenth century English parlour. Pictures were taken before they were left in the room, which was promptly locked.

"At least it's an improvement on our cells," said Jem. "I saw the big bastard yesterday when I arrived, he was grinning then too."

"What does he mean about success, and what are the photos for?" asked Lorna.

"Your guess is as good as mine, sounds ominous with the dammed dresses though, I feel a real tart in this."

"Never seen you in a dress before," replied Lorna.

"Never worn one before, it's not standard police operational uniform," said Jem looking around and trying the door. "To answer your question I should think it's obvious what he intends to do with us, either sells us to some bloody Arabs or worse."

"What could be worse?"

"Use your imagination."

"I hope to God it doesn't mean what I really fear," replied Lorna.

"What do you mean?"

"The Dutchman uses the same words as my father used when selecting girls for his breeding camp in Norway."

"Oh my God, you've got to be joking," said Jem, desperately looking around the room. "We have to get out of here."

"But we don't even know where we are."

"I do, I noticed a brochure whilst they were taking the photos, it's a place called Saba in the Dutch West Indies. That idiot had a Dutch accent, so it fits. We need to breakout tonight before it's too dammed late."

"But how?"

"Desperate times call for desperate measures, here's what I need you to do."

"What the hell is going on?" asked the matronly woman as Lorna started hammering on the door with her shoe.

"My friend is having a panic attack; she needs regular medication or she will die," she shouted, pointing at the floor where Jem was convulsing.

"Shit," mouthed the guard, grabbing her radio. Moving like lightning Jem grabbed the guard's gun slamming it into her head as she did so, just as the second guard gave a great bellow.

"Drop it, in here," yelled Jem, slamming the door shut with both locked inside. "Come on, we need to run before the alarm goes." Together they ran along the corridor as fast as they could in the long dresses. Off to her right Jem saw more rooms. Lorna had been right: it was a maternity hospital.

"It's a nightmare," stammered Lorna behind her, "oh God, I can't believe it, my father all over again."

"Indeed it is, he was a great man well ahead of his time," came the familiar booming voice. "Ladies, if you don't mind, there are three guns trained on you and I really do not want to waste the dresses."

"You bastard, this is a breeding centre."

"You've found out rather sooner than I intended, but it doesn't matter; indeed, Miss Oleson, you are very familiar with such enterprises, a product of one yourself, all very apt. We have greatly improved upon his original version. You know it always amazed me how when he met his end that your colleagues didn't realise he was just the trial, and that we had learnt from his mistakes. The truth was that he was finished anyway, as other smarter people had taken over," smiled Kobus, emerging into the corridor as Jem flung the weapon down. "Natural selection doesn't work, your father improved on the coarse experiments of the Nazis but the real work has been done in recent years with our wealthy enhanced selection techniques. We are now sat on a population explosion and there has to be selection of the species, anyone with half a brain can see that."

"So you get to play God, do you?" snapped Lorna, as they were both handcuffed and led back to the room they had escaped from."

"Sounds good to me, and there are side benefits," said Kobus as the door was relocked and the two sheep face jailors ordered out. "The good news is you two are on the inside and will get to play key roles. Particularly you, Lorna, a second generation breeding machine, the purity of your offspring will be second to none. A very attractive and expensive proposition. I've a mind to fertilise you myself."

"This is obscene and insane," said Lorna.

"Fascinating to see your offspring," smiled Kobus, making sure they were both seated and restrained with handcuffs. The two jailors looked balefully at them as they were led away. "I think I will put you on my shortlist," he smiled looking at Lorna. "Thought you were a bit thin but you have spirit."

"Go to hell."

"The good news is you have already been preselected for partners and it really is very grim for those who aren't part of these programmes, so to justify my selection I need a total change of attitude. There will be no more escaping and swearing like troopers, you shall behave like ladies of decorum."

"You will be stopped," snapped Jem, "you're on our police suspect list so don't think you are immune."

"Ever the policewomen aren't we, but the world doesn't work your way, ma'am. Now you both have a busy day ahead tomorrow. The doctor will be with you both soon to do an intimate examination; can't have you pregnant already, can we. I'll let you stay together but don't damage the dresses." He laughed as he left the room and two new burly looking female nurses entered.

St Bart's

Rose stared around the small airport as she stepped down from the small aircraft. It had been a bumpy flight across from Barbados on the small jet. She gulped as the sloping runway seemed to jump up to hit the small plane, and relaxed as they slowed. She had reflected a great deal on the flight; it had been hard to leave Guy, but she knew they had to address both of the threats, and something was happening here. Ultimately, it came down to her instinct, which was currently screaming that the Caribbean held the answer. It was beyond reasonable doubt that the organisation was under serious threat, a six hundred year history about to be extinguished and all on Guy's watch. Something big was being coordinated and she sensed that what had happened to Jem was linked to their travails in Europe. She took a taxi into the town, amazed at the wealth on display, particularly at the marina.

"The news isn't good," declared Police Inspector Montalban looking at her coldly as she asked about Jem, "the stupid woman wilfully disobeyed my orders and my officer has serious concussion as a result. On top of which, I have my regular yachting customers asking what is going on, which affects trade."

"I thought you were here to protect the general public, not just the wealthy," replied Rose, looking around at the well-equipped office and immediately sizing the Inspector up, "you must have an idea where she may have gone?"

"She was last seen getting onto a particular yacht, and it left soon afterwards. I guess she's with them wherever they are: my Sergeant was left concussed in the water and remembers nothing. We have tried to trace the yacht Fireball without success; besides, I have other important things to do here."

"More important than the disappearance of a police officer?" said Rose angrily.

"Not here on official business, probably met someone and gone on a romantic cruise," sneered the man, sweating profusely.

"I will have to call the Chief Inspector in Bermuda, an officer disappearing is serious."

"Just who the hell are you?"

"Someone with a real concern for the fate of your fellow officers, which is more than you seem to have."

"How dare you, now get out dammit," bellowed Montalban, pointing to the door. "And think yourself lucky I don't have you locked up."

"I'll be back, don't worry," she said, and she went down to the marina and looked around at the large yachts, checking them one by one. She had tried to call Monty to no avail: she would have to do this one on her own. She went up to each yacht to be met by similar negative answers. No one had heard or seen a female two days ago and they generally looked at her as if she was mad. Finally, she reached a particularly ostentatious yacht that looked as if it had never been to sea, and which had no name plate. On closer inspection it had been removed. Rose, who had run her own cruise charter companies with Guy, knew that all boats had names. She went to the gangway to be met by an older man. He looked balefully at her and then, to her surprise, nodded.

"Yes I saw a woman here, few days ago, got a photo of her."

"What time of day was this and what was her name?" replied Rose. She stepped onto the yacht, then cursed as the door slammed shut and two youths approached. "What are you doing?" she yelled, and they knocked her to the ground.

She came to feeling groggy with a horrendous headache, and realised by the motion that she was at sea. She sat up slowly, cursing at the stabbing pain in her head, and heard voices approaching.

"A little runt, not sure she is a suitable standard," said a voice. Rough hands held her down whilst a syringe was produced, and she struggled in vain as she was injected. Her feeling of disorientation grew as time went on and she struggled to sit up on the cold floor, adding to her sense of confusion her watch was gone, finally the door of the room slammed open.

"Nice legs, but very average," gloated one of the guards.

"She's taken, you bastards," boomed a large voice.

"Where am I?" moaned Rose.

"You're the third woman to ask me that in a matter of hours, my luck keeps getting better and better," boomed Kobus. "I do like Asian girls, especially the famous Rose Tresanton, which is not good news for you as I will need to protect you from my superiors."

"Who the hell are you?"

"The master of all you survey, your future lord and master, I fear you're for the guards or the red head."

"Red head, you mean Sabine the evil bitch."

"Perhaps an Oleson mistake but the new programme would eradicate such errors," beamed Kobus.

"What do you mean Oleson, you mean Lorna's father?" gasped Rose.

"So now you get it, a true visionary whose dream did not die, just a pilot programme for the real deal."

"Sabine was a product of the breeding centre programmes," intoned Rose.

"Of course, and she is particularly upset at you escaping from Scotland. But you won't escape from here, the place is impregnable."

"I can take care of myself and have had worse than you to contend with."

"You know the more I talk to you the more I like your guts. We do have need of such talents as yours, the sort of ballsy person I need, maybe after Sabine has finished with you."

"You mentioned others?"

"This is your future now, so I guess there's no harm in you knowing. You'll be part of a great experiment, a great new designer world."

"What do you mean?"

"You and your stupid husband thought you were so clever destroying the Teacher and Professor when they were simply the warm up act, pyrrhic victories, nothing more than small bumps in the road."

"You sound like bloody Hitler."

"He lost."

"Where am I, at least tell me that?"

"A small island paradise ruled by the Dutch. Escape is impossible, so think of this as your new home as we ensure you become one of us. I like you, so I will induct you directly into Project Valkyrie. It's your lucky day: you will have me as an approved partner."

Chapter 9

Venice – Doges Palace

Lucrezia stared absently across St Marks Palazzo at the tourists browsing in the shops. They were oblivious to the real Venice and its challenges, but she would change all that. It was the second day of her Doge meeting, the honorific title appropriate as she was the secret Doge. She had adopted the name for this council also as it gave the proceedings a sense of historical relevance showing symbolically that the old Venetian Republic was returning to life again.

The invasion of La Gomera had taken place in order to break into the secure vaults and find the first of the Prophecies. She alone knew there were others; in fact, there was a trilogy of Prophecies. Her brother had told her of the existence of the Khans' Prophecy long ago, and she had known for some time of tales in Venice around the Pope's own legacy. Her own research with her team of specialists had confirmed there was indeed something tangible, as so many different texts referred to it. The problem was that she was no nearer the truth, although she now knew there was a sister document in the Vatican traced to Marco Polo and an historic meeting here in Venice between representatives of the Catholic and Chinese hierarchies, the two most powerful dynasties on Earth at the time.

She knew there had been a meeting and signature of an accord with far reaching consequences, and that there were two documents. She cursed that Sergei had escaped her clutches. They had to track him down again, a job for Sabine because whatever she may think about the woman's methods they got results. Lucrezia checked her private files on her encrypted mobile. She was a chosen one, the same as the Teacher and Professor had been, privy to the same secrets and plans. It was all hers, except she felt increasingly uneasy that she was losing control. A hidden force in the background was always watching and passing judgement; she had to keep control, and the Mare Nostrum was her answer.

She took her seat and looked around the group of investors, people she needed to keep engaged in the project - something else her brother had not been good at. She knew the Doge's success had been their adaptability, keeping such diverse powers as Suleiman of Turkey and the Catholics onside by appearing to be their friends.

"Ladies and gentlemen, we are pleased to announce we have full financing for MN, though of course higher stake holdings are to be encouraged and some of you have taken that option. From now on you are all shareholders in a new nation beholden to none other, an independent entity; indeed an entity with its own currency, a version of Bitcoin."

"Including Venice?" asked Dorte, a tall dark haired Danish industrialist who had made her fortune in the designer clothes trade.

"Secretly yes, formally at some point in the future," smiled Lucrezia. "With the recent refugee crisis across Europe the world requires guidance. We will provide that, but not like the Elders acting as secret policemen. We are going to do something practical."

"What have the nations and the international bodies got to say?" continued Dorte.

"As you would expect there is considerable scepticism, but we have taken legal advice, which is all in the folders before you. We are on firm legal ground, providing we stay outside national waters. The world's oceans are not owned by anyone and cover the majority of the earth. In a strange sort of way you could say we are returning to the habitat of our ancestors who came from the sea millions of years ago."

"Not democratic though, these elite platforms," said Dorte.

"Democracy brings us down to the lowest common denominator, drags the best down to the lowest level."

"And the Doge plus this council will govern these man made communities," continued Dorte.

"Absolutely, indeed it will truly be a meritocracy, this small group of well-educated people," smiled Lucrezia.

"And the world's media?"

"We have nothing to hide, they will get exclusive interviews to selected journalists when we launch next week in the Mediterranean which I hope some of you will be present at," continued Lucrezia.

"I think congratulations are in order," stated Benedict to Lucrezia's surprise, "there has been much thought given to this programme and I for one thank you for been included in your plans and being central to the Mare Nostrum. We need real leadership, not the posturing and baying of the world's politicians to ensure our offspring have a decent chance to be successful."

"Thank you," smiled Lucrezia, "Mare Nostrum is our passport to success, now if you'll excuse me ladies and gentlemen I have some business to attend to then I will join you all for dinner, my assistant Giuseppe here will take you through the next steps." Lucrezia followed her assistant, who had been signalling frantically from the side door. "What is it?"

"Sabine is on the line says it's urgent."

"It's an amazing find worth at least fifty million US dollars," shouted Sabine into the video screen, her excitement making Lucrezia smile.

"That's fantastic news; you need to secure it quickly."

"I reckon we have about two days grace and there's a complication."

"What?"

"The Russian bitch has escaped, can you fly her friend here for leverage."

"I have other plans for her; sort it out your own way."

"You will have the treasure Lucrezia."

"Then get on with it, I trust you on this and will leave El Hammill out of it, I know you two don't get on, we've lost both Sergei and Tatyana, there's no room for complacency."

Gallipoli

"There she is," smiled El Hammill as he looked across the water to where the Aegean Sea converged with the Dardanelles Strait to the east. In the foreground lay the gleaming superstructure nestling in the shipyard near the infamous Gallipoli beaches. "My baby," he said to his aide Waleed as he looked directly at the structure twice the height of the Eiffel Tower dominating the sea front and covered in green fabric. Two signs proclaimed a fictitious oil company Roald Oil, to keep nosy sightseers away. The accommodation platform itself had sleeping room for four hundred, a luxury city with large penthouses sheathed in black glass. To his practised eye it was everything they had planned, with the superstructure pleasingly proportioned. He knew it had cost millions, funded by the mysterious Tutulus and the new backers in the west, but that wasn't his concern; all he cared about was the operating system, its construction and security. "Everything working?"

"Nearly, just one or two glitches with the security radar system, it's not picking up long distance traffic as well as we would expect."

"You better sort it fast, Waleed, as far as our superiors are concerned everything is working okay." Secretly, he was pleased, marvelling at the central computer system responsible for the entire security system on all rigs controlled through the device in his hand. The rig had been tested in hurricane conditions and he knew the security system would alert a crack response team should anyone unauthorised arrive at the rig. Only the best tradesmen had been involved in the construction, leaving signed agreements which if breached would land them in severe legal trouble.

"The launch date next week is secure Waleed?"

"Yes, the tugs arrive from Istanbul tomorrow."

"How long to the anchorage?"

"Four days to international waters just west of Malta, then we start taking on our guests. It gives us time to make sure everything is working correctly."

"The simulations?"

"Working perfectly, we've learned a lot."

"Excellent," smiled El Hammill, "the next launch in Abu Dhabi is on schedule?"

"Absolutely," replied Waleed, knowing anything other than the affirmative would be trouble. "It starts its journey south to Cape Town next week, The American rig is ready two weeks later for the Atlantic crossing, and the final rig is heading west of Malaysia three weeks later."

San Juan Almeria

It was bitterly cold in the desert as Tatyana shivered deftly circling around where the two approaching voices were coming from. She had quietly left the small hut her senses playing havoc as she felt a presence. She slowed to a walk and looked anxiously around for the umpteenth time, seeing nothing but coarse scrub land. Tatyana was nearly at the end of her resilience, and reaching the top she dropped over the other side and waited using her spetnaz training to sense danger. She was sure they hadn't flanked her but where were they. She dozed slightly senses alert then suddenly jerked into action, her senses on high alert as she looked around for a weapon. She rolled quickly, falling to the ground as she sensed a presence behind her and lashed out with her left foot bringing the intruder crashing to the ground. There was a grunt and then a familiar noise.

"Sergei, it's you."

"What a welcome," replied Sergei, gingerly picking himself up.

"The tracking device in my shoe?"

"Got us to this region. The rest was luck."

"I betrayed you."

"I understand Tatyana, your family, besides your foresight with Segovia got me out of Venice."

"Doesn't excuse what I did."

"Hello Tatyana," said Guy smiling. "I'm glad the old man went first, never seen anyone move so fast, need to make sure I don't make an enemy of you."

"I am the enemy over what I did."

"I would have done the same, besides you led us here with the tracking device and your friend Segovia got Sergei out of Venice."

"She was brilliant, also helped me find out more about what we are facing. How did you escape, and where's this treasure?"

"Long story but we need to get there fast. It's real, that's for sure."

"You know where the treasure is?" asked Guy.

"Yes, but they're moving it."

Dawn was breaking four hours later when they made their way to the Crystal Cave. As they neared it, they could hear the noise of a truck.

"They're still here," whispered Tatyana as she inched forwards. "There's a truck just leaving over there, I hope we're not too late."

"We have no time to find out, I've contacted Monty who spoke to Columba, he says we are on our own unless there's proof. Guess he's a bit wary," whispered Guy as they made their way down to the mine.

"I don't like it," said Sergei, "too easy."

"We don't have any choice," hissed Guy.

"We could wait here and spring a trap," said Sergei.

"We have to go in; it may already be too late."

"You're sure this is it, Tatyana?" whispered Guy as they inched forwards.

"Yes, but it's too quiet," she gasped, as an almighty explosion rent the air and they flung themselves to the ground, rolling instinctively away from the blast. Another blast to their left sent earth flying across them. Someone was throwing grenades.

"We need to get back, get out of range," rasped Guy as machine gunfire erupted around them.

"Too predictable Tresanton," came a familiar voice, "you escaped from those buffoons in Scotland but your time is up. Raise your hands."

"You're surrounded," yelled Guy as he tried to figure out where the woman was.

"I don't think so or they would have been crawling around here already, just you and I and your Russian girlfriend," said Sabine emerging from an adjacent tunnel to their right carrying a machine gun.

"This is government property and they have been notified. You have no chance of getting away, the authorities will block every port," said Guy.

"Don't waste my time, Tresanton. Throw down your guns and come out."

"So you can shoot us," said Guy.

"She can't see us, if we get to the tunnel over there on the left we can get inside. She will have no choice but to come into the open," Sergei whispered.

"Good idea, Sergei. Tatyana, can you head back and get Columba? We have enough to get them in now and it will make him look a star when all this is uncovered, you've done enough and this could get messy."

"I'm better here, Guy. Sergei should go."

"He can't go at your speed," said Guy.

"He's right, Tatyana," said Sergei, "I'm practically immobile and totally out of my depth, this sort of firepower is way out of my league, at least though we can keep them pinned down here until reinforcements arrive."

"Very well, if I can convince them."

"If Columba is awkward call Monty, he'll persuade him," hissed Guy. "Come on, Sergei, we need to get into the tunnel before Sabine moves in." Sergei watched Tatyana shuffle backwards and then broke into a run as bullets slewed around him, before crouching next to Guy in the tunnel entrance.

"We have her at a disadvantage now," whispered Guy, "she will need to show her hand to get us." Suddenly there was a huge explosion above them and they instinctively dived inwards, retreating as far as they could into the cave. They heard another loud explosion and another rumble. "Bitch has triggered a cave in; she must have planned this," gasped Guy.

On the crest of the next hill Tatyana heard the loud bang and shivered involuntarily. She wondered if she should go back and see if they were alright, but the answer was provided by a blinding light.

"You've just cost me the dammed treasure," snapped Sabine, holding a gun at her. "At least those bastards won't last long in there and the authorities will be too late."

"Bitch," snapped Tatyana. She had blindly walked into the trap. She cursed herself, but was too tired to resist and slumped disconsolately in front of the red head.

"Finish loading, we take what we have and go in ten minutes," said Sabine into her mobile. "Get the bitch into the truck, I will be there once we've sorted this mess out and seen to a few private arrangements."

La Gomera

Victoria gasped in the cold night air as she made her way along the secret tunnel into the monastery, her aged bones protesting angrily. As the previous Chair of the Elders she felt partly responsible for the loss of the monastery; she knew the invaders were after the monasteries secrets, secrets that she knew better than anyone else. The invaders appeared to be scaling back: it was time to strike. She had been observing the invaders carefully and had a fair idea how many were up there: not too many. What bothered her was the durability of the vaults locking systems; she knew they were good but had heard a number of explosions over the last few days and wondered how long they could withstand the barrage. If they got into the vaults then all would truly be lost, so it was urgent that Guy returned. She emerged from the tunnel into the monk's quarters and gasped as a figure suddenly emerged. She smiled and relaxed as she saw that it was Hernandez.

"What's the situation upstairs, Hernandez?"

"Victoria, you shouldn't be here, it's dangerous."

"Have you lost any men?"

"Just the two bodyguards killed on the first day, they ignore us, treat us as idiots."

"Who is in charge?"

"A man called Matarife, saw him down by the helicopter talking animatedly, they are either getting ready to pull out or scale back."

"Have they tried to get into the vaults?"

"Many times, but have failed thanks to the special lock system you installed. They've tried explosives and even drilling, it's a good system."

"The best money could buy, so it should be, and you?"

"They leave me alone, beat me up at the start, vicious woman called Danielle did it just for the fun of it, I'm okay and want to do something to strike back, my old police background."

"Good, they will want to access the Prophecy even though it's not here," smiled Victoria. "Cover me whist I get into the vault."

"It's very dangerous, if you are seen they will kill you."

"They won't. Have you got a gun?"

"No, they took it away, that's why the woman beat me up. Said it was an unusual type of monk who carried one."

Victoria made her way quietly down stairs though to the vault where she looked around carefully before using her access codes. Neither she nor Hernandez noticed the figure hiding deep in the shadows.

Germania - Paraguay

She was nervous and excited at the same time, and determined to go through with this after being chosen specially for the assignment. Annaliese Kolb was a pretty thirty two year old blonde Dutch girl who had been brought to Saba when her Uncle Kobus had offered her a job. After a failed relationship in Amsterdam it was just what she had needed. At first her uncle's ways had been shocking to her strict Calvinist upbringing, but the extent of the operations were breathtaking and her disgust had slowly changed to acceptance. She slowly began to adapt and see what was happening in a different way; after all, breeding communities were just a way of managing nature, the survival of the fittest. She had become a full convert when she was chosen by her uncle for the ultimate assignment: to be his key liaison with the Chosen Ones.

Annaliese stared down through the muggy haze from the bridge of the old steamer and wondered if it ever did get cool; the heat and humidity were oppressive, and she was irritated by the ever present swarming mosquitos. After nearly a week's voyage upriver with Berthold, her uncle's trusted right hand man and fellow Dutchman, she prayed for the end. The old man had leered at her at every opportunity, which was disconcerting from someone of her father's generation, not that she couldn't take care of herself. Fortunately he became ill and confined himself to his cabin, until finally they reached the place that her uncle had told her so much about, a place where she would finally learn the grand plan. The old tub finally came to a halt next to a decrepit old jetty and she made her way ashore, glad to be off the stinking craft. Two blonde men made their way across to her, smiling.

"Annaliese, good to see you at last," said the taller man with a faint German accent.

"It's a great honour to meet you all," replied Annaliese, pleased that they knew her name.

"The Philosopher is looking forward to meeting you; we will take care of your servant and your luggage."

"This is a great honour," said Annalise, who had not been expecting to meet the boss so quickly. The Germans followed behind her as they were led across the clearing towards a large and incongruous gothic building.

"Built by our great forefathers Elisabeth and Forster," said the taller man.

"It's spectacular," murmured Annaliese as she was shown inside. "They lived here many years, I assume."

"They were pioneers, living off the soil as they founded the great nation unsullied by the interbreeding of old Germany. Elisabeth Nietzsche was of course the sister of the great philosopher Nietzsche, that why or leader here is so called also, very fitting. This is the spiritual and philosophical heart of the movement you know as Tutulus."

"The Chosen Ones."

"Of course."

"A testament to their great work and to show our supremacy as a race, which of course includes the Dutch," smiled the taller man. "I'm Helmut and this is Wolfgang."

"How's your uncle?" came a curiously distorted voice from the darker end of the large room.

"He sends his best regards," replied Annaliese, feeling an unnatural chill in her bones.

"You have been sent here to learn about our mission, specially selected."

"I am very honoured."

"And so you should be my dear, so you should be, there is much to do as we launch our campaign; you have joined us at a very exciting time."

"I'm ready and willing," replied Annaliese, trying to make out the human form at the other end of the gloom. The voice had a curiously androgynous sound; she had been briefed by her uncle about the Philosopher's anonymity, the person in front of her was a woman.

"There will be things you see here which you may find odd, things that may disturb you and perhaps make you question our mission. Our great ancestors carved this place out of nothing and started our journey of enlightenment: our journey now is to carry that mission though to its logical conclusion." The voice made a shuffling noise as if losing interest lost in its own world. "The Battle of North Cape, have you heard of it?"

"No, should I have?"

"Connected events are very important for our movement, the mystical side which some of my esteemed colleagues struggle with, too focussed on materialism," continued the voice. "Thirty five survivors in the freezing cold Arctic Sea in temperatures ten degrees colder than a house freezer with life expectancy of less than three minutes and yet they survived. They are the heroes of our dear people; young sailors on the Scharnhorst hunted down like vermin by the British battleships in the Great War."

"I didn't know," shivered Annaliese at the unexpected frost in the voice. Her uncle had warned her of the Philosophers predilection for bouts of introspection.

"Fourteen of them survived their ship sunken by the cowardly actions of the enemy, and yet they survived to become people of great vision and determination. Their descendants are here in Germania and are a lesson to us all."

"Why do you tell me of this?"

"Because they were joined after the war and came here for a new start, all the people here are their descendants, the new Germania."

"All ingrained with the survival instinct."

"Exactly my dear, a key part of our plan, strength through adversity, build on top of that intelligence which we will breed in and you have the perfect humans."

"Controlled breeding," murmured Annaliese.

"Yes, and you shall be a direct part of that, you will be shown our greatest achievement. Show her, Helmut."

"Over here on the monitor, we have to watch them all the time."

"A lot of girls, young girls. Some pregnant."

"Our main American breeding centre here in Germania hidden from the public's view, all the girls are of course pretty and intelligent."

"Very impressive," said Annaliese, angry but determined to see it through, to see the reason that had to be behind it all.

"So you see why it's important my own secret is kept."

"That you're a woman?"

"Yes. Some people see that as a weakness, I see it differently but it pays to let rumours grow about a strongman in Latin America; this is not a good place for females, not yet."

"Thank you," said Annaliese. She stumbled forwards and saw for the first time the deep penetrating eyes. Her knees felt weak as she looked into the gloom, and she understood.

San Juan Almeria

Guy and Sergei had burrowed in the dark for hours when they finally saw daylight, a small ray of light that meant their survival. Both were covered in grime and dust as they finally emerged and looked around. For a time they had thought they had been buried alive destined to end their lives in the earth of Spain. "We need to call Columba fast," said Sergei, noticing loose boulders in front of the main tunnel.

"Come on, we need to make sure the treasure is still here first," said Guy.

"Impossible unless you know of a way to get through those boulders; there's a good chance they have locked those labourers in there behind the door but we haven't time, we have to stop them, and there are no guarantees Tatyana got away."

"She's a big girl and can take care of herself," replied Sergei without conviction as they looked at the main tunnel. They climbed the ridge above the cave and Guy tried his mobile with no luck.

"Come on, we can get a stronger signal up the hill over there." They reached the top of the incline just as Guy saw movement off to one corner, a large truck. "We need to warn Columba."

"Monty is a better bet," shouted Sergei.

"Okay, got a signal," yelled Guy as he grunted with relief at the familiar voice.

"My boy, you do get in some pickles," replied Monty. "I've talked to Columba who we shall say has seen the error of his ways and is on his way as we speak."

"Any progress with Jem?"

"Totally disappeared off the face of the earth."

"As has Rose," replied Guy, worriedly turning to Sergei as they both slowly made their way around the cave area. "At least we are narrowing down the search areas to the Caribbean; clearly Rose and Jem have stumbled into it."

"And Venice," said Sergei looking across as the large truck came closer.

"And Venice," acknowledged Guy. "Columba needs to be told the truth about the treasure; these buggers are armed to the teeth, but we can try and delay them."

"Any more ideas on who we are up against?" asked Guy.

"A many headed monster, a hydra that has awoken from its slumber and has tentacles everywhere I'm afraid. Worse still, they're coming after us and we don't know who they are."

"We're like pieces on a chess board where the opposition is always one step ahead of us."

"Not if we get the treasure," said Sergei strongly.

"You're right," replied Guy as he saw a dark shape in the sky, a police helicopter at last.

"Well done Monty," breathed Guy to himself. "That will put the cat amongst the pigeons," he exclaimed as he saw the familiar figure of Inspector Columba making his way across to them.

"Well done," the man acknowledged as he surveyed the scene, "seems we have caught one of the top gangs operating in the south of Spain."

"And recovered a great deal of treasure," smiled Guy.

"We will see when we get chance to go in there, at the moment it's unsafe."

"We have to get after them, the ring leaders will get away"

Chapter 10

Tenerife

Two days later Guy and Sergei arrived on the largest of the Canary Islands having finally satisfied Inspector Columba that they were not complicit in the treasure investigations. They arrived late at night and headed to a luxury hotel named the Melia, which looked directly across the sea to La Gomera, a view of his new homeland Guy had not seen before. It had taken two days to convince the Inspector that they were totally on his side and that they were not somehow embroiled in the events with the treasure. He had proved to be a tough operator and had held them all under semi-arrest for a day whilst he discovered the true nature of the treasure and what had happened. It was only after Monty had got involved that he had begrudgingly let them leave for Tenerife on the understanding that they would immediately return if required. He had offered little help in trying to find Tatyana who had disappeared off the face of the earth. In addition, a warrant for the arrest of Jose Barr had gone out.

"There's something about the truck that bothers me," said Guy as they started to descend to the island.

"What do you mean?" asked Sergei glimpsing across to his trusted aide Rostov who was currently planning the assault of La Gomera in great detail with his three man team, Kirov and the Spassky twins, Ivan and Adam.

"It's not like Sabine to give up so easily, she would have fought back more. The problem with the treasure is there was no inventory before the find so no way of telling what has gone and where."

"That's Columba's problem and why he held us," replied Sergei, "so where is the red headed devil?"

"No idea, but she has Tatyana, I'm sure of it, along with some of the treasure."

"Tatyana can look after herself; we're doing the right thing coming here Guy, Victoria was insistent and worried. God, the dammed police interrogation was painful, reckon they are acutely embarrassed. Turns out this Mare Nostrum bank were in it up to their necks. They'd known of the treasure for decades and didn't alert the authorities."

"Just goes to show, you can't trust a banker."

"Apparently they have now found the Chairman Jose Barr, that's why they let us go."

"Good to hear," said Guy frowning as his mobile picked up the signals from Tenerife and buzzed into life. It was Victoria.

"You're in the vault?" he exclaimed, looking at Sergei, "that's dangerous."

"Using the secure communications unit we put in here for emergencies, they can't get in but you need to get here fast."

"Tomorrow," replied Guy, frowning as the line suddenly went dead.

"We go tomorrow, very early," said Rostov, taking charge, "we need to move forward our plans, keep the element of surprise, that call could have been traced."

"She said it was secure."

"At this end I meant," replied the Russian.

"We're in your hands," said Guy, increasingly worried about Rose. Enquiries to the police in St Bart's had revealed nothing other than that she had ignored Inspector Montalban's recommendation, a point he had made very clear.

"It's all down to moving fast and hard now," explained Rostov. "We go in at two in the morning," he told his three men from Vladivostok.

Guy's mobile rang again, and Monty asked him where he was.

"About to recover the monastery."

"I've picked up a lead, a Dutchman called Kobus, larger than life character that Interpol have been watching for some time, the underworld has been abuzz, I'm going to check the man out."

"Give me a couple of days Monty, I need to be with you. Remember your age."

"Retirement is vastly overrated; we don't have the luxury of time but I will go to St Bart's first."

"We go first thing," confirmed Guy to Rostov, "as fast as possible, I'm wanted elsewhere."

"Good, then you all listen to me for the next twenty four hours," replied the Russian as he carried out the briefing. "This will be tricky if they pick us up before we land as there's no natural beach; it's basically clambering onto rocks, we'll be very vulnerable."

"Why not the village?" asked Guy.

"Element of surprise, they are bound to have it watched, we go this way," grunted the big man.

"You okay?" whispered Sergei, half listening to the briefing.

"I'm worried about Rose and the reception we'll get. It still bothers me that there was no sign of Sabine and Tatyana in Spain."

"Sabine has to fail eventually, how many lives has she had?"

"Never underestimate her; I've learnt that the hard way, we should be hunting her down."

"Perhaps, but we need to fight back, and instinct tells me Victoria is right and the archives are critical," replied Sergei. "It's a fortress over difficult terrain and they'll be well armed.

San Juan Almeria

Inspector Jose Columba puzzled again over the facts in front of him. He had delivered an amazing hoard of treasure and his superiors were ecstatic, though he had been ordered to keep the whole affair secret as the government didn't want it getting out that a national treasure trove had lain unclaimed for centuries, particularly as one of the state banks had been complicit. Still, that wouldn't stop Columba getting a reward, but that was of little interest to him at present. His policeman's instinct was bothering him; something was wrong with the trucks, heavy and old and driven by terrified immigrants from Morocco. It was almost as if they expected to be caught. They had given up without a fight and there had been no arms aboard the truck. They were currently surveying the treasure but it was impossible to say what had been taken. He was sure that diamonds and gems were missing, and that they had been what the thieves had been after all along, the gold merely a diversion. He looked around the site one last time before leaving. It was now teeming with government officials, recording everything diligently, and headed to his car when one of his assistants came over.

"We have a sighting of the Toyota cruiser you asked for."

"Where?" replied Columba excitedly, as he had been able to assess the tracks from the dirt marks in the gravel near the tunnel, instinct telling him that whoever was driving the car was in charge.

"On the E15 to Granada heading west, it's gone through two toll gates and we're tracing it heading toward the Sierra Nevada."

"Follow it and don't attempt to intervene, I want to know where it is at all times," he barked, accelerating away from the site. He needed to get the Russian or Tresanton back as he felt that there was more going on than met the eye.

Tenerife

Matarife scowled as he looked down at the expanse of forest from the monastery. He was bored witless and had not signed up to sit in a room looking after monks. His men had reported nothing for days now and he looked forward to returning to Gibraltar in two days' time

The breeding centre in the caves complex there had been his creation, and he had seen many females come and go. He had high hopes that he would be chosen as one of the breeders and could sample the merchandise for himself. He looked up as the door opened.

"You?"

"Yes, me," said the small wiry man with the piercing eyes, which made Matarife feel as if he was shrinking every time he saw him. "I'm going down to the archives and want protection whilst I spend time there."

"You can't get in; we've been trying for some time to get in there without success."

"There's always a way. Make sure I am covered, understand?"

"Very well," growled Matarife, disliking the man intensely but knowing he was highly recommended and had powerful friends.

The early sun was slowly rising against the magnificent backdrop of Los Gigantos rock in the distance as Guy and Sergei made their way down to the launching area just below the hotel. He could see his home island silhouetted by the early morning sun behind them and listened intently as Rostov gruffly issued instructions. They climbed into the three rigid inflatables that had been flown in the previous evening and he held on tight as the craft sped across the water. Rostov had a map of the island, and the place where he had earmarked to go ashore was a small area just to the north of where Rose and Guy had been picked up by Sabine. Slowly they started to make out the details of the island as they headed for the landing cove to the north of the island. They were in camouflage with blackened faces, and they felt the sudden swell take them ashore and braced themselves as they slammed against the rocks. The men ran ashore whilst Guy and Sergei stumbled through the waves soaking wet, before swimming the last part, their weapons protected by plastic covers.

"Hold," shouted Rostov, raising his hand as his men disappeared and then rose as he signalled them forwards while Sergei struggled with his vast bulk. They followed the path away from the sea, climbing past a craggy output and then into a forested area. The soldiers broke into a steady gait which left Guy and Sergei breathless before finally they breeched a steep incline to stare down at the familiar grounds of the monastery. Thinking of Victoria down in the vaults spurred Guy on, and he was determined to help her protect the Elders' greatest asset.

Guy used his knowledge of the topography as best he could, conscious that they were at their most vulnerable as trained marksmen on the walls would be able to pick them off one by one. He pointed to Rostov as they climbed, indicating a short cut across a small bridge which was out of sight of the monastery but would expose them to anyone looking. The Russian shook his head and ran down the narrow incline, gesturing to his men to follow. Finally, they made a dash for the same tunnel Guy and Rose had escaped from on what felt like months ago.

"Stay here," said Rostov, "don't move until I call and bring Sergei with you when I call, not before."

"Pity the poor buggers if they get in his way," said Guy to Sergei as the big man collapsed in a heap.

"What the hell?" exclaimed Matarife, as his morning breakfast was interrupted by a short burst of gunfire. He ran to the door and shouted to the other men before running along the corridor. "Move it, we're under attack," he yelled, seeing shadows in the distance. He saw a figure moving down the corridor and had raised his machine gun to fire when something caught him on the side of the head and everything went black.

"They won't survive long that's for sure; they're elite Spetnaz troops looking for revenge after my kidnapping," said Sergei. The two of them sat a while and Guy thought he could hear the familiar pop of gunfire, but with the thick walls couldn't be sure. His phone crackled.

"Objective secured," snarled Rostov's voice and they made their way through the tunnel and into the building. The place looked like a bomb had hit it, which he guessed in a way it had, and there were at least five bodies strewn around. "Five dead and the others on the run, bloody amateurs," said Rostov in disgust as he pointed to Matarife, "led by a bloody incompetent, you have your HQ back."

"I need to get to the basement," shouted Guy, rushing down to the vaults without waiting for anyone. The large steel door confronted him and he entered his private codes.

"So you came at last, I wondered how long it would take you," said the small wiry man, lifting his revolver.

"Who are you and where is Victoria?"

"The old woman got in my way."

"Bastard," cursed Guy, seeing Victoria on the floor in the distance. "Why?"

"She's only sedated; I'm not finished with her yet, now show me where the Prophecy is."

"I have no idea what you are talking about."

"Come, Tresanton. I know all about you, you have one minute to tell me or I blow your head off."

"Who the hell are you?" asked Guy trying to place the European accent.

"The name's Tago, but to you that's irrelevant. Twenty seconds and counting."

"I told you I don't know about the Prophecy, Sergei managed that."

"Then get him before I kill her, you have five minutes, I know he's here."

"He doesn't know either."

"Very well, maybe this will aid your memory." Tago raised the gun and pointed it at Victoria's head. "She's dispensable now you're here." He started to pull the trigger and then crumpled to the floor.

"Good job I followed you," said Rostov as he looked down at the man he had shot. "Now what's that scum Tago doing here, last time I saw him he was heading up a major crime syndicate in Russia."

"You knew him?"

"Unfortunately yes, a rabid Ukrainian fascist, went into hiding, was last heard of in Latin America. They don't get much worse than him, a real viper."

"Thanks Rostov, you saved my life again."

"Victoria, she's moving."

"I've had better days, I must admit," murmured Victoria, looking dazedly around as Guy cradled her. "Thanks."

"Thank Rostov here, he saw to the intruder."

"I am puzzled why they would send a top hitman down here," said Guy.

"Because they are desperate. He used chloroform. Still, the vault is secure, there's something there they want desperately and I can only think it links to the Chinese. I remember reading about it at the time of a football match at the turn of the last century. There was a Chinese presence there, a ghostly figure in the background. I've done some quick research and found a connection to Zheng He."

"Zheng He the Admiral?" asked Guy.

"Yes, the same, the interesting fact is there are writings by him talking about an enemy, an enemy so great that it would test all the courage of those committed to his ideals to fight them off. This Chinese link permeates all his later writings recently uncovered. I believe this provides the key to everything that is happening, only I've no idea how."

"So this Tago was brought in by them."

"Probably, what's happened to Brother Francisco?"

"Didn't notice him," replied Guy, looking across at a monk in the corridor lying at an unnatural angle and clearly dead.

"Well done Guy, you've rescued the Elders just in time."

"Thanks to Sergei and Rostov, Rose is still missing, I have to find her now, "the rest of the place is secure and all the invaders taken care of, "Rostov's gone to check the island out and make sure there are no vipers left." It felt good to be back in charge; Victoria had got him thinking.

An hour later they all assembled in the main lounge amongst a mess of broken glass and furniture. "How the hell did they take over so easily?" asked Sergei as they reviewed the day's events.

"They came in under the radar, a specialist unit, Hernandez was warning me of the same when it actually happened. We need to tighten up on security."

"Mixture of Europeans and Latin American mercenaries," replied Sergei, "I am more concerned about that rat Tago down in the vaults; Rostov tells me he's more than a fascist, he's a high level hitman and on every watch list in the crime scene. Last he heard he was involved in Latin America with drugs earning millions, so why would he come here?"

"Why not?"

"He has millions," said Rostov, entering and wiping his brow. "I heard a rumour he was setting up his own business in Paraguay, so it doesn't make sense."

"Not when they went out of their way not to hurt anyone, including you, Guy. This Tago is the one who killed your two security guards cutting their throats."

"So we have a renegade?" asked Guy.

"More likely someone who is being paid a lot of money and working for a different organisation funded separately, perhaps we have a rift at the top," speculated Sergei.

"There's something else you should know," continued Victoria, "we heard Sabine talking about a Project Valkyrie through the listening system you had installed. It was very revealing; she was talking about human experiments led from Latin America, she was dismissive of Lucrezia, and also talked about artificial islands."

"Latin America, are you sure?"

"That's what we heard, didn't we Jane?" said Victoria turning to Guy's mother.

"We did, she's a nasty piece of work and had someone with her called Danielle who sounded as bad, and they were gloating about how they were going to kill you both."

"I almost miss the good old days of the Teacher; at least he was a straightforward threat."

"Perhaps not," murmured Victoria, "this Chinese angle bothers me, I'm beginning to wonder if he was only one in a long chain of mandarins, and the real danger is elsewhere."

"Makes it more important than ever to stop them getting the Prophecy," said Sergei.

"We need to convene the Elders for an emergency meeting," said Guy. "Great job Rostov, my eternal thanks."

"My job," replied the Russian gruffly. "What now?"

"I'm going to the Caribbean, Monty has gone too quiet."

"It's important you show the Elders that we are back in control and fighting."

"Of course, tomorrow, then I head west, and you?"

"Inspector Columba has asked me to return urgently, reckons he has a lead on Sabine," replied Sergei, "I've always believed attack is the best form of defence, they have been making all the moves, we need to strike them where it hurts."

"And where would that be?"

"These platforms, the Mare Nostrum, that's where we can hurt their credibility. Rostov and his men can cause some serious damage."

It was a sombre Elders meeting, and was down to eight members, although Victoria had been working hard behind the scenes to recruit more members from the long list. It was an ill wind that blew no good and the loss of members had brought others to the fore.

"Seems a great deal has happened since the last meeting, most of it bad," boomed Jackson, a man used to getting answers.

"We were unprepared for what happened," conceded Guy, looking at the assembly, five letting their faces show in an act of defiance. "We are faced with a threat to our very existence with foes on many fronts. Indeed, the very survival of the Elders is at stake," he continued.

"Be more specific," growled Jackson.

"We have faced attacks from Venice to St Bart's, my wife is missing, and we are no closer to finding out who except a Venetian woman. The more we uncover the more complicated it gets."

"What of the Prophecy?" asked Giraud, the French delegate.

"Let me answer that," replied Sergei, standing up. "As your President I think the time for secrecy is gone in these desperate times and I note many of you have already forgone your right to privacy, can I assume that is the case?"

"You can."

"As Guy says, we are all in grave danger and need to protect each other."

"Secrecy has always being our way, for centuries," said Madam Ramping.

"I myself have been kidnapped; we face an extremely smart foe who will think nothing of killing us off."

"So you want us to help attack this many-headed hydra," intoned the deep accented voice of Charlotte Winnie.

"Madam Senator, good to hear from you," replied Guy, feeling sympathy with her as she had mentioned the plight of black women she suspected were linked to this hydra. She had refused to travel in the offered private jet and had instead taken a scheduled flight to Madrid; he respected that as she was a fighter looking after the neediest.

"Thank you, we heard about this pirate in the Caribbean and the disappearance of girls, I too have heard similar disturbing stories about girls disappearing from my own state in the south. Always pretty ones disappearing to the Caribbean, and of course the recent tragic death on Bequia."

"My own wife Rose has also disappeared in the region and Monty's niece Jem."

"As you say, the very future of this august body is in danger, I must admit when I heard you had been attacked here I wondered whether to quit. Now I realise we have a unique opportunity to fight something that doesn't abide by national boundaries. We are put on this planet to make a difference, these people you talk about have been corrupted, and we have to stop them.”

“Thank you, ma’am,” said Guy with feeling. She had articulated far better than he had and there were nodding heads all around as all the members came down into the light, an unprecedented show of unity.

“You need to give us some guidance. These sea platforms, do we know any more?” the Senator asked.

“Not a great deal. Sergei will head to the Mediterranean to find out and neutralise them if possible, they’re called Mare Nostrum’.”

“Roman word for the Mediterranean sea,” commented Huang, the Chinese delegate, a squat little scholar turned entrepreneur. “The Romans used the term to embrace their empire; perhaps these people have a similar plan.”

“I have a hunch the raid here was a diversion,” said Guy. “They are striking in many places but we have had our first success in stopping them acquiring the treasure.”

“The Caribbean and the Mediterranean are two big places,” said Ramping.

“And the Khans’ Prophecy?” asked the Senator.

“You all know the story of how we got it, it is well hidden, I have not opened it,” replied Sergei.

“Why not?”

“It’s a kind of Pandora’s Box; we don’t want to know what’s inside, it’s now well-hidden away from here and needs to stay that way”.

“Why not hide it here?”

“We planned to before the place was invaded,” replied Sergei.

“Seems to me we follow the only lead we have, the disappearing girls, they should lead to the head of the hydra,” said Charlotte.

“I don’t believe they will come back here again,” said Guy, “so I’m going to the Caribbean to find my wife whilst Sergei keeps Inspector Columba happy.”

“Only briefly, I’m going to find the dammed rigs,” replied Sergei quietly, “I’m convinced they are at the heart of the issue and there’s one somewhere in the Mediterranean.”

"Perhaps I can be a practical help," came a new voice, a recent delegate called Pasha, a Turkish billionaire who had made his fortune in electronics. "My friend owns factories in Turkey, including one near Gallipoli, and may know your rig. For some time a large rig there has grown into a behemoth; last year he was asked to tender for it under strict secrecy and we assumed it was Russian for oil exploration in the Black Sea. What you have been saying about these Mare Nostrum rigs may prove it's the one: he told me about an unusually large superstructure which could be luxurious living quarters. He said it's twice the size of a normal rig, that he wasn't allowed to go there and had heard of others being taken from the area."

"Where is it now?"

"That's the thing," replied Pasha. "Yesterday it left the yard. He told me it was heading south west."

"It all adds up," said Sergei excitedly. "I've just googled the rig builds and there's nothing about an oil platform, it's all very secretive."

"I just spoke to my friend, he says his men have been called to the rig to work on finishing touches for the electronic security systems as there are teething problems, we could find a way of taking extra men with his."

"Brilliant, fantastic," smiled Sergei, "we will leave immediately."

"You have to fit in with the strict schedule his men have but yes we suggest two of you go to the rig as part of the repair team for the security system."

"I will take Rostov with me; don't think I look like an engineer."

"You're the supervisor and electronics expert," smiled Pasha.

"Sounds good," replied Guy, looking around the room. "Ladies and gentlemen, I came here tonight fearing that you would want to concede to these forces that are assailed against us. I won't deny it has been a rough few weeks, the hardest ever, but working together I am convinced we can beat these forces."

"I have something proactive for the Caribbean side also," said Charlotte, "there are sinister events being reported in Latin America and I will make it my business to find out where and why."

"We have no have no resources down there," said Guy.

"I have a good friend called Jacques Emerson, a Brazilian, he's near retirement as Police Inspector in Rio and told me recently he was investigating girl disappearances around Rio. We were due to exchange notes anyway but with this added urgency I will go and see him, maybe he could also join this group," she continued. "I can get him on the line if you want."

"Excellent," replied Guy, pleased that the group were reacting actively, "until the next meeting then, and hopefully there will be some good news."

"Pleased to join your crusade," said Emerson on the conference call.

"Thanks Jacques, I will join you in Rio."

"I'll work my contacts in the favelas, the rumours we are picking up come from countries like Paraguay, where there are some tales of Germans."

"That could be significant," said Guy as he sat with Sergei. "Germans keep cropping up and I don't believe in coincidences. For the first time it feels like we have a plan. These girls disappearing, it has a disturbingly familiar feel to it from events a couple of years ago with Lorna's father, a dreadful business."

"The signs are familiar," conceded Sergei.

"I hope to God it's not a continuation of that nightmare, something that took the life of someone I loved dearly."

"Where will you go in the Caribbean?"

"Only St Bart's, it's as good a place as any, I feel guilty leaving the heavy stuff to you, Sergei, particularly after Tatyana disappearing."

"We have to divide our forces and she's trained to cope with adversity. I will leave in the morning; Columba is chasing me by the hour, tells me he has a lead on Sabine."

"Really, what sort of lead?"

"Tracked to the Gibraltar region, he wants me to help with the search."

Gibraltar

The heat simmered on the limestone rocks as Sabine entered her familiar cave, where she had recuperated after her horrific injuries. Next to her sat Danielle with a manacled Tatyana. "We go tonight so be ready for a fast departure," Sabine said as she made arrangements with the staff there and glimpsed the inmates in the next cave.

"What do we do with the bitch? She's slowing us down."

"We may need her as a bargaining tool, so keep her. I need an hour to sort something out, go and make sure we haven't been followed."

"This place is amazing; the cave entrance is so well hidden I would never have found it."

"Courtesy of the British in the Second World War, they built a network to protect the place against attack from both the sea side and the land. It's a hidden city with many surprises, some of which I won't share even with you." She turned and walked deeper into the cave, taking with her a large bag. It was her insurance policy; a veritable fortune, and something not even Lucrezia would be made aware of. She would give them some of the Venetian gems, but she would keep the bulk of them. It had been a close run thing at the mine, and they had used the last gold truck as a decoy heading east whilst they headed west. The need for contingency plans had been instilled in her years ago and had kept her alive so far. At last she now had her own wealth after years of building it for others. Lucrezia would get over her disappointment in time, though she had ordered her to report to Venice urgently.

Inspector Columba put down the powerful binoculars and smiled coldly. He had managed to get across the border into Gibraltar after persuading the local police that it was in their interests to collaborate with him in finding a major terrorist. He hadn't been on the rock for many years and appreciated the support. He had finally seen what he wanted to see on the far side of the rock, away from the tourist hordes.

He had combed the rock for over an hour, and had puzzled over where any caves could exist, but was finally rewarded when he saw Danielle emerge from a crevice, making her way behind a clump of trees to a Toyota that had been carefully hidden.

Chapter 11

Saba

The island looked as if a giant had left a boulder in the sea by accident, a mountain fortress that few would be able to penetrate without an army. Kobus took great comfort from that thought as he looked down across the vista, his vista. Across the small valley in a university research complex Rose awoke feeling groggy and not a little disorientated. She had slept badly for the hundredth time, and had been pondering her situation and trying to make sense of it. The Dutchman was a power-mad zealot who had known she was coming. Her stomach rumbled and she realised she hadn't eaten for over twenty four hours. She heard footsteps in the distance coming towards her cell and winced as the door was unlocked and a surly guard poked his head in.

"Against the wall or you'll get no food," he snapped, slamming the tin tray down and turning to leave. She wrinkled her nose at the foul-looking porridge, but knew that beggars couldn't be choosers, and needed to eat something. She swallowed with distaste, turning her nose up but feeling her energy levels rise. When she had eaten, she thought of what she could do about Guy. She had to do something, she thought, or she would go mad. Rose looked up, and had an idea.

"Make way," boomed the jailor, opening the door and cursing as he was confronted with nothing but an empty cell. He whirled around in confusion, and saw the blur of something moving out of the corner of his eye. The jailor grunted in pain as Rose fell down on him from the beam and crashed to the floor. Hot coffee had spilled all over him, and he screamed in pain on the floor while Rose dashed to the door. She slammed it shut before looking around for her next move.

A narrow dark deserted corridor lay ahead, and she took a chance. She was in a building on the side of a laboratory complex, which explained why no one had come running when she attacked the guard. She saw her shoulder bag hanging in the corner of the front office and grabbed it, needing to put as much space as possible between herself and her captors. To her left she saw row upon row of identikit red and white houses, whilst further down the road stood a police station with two policemen outside. She cursed as there was a shout behind her from the struggling guard and one of the policemen looked up. Grateful for her practical attire of her light tee shirt and shorts, she started to move in the other direction as the two policemen approached her. She had three advantages over them she needed to exploit; her weight, her light clothing, and her elevation. She broke into a jog, heading uphill into scrubland and gasping as the sharp undergrowth scrubland ripped at her bare legs. She kept on climbing, seeing a sister outcrop along with what looked like the biggest building on the island, a Dutch flag flying from its mast.

She looked down and cursed as she saw the policemen climbing into a police car, her advantage now gone. The road swept around above her; she would have to get above it, and quickly. She turned a corner and saw a similar building to the one in which she had been held captive, which was enclosed in high fences and was, according to the sign outside, a medical school. She ventured closer, and saw security lights and a fence: a strange medical school, she thought. She edged closer and gasped as she saw a familiar figure at one of the widows. It was Jem. She had to get down there and take a closer look, and she cut her legs on sharp plants while trying to avoid the barbed wire. The fence appeared to be impenetrable, but suddenly a gate opened and a man in a surgical gown came out to deposit something. He lit a cigarette before turning and walking back inside, leaving the door ajar. She ran the last few metres, finding herself in a narrow corridor and made her way to a large door, gently opening it and exclaiming in astonishment.

"You idiots," shouted Kobus at the two policemen from his veranda. The Flying Dutchman didn't feel particularly mobile as he waited for his niece. "What the hell do I pay you for? This is her second escape."

"She can't have gone far," replied the taller of the two men.

"Then find her and bring her here immediately," snapped Kobus, as if he didn't have enough to concern him the bitch was loose on the island, his island, prying her nose where it wasn't wanted. "Now, or you lose your jobs," he added, heading insidehis house he called the Eagle's Nest, a former luxury hotel that he had appropriated. It had the best views of the island, and the Caribbean lay out before him. He turned to his faithful assistant. "Dirk, get down to the school and make sure the others are managed, I don't want anyone else getting loose. And take a couple of the men with you. Leave one here, that bitch is going to suffer."

"What if they can't capture her?"

"There's absolutely nowhere for her to go unless she grows wings," he said, turning to his computer.

Rose gasped in horror at the scene in front of her. Horrible memories flooded back from her time in Norway. It was a maternity ward, much larger than what she had seen in Norway, and her instincts told her that it was a breeding camp. A door slammed behind her, and she looked around in horror trying to identify where she was, before running back down the corridor checking room after room and hearing voices. It was Jem's voice, it had to be. "Jem, where are you?" she screamed as the other shouts came closer.

"Over here," came the familiar voice. They had her surrounded, and Rose spun as men arrived at either end of the corridor, and she had to move fast back onto the rocks. She ran straight at the smaller policeman and kicked him hard in the stomach, dashing past as he fell backwards in astonishment. Slamming open the door, she ran back to the rocks, making it onto the scrubland and heading upwards, the two policemen panting behind cursing. She was losing them, as her fitness was to her advantage, but then her spirits sank as she heard the sound of bullets. Instinctively she ducked and kept running, swerving constantly, her lungs bursting as she ran on upwards until finally reaching a ravine. She stopped to get her breath back. No one followed her, and she thought that it was probably because they knew she had nowhere to go and would simply wait for her to come back down. Her gaze travelled across to the far side of the rock, her height giving her breath-taking views, and then she saw something to her right.

Kobus stared through his telescope and cursed, seeing what she was trying to do, before smiling wryly to himself. She was caught and didn't know it. He checked the monitors on the room cells, relieved to see that Jem and Lorna were still locked inside.

St Bart's

Monty cursed as he looked around the marina for the umpteenth time, conscious that he was getting nowhere and would have to take more direct action. It had been a week since Jem disappeared; the local police had been unhelpful, and Inspector Montalban positively obstructive, and Monty still fumed at the man's attitude. He would make a formal complaint when he could get back to Bermuda, and something would be done about the Inspector immediately. Monty looked around with distaste at the harbour of garish yachts, floating gin palaces obtained through ill-gotten gains. It was not his world as an ex-copper on a police pension, and he wondered how on earth people got hold of that sort of money outside of crime. It almost made one want to become a socialist, he thought. He shook his head ruefully and made his way along the harbour front back to the police station when the young sergeant Murat greeted him.

"No luck."

"Do you expect me to say yes?"

"Not really."

"So where is she?"

"We have no idea."

"You do, you were with her and know the boat she got on as you know them all, give me their details."

"I gave you them."

"That was the official line, I want the real stuff, the stuff that you know because they pay you backhanders," he snapped. "Where's Montalban?"

"On a social visit."

"Collection time from his paymasters," snapped Monty, out of patience.

"We have a peaceful island with no trouble, that's what attracts all the money."

"So how do people go missing?"

"Perhaps through choice. She may have met someone; after all, there are a lot of rich men here," smirked Murat.

"I know my niece and she's not like that," said Monty. "Take my advice and get transferred out of here before your career comes to a premature end. I will be making a formal report, and you can tell your boss that."

"I don't think that would be a good idea."

"What's more I am going to make a nuisance of myself until I find what I am looking for. They may have money but I can get them for drugs which I will find with or without your help."

"Those are serious accusations, Inspector," said a familiar voice as Montalban waddled into his office. "Would you care to substantiate them or apologise?"

"Oh I will substantiate them, and you will be drummed out as a disgrace to the uniform and to all the honest cops out there."

"You'd better leave before I file a complaint," snapped Montalban. "I've checked on you and you're not even on the force so I can arrest you for any number of reasons. As for your girl, she went off on one of the yachts. She probably saw the chance to make a few dollars as a hooker, nice arse on her." He ducked as Monty swung at him. "Assault now as well, get out of here, old man, before I lock you up."

Gibraltar

Inspector Columba looked intently at the video screen and saw that his hunch had been right, that he had indeed seen that woman two years previously. He was encamped outside the cave where he had seen Danielle go to the Toyota, waiting for something to happen.

"We have nearly thirty tonnes of gold, Inspector."

"But no diamonds or gems, and there were plenty," said Mendoza, scrambling to get his mobile. "Block the dammed port. That woman is up to something," he shouted over the phone as he ran they were following the wrong person instinct told him the dammed The Toyota was a decoy, but he had no choice now. Surely there weren't many places they could reach, he thought. The questioning of Jose Barr at the Bank Mare Nostrum had revealed that there were millions of Euros of uncut diamonds and gems, all with the red headed woman. He looked around down at the port and saw the Toyota next to a large cruiser. "Down there, quick," he yelled as they screamed down the narrow road with a local police car in attendance. They surrounded the Toyota and yelled for the occupants to come out. Nothing happened at first, but then he spotted movement over by the cruiser.

"Hands up and come out slowly or we shoot," he yelled, and a frightened-looking Danielle emerged.

"What's the problem, officer?" she said, looking at the drawn guns.

"The woman Sabine, where is she? Where are the diamonds?"

"I've no idea what you're talking about, Inspector," said Danielle sweetly. "I'm going about my rightful business getting the cruiser here ready for a short journey."

"Where to?"

"Around to Portugal for a little holiday."

"You're coming back up to the cave with me now," shouted Columba angrily as they made their way back up to the cave, Danielle leading the way. It was an empty cave, though clearly one that could be lived in with electricity and water. "Where is she?"

"I've no idea what you mean," replied Danielle smiling sweetly.

"What was that?" he said, hearing gunfire in the distance.

"Can I go now or are you going to charge me?" said Danielle.

"You stay here under suspicion until I get back," snapped Columba, jumping back into his car. They screamed down to the harbour area to see Danielle's cruiser making its way steadily out to sea.

"You've got to stop it," he yelled to the local policeman, a taciturn Scot named Renton.

"It'll be outside our waters any minute now," shrugged the Scot.

"Stop it on suspicion of drug offences."

"I've told you, it's now in international waters. We have no authority."

"Then let my men take her."

"That's illegal, you should know better."

"The bloody woman is escaping with millions, for God's sake," said Columba as he saw the craft pick up speed, "laughing all over her face, no doubt."

"This is my jurisdiction," spluttered Renton, shaking his head at the Spaniard.

"Yes, what is it?" asked Columba as his deputy came over.

"The woman Danielle has gone."

"What do you mean, 'gone'?"

"She asked to go to the toilet and never returned."

"For God's sake," spluttered Columba, staring helplessly out to sea.

"There's a man here for you, a big Russian called Sergei." That was all he needed.

"So you let her get away. My men would have stopped her, in fact I can go after her now," said Sergei, appraising the situation.

"Not under my authority you won't. There is no proof they have the diamonds or indeed your assistant, it's all supposition."

"You know that's not true, they're both out there and we're going after them," said Sergei.

"Then I'm afraid I will have to arrest you," replied Columba calmly.

"On what grounds?"

"How do I know you are not in cahoots with this woman, you say she has your assistant with her called Tatyana, perhaps she is the leader and you are diverting the police."

"Would I have come back to you if that was the case?"

"Just get out of here, I will track the cruiser and I will let you know."

"You are making a mistake," said Sergei, realising that he had little option other than create a major scene. He was dammed sure that Tatyana was on that yacht but he and Rostov knew it would be difficult. It would be better to head to Turkey, he thought; after all, Tatyana had always told him she could take care of herself.

Rio de Janeiro

Charlotte was feeling her age as she looked around the throngs of young bodies on Copacabana beach, some wearing little more than what appeared to be dental floss. She had always fought the most difficult of causes as a politician and knew that this one was no different. She had had a long and successful career and now chose her battles carefully. For some time she had been concerned over the disappearances of young girls. Her health wasn't good with cancer diagnosed in her stomach, this was one last fight. She waited for her colleague in a deprived area next to the favelas, then saw the distinctive form of Jacques heading her way and smiled.

"It's a dangerous area, Charlotte, even for me with police protection. You should have waited," said Jacques Emerson, a tall stooping figure.

"I wanted to see what it was like, although I must admit I was beginning to get a bit worried."

"Come on, I have the address, it's inside the favelas so go careful. I have armed men watching us." They drove around behind Christ the Redeemer and finally pulled up in front of a small shop front. "This is the only address I have that traces back to the holding company Tutulus," said Jacques, knocking on the door, which was opened by a middle aged man in a faded suit.

"No visitors."

"Police, so open the dammed door," growled Jacques. "I want to talk to the owner of Tutulus Corporation, which is registered here."

"Not here."

"I have come a long way, young man, so I suggest you let me in," snapped Charlotte, angered by the man's attitude.

"You have a warrant?"

"I can get one."

"Very well," replied the man standing back and watching as they entered through to a back office.

"How can we help you?" said a blonde haired man with a German accent, "this is a private company, I don't see what possible interest we could be to an American Senator and policeman."

"How do you know that?"

"My business to know everything," smirked Helmut, "that's how we are so successful. Computer technology at the door took your photos and matched them immediately."

"Are you linked to the Germans over in Paraguay?"

"What if I am, it's a free country isn't it?"

"Yes, so why is such a large corporation tucked away in the favelas?"

"We don't seek to draw attention to ourselves; after all, we are doing charity work helping youngsters carve out a career."

"Oh really, what sort of career?"

"Modelling work, that sort of thing, it's all here in the books."

"I bet it is," said Charlotte, disliking the man's smugness, "the name Tutulus has been linked to girls disappearing."

"That's dreadful and a smear on our name."

"Then you won't mind my men taking a look at your trading files."

"We are a talent spotting office," replied the German, "totally legal and above board, I do mind but you two can have a quick look to put your minds at rest, come through here," he gestured, pointing to a filing cabinet.

"This is full of young girls."

"We don't do male models and we are looking for talent, modelling is very demanding these days."

"Talent for what," asked Charlotte.

"Our clients are film companies here in Brazil and the Caribbean," replied Helmut, "aspiring talent for adverts and television."

"This file is headed Mare Nostrum, what does that mean?" asked Charlotte, her eyes glancing across to Jacques.

"Location sites, it's an internal code," replied Helmut.

"It's been associated with elitist communities in Europe, and with potential breeding sites for young girls."

"I know nothing of this."

"Too much of a coincidence," said Jacques raising his phone, "you will accompany me to the station."

"It's unfortunate for you that you have taken that view," smiled Helmut coldly as the door to the room slammed shut. Jacques started to turn when the lights went out and the room was plunged into darkness.

"Gas, we have to get out of here," yelled Jacques, reaching for the door.

Helmut turned to his assistant. "Get the truck, we need to get them out of the country, they're high profile."

"Where to, boss?"

"Just get the truck, I will handle the rest." He needed to contact the Philosopher urgently, and they needed to speed up their plans.

Istanbul

Rostov and Sergei left Gibraltar after persuading Columba they had no more information. It had been disappointing to see Sabine getting away, but they had little choice if they didn't want the might of Spanish law bearing down on them.

"You think they have a base on Gibraltar?" asked Rostov.

"I'm sure of it, but we haven't time to explore. We're lucky to still have our liberty with Columba. The caves there are holding something, I'm sure of it," replied Sergei as they arrived tired and weary on a night flight from Spain. To their relief they were met at Istanbul airport by Pasha himself, who swept them away in his limousine, driving along the west of the Sea of Marmara before reaching the town of Sarkoy. Sergei fretted about what had happened to Tatyana in Gibraltar, and began to doubt whether she would survive.

"Thanks Pasha, this is great," he said in appreciation, and they were shown to a very comfortable villa overlooking the Dardanelles before being left to sleep. The next day they met for breakfast, where the businessman greeted them, along with two colleagues carrying bags.

"My friends, here are your company uniforms."

"Thank you. I'm the supervisor, and Rostov here is the muscle."

"The rig is bristling with armaments, I need my back up team," said Rostov, looking over at Pasha.

"No deal, they have long distance video surveillance which fortunately we can modify to get you through, but we can't make it too obvious or they will suspect something," replied the industrialist.

"Where is the rig?"

"Just west of Cyprus, rumour is that it's moving down to Santorini, we've arranged for the visit and it's been confirmed for eight this evening. Three of you can go in, and the real expert will join you. Our helicopter has landing rights, so I suggest you get some rest before we take you through the equipment training."

Sergei groaned as he saw the flimsy helicopter and even more so as it rose sharply into the evening sky, heading west into the proverbial lion's den.

"Target off the port bow," ordered the pilot, and they held tight as they hovered over the rig.

"Pretty piece of work," whistled Sergei as they hovered beside the luxurious platform.

"Five star luxuries on an oil rig," exclaimed Rostov as they jerked and then moved to one side over the rig.

"If I didn't know better I'd think we were in a luxurious hotel," said Sergei as the sea came out of his periphery vision. Pristine buildings towered above artificial grass the size of three football pitches with ambient lighting and mood music. He saw a game of tennis in the corner and a spa high above.

"We have a short delay before we can land, remember just follow me and do as I say, pretend you only speak Turkish," said Kemal, the security systems expert.

"What do we do first?" asked Rostov feeling distinctly uneasy without his men.

"The main tower over there is where the security system is based, we've come at a bad time," continued Kemal. "They've got a VIP chopper coming in bigger than ours." They watched the larger helicopter land below, and they saw an elegantly dressed woman climb out and make her way across a red carpet stretched out over the green AstroTurf.

"Someone important?" asked Rostov as they hovered to one side waiting.

"My God, that's Lucrezia," gasped Sergei.

"Keep your head down," replied Rostov as their own helicopter came into land, jerking as it hit the deck.

"She's gone," said Sergei with relief as Lucrezia didn't even look back as she swept across the carpet and into the main building. They were greeted by a maintenance man.

"Took your bloody time, the dammed system is all over the place, were having to wing it with the big boss here, they shoot people for less than this so sort it quick."

"We'll fix it," smiled Kemal, and he and his two colleagues made their way to the tower. They reached the main switchboard to be confronted by a bewildering array of consoles.

"Like a bloody aircraft flight deck," said Sergei.

"Leave it to me and just look busy, it won't take me long to correct the remote activated fault," smiled Kemal, going to work. "You have twenty minutes."

"Time to explore," said Sergei. "You go that way, and I'll go over here; you know what we are doing."

"Small amount of explosives, all I could get in my jacket, just enough to cause a psychological effect."

"It's enough to shake them and hopefully affect confidence. It'll give them something to think about, anyway. Go to it whilst I try and find proof of the breeding centres, and then we can get the authorities in." He made his way across to a larger area and noticed in the distance a small crowd gathering around Lucrezia. He edged closer hiding behind a retaining wall.

"Ladies and gentlemen, this is an historic day that will go down in the annals of human history; you are here at the start of a new era in human affairs, the first new society subject to no nation or to the rules of nation states. You are all privileged to be in the first launch and in decades and centuries to come people will talk about you as the true pioneers. My congratulations to you all," said Lucrezia. She cut the gold ribbon and smiled across to the cameras.

"Sergei, you need to come back," hissed Rostov into his earpiece.
"What is it?"
"Kemal says there's trouble brewing."
"Get the command centre Rostov, a twenty minute fuse."
"The chopper goes in ten minutes," shouted Rostov, "Kemal says they are getting suspicious, otherwise we have to fight our way out."
"We'll go down to the command centre together, then," said Sergei, turning and heading for the lower floor, where he looked around in amazement. "This is some advanced kit, the command module looks as if it's run by robots and there are screens everywhere. There won't be much privacy on board this thing. It's all centrally controlled, whoever is running the show here knows everything, real time tracking, no one will have privacy, I'm beginning to realise what they have here and can see a room over there that looks suspiciously like the breeding centre arrangement with girls."
"A voyeur's haven," nodded Rostov, looking around in appreciation. He toggled the switch and grunted in amazement as it took him into at least thirty rooms all on one screen. "The perverts, this place is wired big time, a luxury home for the unsuspecting, but for what purpose? Assume the cameras for this lot are so well hidden that they can't be detected. We need to go," he said, attaching the small magnetic explosives to a module. "A little present that will make them think twice," he said grimly, "these beauties should do the trick, disable the control room for a week or so and show them we mean business."
"More importantly, it will draw them out and make them make mistakes, particularly as Lucrezia herself is here."
"Time to go," shouted Rostov as they headed for the helicopter pad. "Shit," he exclaimed as their chopper rose into the sky ahead of them and they were bathed in searchlights. "Get down," he yelled to Sergei as gunfire raked the area.

"Oh no." Sergei looked around in resignation. They were trapped.

"Come on, there's still a chance," said Rostov. "The dammed cameras are following us whichever way we turn."

"We do this together," said Sergei firmly.

"They want the Prophecy; we have to keep you away from them."

"I said no."

"Very well, follow me," said Rostov. They ran down to the far end of the rig, hoping Kemal would come back for them. "He's still rising," shouted Rostov in despair, "the water is our only chance."

"Not sure I can do that," said Sergei looking down into the cold water with foreboding.

"You need to jump," said Rostov as they ran to the side.

"No Rostov, I'm too old, you get away or they'll kill you, they need me alive."

Rostov grunted as a stray bullet hit his shoulder, and he stared impassively at Sergei. The men were coming for them, in the distance he heard a dull thud and knew it was his only chance, with a shrug he launched himself into space, tumbling as he fell into the dark sea beneath.

St Bart's

The island was exactly as Rose had described it. Guy landed on the sloping runway at nearly midnight, having experienced frustrating delays on the scheduled flights. He was desperate to find Rose, having realised how much he missed her; they were a team, and shouldn't have split up. Sergei had called him from Gibraltar, fuming at the loss of the treasure and the fact that Sabine had escaped yet again, yet Guy felt pleased to have done something at last rather than react. He took a taxi down to the police station and knocked on the door.

"I assume you are like the rest, here to snoop on us," said a clearly drunk Montalban. "Into the cells with you," he ordered.

"What the hell for? I've done nothing," protested Guy.

"Exactly the reason you are going in the dammed cells, I should have done exactly the same with the others, thanks to them I have lost years of good work up in smoke. Modern policing is far more than just chasing the bad guys and you idealists don't get that," he slurred as Guy was led to the cells by an embarrassed-looking Murat.

Mediterranean Sea

Sabine looked back at Gibraltar as they made their way out to sea, smiling at the deception played on the police. She had secured the diamonds and ensured they were fit to fight another day, but it had been a close run thing and the Russian girl would pay later. The worst thing was the danger of their secret cave system being discovered on Gibraltar, along with her own secrets, plus, of course, the breeding centre there.

"We have some gems but not a great deal, we were betrayed," she said into the video line to the scowling Lucrezia.

"So another failure," snapped the Venetian, still coming to terms with the explosion on the Nostrum and the work she'd had to do with the customers. At least they had Sergei in their custody again and this time would keep him.

"There must have been a leak," said Sabine, deciding attack was the best form of defence.

"You have a week to sort this mess out."

"I still have the Russian girl, the one Sergei will do anything for. Recaptured the bitch after she played games, even though we hold her mother and father."

"Good, that should ensure Sergei squeals this time, can't believe he was stupid enough to drop in on us the same time as I opened the first Nostrum."

"Then we will get the Prophecy?"

"Get the girl to me fast, I want you in the Caribbean, this dammed Project Valkyrie is causing me grief and I want you to go to Germania."

"Where the hell is that?"

"Paraguay, we have a few issues, call it an insurance expedition and your chance to redeem yourself, without the treasure we need to ensure that we maintain control of Tutulus."

"What's happened at the Nostrum?"

"Our enemies have had the audacity to try and disable our new rig, they have failed and no harm done but it's bloody annoying, just as well the bulk of the new arrivals aren't there yet."

"But Paraguay?"

"Yes, Paraguay and practice your German. I'm trusting you here Sabine, I want you to check a few things out before I get involved."

"Very well," replied Sabine, thinking that it was time to build herself a little security plan of her own.

Chapter 12

Grenada - Grenadines

The sun shone harshly across the bay, amplifying the effect of Fort George Castle overlooking the harbour. The island itself, like many in the region, had changed hands rapidly in the past centuries and the old fort had seen a great deal of action, primarily between successive French and British fleets. More recently in 1984 it had been centre stage when the island's Prime Minister had been gunned down by rebels aligned to the communists, sparking an invasion by President Reagan. Signs of the invasion in the Eighties' were still clear on the older houses, where graffiti daubed the walls.

None of this was of any interest whatsoever to Wolfgang Fein as he made his way from the airport having taken charge of the human cargo from a grinning Helmut Schwab at the small airport. It was his responsibility now as the senior manager to handle the VIP prisoner with care. They had agreed it was politically too dangerous to bring the American senator here, so she would be held until it was safe; the complication was that she was clearly ill and unlikely to survive at all. The gas attack had sent her unconscious, and they were monitoring her. Fein gave very little for her survival chances and they would need to distance themselves carefully. The Police Inspector was a different matter, and there were scores to settle, so Jacques had been drugged and transported in the private jet where others would decide his fate. It was always useful to have hostages, and this one would bring a decent price if they went down that route. He looked at the castle in front of him as the car came to a halt; the Philosopher as always had made a good choice in choosing the island for operational reasons halfway between their base in Paraguay and new operations in the northern Caribbean.

The local bank was convenient as a staging post for their supplies, located next to Bequia where one of the camps had been built, and now served as the front for the Tutulus financial empire across continents. He felt very satisfied as he looked around and climbed from the car; he must surely have earned some points with the Philosopher for this campaign, sending Helmut to Rio to oversee the emerging problem, always keeping one step ahead of the enemy. He was glad that he had been tailing the Senator for some time as she had enquired about the disappearing girls. It had been a simple matter then to reel her into the Rio office, a temporary affair. His success would enable him to press his case for Annaliese as his approved partner, for she was the one he intended to marry, after all that was Germania's way, and he could see their offspring ruling the whole enterprise in the future.

He drove past Fort George Castle and up the main road towards the Prime Minister's residence, before reaching a large white mansion called the White House, which was set off the road and partially hidden by trees. They had registered the name Tutulus here since moving their headquarters over a year ago and he for one had thought it would remain hidden beneath layers of other companies' names for some time. It was especially galling therefore to find that the American Senator Charlotte had tracked them down, and, worse, subjected them to an official search request by the American authorities. For that alone she would pay the ultimate price. Aside from that, all was going well, and Germania was spreading its wings across the Americas, it was all coming to a climax here in Grenada in the following few days and he needed to make sure it was a resounding success for the Philosopher, particularly as he as well aware of divisions in the ranks.

"Well done Wolfgang, the actions in Rio were effective in a difficult situation, how many more know of this American Senator?" came the familiar voice.

"Just the police inspector who doesn't know she is dying."

"We have to move faster than we thought, American Senators, particularly dead ones, are bad news."

St Bart's

"This is ridiculous," said Guy as he found himself in a small cell under the police building. The Inspector was a disgrace and yet what could he do, he was powerless and worse no one knew he was here. Tiredness took over eventually and he fell into a deep sleep, punctuated by the noise of someone in the next cell snoring deeply and drunkenly. He cursed Montalban repeatedly and wondered how long they would dare hold him here without charge. Dawn was breaking as he finally heard the rattle of breakfast tins. "How long are you intending to keep me here?" he asked the young police officer.

"Up to the boss," replied the young man turning to leave. It was another hour before Sergeant Murat came down and took him upstairs to Montalban.

"Why are you here?"

"I told you I am trying to find my wife, if you had let me get on with that instead of locking me up I might have found her by now."

"This island is my business, I don't like others poking into it."

"Perhaps if you worked within the law rather than against it would help."

"You could go to prison for a long time for that remark," snapped the Inspector, "I can make you disappear just like that."

"I just bet you can," said a familiar voice from the doorway, and to Guy's relief Monty entered, followed by a stern-looking man in plain clothes. "I believe you know Chief Inspector Garston, your boss, he has some rather interesting questions to ask you," said Monty, "including why you've been taking bribes."

"Rubbish," said Montalban, "you have no idea what you are getting involved with."

"The Inspector here has told me enough," said Garston. "You are under arrest."

"Thank God you came when you did Monty; things were getting a little sticky," said Guy.

"Sorry you were stuck for the night, it took a bit or arranging but I couldn't see another route except calling in favours from the top. The whole region is riddled with corrupt cops, there's been a systematic attempt to bribe officials," said Monty. "First, though, Victoria needs to talk to you urgently, we've set up a secure call."

"I've been digging into the Chinese section of the archives and found a document so well hidden even I didn't know it existed. It's in Chinese script but I've had a colleague translate it, and what they came up with is very interesting."

"Go on."

"An old note stuck in the front on a scrap of paper that looks like it was put there accidentally, it talks of three holy documents, and they talk of the righteous destiny for those who control them, along with a great meeting in the desert on the old Silk Road, a global summit of the north, the west and the east."

"North?"

"The Mongols, the Chinese in the east and the Catholics in the west."

"The Catholics?" asked Guy.

"Don't forget they had a head start in the east through Marco Polo."

"So a global summit?"

"Yes, and the word they used was Tutulus, the same as the holding company we are tracking down."

"A connection."

"Exactly, this summit they talk about was deemed so important that the respective emperors and the Pope himself were all made aware, it was kept under the utmost secrecy."

"Its purpose?" asked Guy, intrigued.

"To pave the way for a new order signposted through three guiding documents."

"So the prophecy is only part of the story?"

"Yes, the second was the Pope's Covenant and then a new one."

"Don't know its name, that's the great mystery."

"Old Zheng He's artefacts were a diversionary tactic away from the documents."

"It also talks about Zheng He as part of the legitimising process, it's all in a very old dialect that has taken the monks here some time to decipher. But here's the most interesting part, which starts to explain the problems we've been having. Seems that Zheng's mandate was to set up the Elders but there was a schism, much like the Shi'ites splitting form the Sunnis or the schism in the church when Protestantism split from Catholicism. Effectively there is a rival organisation that has kept itself very secret."

"Not this so-called Doge."

"Further east than that. Asia."

"Asia, my God, the Chinese and a competitive organisation based there, that would explain a great deal but I thought we got rid of all that with the death of the Teacher."

"Perhaps not," continued Victoria. "I always wondered about the Chinese element and now we have part of the answer, there are other forces."

"What forces?"

"I don't know, but my money is on this being the item they wanted to recover. I've always thought there was a Chinese link at the very core, but now I'm even more convinced."

"Thanks," replied Guy.

"We are looking at something on a grander scale than we ever thought possible, that would explain that assassin who nearly killed me down in the vaults, a big time thug who plays only for high stakes."

"Any ideas on who they are?"

"There are many rumours about a secret German organisation in Paraguay expanding across the Americas."

"I'm beginning to think this goes all the way back to Zheng He, manipulated for centuries by others. The Khans' Prophecy was the core but these references open up new avenues."

"There must be a link," said Guy, thoughtfully looking across at Monty as he did so. They were using Montalban's office as the Inspector wouldn't need it any longer.

"There is something else, Guy."

"What?"

"There are frequent references to a 'Quintet'."

"Quintet?"

"So we're facing a global operation with seemingly infinite resources and a conspiracy involving Germans and Chinese including slave camps, disappearing girls and mysterious elite platforms in the sea," surmised Guy.

"Just about sums it up, and no official help because there are no international agencies sufficiently interested," continued Victoria.

"Surely the United Nations is?"

"With no proof it isn't, they have enough on their hands, we also have the problem that the international policing through Interpol is only helping because of Monty, I suspect that they, like many bodies here, are compromised in these elite platforms so we are on our own."

Grenada

"Good to see you again, Annaliese," smiled Wolfgang as the blonde girl stepped down from the car and entered the White House.

"You look as if you've been successful," she replied, looking around at the opulent living quarters.

"All part of the new empire, has to look the part, I was thinking perhaps we could take a drive up to the north of the island, I know a great place for a meal."

"We have work to do, the conference is next week, we don't have time for such fripperies and I'm sure the Philosopher would object."

"She's authorised it; you need to learn how to relax, there's plenty of time for the work."

"I've been told I need to complete an inspection tour on the islands."

"When?"

"Tomorrow up at Bequia in the Grenadines and then back to my uncle on Saba."

"They must trust you."

"Indispensable," smiled Annaliese, "apparently we have an American journalist named Zelda at the camp, we need to keep her quiet."

"The worst type, seven o'clock then," smiled Wolfgang, "no one will miss us."

"Just for a short while."

"Don't worry, everything has been a long time in the planning, the boss's mantra is that you fail to plan and you plan to fail."

"I need transport over to the islands."

"Take the seaplane, no one else needs it and the boss only goes by private jet, we have one anchored down in the harbour, your own pilot, guy named Toto, the boss wants to see you."

"Annaliese, are you ready to take over the northern operations?"

"Of course."

"It's time you heard more about who we are and where we are going. What you see is only the surface. You have all the requirements to be one of us but it requires uncompromising loyalty to the movement, do I make myself clear?"

"You do."

"Good, then let me explain our objectives. I assume you have heard of the Silk Road?"

"It leads from China to the West over land."

"Yes, the first real trading route between nations, long before Columbus came over here. This is at the heart of who we are as a movement; do you know the fastest growing new Silk Road?"

"No."

"Between Germany and China by rail; every day a long train leaves China laden with goods and gets to Germany in two weeks instead of two to three months by sea, a distance of 12,000 kilometres. That's why our two nations will be prominent in the future and we are at the vanguard."

"I had no idea."

"Kill him."

"Are you sure?" asked Wolfgang, taken aback.

"Make it look like he was killed by the Elders, which will get the full weight of the Brazilian police on their tail, keep him in Bequia until then."

"I have a favour to ask with Annalise."

"I know, and the answer is you are my chosen successor so make it happen but she is a strong minded individual and I sense does not agree with Project Valkyrie."

"Thank you Philosopher, I have your backing and that's all that counts."

"Call me Elisabeth now; it's time to end formalities amongst our leaders as we reach the key moment."

"I will be travelling with you tomorrow with a prisoner," explained Wolfgang as he drove Annalise south west on the island in a hired Mercedes, stopping at Parc a Beouf beach.

"I've other things I need to do," replied Annaliese.

"Probably just as well," replied Wolfgang, explaining his latest instructions.

"Guess it has to be part of the bigger cause," she replied as they parked and sat down on a rock overlooking a stunning view of the Grand Mal Bay.

"I'm her chosen successor," smiled Wolfgang as he sat beside Annaliese.

"Why the subterfuge originally over the name and hiding her gender?"

"The Germania movement has always been very macho; it's the German part I guess, so she felt it had to be done carefully. There's still only a privileged few who know and she's very cagey over that. There are major challenges coming at the top of the movement."

"From whom?"

"Principally a person called the Composer, who is part of the ruling Quintet, I know nothing of this person other than she is extremely elusive, a puppeteer holding the strings."

"From where?"

"From everywhere," replied Wolfgang.

"But someone must know of this person," she said, but got no further as Wolfgang launched himself on top of her trying to kiss her.

"What on earth?" she gasped, struggling free, "I'm not ready for this Wolfgang."

"But your commitment to the cause…"

"Does not involve succumbing to your desires," she snapped, standing up angrily. "Now take me back, you are an example of this macho culture, I want none of it."

"You will marry me," said Wolfgang standing up, "it's the Philosopher's orders."

"I said leave me alone," snapped Annaliese, and he reached out to her, grabbing at her blouse and tearing it.

"I really think you ought to leave her alone," came a voice dripping with menace. "The movement doesn't behave like this, no matter what you think."

"Who are you?" gasped Wolfgang.

"You know who I am," said the voice. "It appears I arrived just in time, I suspected this was your intent, a total and utter misuse of the powers invested in you," said the Composer.

"I don't report to you, the Philosopher will hear of this."

"Oh yes, she certainly will," replied the woman, turning to Annaliese. "Come with me my dear, I don't believe this man is safe."

"Just who are you?" replied Annaliese, and she climbed into the back of a red BMW.

"You will find out when the time is right. One piece of advice, however: keep your options open. Here is my private number."

Bequia

Jacques opened his eyes and groaned as he looked around the room a cell like structure. His last memory was the gas in Rio de Janeiro and then the dizziness. He stood up and looked around, seeing a small sky light but no windows. The door opened and food was pushed in by a scowling man. "Where am I?" he asked.

"No questions," the man growled. The door slammed shut and Jacques ate the food feeling nauseous. He could sense by the warmth that he was in the tropics and chewed the stringy meat as he tried to figure out what to do and where on earth Charlotte was. The day passed monotonously before the door was flung open and a blonde German gestured him out. "Who are you and what's going on?" Jacques demanded.

"I told you, no questions," snapped Wolfgang, still bruised by what had happened and determined to do this one right. "You have caused us enough trouble."

"Why am I here?"

"To stop you causing further trouble," said Wolfgang. "Now here's what I am going to do as I'm a reasonable man. You're going free here but don't bother going near the water or I will hunt you down myself."

"I don't understand."

"You don't need to understand, now get away, if you're still in this vicinity in half an hour I will set the dogs on you."

Wolfgang watched as the policeman made his way up the hill behind the house. The areas were practically deserted and it was over ten miles to the next habitation. The man looked unfit, and Wolfgang thought that if the weather or wild animals didn't get him, then his planned arrival would. Despite his predicament with the Composer and Annaliese he smiled to himself. This little trick would have the American authorities down on the Elders heavily and leave the easy clear for him to make his case for Annaliese.

Venice

Segovia looked around carefully and smiled coldly. Since setting Sergei free she had deliberately kept a low profile, working on tedious accounts for Giuseppe and smiling at the right times to the old man. Freeing Sergei had made her feel satisfied that the subterfuge was all worthwhile. Tatyana had been her childhood friend, and she owed her, so when she had been asked to help she had jumped at the chance. They had been firm friends in the spetnaz, two good looking girls amongst many macho men, and they had had to learn to take care of themselves quickly. She had happily agreed to take the assignment in Venice; the American Stanton had approached her through Tatyana and had enabled her to successfully free Sergei, now he was helping her on stage two. His story to the Doge was that he had defected from the Elders, when in fact he was helping them. Together they had carefully planned the next stage, a chance to hit at the heart of Lucrezia's plans.

"I have identified an opportunity," said Stanton as they sat in a coffee shop in St Mark's Square. "There is a special document I have heard Lucrezia is desperate to find."

"What sort of document?"

"That's what we need to find out, along with its location. I am told it's here in Italy but we need to find out where, if we can then we can get it to the Elders and stop Lucrezia."

"Any place that it's likely to be?"

"No, only that it's got Papal connotations."

"You're taking a major risk going undercover," said Segovia looking across at the corpulent American.

"We have to stop this evil, I've spent over ten years on the Elders and I figured what better way than to strike from the inside, so here I am."

"Where do we start looking for this document?"

"You are in the ideal place. Giuseppe has the key to all the Doge files, he trusts you, and you can wander at will. I will try and help from my side."

Saba

Rose groaned as she made her way down the steep mountain side to the sea front, where waves pounded the concrete pier. She had fallen down the rocks and her legs were bleeding from multiple cuts, but all she wanted was to get off the accursed island. Ahead of her was a small jetty upon which stood two uniformed men, who Rose suspected worked for the Dutchman, struggling with diving equipment. The pain from her cuts and bruises focussed her mind and she saw a solo yacht, its mast bobbing in the swell, crewed by an older man, who was busy with provisions.

"You heading off soon?" she asked, keeping her voice low.

"In about half an hour," smiled the man behind his white, bushy beard.

"Can I hitch a lift? I have to get off the island urgently."

"Why would that be?"

"Family problems," she improvised as she heard raised voices behind her on the hills.

"Can you cook?"

"Yes."

"Very well, my name's Joe, I'm heading over to Virgin Gouda, you need to get those cuts looked at, missy. Did you fall?"

"I had a small accident, nothing serious."

"Jump aboard."

"Thank you," said Rose, breathing a sigh of relief and climbing aboard. She went down below immediately, relaxing in the bow cabin as the gentle motion of the craft told her they were moving. She fell asleep for a short while, and awoke with a jerk, scrambling up on deck to see a sky full of stars.

"Beautiful, isn't it?" shouted Joe from the helm. "Guess we ought to get to know each other. I'm from North Carolina."

"Rose, and from many places but I guess you could say Chicago is my home."

"A fellow American then, could you rustle something up to eat whilst I trim the sails for the night sail?"

"Of course." An hour later they sat on the main deck eating Rose's hastily prepared stew as she embellished her story about a jealous lover on Saba. She offered to pay her way and Joe shook his head, which was fortunate when she realised she had no money or personal documents. She sat on the bow and tried to relax, finding a sail to cover her legs. She had to find a way of contacting Guy and raise the alarm.

She sensed the old man's eyes boring into the back of her head, and decided it was best to head below as Joe announced he'd set the auto pilot. She locked the door, though it was flimsy. She was exhausted and needed rest before trying to communicate; she would need to persuade Joe to use his radio. It was essential that she get help and explain what was happening on Saba. Instinct told her that Joe was not the person;

she closed her eyes and was drifting in a sea of unconsciousness when the door burst open.

"It's dangerous to lock the door on a boat, want some of my bourbon?" said Joe, stumbling into the small cabin.

"I don't want any," replied Rose, "I was trying to sleep."

"Aw come on, just a little drink and a friendly cuddle," slurred Joe, struggling to keep himself upright and stinking of alcohol.

"Who's sailing the boat?" asked Rose, cursing her luck.

"She's on autopilot, I am only looking for a cuddle, little enough for free passage."

"I told you I would pay," snapped Rose, stopping his hands reaching her breasts. He lurched forwards and she swung a wooden pole she had found earlier, hitting him hard on the head. Joe sank down with a groan, his head bleeding. Rose quickly checked his pulse before locking him in the room. He would live. She clambered up on deck, grateful that she was familiar with yachts of this type from their charter business. She familiarised herself with the controls and took a heading on the GPS before disconnecting it and resetting the autopilot. She reckoned they were about four hours from Virgin Gouda, and noted the position, before reaching for the radio and cursing when she saw that it was password-enabled. Even the emergency call units were immobile; she checked the headings to Virgin Gouda directly heading south, and found a larger pole as a suitable weapon. She locked the main hatch and settled down into a fitful sleep.

Dawn was breaking and she saw seagulls in the distance. She took manual charge and eventually moored at a small jetty, Joe still banging and cursing under the main hatch, before stepping ashore to look for a telephone. The coast guard's office lay ahead and she started up the road.

"Where's Joe?" asked a female voice, and Rose turned to see a tall leggy blonde girl heading towards her.

"I left him on board, he didn't feel very good," she improvised.
"And you are?"

"A friend, he was to pick me up for the transfer."

"When?"

"About now, so I think we have a little problem," said Annaliese, pulling a gun from her pocket. "The problem is I know all about you, Joe is one of our more reliable couriers and had the auto pilot preprogramed so you came nicely into the trap all unsuspecting. Told us last night he was heading down here and picked up a dubious passenger, it didn't take long for my dear uncle to work it out, and here we are, though I can barely afford the time."

"He offered to give me a lift and I'm looking for a doctor," Rose continued. "I need to get to a phone."

"I don't think so. I would strongly suggest you come back down to the boat with me. Uncle Kobus is very angry with you, looks like I've saved him from an embarrassment."

Lorna stared out of the window and whispered across to Jem, hoping the other girl would hear her. They were in different cells but had found out they could communicate providing they knelt down and talked at the bottom of the wall without the guard hearing them. "Are you sure you saw Rose?"

"Certainly," replied Jem, "it was hazy out there but I recognised her."

"So where has she gone?"

"They were chasing her so she must have got away, no idea where she was heading but we need to get out."

"No one will be going anywhere," boomed a horribly familiar voice as Kobus opened the door, hustling them out and across to the larger room where two female guards ushered them to seats. "You two need to pretty yourselves up with the red dresses, we have important clients arriving in an hour and they need to see you at your best."

"Slavery was outlawed over a century ago, it's disgusting," said Lorna.

"I learnt it all from your father, and it's all exactly how you arrived into the world, my dear, he taught us everything we know. The good news is you have both been classified in the highest category so you should be very pleased, you're good breeding stock."

"I cannot believe this," said Lorna.

"Breeding machines, and dammed pretty ones."

"I'm a police woman, you will be locked up for decades for this," snapped Jem looking at Kobus in horror.

"There's no law here except mine, and as you've insulted me I am going to stay and watch. Strip them," he snapped, "a little humility will help before their clients arrive." Both were forcibly stripped in front of him by the two burly female warders as Kobus smiled. "Don't think your little friend will make a difference, she's being brought back here as we speak. Yes, I think you both are of ample quality," he smiled as Lorna and Jem stood naked in front of him trying to hide their genitals. "I suggest you pretty yourselves up, we have industrialists and politicians queuing up, even a minister of the church would you believe."

"This is barbaric," snapped Jem.

"On the contrary, it's the future of our race, the chance to have perfect human beings without all the inadequacies. Why should valuable resources be used up by halfwits and those that barely can string a sentence together? What we need is a super race. Nietzsche had it right: we need a race of Supermen."

"I won't do it," said Jem.

"Then it will be done for you, and my men are none too careful," replied Kobus. "Your choice, ladies," he added, and closed the door.

Germania

The dark, swarthy man looked around the place they had called home for so long and cursed as he realised the depth of the betrayal. He had devoted his entire life to the mission and to the support of the person he had called his partner to now find out she had moved on. He cursed again in his mother tongue and saw Helmut bearing down on him.

"Is there a problem, Aitor?"

"None at all," replied the Spaniard, standing up. "We have much to do, so I suggest we get on with it."

"We are cogs in the wheel," smiled Helmut, as if reading his thoughts. "It's all worth it for the greater mission."

"Of course," replied Aitor, "I suggest you go and do as you are instructed, I am in charge here and have things to do."

"Of course, our great nations will prevail and we will all be part of the great new world," replied Helmut turning away. "You are a great man, as is our leader, and the world will be astounded."

"That's your version, mine is different," said Aitor, turning away. "She has betrayed me but I will stay loyal to her, not to your imposter."

"There is no difference, we are all the same movement."

"You think so? really? I'm sick of all this German stuff, this place was built in a bloody swamp and isn't fit for human habitation. I want to be with my own people."

"We are cogs, Aitor: we do as we are told."

Berlin

The rain hammered down on the King Wilhelm Church on the Kufurstendam. Inside the modern building built around the ruins of the bombed out original church an organ recital rang out in the night sky. It was a movement from Wagner's Lohengrin opera, played with gusto by a lone woman. The weather was consistent with the piece and with her mood as she glanced up at the skeleton of the original church. She turned as her mobile bleeped, the call she was waiting for.

"Good to hear from you."

"Good flight from Panama?"

"Always the same on the private jet," she smiled wanly, "problems with some of the staff and our mutual friend but nothing that can't be taken care of."

"You don't sound sure."

"Our mutual friend is getting too dominating; some of her followers concern me."

"We must all work together for the common good, Composer."

"I accept that, but we must mitigate against risks; they work on emotion not logic which is always dangerous, that's why this place was nearly destroyed."

"Very well, I have total trust, what do you propose?"

"We can use the Europeans here to our advantage and watch," said the Composer. "All it takes is a little balancing act for them and sparks will fly," she smiled, before placing a call to the man called Giuseppe.

Chapter 13

Saba

Rose cursed as she saw the now-familiar high cliffs of the island citadel rise before her. Locked in the stern cabin with her hands tied behind her back, Joe had said nothing, but his eyes said everything. She was glad Annaliese was there, though the girl studiously ignored her, spending most of the time on the radio. She felt tired, hungry, and seasick, made worse by the yacht's precarious wobbling as they entered the small harbour. She had to get a message to Guy but how, everything she had tried had failed and she began to feel the spectre of defeat. She was dragged ashore, her hands till tied behind her back, and was bundled into a small jeep for the ride to the university building, where she was unceremoniously thrown onto the floor at the feet of Kobus. "Look what I've found."

"You have caused me a great deal of trouble, missy," snapped the big man, "so much so that will put you on the programme. You have strength, and I like that, we need to replicate it."

"Go to hell," said Rose pulling herself upright with difficulty.

"Take her through to the back room and keep her separate from the others. You have done very well Annaliese, now come and tell me all about the Philosopher, I am eager to hear."

"Great plans," replied Annaliese enthusiastically as she followed her uncle up to his house.

"You are honoured to be included in the inner circle," said Kobus, listening and smiling across at his niece. She was part of his long term plans though it did bother him how she enthused over the Philosopher.

"The future is about meritocracy and I was considered a suitable subject for certain tests."

"What tests?"

"Intelligence tests and assessments, we all have to have them in the inner circle."

"Inner circle?" asked Kobus. He hadn't been asked to sit any tests.

"I have my instructions and portfolio," continued Annaliese, not registering her uncle's discomfort. "There is room for only a few in the inner circle."

"So I see," replied Kobus.

"I have been selected by more than the Philosopher."

"What does that mean?"

"I met the Composer, in fact she saved me from an assault, she is behind all that happens, but I can't share all the details with you."

"The Composer, eh? Praise indeed. So I am on the outside. Fine, but make sure they leave me alone here, And watch out for the politics."

"We will make this work, Uncle."

"Guess we'll have to," said Kobus. This wasn't in his plans but it wasn't insurmountable: they had reckoned without Kobus the fighter. People like him didn't fit the mould and they couldn't control him; probably, he thought, the reason they sought to indoctrinate his niece. He looked up, his attention caught by Dirk. "Just a minute Annaliese," he said, and motioned Dirk over.

"Keep the Chinese bitch for me; I want her cleaned up and here tonight."

"So, Annaliese, this meritocracy thing, will you be in charge?" he asked, seeing in the girl's eyes that he had lost her to the movement.

"The world's most enlightened states have been governed by meritocracy - just look at Singapore and Lee Kwan Yue. Real leaders rule by ability not inheritance, just as with Napoleon and the Code Napoleon. Meritocracy will replace the aristocracy."

"Napoleon had the advantage of following a revolution and anarchy," replied Kobus. People needed order and he provided it, but yes, I agree, there is merit in what you say, except it's more than just brains; Napoleon was also a street fighter like me who clawed his way to the top, so don't get too obsessed with these Germans, you've seen how they can behave if they don't get what they want."

"Dear Uncle, please let's not argue tonight. I am tired, and together we have much to do."

"Of course you are right my dear," beamed Kobus, gesturing to Dirk and looking forward to his later meeting. He had always had a thing for the slender Asian girls and particularly enjoyed when they fought back, that made it twice as exciting.

Abu Dhabi

El Hammill looked across in delight at the two rigs towering over the skyline. The first was being fitted out in Turkey, and these two would be next: one for Africa and one for the Americas. The timing was critical and he looked down at the myriad of workers labouring in the hot daytime sun on what they believed were natural gas extraction rigs. The place was guarded by the best security men he could find and he reflected that in the three years of its construction there had been no incidents. With the first rig nearly ready, attention was also on the final one for the Asian market, which was being built in Jakarta. It had been his idea to keep them in different locations before moving them for final assembly so they wouldn't attract too much attention. Security was paramount, particularly as they started to construct the top levels. He watched as the more advanced rig was slowly towed across the harbour area by three huge tugs, its legs sticking up in the air resembling a giant upturned beetle. This was the future and Mare Nostrum was now real.

"You've done well, El Hammill," said Lucrezia, watching on a video screen as the mighty beast moved. "All on time and to plan, I assume that one is for Africa and will go to final assembly in the Seychelles?"

"As planned, yes, and a fitting memorial to your brother."

"Thank you, very appropriate."

"My only concern is the central security systems, they need time to be embedded and didn't work properly on the first rig, hence the attack."

"The timetable is sacrosanct," snapped Lucrezia, "we have to keep to schedule people are lined up waiting, this will be the greatest demonstration of sea power for a generation."

"Probably since the Venetian Republic," replied El Hammill, well aware of Lucrezia's influence.

"What's the latest on the attack on the first rig?"

"The Russian must have drowned, he can't have survived that fall from the rig, the waters were freezing and they won't try again."

"But they got through, which is not acceptable."

"Only through subterfuge and those responsible have been suspended, the Turkish contractor included."

Minorca

Rostov staggered ashore more dead than alive and collapsed in a heap, having survived at sea for over six hours before his trusted deputy, Kirov, had rescued him and brought him to Minorca. He sat on the waterfront overlooking the deep-water harbour and stared at Kirov. He had no idea what had happened to Sergei and felt wretched for leaving his boss, but he had had little choice: they would have shot him down like a mad dog. He watched as his men gathered around, and then outlined his instructions. It was time to fight back by going to the heart of the enemy and he knew the only place where he could do that.

Abu Dhabi

It was a blisteringly hot afternoon as Rostov and Kirov landed and made their way with the Sparkasy twins across to the futuristic area around Ferrari World, near the port. The area was bristling with security men, and they had limited time. He looked around grimly at the array of security towers thinking that somehow they had to find a way of stopping them. If they cut out the heart of the hydra beast then the whole edifice would falter, stop the rigs then the whole programme would grind to a halt, with loss of confidence from their investors.

"Get some rest until dark," he announced to Kirov and Spassky twins as they checked into the luxurious Intercontinental hotel. "Any ideas, Kirov?" he asked his second in command as they checked into rooms. "This is going to be tricky, that rig is enormous."

"Create a diversion to allow us to get into the yard and place explosives on the four retaining legs," replied Kirov. "They look relatively unprotected and are very low tech; I've bought both the explosives and guns from the locals."

"Good thinking, then we have a plan," replied Rostov grimly. "I want to do real damage to them this time, there's five times the explosives here that I had before."

It was early dawn as they made their way out of the hotel in the hired car and made the short journey across to the year, already bristling with workers on the early shift. Rostov took the most expeditious route open to him, driving the hired Toyota Land Cruiser straight into the front dock gate. The twins simultaneously opened fire with machine guns as the gates buckled and the guards dived for cover. They drove through at speed and Rostov grunted as he saw groups of men run towards him. He swerved hard and drove at speed along the dock side; the truck jerking as gunfire hit them, and he began to wonder if they would make it when suddenly they were through and into the special area of assembly. Rostov slammed the accelerator down as they hit another gate and bounced through, before finding themselves in a welding area, seeing startled workmen high up on the girders. "Quick, set the charges on a two minute fuse."

"But the workers," asked Ivan Spassky, the taller twin.

"Thirty second warning."

"Not long enough for those at the top."

"They can jump into the water," said Rostov, seeing a speaker unit in the nearest hut. "Over there," he shouted whilst he scrambled back to the truck, and the Toyota's tyres on the driver side shredded.

"Same again," said Rostov. The charges were laid and they accelerated out as the first explosion shook the yard.. He saw one of the large legs buckle as simultaneous explosions shook it. They had concentrated all of the explosive power in the same leg, reasoning that it would take months to repair it. What did concern him, however, was that the leg only bent a little, meaning that it must be made of toughened steel. He looked to his men grimly as they drove down the dock side; there was no way back from this assignment, it was every man for himself, and he saw one of the twins falter. He hoped to God that Kirov had got the powerboat ready as he drove at speed back alongside the dock, wanting to put distance between them and their pursuers. "Each to your own," he said. "You know where we meet." He slammed the truck into top gear and drove for the dockside, jumping for the water as it went at pace over the edge.

He hit the water hard and gasped involuntarily as the now familiar feeling of sea water filling his lungs took hold of him. He cursed and started swimming with long purposeful strides out for the powerboat he could see dimly through the chaos. He spotted Kirov on the powerboat, and shouts came from the side of the docks as two guards started unfastening their rifles. He flung himself aboard as Kirov accelerated hard and fast. The Spassky twins were dead.

Casablanca, Morocco

She looked around desperately as she was pushed and shoved onto a small privately hired plane. Her last recollection had been hiding in the Gibraltar tunnel and then being forced on board a fast cruiser, heavily drugged. She had then known nothing until awakening here feeling sick and disorientated unable to remember how on earth she had got across the small gap of the Mediterranean Sea separating Europe from Africa. She looked around as the flight levelled out and saw only Sabine with her. They had been flying for two hours when she heard Sabine give the pilot the instructions to descend.

"Where are we?"

"Be quiet," snapped Sabine. "I will deal with you later. You think you can outsmart me? I know you led Tresanton to us, but luckily for you we need you."

"I just asked a civil question," replied Tatyana, noting that they were landing in mainland Spain. They taxied to a halt on a grass airfield and she saw a sign for Galicia before being bundled into a car. They drove for half an hour along winding narrow country lanes, and she wondered how on earth she could get a warning to Sergei. She started to feel nauseous again when at last they turned up a track towards what looked like an old monastery. She was ushered into a cell-like room and the door locked. She must have dozed when the door opened to reveal a grim faced Sabine. "You will sleep here tonight and don't get any ideas; this place is a fortress."

"Go to hell," snapped Tatyana as the door slammed, and to her surprise she heard voices next door. Sabine was talking to someone and she realised an air vent at the top of the door was responsible. She went closer to the vent and tried to listen. The voices were indecipherable but she could make out some words.

"It's a well proven route; it's worked for over sixty years, they will be watching all the airports and we move all the girls across continents this way, it's well tried."

"She's my prisoner and I don't report to some German in Latin America called Wolfgang."

"There are other plans for you and I suggest you obey the Germans," replied a heavily accented Spanish voice. Sabine was not in charge.

"I don't take my orders from you," said Sabine.

"The architect is responsible to my boss, at the end of the day life is all about making good choices, Sabine, and I thought you were smart enough to know that. Be very careful who you align with, the wrong choices can be very dangerous."

"I thought we were one team?"

"There's politics like any organisation."

"I make my own decisions."

Tatyana couldn't hear the reply as the voice dropped, She tried to press her ear closer but to no avail, and she scrambled backwards as the door opened.

"What the hell are you doing, trying to snoop?" asked Sabine, trying to smack Tatyana's head against the door. Tatyana saw it coming and managed to evade the worst of the impact, before grabbing Sabine's arm and twisting hard, causing the redhead to fall screaming to the floor. Tatyana grabbed her hair and pulled hard, but Sabine pushed her leg under Tatyana, who lost her balance and fell to the floor. She hit her head upon impact, and Sabine began to pummel her mercilessly.

"Feel better, Sabine?" resounded the male voice.

"Bitch had it coming," snapped Sabine as Tatyana dragged herself away, bruised but not broken.

"We need to patch her up for the programme, Wolfgang needs her," he said.

"This is outrageous," stammered Tatyana.

"You've seen nothing yet," said Sabine, adjusting herself, "enjoy your journey to hell, bitch."

"What journey?"

"The Nazis' escape route after the war, this Catholic monastery is part of it, they were ambivalent towards Hitler, and they must have streamed through here after the war like rats from a sewer."

"Enough," snapped the man, looking across at Sabine.

"Clever bitch, isn't she, Jose?" said Sabine.

"Perhaps," replied Jose, a swarthy mid-sized individual, "anyone finding out about the route has to be contained."

"She won't last long where she's going," smiled Sabine as she slammed the door turning to Jose. "She has the required genes, believe me I would love to dispose of her." She turned away as her phone rang. "I have to go now, be careful: she's Spetnaz trained."

"I have plenty of experience, the fighters are more interesting company anyway, makes it all the more enjoyable," said Jose.

"Couldn't agree more, but no package damage, how many in the first shipment?"

"The full complement of Project Valkyrie per rig is fifty."

"That many?"

The next morning was cold and wet, and Tatyana shivered as she was bundled into a small car and taken the short journey down to the coast from the monastery. It was dawn as they headed south approaching a dirt track down to a small cove. She saw something large and dark in the ocean swell down in the bay. "Oh my God, we're not going in that thing," she exclaimed with disbelieving eyes as a submarine broke the surface.

"Just as our descendants did decades ago," snarled Jose producing a gun and pointing, "there are six men aboard just looking for a chance with an attractive blonde, I will protect you providing you behave, do we understand each other?"

"Yes," said Tatyana, desperately looking around at the deserted area as Jose got out of the car. Momentarily distracted as he closed the car door, she slammed her foot forwards, knocking him down, and tried desperately to find his gun. She saw the two men below looking up in puzzlement from the inflatable; she had seconds to make a decision and ran upwards onto the cliff away from the submarine. Turning she saw Jose angrily running after her, she looked around in dismay but saw nothing but moorland; she had to keep running. She lengthened her stride and in the distance saw a lone cyclist on a dirt track. She tried to attract his attention as he came to a halt looking at her, and with shouts growing louder behind her she pushed the man to the ground and grabbed his bike.. She needed to get away from the road and turned onto the rough ground, pedalling furiously. Suddenly, the bike lurched and shuddered as she hit a hidden rock, and she flew through the air, hitting hard ground. Semi-conscious, she tried to stand up, blood pouring from her head.

"Told you there would be consequences," said Jose, punching her in the stomach as he dragged her unceremoniously back down the road to the water's edge.

Sabine reflected on Lucrezia's order to head west, which suited her better than returning to the unforgiving and frozen wastes of Russia. She also reflected on her late night conversation with Jose, a long standing supporter of Germania. He had told her about the Quintet, a special order riddled with politics, and it made her more determined than ever to play all sides. Experience told her to stick with the situation she knew whilst always looking for opportunities; that was how she had acquired the diamonds in Spain and also what had kept her alive for so long.

St Bart's

"Taped to the top of his safe where no one would see it, obvious really and proof that he was in the pay of Tutulus, there are a list of bank transfers, regular as clockwork 20th of every month, look at the dammed amounts, no wonder the bastard has a plush office," said Monty.

"Won't do him any good where he's going," said Guy.

"They always say follow the money," reflected Monty, opening another file marked secret. "Talks about the islands of Saba and Bequia as key refuges should he ever get in trouble, mentions a Dutchman."

"The pirate, the Dutchman you mentioned, where is he?"

"Saba."

"Any other names?"

"Nothing else, but we have what we need, proof at last that they have a tangible presence."

"So we follow the money?"

"No, we go to Saba and this pirate Kobus, I've a feeling that will provide answers, don't you?"

Grenada

To the various dignitaries gathering in the grandiose building the White House looked spectacular.

"Welcome," smiled Helmut as the Philosopher arrived with an entourage, the staff taking care of the luggage.

"I assume all is as it should be."

"Most of the others are here; we are ready for the meeting," replied Helmut.

"Including our European colleagues?"

"On their way."

"The long awaited meeting of the Quintet, or what's left of them," mused the Philosopher looking around, "the first for many years and I suspect not again for many more, still it's a momentous occasion and one that should be appropriately honoured."

"As indeed it will be," smiled Helmut, turning as he saw the Composer approaching.

"Our special arrival."

"Wolfgang is a liability," said the Composer to Helmut entering, "a word of advice Helmut, spend time with Annaliese."

"Of course," replied Helmut, smiling. Revenge on Wolfgang would be very sweet indeed; the Philosopher's favourite had fallen foul of the Composer, which was just what Helmut wanted to hear.

"Her uncle is also a liability," said the Composer, "we can't afford to have a loose cannon around."

"He's a loyal subject."

"Keep an eye on him, should be easier if you and Annaliese were an item, a fine looking girl."

"She is indeed."

"Composer, would you join me please?" said the Philosopher, annoyed at the delay, "there are a number of important items we need to discuss prior to the arrival of the Europeans."

Bequia

It had been a long arduous journey and Tatyana felt ill as she was pushed ashore onto the little island. She had hardly slept in the metal can they called a submarine, the whole thing being unbearably noisy and smelly. They'd taken five days to cross the Atlantic, surfacing at night to avoid preying eyes. Her ordeal had been worsened as she felt constantly exposed to potential attack by the crew. The worst was Jose himself, who glowered at her whenever he came into the locked room where she was held captive and had twice deliberately groped her. She had spent the time productively fashioning a small metal fork into a stiletto blade that she'd concealed in her shoe as a precaution. She was relieved when told that Jose would be heading back with the submarine, along with three scared-looking girls she saw in the distance. The hard land under her feet made her wobble as she re-acclimatised to the new surroundings before she was bundled into a jeep and driven across the island to a large house on a hill.

"This is your new home before you are sent to the operating area," said Wolfgang as she was pushed into a cell like room.

"What operations?" asked Tatyana, detecting a German accent.

"It's like this, either you go straight to the breeding centre or you carry out a little task for me that involves some of your particular skills," intoned Wolfgang, still smarting from Anneliese's rejection. "You would do well to do as I say, Russian," he smiled as the door shut. "You have two hours to get cleaned and then I will be back for your decision, there's a bathroom through there, make sure you use it."

"Shit," exclaimed Tatyana. She was under no illusions as to what was coming her way as the door slammed shut, she had to escape; however, she couldn't resist her first bath in weeks and luxuriated in the warmth for ten minutes before quickly getting dressed, pleased to note that whilst she had been in the bath her old clothes had been washed and ironed. She dressed and then prepared herself.

"I've heard Russian girls are particularly willing to please, apparently it's in your blood from when our master race invaded the steppes," smiled Wolfgang, locking the door behind him. He would let her hunt down the Brazilian after a little pleasure.

"I doubt you have what it takes," said Tatyana, steeling herself as the German lunged forwards and grabbed her blouse. Instead of resisting she let herself be pulled forwards, which briefly knocked him off his balance, before driving the small blade into his shoulder. He screamed and collapsed, blood pouring from his shirt.

"You bitch, you should be grateful Helmut uses a whip."

"My normal response to rape, the way we Russians have dealt with Germans," she smiled sweetly.

"You'll pay for that," he snarled, pulling himself up before Tatyana hit him hard with the table lamp and he slumped to the floor unconscious. She ran out of the room and quickly found her way onto the small track behind the house heading upwards into the desolate mountain. It was pitch black, and she had to be careful, but she made good time. and after nearly an hour found a sheltered shepherds shack.

She slumped down and relaxed for a moment, then was startled as the door opened and a man stared at her. She raised her blade, shaken by how quickly she had been discovered.

"Whoa there lady, I think we're on the same side, I saw you escape from the same house I was held in," said Jacques.

Wolfgang cursed to himself as he staggered into the first aid area and got the warden to fix his shoulder, the cut wasn't life threatening but his prisoner was out there with Jacques who she was supposed to kill after he had published news of her capture as one of the Elders. Now it had gone badly wrong all because of his own lust, he needed to kill them both, but felt dreadful as the loss of blood took its toll.

Venice

It was past midnight as they carefully made their way into the innermost sanctum of Lucrezia's office complex, knowing that she had left the country earlier. Segovia led the way with Stanton checking her back as together they searched her files looking for anything to do with the Papal Covenant. After nearly twenty minutes she spotted something in the top filing drawer stuck to the roof of the desk.

"Over here," she smiled.

"Well done, my dear," said Stanton, before reading it carefully. "This mentions Marco Polo taking a document from his meeting with the Chinese mariner Zheng He, the founder of the Elders, and this has to be it." He looked carefully at the writing and shrugged. "We need to get back to our offices, we have what we came for, how did you know it would be here?"

"Because Sergei and Tatyana told me there was a special second document and this proves it, we need to go and get it."

"But it talks of the Vatican."

"Into the Lion's den, if we can find this it will save the Elders, think of it."

"You know I'm glad we met Segovia, you are very resourceful, and this way we can destroy Lucrezia and the Doge. Call me Ed."

"Hopefully, yes, but it's fraught with danger, however ever since I freed Sergei I've felt exposed, now we have the way out, thanks for your help Ed, strange that I wasn't briefed about you in advance."

"Too risky," replied Ed Stanton, "cells within cells, none knowing about the others, always safer that way."

"I suppose so. Come on then, we need to drive there now before we are discovered."

"Not tonight Segovia, we need rest first, let me make some arrangements and we leave at first light."

"Perhaps you are right," conceded the Russian, heading back to her room. She was in the deepest of sleep when rough hands shook her awake and pushed her out into the corridor clad in her nightie.

Chapter 14

Venice

Lucrezia sat deep in thought as she watched the myriad of coloured gondolas make their way slowly along the narrow waterfront outside her private home. The loss of the Spanish treasure had been externally irritating, as was the recent attack on the rig, but she had the Russian Sergei in custody and therefore the key to the Khans' Prophecy. That gave her what she needed for her imminent meeting with the Chosen Ones. She reflected on her own title of the Architect, after all she was the designer of the rigs, of the future living platforms, the designer of a new way of living and richly deserving the title. She took her role in the Quintet seriously; after all, it had been a momentous occasion when she had been chosen. The problem was the others; the Teacher and the Professor had both had their time, but the three surviving members of the quintet were a problem. The Philosopher was too emotional without pragmatism, she needed insurance, and Giuseppe was her insurer, hence their private meeting in a very different part of Venice.

"You look troubled, my friend."

"Two things, Lucrezia," said the Italian, looking flushed, "the Russian girl I employed in the ledger department, she found this."

"Did she indeed?" replied Lucrezia, frowning. "That's private property and highly

sensitive, send her to me and the other?"

"Your insurance plan, I've got something."

"What?"

"A place in Belgium."

"What makes you so confident?"

"I had a call from a source connected to the Quintet," replied Giuseppe, "it's served me well before, I trust it."

"Check it out quickly."

"But the meeting tomorrow…"

"I can manage without you; I need this insurance before I head into the lair."

"It sounds dangerous."

"I need ammunition."

"Ammunition against whom?"

"My esteemed partners on the Quintet. Tell me about Belgium."

"Connected to the First World War."

"Tell me more?"

"The Flanders Field museum, in a place called Ypres now called Leper, name changed to disassociate it with the War; it was practically rebuilt but contains a secret."

"What sort of secret?"

"Something embarrassing to one of your colleagues, I'd rather not say more until I check it out."

The midday sun was beating down as Lucrezia made her way along the canals from her home to the Doge meeting room, nodding curtly to El Hammill and gesturing him to one side as they entered the small ante chamber. "You know where the Prophecy is?" she asked.

"St Petersburg, my men are working on him as we speak."

"Another attack?"

"Two men were killed and the damage will be repaired. We have spare legs so we are still on schedule."

"Good, get the Prophecy, I'll handle this," said Lucrezia, heading through into the main room and greeting the assembly. "Ladies and gentlemen, I am pleased to report that Mare Nostrum One is running successfully, feedback from the guests is very positive. The appropriate countries in the Mediterranean have accepted the loss of their respective tax paying citizens." Lucrezia looked around the room, it was important that all believed in the concept as a viable idea before she started to introduce the non-democratic elements. She had designed the whole concept of living platforms from the drawing board funded by Tutulus, although the cost had run into billions before she had achieved the necessary funding. That was why the Spanish treasure had been so important, to give her control, and now she needed something else. "We are one person short tonight, and that is the banker Jose Barr from BMN, who unfortunately has left us."

"I thought once we were in we stayed in," commented Benedict.

"He has been arrested by the Spanish authorities for malpractice, so it was not appropriate that he stay on as we are a law abiding group. Now, ladies and gentlemen, onto happier things; I want to tell you about a fascinating document called the Khans' Prophecy, a prophecy that will help us all."

"Why is this of interest to us?" asked Contessa Gerhard.

"It's important to have insurance policies in case some countries don't accept our alternative way of living and the attendant loss of tax revenues. Therefore it's important to know secrets that will make any nation state think twice before taking action against us. We have the best security systems money can buy, but of course we cannot defend ourselves against an army, that's where insurance comes in."

"I never thought we were entering into potential conflict with nations," replied Gerhard. "I would have thought twice about my investments if that was the case."

"Of course you would and no we aren't," smiled Lucrezia. "Let me assure you all that what we are doing is totally legitimate and within the rule of law. I even have tacit approval from the United Nations for our plans. No, what I am talking about is more autocratic or dictatorial nations who may be tempted to use force against us. Against those people we must have protection, and over the centuries the one sure form of protection has always been knowledge that can be leveraged, hence this Prophecy is an insurance policy."

"The Khans' Prophecy does I take it mean Mongolia?" asked Benedict.

"Initially, yes, and the country has huge influence across growing Asia with its huge natural resources and the re-emerging Silk Road."

"What do you mean 're-emerging Silk Road'?"

"The oldest global trade was the original Silk Road from Xian in China to Istanbul, we are seeing the dawn of the new Silk Road, what the Chinese President calls the 'one belt, one road' policy that envisions world trade being predominantly driven through the Asian land routes with their huge mineral deposits, so real power is knowledge of secrets that can damage the credibility of nation states."

"It sounds problematic and ambitious," said Hatari the Japanese delegate. "What's the latest on the Elders, as I hear on the grapevine they are reforming?"

"It was never intended to abolish the Elders, only to redress the balance of power, for too long they have sat in secret judgement."

"We will have the Prophecy."

"There does seem to be a lot you aren't telling us," said Antonio.

"You have to trust me. Look on the positive side; your investments have already gained twenty percent."

"Lucrezia is right," said Contessa Gerhardt, "I for one am delighted with the new platforms, they are already the talk of the wealthy classes, a new mode of living far removed from the vagaries of democracy and the masses."

"Thank you," said Lucrezia. "It's important I know I have your support."

Saba

Kobus busied himself with the final arrangements, noting the two large private yachts moored at the landing place and buzzing with clientele. They had all paid handsomely for the privilege of taking part in Project Valkyrie, where they had a chance to create the world's future leaders. They had arrived from all over the continent, and had been chosen for their influence, their intelligence, and their money. Kobus saw it as a kind of huge dating agency, and he intended to make sure that he got as much credit as possible. Conditions on the island were too rudimentary for the people arriving, so they would spend the appropriate time at his 'university' then retire back to their flashy yachts and head off to another site. It was a special type of cruise that was earning them a fortune in the process, only now it wasn't his organisation, it was the Philosopher's.

Months in the planning, he was pleased as expectations from the special guests were high and nothing must be allowed to get in the way of their satisfaction. He sat watching from his mountaintop retreat as the yachts disgorged their rich passengers, and reflected on his own journey from the bottom in the Amsterdam drugs world and then working hard until he was where we was now, master of all he surveyed. His thoughts turned fondly to the Chinese girl later that evening after the guests had gone and looked up as Annaliese entered the room.

"Hello my dear, are you settled?"
"I take it you want me to oversee the girls tonight?"
"Yes, make sure our privileged guests are taken care of."
"There was a time when I would have been disgusted by this."
"But the means justify the ends, right?" smiled Kobus, "we will take a few days break after tonight you and do some catching up, maybe go over to that luxury island and avail ourselves of their hospitality."
"Sorry, Uncle, but I have to be at Bequia tomorrow, another assignment."

"Which assignment?"

"Arranged by the Philosopher directly," replied Annaliese, seeing her uncle's discomfort.

"Very well, we have eight visitors arriving and I believe eight girls are ready."

"Including the two captives yes," replied Annaliese, "what about the Chinese girl?"

"I have other plans for her."

Lorna and Jem were ushered into the small room and then separated. Jem had resorted to drinking wine for the ordeal she suspected lay ahead, though she couldn't quite believe it was about to happen, not in modern times, and she would fight it. The woman who was dressing her spoke only a local dialect that sounded like a form of Dutch, and she was clearly afraid. Jem was ushered to a separate room and the door locked. In front of her was a note saying to expect a guest for dinner in the next hour, and she wondered what sort of person would come through the door, unable to believe the situation she was in and steeling herself to fight.

Next door, Lorna was tearful, also unable to comprehend what was happening to her and devastated that her father's legacy had returned from the grave.. Both Lorna and Jem had lost their private medicine and any form of contraception, and Lorna felt herself grow angry at the thought of what could happen and looked around the room for a method of escape. She didn't have Jem's training to fight off an attack and somehow doubted whether it would be that simple: Kobus would have thought of that.

Half a mile away, Rose looked again at the cold walls. Guy would be frantic with worry but she couldn't see a way out. She was under a double guard; there wouldn't be a second chance to escape easily. They also weren't feeding her anymore, and she looked up as a small note was pushed through her door and she read the words with mounting horror as she realised the implications. The Dutchman wanted her, but she had no intention of letting that oaf anywhere near.

Rio de Janeiro

The room was still spinning badly and Charlotte felt like she was dying; she was disorientated and realised there had been a reaction to the gas. She managed to stagger across the wooden room to see she was in a shack on the edge of the favelas, and heard the sound of a woman crying coming from next door. She looked around and felt immobile, then saw the door open as if in slow motion, and a large man entered.

"You're trespassing."

"I'm an American Senator," she shouted, but it came out slurred.

"Well you're in the way; I've got much to do." He walked past and opened the next door. Three attractive but scared witless teenage girls were pulled out.

"Those girls, you are holding them against their will."

"My property."

"This is slavery," yelled Charlotte.

"You've seen too much."

"Who put you up to kidnapping these girls?"

"They came to me for modelling assignments," he grinned through gapped teeth, "there's good money to be earned in the Caribbean."

"Spare me the lies," snapped Charlotte, "they're for the sex slave trade, I have seen too much of this sort of thing, you will release them now." With mounting horror she watched the man reach over and lift a machete.

La Gomera

Victoria half-smiled to herself as she took the familiar chair for the extraordinary meeting of the Elders. "I never thought I would be sitting here again."

"It suits you," smiled her secretary, who activated the phone. Guy came on the line with Monty.

"Everyone there?" asked Guy.

"All except Charlotte," replied Victoria. "We seem to have permanently lost contact. The floor is yours, Guy."

"There have been a number of developments that need to be brought to your attention that Victoria will explain in a minute. Firstly the enemy, or Hydra as I now call them, have many heads; the Doge is based in Venice and led by Lucrezia, the sister of the Professor," said Guy from St Bart's police station. "They are part of a wider group called the Quintet, who are involved in the female slave trade, or, to be more precise, breeding centres, the same group that we uncovered in Norway a few years ago. We have a mammoth task ahead of us trying to uncover the real nature of what's happening."

"What exactly have you got?" asked Harry Jackman, the American.

"Very little, except that Tutulus have moved their operating headquarters to Grenada."

"It's unlikely they are operating in any other places in the same way, as we would have heard of them," said Victoria. "I have examined the vaults, which fortunately are intact, though a master criminal got access. Interestingly, I have found what I believe they were really looking for, and it wasn't the Khans' Prophecy, but a document in Chinese. It does seem that this quintet see themselves as guardians of the original Zheng He legacy. Two of this Quintet were the Teacher and Professor, this Lucrezia, called the Architect, is the third."

"So two other names running around and I take professional names?" asked Contessa Gerhard.

"Yes, and Guy has heard of the name Philosopher," replied Victoria, "it seems that the Prophecy is linked to other documents that lay out a vision of the future, plus we appear to have an Asian dimension. I don't know any more, except that the Doge desperately wants access to these documents."

"So we have a situation where the particular plot we uncovered has been reactivated on a larger scale," continued Guy.

"These breeding sites are related to the rigs you mentioned?" asked Jackson.

"We can only speculate," continued Victoria. "From what we understand of the sea platforms or rigs they are for the richest, a simple form of tax avoidance."

"The Nazis reborn," murmured Jackson. "This is a nightmare in the making."

"A nightmare that's already with us," said Monty on the phone. "We have every available police force investigating and unfortunately have lost all contact with Charlotte."

"What of Sergei?" asked Madam Ramping.

"Disappeared, though his men have attacked one of the rigs under construction," said Guy. "We have lost track of both Sergei and Tatyana, his associate."

"Thought she had turned against him," said the African.

"She was coerced."

"That's why we need your help," continued Victoria, "what we do have is the Prophecy, at least for the moment, along with the document in the vaults."

"If Sergei is captured then the Prophecy is lost," said Jackson. "These rigs, why can't we stop them by going directly to the police?"

"Because they're not illegal, in fact they're far from it, because they have been condoned by rich and powerful people."

"So what exactly do you want us to do?" asked Ramping.

"Use your contacts to track down Tutulus and find who is behind all this," said Victoria.

"Also I need help to find my wife," said Guy. "So far we have narrowed the search down to two islands, Saba and Bequia."

"Saba is Dutch, I may be able to help there," said the Dutch delegate Dorte.

"In what way?"

"I have links into our government's overseas operations as there has been a problem with the local governor on Saba, I am aware that he has just been asked to retire early."

"Why?"

"Complaints from residents who have been threatened, and rumours: apparently a renegade Dutchman has styled himself as the de-facto king of the island."

"You've only just found this out?" gasped Guy.

"It's an embarrassment to our government, they don't want this becoming public knowledge as Saba harbours a community of over two hundred on top of the rock. I would suggest you go there first."

"So we have something concrete and we know where their organisation is getting its money from. Mr Huang can I ask you to help with the translations of the documents," continued Victoria. "Senor Giraud, can you commence an investigation into the potential routes the Nazis used and indeed where they ended up in Latin America."

"Nazis," exclaimed Giraud, "why the Nazi's?"

"The idea of breeding camps started with those horrible people, if we can track down the routes they used we may well get useful leads to where this new organisation operates from."

"We have missed you as Chair," said Huang.

"Make the most of it, I have retired once and will do so again."

"I do know a little about the Germans in America," said Giraud, "Latin America and particularly Paraguay became a stronghold for escaping Nazis, and Germania in Paraguay was a German stronghold at the turn of the last century."

Bequia

Jacques and Tatyana had decided to work together, having no idea that Wolfgang had planned for one to kill the other. They made their way back to the outskirts of the house, both hungry and tired after a day scavenging across the island, and finally agreed that the best course of action would be to confront the enemy and free the others.

They approached as dusk fell, taking care to stick to the shadows and armed with no more than two wooden clubs fashioned during the day.

"Let me take the lead, I'll make it official," said Jacques as they approached.

"I will take the back door," replied Tatyana.

"Very well," said Jacques. He banged on the door and braced himself.

"Well you've got a nerve," snapped Wolfgang, opening the door in amazement. "I was just about to come looking for you and you come to me, my salvation on a plate."

"The police are on the way, I suggest you surrender now," said Jacques.

"Highly unlikely," smirked Wolfgang, drawing his gun as Jacques lifted his wooden club, already regretting their direct approach.

"You wouldn't shoot me in cold blood," said Jacques.

"Afraid so," smiled Wolfgang, and he fired. Jacques gasped as the bullet hit him in the chest. "No one said I had to keep you in one piece, where's the bitch?"

"No idea," said Jacques, struggling with the pain.

"Well you're not of much use to me then," said Wolfgang. He raised the gun again, determined to finish the man off, then felt horrendous pain on the back of his head as Tatyana hit him with her wooden club. He fell to the floor with a grunt then rolled to one side, grabbing at his gun.

"Stay down or I shoot," she shouted.

"Idiots! You have no idea what you are playing with here, this is way too big for you," snarled Wolfgang. "Help," he yelled into the house, and three men came running down the corridor.

"Come on Jacques, we need to move," hissed Tatyana.

"You will have to escape, I'm injured," gasped the Brazilian. "Go!" he yelled as two shots from inside the house hit him in the chest.

"No!" screamed Tatyana firing back and seeing Wolfgang crumple as three men burst out into the entrance area. She fired three more shots and then ran as fast as she could, shots pinging around her as she desperately tried to put space between her and the building. The bullets kicked up dust as she made it to the nearest treeline, where she had the advantage of knowing where she was going, she was all alone now but at least the German was down.

Grenada

"You wanted to see me?" asked the Philosopher as she met with the Composer in the main reception room.

"Time for a few home truths Elisabeth, we need clear lines of demarcation, you are trying to blur them."

"What do you mean, the movement is here."

"Yes, but you are trying to impress your movement's standards on all of us, we agreed that the quintet would operate regionally, that was all agreed long ago, you also must accept my prominence in matters of politics."

"We are the thought leaders."

"There are many areas of necessary ambiguity; however, our movement needs clear leadership."

"What about Aitor?"

"He played his part and now times have moved on," said the Composer. "I make the plans, Philosopher."

"Aitor was a loyal servant; you need to be careful with trust, Composer."

"Don't talk to me about trust; your chosen successor is dead, a huge disappointment who put his personal desires above those of your movement. You need to choose more wisely, understand?"

"Of course," mumbled Elisabeth, uncomprehending, Wolfgang had been her favourite, her future.

"We must work towards our common goal; the movement is far bigger than both of us."

"You are assuming full control?"

"I have full control and responsibility, my pedigree is unquestionable and you of all people know that. I'm pleased we can see eye to eye on this, and our friend in Asia will also be pleased. Now, here is what we are going to do."

Chapter 15

Saba

"Evening, I trust you are well rested?" announced Kobus, smiling down at Jem. "Wouldn't want you falling asleep on us at the wrong time."

"You are sick," said Jem, "this is an assault on a police officer, I cannot believe you're seriously proceeding with this, it's morally repugnant, and do you really think I will produce better human beings?"

"It's scientifically proven."

"No it isn't, and if I get pregnant from this I will sue you and the rest of our sick people for every cent you have."

"You don't get it, do you?" said Kobus. "You're never going back to your old world; this is it for keeps, so you better get used to it, lady. Don't think there will only be one child either, you will be told how many, and you will have to help with its education but it won't be yours. Once your breeding days are over you will supervise other girls until the day you drop dead. Get it? You are ours now."

"You'll be stopped."

"You forget that this will all be done beyond national borders, the routine today is an exception as the rigs aren't quite ready but you will have the child away from national status, you will be ours subject to our laws."

"I will refuse to be raped."

"Really, well I would have thought being a police officer you'd have seen enough to know that doesn't make a blind bit of difference, there's either a pleasurable way or a medical way to precede, your choice," said Kobus, "I'll leave you with my niece."

"I cannot believe this is happening," said Lorna, also wearing a tight, red dress, in her separate room.

"As my uncle says, it's your choice," said Annaliese, entering.

"We have no choice, we do what you tell us or else," replied Lorna.

"You will go with the suitor of our choice. Now, let me see to your friend."

"You are a disgrace to the female race," said Jem.

"Think of yourselves as fortunate to be chosen for this great new world," smiled Annaliese, "just do as you're told or face the consequences, you will soon see the bigger picture."

"Go to hell," snapped Jem, trying to adjust the tight fitting dress as Annaliese closed the door, not totally comfortable with proceedings but convincing herself that the end would justify the means.

"It's time, ladies, your gentlemen guests are in the main rooms and will be brought through," intoned the larger of the two matronly figures looking at the adjoining rooms.

In the Eagle's Nest, Kobus smiled as Rose was ushered in. "I always save the best for myself," he leered.

"You'll wish you hadn't," said Rose, looking desperately around for possible escape routes as Dirk handcuffed her and took her to be prepared by a woman.

"I figured you might take a little persuasion, I'll be there in a moment," purred Kobus, checking the monitors at the University building. "I don't want any dissatisfied customers so need to wait and make sure all is proceeding as planned before I join them. Business before pleasure."

"I can watch for you," replied Dirk coldly.

"You're more interested in men, Dirk, so it is business only, take care here then."

"What about her?"

"I can manage here on my own."

"She's a little vixen."

"So much the better."

"What would your darling niece say if she saw her uncle raping a non-Aryan Chinese girl?" asked Rose with one hand cuffed to the bedstead and in a flimsy nightdress as he entered.

"The master race doesn't include me."

"There must be high penalties for non-compliance."

"Just do as you are told," snapped Kobus, closing the blinds and smiling at Rose.

"The handcuffs…are you afraid of me?" she spat.

"Just a precaution."

"Some coward if he resorts to such things," sneered Rose.

"Well I had heard you Chinese were very forward," smiled Kobus, "I thought you would put up a bit of a fight."

"Well you were wrong," snapped Rose.

"Very well, the cuffs come off," replied Kobus, undoing the manacles and then grinning as he reached out to release her nightie exposing her. His grin suddenly turned to a grimace as he felt a sharp pain in his abdomen, which spread quickly, and he bellowed out in agonising pain. "What the hell?" he cursed as something warm and sticky flowed over his hands, his own blood.

"Letter openers are useful weapons," said Rose, rolling to one side as he fell forward at her looking in distaste at the blood spurting out of the gaping gut wound she had caused.

"You've cut me," snarled Kobus, staggering up and pulling the knife out of his stomach. He staggered towards Rose as she desperately pulled on her shorts, massaging her knife arm and realising that he would survive the gut wound, that it wasn't over. She nimbly ran to one side, grabbing her tee shirt and fleeing out onto the balcony.

"Bitch," Kobus bellowed like an angry bull, and she hit him hard with the lead door stop. He staggered badly, blood now pouring from his head, then managed to right himself.

She realised in horror that he was still functioning and looked in despair at her situation, stuck on the balcony with nowhere to go and a huge fall to the rocks below.

"Get ready for a long fall, bitch."

With superhuman strength she climbed over the balcony railing as Kobus lumbered across bellowing and saw a rocky outcrop about four feet below her. She reached out desperately and felt her foot engage, dropping down just as the man swung at her. She looked down to crashing waves and sheer rocks below, only a narrow metre-long piece of rock saving her. Kobus leaned over, and she took her chance and grabbed his outstretched arm, pulling hard. He stumbled and yelled, before losing his balance. Caught unawares, Kobus flailed helplessly in the air and then released a great bellow as he fell. Rose quickly disengaged her arm and crouched down, the flailing body narrowly missing her as it fell over the edge, bouncing off the jagged rocks on the way down.

Rose shivered at the sight as she hauled herself up cold and desperate, quickly donning all her clothes. She knew that she had to escape before the alarm was raised. Looking down she saw Kobus laid at an unnatural angle on the rocks below. No one could possibly have seen him unless looking at the house, so she had a little time. She went back to the bedroom and took a quick drink of whisky to give her courage. She looked down to the main village saw a minibus pull away from the University building, no doubt taking the clientele back to their cruiser. She found car keys and tried the jeep, sighing with relief when its engine sprang into life, and she careered frantically down the winding road. The fact that his staff had made themselves scarce had bought her a few precious minutes. She stopped at the university building, taking care to park out of main sight, and checked for any signs of movement. Armed with a knife she had found in the kitchen, she walked down the corridor to the main rooms trying to get her bearings then she heard females sobbing.

"Rose, thank God," exclaimed Jem, a man comatose on her floor, "my self-defence," she half-smiled.

"Where's Lorna?"

"Next door."

"I couldn't stop him," wailed Lorna as Rose got her dressed, "it was obscene."

"You're safe now," said Rose seeing what had happened. "We need to go quickly, I've killed Kobus."

"What?"

"I'll explain later, come on," replied Rose, "the beast is dead and sprawled down on the cliffs; we have little time to get away."

"Where do we go?"

"Off the island

"Can't we tell the police?" asked Lorna.

"They're corrupt, that's why," said Rose, seeing a police car ahead.

"So how do we get away?" asked Jem.

"The airport is our only hope, providing there is a craft there. Come on." They ran back to the jeep and Rose gunned the engine, lurching forwards and then gasping with shock as a Land Rover slammed into their side. She scrambled to the door and jumped out, brandishing the knife.

"So where would three pretty ladies be going in such a hurry?" said Annaliese. "There are more clients to see and I've had a complaint that one was assaulted. Take them back in," she said, looking across puzzled at Rose as her men raised their guns.

St Petersburg

"This better be good," snapped El Hamill to Sergei as they frogmarched the Russian across the harbour area. They had arrived overnight in a private jet from Marseille, with Sergei tightly bound in the back of the plane and surrounded by El Hamill's bodyguards. From St Petersburg airport they had been ferried to the waterside front, and they surveyed the cold morning scene as Sergei was pushed forwards. He was hallucinating from the drugs and he was scarcely aware of where he was until the unique cold of the country hit. He had given away the location of the Prophecy under the torture, and had accepted that the Prophecy was lost unless he could think of something fast.

"I told you it's here," he replied as he was pushed out of the car.

"We need to keep a low profile, the fat man will have friends in this city, let's get this over with fast," said El Hammill. "I should have brought more men with me," he said, annoyed that Lucrezia had demanded he do this errand. This was Sabine's department, he didn't like getting his hands dirty, and on top of that he hated cold weather. He looked up as a large old man towered over him, Georgiou, Sergei's uncle, and someone he wouldn't want to meet on a dark night. He signalled to his three men, and they told Sergei and Georgiou to board the powerful boat, before speeding out into the harbour. The wind chill was unbearable for El Hammill, and he shouted to Waleed to slow down. Lucrezia had also let him have the Vespucci twins, her best men, which was a consolation, but it didn't make him feel a lot better in this alien place.

"You scared?" asked Sergei, taking some pleasure in the man's discomfort.

"Shut up, the old man had better deliver."

"He knows the coordinates."

"Don't trust him."

"No choice, really."

"He had better do his stuff with no tricks, or you get a bullet," sneered El Hammill as he looked down at the map Sergei had drawn. He tried to relax as they finally reached a half-submerged and seemingly abandoned ship.

"This is where we go down," announced Sergei as Georgiou gestured. El Hammill gestured to the Vespucci twins to get ready with dry suits. "Get the old man down there and find the Prophecy."

"My uncle will take your men; if you make me go you'll have a dead man on your hands."

"You two go down with him, and Luigi, you watch the fat man here, he'll be dead soon anyway," murmured El Hammill. "The twins have orders to kill him immediately if there's anything unusual."

"Whatever makes you feel better."

"How do you know it's here, the Prophecy?"

"Because we put it here," said Sergei. "Hidden with great care to ensure the wrong people did not get their hands on it unfortunately I failed."

"What's so dammed special about it?" asked El Hammill as the twins got ready to dive.

"You mean your boss hasn't told you? I am surprised," said Sergei, "she obviously doesn't trust you."

"Tread carefully, old man."

"It's already killed a lot of people," murmured Sergei, feeling powerless without Rostov and Tatyana.

"Get on with it, the sooner I get out of this godforsaken place the better," snapped El Hammill, walking around the deck and keeping his eyes on Sergei whilst watching the spot where the men had gone down. He trained his gun on Sergei.

"Can't see a dammed thing down there, it's like mud," said El Hammill getting up and looking around, "how on earth can he tell it's there?"

"He knows what he is doing," replied Sergei.

"He'd better," said El Hammill, becoming more annoyed as time dragged on. After nearly an hour he saw one of the twins surface with a large box. "At last, I'm bloody freezing," he said as he watched the box hit the deck. "Where's the old man?"

"Lost him in the murkiness," replied Luigi Vespucci, the larger of the twins. "It doesn't matter, you have what you want."

"You sure?" replied El Hamill suspiciously. It saved a bullet if the old man was already dead." Open it, make sure this Prophecy is in there." Luigi hammered on the lid as his twin arrived, and found a set of leather looking parchments. Checking that the box was as genuine as possible, El Hammill looked across at Sergei. "What funny trick is the old man pulling?"

"You have what you want, dammit," snapped Sergei, "your thugs probably killed him, and maybe they hid the real one, you need to check the parchment to make sure it's genuine."

"Luigi knows whether it's real or fake, don't you?" replied El Hammill, looking at the parchments. They looked suitably old and weathered. A sudden movement caught him unawares and he spun around. "Shoot the bastard," he yelled as Sergei made a dash for the side. Luigi fired two shots and grunted in satisfaction as he saw them hit Sergei. "Got the bastard," he shouted.

"Good, let's go, I'm freezing," said El Hammill.

Bequia

Tatyana foraged around the clifftop, having escaped a second time, and was dismayed over the death of Jacques. She had used all her training to keep ahead of the tracker dogs, climbing trees and sleeping in a cave the previous evening, which was where they had found her. She reflected on her nightmare journey across the Atlantic on the Nazi escape route. Since joining Sergei she had expected hardship, but her current ordeal was worse than her experiences in the Russian Special Forces in Afghanistan. She had no idea why they had brought her here.

She must have dozed off, as the dogs finally found her, as they always did, and she emerged from her cave sanctuary to be greeted by three snarling men, who kicked at her as she was forced in front of them. They made their way back to the house, where she was unceremoniously flung into a cell-like room. After five hours the door slammed open and a large matron like figure threw some clothes at her and gestured to a bathroom.

Tatyana was pushed through into another room and gasped at the sight of eight girls of varying ages.

"Welcome to the hell house," said a tall brunette girl closest to her.

"What is this?"

"A harem, or, to be more precise, a breeding centre. My name's Zelda, I was abducted two weeks ago in full view of the police."

"Russian special services but working privately," said Tatyana looking around. "A harem, you say?"

"We have had videos and been instructed on how to comport ourselves to entertain male clients. It's not a brothel, though, oh no, we are exclusive," said Zelda bitterly.

"You're a journalist?" asked Tatyana, taking a liking to the feisty American.

"A great story here only I can't get out, perhaps you could help."

"I've already killed one of them, so my days are numbered."

"Heard about it and you're trouble, this place is heavily guarded, rich men's playthings, breeding machines."

"I've already escaped once and I can do it again. There's a beach with boats; if we can get there we can escape. What of the others?"

"They're zombies and scared witless, and not that many speak any English: it's you and me, sister. There are some pretty nasty individuals here threatening dire retribution on their families, you really think we can get away?"

"Yes, of course, this is a holiday island, I've seen the cruise ships coming in across the other side of the island."

"We need to get out first, they have doubled the guard and are sending reinforcements after what happened to the German. They've tried to rape me a couple of times but the head man stopped them, saving me for the paying customers."

"My hunch is that this is just a holding camp, they will be taking you all somewhere else. I think I know a way," replied Tatyana.

"I've nothing to lose except my self-respect and I want the exclusive on all this."

"Yours as they won't let me out alive, I know too much about them."

"You've had military training."

"Special training with the elite Russian security forces, that's why they sent me here to be conditioned."

"What sort of conditioning?"

"I expect to kill someone who has died anyway, but ultimately they made it clear I would be part of your programme."

"It's a controlled breeding programme, all very scientific, and in fact they reckon it can all be done without physical contact, but of course that's part of what attracts the wealthy clientele. I think they want to create some sort of master race like the Nazi vision. I think you're right, by the way: this is just a feeder camp to something else."

"Why do you think that?"

"The men here talk of a new life, an elite colony outside normal rules and national boundaries."

"How many girls are here?"

"Seven plus me and you, I haven't seen them all as we are kept in small groups."

"Guards?"

"Two female and three male, though I think another German has arrived and there are more coming."

"So we have to act fast, do you know if there are any others on the island?"

"Trust me and be ready to move fast," whispered Tatyana, a distasteful but necessary idea forming. She called for the guard and told him she wanted to speak to the top man.

"The only reason you are still alive is your selection for our special programme," snapped Helmut, staring disdainfully at her, "my boss is calling for you to pay the full penalty," he said as Tatyana was ushered into a small room.

"To be raped and forced to breed a little German bastard," snarled Tatyana, realising that pretending to seduce the man was going to be difficult.

"That man you killed was my cousin," replied Helmut. "Throw her into the punishment tank," he ordered one of the men. "And turn the video camera on, I shall enjoy watching her as I eat."

Tatyana was grabbed by strong arms and wrestled to the floor, then pulled through into a back room with a large plunge pool in the middle. One of the women held her down whilst the other forcibly stripped her. The water was freezing and Tatyana gasped in horror as she realised how bitterly cold the water tank was, glass walled with absolutely nothing to grab hold of but a small narrow ledge. It would take superhuman effort to get out before hypothermia set in. Breaking the surface and oblivious to watching eyes she pushed with all her might and grabbed a finger hold, slowly pulling, her muscles straining upwards until she managed to heave herself over the ledge. She lay there panting and exhausted as strong hands propelled her in front of Helmut.

"Impressive, you know I think you're strong enough for the whip next, only used that once before, put her into the solitary cell and keep her naked," commanded Helmut.

She sat shivering trying to hide her nakedness, until finally the door opened and some food was pushed forwards. She was struggling to survive and willed herself to slow down her metabolic rate. Eventually her breathing returned to normal and she fell into a semi-peaceful sleep for a few hours until the door slammed open.

"I must admit that was impressive," smiled Helmut, looking down at her, "rarely am I impressed but you did, in fact so much sothat I think you and I would produce an ideal specimen," he said, and undid his dressing gown. Tatyana tried rapidly to get herself ready, her plan reactivated. She felt his clammy hands on her breasts, and grimaced before springing forwards, grabbing his dressing gown cord and wrapping it round his neck, pulling as hard as she could then delivering a viscous karate chop to Helmut's neck. He fell unconscious, and she ran out of the room, locking the door, and found her clothes quickly, dressing before making her way upstairs, reasoning that the best way out was via the roof away from the dogs. She groaned as the stairs creaked from her weight, and looked around trying to get her bearings and find out where Zelda was, before seeing guards in another room full of girls.

She heard a sudden commotion down below, and thought that Helmut must be stirring, meaning that it was time to move. Crouching down, she ran along the corridor, realising that it was a viewing area into individual cells, seeing with disgust that the guards used these to spy on female prisoners. Finally, she found Zelda's cell. "We need to move quickly."

"I never thought you would do it," smiled Zelda, grabbing a shawl. "Who would have thought a Russian and American alliance?"

"Needs must," replied Tatyana, heading fast down the corridor and then down steps.

"Where are we going?"

"Across to the next bay, replied Tatyana. "Come on, we don't have much time, this place is disgusting."

"This way," gestured Zelda, "it goes down through the kitchens then out into the open." They gasped at the humidity and taking a minute to get their breath as Zelda led the way, then they heard the ominous sound of dogs.

"Those bastards have my scent," said Zelda, "I will divert them."

"No, we do this together."

"Don't be stupid, look at the speed of them. Go, go!" She turned away and ran towards them, holding up her hands as Tatyana cursed, realising Zelda was right. She turned and ran upwards, getting into her stride and gathering pace, and she looked briefly downwards to see Zelda being circled by the dogs. She headed upwards back into her world, and she ran on, finally cresting a familiar hill. In the moonlight, she saw a long deserted beach area with scrubland to the rear, and she was safe for the time being.

Venice

"You did very well, El Hammill," said Lucrezia, listening on her secure satellite phone. She was pleased to at last have the Prophecy, and was now after the next one. She signalled for her car and motioned the girl to be brought in. "Segovia, what are we going to do with you? Did you really think I wouldn't have cameras on my offices, going through my files was a dangerous thing to do?"

"I did you a favour."

"Indeed you did, and perhaps you will see the need to rethink your alliance."

"What have you done with the American?"

"Not your business, now this is your chance to come with me and my expert to Rome to check out what you found." She was bundled into the Alfa Romeo, her arms tied. "So, time to tell me more on the drive. You've done well uncovering the Popes Covenant, now you can help me find the real thing."

"They are historical documents," said the Russian, struggling with the ropes.

"I don't have much time so let's get moving," smiled Lucrezia, signalling to her assistant to join them.

Germania Paraguay

"This is unacceptable," snapped the Philosopher as Helmut walked in, still angry at what had happened with Tatyana in Bequia. "Not only is Wolfgang dead but you've again lost the Russian girl who killed him. "Why is that?"

"She won't get off the island," said Helmut, embarrassed.

"Get Aitor in here, I want to talk to him alone before the Composer arrives," said the Philosopher, "and make sure everything else is organised. We need more men from Paraguay, and bring your brother, Karl."

"Karl is too young."

"He is old enough and certainly ruthless enough," replied the Philosopher. The phone rang and she answered it. "Annaliese, to what do I owe this unexpected pleasure?"

"My uncle's dead," said Annaliese.

"How?"

"Killed by the Chinese bitch, thrown down the cliffs."

"You know what this means, you will personally take charge."

"We did complete the first breeding event."

"Do you have the killer?"

"Yes."

"Make an example of her and you are in charge of the northern operations."

"Thank you," replied Annalise, replacing the phone and looking across malevolently at Rose, an idea forming.

"I am sorry, my dear, it must be a shock," said Helmut, calling on her private mobile.

"Thank you."

"I need to see you urgently Annaliese, on a matter of utmost importance."

"It will have to wait, Helmut: you heard the Philosopher."

"Be careful, Annalise. There is a schism in the Quintet, and I don't want you choosing the wrong side. I need to protect you at the coming conference, internal politics are intensifying. Join me at Grenada today, we must meet."

"What specifically worries you?"

"Aitor is opening up the whole can of worms, and heads will roll as a result. The Composer is all powerful, and you have to remember that."

"Aitor is one of the Chosen Ones."

"He is purely window dressing."

"Very well, I will be there," replied Annaliese.

Helmut smiled coldly to himself. He needed allies if he was to survive the grand meeting of the quintet; with Wolfgang out of the way, the power battle was about to start. His mobile rang again and to his surprise it was a special number.

"Helmut, you and I need to talk."

"Aitor, I told you there are things I need to do, important things."

"You will talk to me if you want to survive," threatened the Spaniard.

"Don't threaten me Aitor; you know you are on dangerous ground, no protection as you're not a chosen one."

"I can help the Philosopher," said the Spaniard, "but you need to get me access."

"Why would I do that, even if I could?" said Helmut warily.

"Because I know how to stop her."

Chapter 16

Germania

Sabine looked around the large gothic entrance hall as she was ushered into the old house. It had been a long and exhausting journey from Europe, particularly the last part up into the jungle. A small propeller plane that skimmed the tops of the rainforest had brought her into Paraguay, and then she had embarked upon the short river journey into the middle of nowhere, to the land that time forgot. She entered the large reception room and made herself comfortable while she waited to meet a man called Helmut, who would acquaint her with the details. The door opened and a tall blonde man entered.

"Sabine, is it?" said Helmut. "Pleased to meet you."

"What's this about?"

"Just making sure the Quintet meeting goes smoothly, my boss wants to ask you some questions, I assume you appreciate the significance of this house."

"Why should I?" replied Sabine irritably.

"Germania, a new world set up by Elisabeth Nietzsche."

"Wasn't there a philosopher called Nietzsche?"

"Elisabeth's brother, hence the current boss takes the title Philosopher as she is a direct descendant of the same family and at the heart and soul of the movement."

"What movement?"

"Germania didn't really work in the early twentieth century as the land is not fertile but all that has changed now. We have many groups coming down from Germany; you know Hitler was an admirer of Elisabeth?"

"Sounds like they are all nutters."

"I've read up on you, you're a bit of a loner aren't you, you would do well to contain your views in front of the Philosopher."

"So the Nazis came down here after the war and played with submarines and the like, I get that stuff."

"Many made the pilgrimage to our heartland and the base of the new movement, Project Valkyrie."

"A Nazi revival."

"Germans, not Nazis, we don't like that term."

"You will be called it when the press get this."

"This is the headquarters of the Germania party in Latin America and has been for some sixty years, although of course it's a well-kept secret."

"What's that got to do with me?"

"All will become apparent," replied the man as he gestured to the drinks.

"No thanks."

"After the War many prominent Germans fled the fatherland to a new life here."

"After they had ruined Europe."

"Depends which side of the fence you sit on."

"So a hotbed of old Nazis intent on relieving the glory days, I hardly think this is relevant."

"Oh it is very relevant, we are in the new age and the old ideas are rising again, protectionism and populism. Democracy particularly here in Latin America has never worked, it needs strong leaders, and that's where we come in."

"I thought you were secretive."

"We stay under the radar but we have tentacles in most Latin America republics."

"And this is the power base for our Tutulus."

"Yes, and Valkyrie."

"Ah Valkyrie, tell me more."

"The continuation of the pure blood lines, to ensure the elite prospered. That's what Nietzsche wrote about, and his sister's daughter is here to make it work through Valkyrie."

"The caves in Gibraltar were part of this."

"One camp only, there are many more, particularly here in the Americas where suitable women are been recruited."

"Breeding machines."

"We prefer to call them partners for the future, they are well looked after."

"Providing they do as you say."

"They are carefully selected, and the process must not be misused."

"Look I am not here to pass judgement, it seems a good idea in essence, so what is it that was so urgent?

"There are tensions in the movement and your own leader the Architect needs to understand who to support."

"Who would that be?"

"Depends."

"Go on," said Sabine, growing increasingly impatient, "these people are now here."

"Under the Philosopher, the reincarnation."

"This stuff went out with the conspiracy nutters."

"I can assure you what I have to tell you is a matter of life or death. A new generation has emerged in our spiritual home, the place where the new Fourth Reich will start, founded by the pioneers but with securities on the blood lines."

"Offspring of the old Nazi leaders."

"Differences of opinion have emerged on the right way forwards, the escape route wasn't just for Germans but also sympathisers, and of course that included the friendly Franco regime in Spain."

"Go on."

"One person who came over was Franco's own newly born son, he wanted to encourage his own bloodline to become part of this new Reich. His son grew up here amongst the German faithful speaking German and rose through the hierarchy."

"How is this relevant?"

"The son has fallen out with his allotted partner, who is one of our aspiring new leaders."

"This Composer you talk of, why have they fallen out?"

"Because of his partners infidelity," came a voice from the door and Aitor walked in. "Been filling the pretty ladies head with lies, have you Helmut? Let me introduce myself, I am Franco's son, Aitor, and I am looking for sanity in a crazy world. This bastard is the cause of that craziness, playing politics with a great organisation built by the Composer, who is still all powerful despite the Germans believing there's an opportunity."

"This was a private conversation on my instigation," snapped Helmut.

"Get out Helmut; you are not the Venetian woman."

"I work for Lucrezia, if that's what you mean," replied Sabine as the tall dark haired man looked disdainfully across at her.

"Sorry about the dramatics but that bastard was about to mislead you and cause trouble, we have these bloody Nazis everywhere, purists who need taking down a level, the extremists who always go a step too far. I have indeed been a part of all this, an accident of birth but have recently seen the light. I was attached to a great and powerful woman who puts the movement first, unlike these bastards who will try and infiltrate the good work Lucrezia is doing in Europe, mark my words."

"Why should I believe you? You're Franco's son," exclaimed Sabine.

"You're not what I expected, a refreshing change."

"Flattery will get you everywhere," smiled Sabine as she assessed the man, still dark haired and handsome, with signs of greying. "I guess you and I have a common enemy so we can be friends."

"Why not, we will fight as the underdogs, I want you to arrange a meeting with Lucrezia in Grenada, she has asked for my help which is why I am here, Helmut intercepted you."

"Tell me more, then," smiled Sabine, thinking that this had all the hallmarks of an opportunity. "Essentially I need to know what's in it for us, as this will be dangerous." After Spain this was her second big break: a schism in the movement meant opportunity.

"You know, I think we could perhaps take our little alliance further," smiled Aitor putting his arm on her shoulder, "let's go for a drink, I know a little bar."

"Sounds good to me," smiled Sabine. She always got what she needed, and this man would be no exception to the rule. He would confess all in bed. Power struggles always created vacuums, and she would know more of what was happening than her boss so could watch which way the cards were falling. She smiled as Aitor passed her a gin and tonic.

Vatican City

It was a dark and miserable Rome evening, and Lucrezia and Segovia made their way to the home of Bishop Gorton, an Irish cleric who Lucrezia had known for years. The atmosphere in the car had been frosty as Segovia tried to come to terms with her new position. As for Lucrezia, she reckoned the Russian could be useful with her enquiring mind. Lucrezia had also brought with her a document expert called Fabio from her team. The Bishop met them at the gate and got them past the Swiss Guards and into the inner sanctum of the Vatican, leading them through the magnificent St Peter's Cathedral and into the innermost sanctums of Casino Pio and the Pontifical Academy of Sciences. She felt privileged to be walking into the hallowed buildings of the inner Vatican, which had been such a large part of her life; it was hard to avoid its tentacles in Venice.

The Bishop walked ahead of them nervously. "This room in the Academy was boycotted by Popes for years as the decorations on the ceiling were deemed too risqué," he commented as if leading a tour group as he pointed to the erotic carvings. "We are now in Casino Pio within the Pope's private domain."

"Fascinating," replied Lucrezia, knowing that Gorton had once been a supporter of the Irish Republican Army in Belfast and a number of other far right political groups. She felt that this knowledge gave her a useful hold over him.

"The Casino Pio is mentioned on the document I found," said Segovia, excited despite her predicament. Lucrezia was being inordinately friendly, which made her uneasy. Freeing Sergei was a hostile act and yet the woman seemed to gloss over it, and she turned her attention back to the documents.

"We need to examine this room, the document trail shows that this room is the likely place," said Lucrezia.

"Unlikely, as the central archives are for that purpose, besides we can't just start ripping this room apart," snapped Gorton, frowning. "I will need more than that."

"Tell him, Segovia," said Lucrezia, "and be quick: I don't have a great deal of time."

"The dairies of Marco Polo refer to a covenant placed in Casino Pio," she replied, "so this has to be the room according to both Fabio and I."

"I will need more than that."

"It's called the Pope's Covenant and dates back to Venice in the fifteenth century, a very important link to Asia."

"That's not enough and is all conjecture."

"Your past is safe with me," replied Lucrezia meaningfully.

"Is that a threat?"

"Just a fact."

"The Pope's Covenant was deposited here by merchants of Venice," continued Segovia. "Is there an area where tributes were placed under the protection of the Pope?"

"In the corner there's a small metal grill just off the floor," replied Gorton resignedly.

"Excellent," smiled Lucrezia.

"The document is an original signed by the Mongols and the Pope and also Kublai Khan." Segovia knelt down and lifted the grill, revealing a number of recesses each with chests laid within them. "There are a number of boxes down here, which one?"

"It will be distinctive," said Fabio. "I have translated document that says it has the inlaid shape of a dragon on the top."

"Over there," said Gorton resignedly, looking around in anguish. There is a gold chest made from melted down Turkish cannon, it's got a dragon on the lid," continued Gorton.

"Segovia, over to you," said Lucrezia excitedly.

"You must not do this, Lucrezia, I could be ex-communicated."

"Life is a risk, Bishop, it's that or the British."

"Let me see." Segovia worked at the box with Fabio managing to free it and finally lifting it out.

"Open it, Segovia, and make it fast," said Lucrezia.

"Please do not make any noise," whispered Gorton.

"It's moving slightly," replied Segovia, moving the lid and reaching inside. "It's empty," she exclaimed, "ah, there's a little recess in the lid, let's try and open it."

"There is a leather parchment," said Segovia excitedly pulling out leather bound wallet.

"What does it say?" asked Lucrezia.

"It will take time but it looks like a formal agreement between two great powers to create a new world order to fight the infidels."

"The Turks."

"It talks about Shamanism and Catholicism forming a special bond."

"We have it," smiled Lucrezia.

"So our church and the heathens signed a pact," said Gorton incredulously.

"Tell him, Segovia."

"The Pope was invited to meet Kublai Khan, but was not prepared to undertake such a long and hazardous journey halfway across the known world, so Marco Polo brought the deal to the church. You have to remember the Mongols were land creatures and realised others ruled the water. Poland was as far as their own tenuous supply lines could stretch, as the distances were too great, so they came to an understanding with the Catholic Church rather than pushing further west, now for the first time we have the proof that it did actually happen a century later."

"But they were heathens," said Gorton, looking in horror at the document.

"Not the first time that the Catholic Church dealt with the devil Mussolini and with Hitler, to name but two: I guess you'd call it pragmatism."

"This document cannot be allowed to be made public; it will damage the church, I would never have helped you if I had known."

"I do not suggest that you try and stop me."

"Our church may never recover."

"Nonsense, it has done worse," said Lucrezia, "Fabio is a trained bodyguard as well as an expert on antiquities if you want to debate the point."

"This document will never leave the Vatican."

"Fabio, over to you, I don't want to know the details."

Saba

Rose was feeling sick, largely because of the motion of the small Lear jet but also because she had been drugged. Her feet and arms were bound and she was wedged in the tail section of the plane so that she could hardly move. She saw Annaliese up front talking animatedly with the pilot, and overheard him explaining the new flight system on the turbo jet.

"Got the latest EFI or Electronic Flight Instrument system, this baby can fly herself," boasted the young man called Immingham, who was clearly trying to impress Annaliese, who yawned in response.

"Where are you taking me?" cried Rose.

"You're only still alive because of factors beyond my control," said the girl. "I'll make you regret killing my uncle."

"I'll be a heroine to many women," said Rose, struggling and manoeuvring her wrists as Annaliese unbuckled the co-pilots seat and made her way down to her.

"Don't push it," she snapped, "my uncle was a visionary who built an empire so nothing would give me greater satisfaction than throwing you out of this plane."

"Perhaps you fell out whilst trying to escape," she looked at the back of the pilot, just the two of us and a tragic accident.

"He was an animal and a rapist, it was self-defence," hissed Rose.

"Bad mistake," said Annalise, reaching down to grab Rose's hair and cursing as Rose twisted to pull her hands free. The two fell on each other locked in a deadly embrace as they rolled around the cabin floor, clawing viciously. Rose managed to get a thumb into Annaliese's eye, but the blonde girl was strong and managed to swing around and hit Rose hard across the jaw with her right fist. Rose staggered back as with another jab Annaliese pushed her down to the floor and dragged her across to the door. "Captain, open the door," she yelled up to the pilot.

"For God's sake, we have orders," replied Immingham in horror, engaging the autopilot, "she has to be delivered over to Europe."

"I don't give a shit about your orders, I want her out of this dammed plane," screamed Annaliese, trying to move the door herself. Rose swung a fist, catching her on the nose and knocking her down, before climbing on top of her and pummelling her fists into the blonde girl's head.

"Shit," cried Immingham, unbuckling and racing back. He pulled Rose off Annaliese as the plane bucked violently, and then found himself being attacked as Rose launched herself blindly at him. He held up his fists as Rose swung left and right, until eventually her strength gave out and he pushed her to the ground, lashing her arms together. "That's enough from you, missy." He took a needle from a bag on the wall and Rose watched numbly in terror as he injected her, before everything went blank.

Five hundred miles to the north another private jet with police markings banked and started its approach to what was known as a difficult landing on the small Saba airfield. Approaching at speed, he dropped quickly and hit the runway hard, the jet engine screaming hard in reverse thrust on the short runway as they landed. Two delays had been extremely frustrating, but Guy thanked the young pilot as he looked around the airstrip and spotted a dilapidated taxi. Thirty minutes later, he and Monty approached the governor's small residence.

"Let me do the talking, Guy, don't forget he's about to be replaced anyway so he may clam up, he'll respond better to authority."

"There's no one here of that description," said Governor Van Helst, a grey-haired, worried-looking man who looked at them suspiciously. He was already on notice from his government to leave the island, fifteen years of the easy life wasted.

"I would suggest you speak honestly, my friend here has his wife missing and suspected captured by the gang that are rumoured to be based here."

"I don't know anything about this, we are a Crown Colony."

"Look, Governor, it's not going to work, see I know you worked with this Kobus, a lucrative arrangement I would guess for both parties."

"I don't like your insinuations."

"I have proof of your backhanders," snarled Monty, "there's nothing I hate more than bent officialdom and I'm coming across a great deal of it at the moment. You let the biggest thug in the Caribbean walk all over you."

"You have no right."

"Look, Governor, you are being recalled so let's cut the bullshit, I've just had your mate Montalban on St Bart's arrested and you will not have diplomatic immunity. If I find more proof you were involved with kidnapping girls on this island then you will go to jail irrespective of diplomatic immunity."

"Breeding camps? The girls were on a modelling course, though we have had a sudden death on the island which is the man you talk about, this Dutchman on the hill."

"Kobus is dead," exclaimed Guy, looking at Monty.

"Your pirate on the hill fell to his death, I thought that was why you were here, and we're looking for a Chinese girl who was seen with him."

"Rose," exclaimed Guy. "Where is she?"

"We don't know."

"Not good, is it?" said Monty, "You're in his dammed pay, aren't you supposed to be running the island?"

"He forced me to collaborate; my family in Amsterdam."

"You're a dammed disgrace. You knew about the camps. Talk fast."

"Come on Monty, we need to find Rose, this idiot isn't worth spending time on." They ran up the road to the University and Guy knocked on the door. It was answered by an older woman then they heard the screams. "Out of my way, dammit," snapped Guy, pushing up the steps, trying to identify the source of the scream as he recognised the voice. His blood curdled when he heard it again and he ran to a top floor bedroom to find Lorna bloodied and unconscious.

"Watch out, Guy," shouted Monty as two matrons ran past him, "there are more girls down the corridor."

"My God," exclaimed Guy with mounting dread as he saw all the other girls, seeing a repeat of the nightmare in Norway. "Lorna, can you hear me? You're bleeding."

"Nose bleed, we were attacked; Rose was brilliant, she killed Kobus, the Dutch girl took her."

"Who?"

"Kobus's niece and a nasty piece of work, said they were flying somewhere, one way ticket, Guy, my father," said Lorna, collapsing in tears, "they raped Jem and me."

"Jem was here?" gasped Monty.

"Yes, but they took her away by sea."

"We have all the proof we need now," said Monty, pointing to the horrified girls lying around, some of whom were unconscious or semi-unconscious.

"It's even worse this time," said Lorna, struggling to keep her composure, "my father's plans were a first step, but they have now perfected the programme, perhaps I deserved it as I'm the product of the same," she said, stumbling as they made their way to the main room.

"Don't say that," said Guy fiercely.

"I will need to trace these girls and put the Governor under house arrest," said Monty. "I have temporary powers to complete this investigation under the Caribbean policing agreement," he continued, having no idea whether that could include arresting a Dutch Crown official. "You need to look after Lorna whilst I take care of things here, she's in shock: I've seen it before."

"I will," said Guy, looking sadly across at Lorna. At times like this she reminded him of Leila. "First, though, we need to check out Kobus' house and see if there are any more clues to Rose's whereabouts."

"That's my job, Guy. I also need to check out the scene of the crime."

"You mean whether Rose murdered him."

"I have to do my job."

Bequia

Tatyana had spent a day wandering around the small island, unsuccessfully looking out for a means to escape. She felt guilty about Zelda, who had sacrificed herself to allow Tatyana to escape, and swore to herself that she would rescue her: the only problem was how to do it. Later in the day she saw a small powerboat approaching on the horizon. It looked like it was heading around to the south of the island and moving fast in her direction. She took a chance and raised her head, her relief turning to despair as she saw that it was manned by two of the guards she had seen at the house. She made to run before she realised they had someone handcuffed in the bottom of the boat, another terrified girl. She was done with running, and this would be a fight according to her rules. She raised her hands and the taller guard came closer. Leering, he raised his gun, and she hit him on the temple with a rock in the palm of her hand, before finishing him off with a vicious karate chop to the head. His colleague tried to get out of the boat losing his balance as the girl in the boat took her chance and pushed him overboard. Tatyana turned back to the boat. "Get the engine going," she yelled, grabbing the guard's gun and training it on the two spluttering men.

"Brilliant," smiled Tatyana as they got underway. "The name's Tatyana," she said, holding out her hand.

"You were amazing," said Jem, smiling for the first time in days. "We may have a common ally: Guy Tresanton?"

"Fantastic, then let the fightback begin," smiled Tatyana slumping down as they headed out to sea, "I need to contact him on these radios."

Chapter 17

Saba

The drink, the stress and the despair were a heady brew, and as the night drew in Guy let the alcohol take its toll. Memories were reignited, desires were recalled, and Lorna encouraged him as she lay in his arms. For Guy it felt like Lorna's sister Leila was laying there, and he found himself becoming aroused. They awoke the next morning in each other's arms in the Eagle's Nest looking out across the Caribbean Sea, across a tide of memories and a sea of regret. He was happily married, and yet she was so beguiling…He looked down in horror at the sleeping form of Lorna beside him and tried to justify to himself what he had done.

"Morning, Guy," mumbled Lorna, sitting up.

"I am so sorry; I didn't mean this to happen."

"We needed each other, that's all that matters. It stays here."

"I feel guilty as hell."

"I needed someone, you did that so thank you, it changes nothing."

"You sure?"

"Come on, let's get out of here before someone comes looking."

They had spent the night up at Kobus' house, utilising his drinks cabinet and master bedroom, and now Dirk was outside fixing their breakfast as obsequiously as he could get away with. He looked at them with enquiring eyes, but knew he was compromised himself and said nothing. Guy made his way down to the main office.

"Sleep well, my friend?" asked Monty quizzically.

"Guess so," replied Guy, feeling out of his depth. Not only had he messed up professionally since taking over as Chair of the Elders, but now he had messed up his marriage. His phone rang and he looked puzzled.

"Tresanton, your wife is our prisoner, you were warned."

"Who is this?"

"Tell the Elders to back off looking into Tutulus or she will suffer, we have killed two of the Elders and she will be a third, stop or suffer the consequences."

"Where is my wife dammit?"

"Somewhere where you will never find her, and your fat Russian is dead, go back to your quaint little island."

"They're getting worried," said Monty, "let me see if we can get a trace." He disappeared and came back puzzled. "It's a call from Grenada."

"Shit, Monty, they've got Rose and maybe Jem too, we have to do as they say."

"Trust me, we have them rattled, sounds like poor Charlotte is dead and Sergei too, it's grim."

"They have her, they have my wife, and I have betrayed her," he said to himself.

"We have to play this our way Guy, trust me I don't want to lose Jem but Rose will be safe, she's a major asset for them."

"I hope to God you are right Monty, I really do," replied Guy fiercely as his phone rang again.

"Guy, it's Tatyana."

"Tatyana, where are you?"

"In the Caribbean, on a boat near a small island, I have Jem with me."

"Jem," repeated Guy, looking across at Monty.

"Yes, we have just reached an island called Tobago Cays in the Grenadines, we escaped from place called Bequia that houses one of their camps, we need to meet."

"You need to get across to St Lucia," said Guy, thinking of the Hidalgo, a safe haven. "Padraig is with Hidalgo there, I'll call him; it will keep you out of harm's way until I can get to you."

"We've stepped into a hornet's nest," said Tatyana, explaining about Grenada and the deaths of Jacques and Wolfgang.

"German, that was it," exclaimed Guy, "the voice was German that called, we've just killed one of them, they're panicking," he said, looking across at Monty, who was nodding.

"Down in Grenada, that's where the answers are, Guy."

"Any sign of Rose?"

"No, but she was an absolute star in Saba, they took her away."

"Go to St Lucia, and to the main harbour," repeated Guy, thinking quickly, "I will meet you there."

"Wheels within wheels," murmured Monty. "It's strange that they are panicking when everything appears to be going their way, I wonder if there's a schism in their movement?"

"Rose would have wanted you to go after the girls," said Monty.

"That's not helping my wife."

"Tatyana and Jem need help and I have to sort out this mess. Can we trust Tatyana if Sergei is indeed dead, is she really with us?"

"I trust Tatyana, she's been through too much," replied Guy, looking across as Lorna entered, passing through to the office oblivious of his conflicting emotions. "What do I do about Lorna?"

"Look after her, she's very fragile, take her with you."

"That will make the situation worse."

"She has suffered enough, Guy; give her the chance to fight back."

"It's difficult."

"She hates what these people are doing, I would help you but I have to stay here, we have a major potential diplomatic incident on our hands, I'm officially seconded and also have to clear what Rose did.

Also I can look for Rose; it's likely that some of the guards will know where she was headed."

"Very well," said Guy as Lorna came back through. "We're going on a little journey to sort this mess out if you want to come."

"I need to help more girls in these dreadful camps, that's my mission, so yes I would like to come, I suspect there are many more camps, where are we going?"

"A short flight to St Lucia and then the Hidalgo for a rendezvous with Jem and Tatyana."

St Lucia

They arrived early morning on the short flight from the Grenadines and both took the opportunity to rest and recover in a local hotel, which Jem recalled was not far from where Zelda had been kidnapped. She had shared her experiences of the journalist with Tatyana and they had both agreed that saving the American had to be a priority as soon as they could return to the island. Jem was also suffering from the attack at Saba camp, and was coming to terms with her own vulnerabilities, but the anger and sense of injustice soon returned. They made their way to the main port and down to the Rodney Bay's new marina complex. It didn't take long for them to spot the Hidalgo and they were greeted heartily by Padraig.

"A sight for sore eyes, aye that you both are," he said warmly, "had to sail this bugger across the Atlantic on me own after the attack; still, you are here now, and the boss himself is on his way. Get aboard and we will anchor out at sea, it's safer that way." Tatyana reflected on the situation as Padraig motored out to sea away from prying eyes near the agreed rendezvous point, Pidgeon Island.

Three hours later, Jem gave a whoop of joy as she spotted the familiar figure on the water edge of Pidgeon Island, waving as they arrived in the inflatable to pick Guy and Lorna up.

"My God, it's good to see you both again," smiled Guy gesturing to Lorna and the Hidalgo.

"What about me?" winked Padraig.

"Well done getting her over here. God I've missed this place, it was my home for many years."

"Where to, Captain?" smiled the Irishman as Jem and Lorna joined Tatyana on board.

"South, I'll give you more details in a while but we need to get south whilst we plan, if you see anyone out there snooping around let me know."

"Good to see you both again Tatyana, Jem," smiled Guy as they all relaxed whilst he brought them all up to speed with latest developments, and Tatyana shared her own traumas, including the loss of Sergei.

"Do you really think he's dead?" asked Jem.

"They were trying to scare me, there's nothing certain about it, maybe the man was just trying to rile me, and Sergei is a survivor."

"So what's next?" asked Lorna, bringing them all drinks.

"We have two choices, both down south. Either we liberate the camp in Bequia or go straight for their HQ in Grenada, where we have evidence that Tutulus is based, my personal preference is to take the easier one first as we know the size of the challenge and it's closer."

"Makes sense, I also want to rescue Zelda, we need time to confront these people," agreed Tatyana.

"I will let Monty know. In the meantime, we could all use the opportunity for a rest."

For Guy it was great to feel the wind in the sails again and the sheer exhilaration of the Hidalgo as they headed south towards the Grenadines. He managed to relax a little as they picked up speed whilst Tatyana and Lorna slowly got to know each other. After a couple of days an easy routine developed, supported by Padraig's humour. For the old man having three females on deck in increasingly skimpy costumes was nirvana, whilst Guy used the time to reflect on the seriousness of what was happening. They were dealing with an organised group and the Nazi thing worried him as fanatics were unpredictable. They made good time with the prevailing winds in their favour, and it was dusk when they approached the island of Bequia.. As the light went Tatyana pointed. "That's the place over there."

Annaliese looked around the room angrily, having torn strips off the staff over Tatyana and Jem's escape. After the fight on the plane, she was angry and tired, having been deposited by the pilot, who had flown straight off towards a refuelling point before tackling the Atlantic. She was in a foul mood as she looked over the camp. The terrified girls, including Zelda, the American journalist, were uselessly whimpering in the corner. She turned to the chief warden, a formidable woman. "Any progress on the quota?" she asked.

"All to schedule, first seven deliveries due next week, including the American. Good riddance to her, she makes a lot of noise."

"So you will meet the criteria?"

"Yes, and the mothers are in good condition."

"I want to rest before the next stage." She was slowly getting over the shock of seeing her uncle dead; he had been a huge guiding influence but her newfound control of the north Caribbean theatre was some consolation. "I need to fly to Grenada in the morning see to the sea plane, please."

"The forest behind gave me cover to get out twice," cautioned Tatyana as they approached within a hundred metres. Guy nodded surveying the areas; the place from the sea was quiet with a single front street and little else. The building Tatyana pointed to was away to the left behind a sheer cliff, and was accessible by what looked like a narrow rope walk. The Hidalgo was out of sight, so Guy decided to moor at the small jetty to facilitate a quick getaway. Padraig, Lorna and Jem would stay aboard, whilst Tatyana and Guy went ashore armed with a single revolver and knives.

"This way, the house stands on Princess Margaret Bay."

"We go in two hours when the moon is full," said Guy, checking his tidal tables. "I don't like the rope way, it's too exposed, we will take the inflatable round, they won't see us under the cliff overhang and Hidalgo is out of sight."

They set off rowing slowly, keeping the engine for the return trip, a plan forming in Guy's mind. They landed quietly and pulled the inflatable into the bushes.

"The place up there on the headland is owned by an eccentric Scotsman."

"I've had my fill of eccentric Scotsman," replied Guy, looking carefully around using a small flashlight. "It looks like it's quite a climb."

"This way," hissed Tatyana. They made their way up the familiar tracks and finally reached the edges of a ridge next to the building. It was slightly down to their left, still aglow with light at the front, the back shrouded in darkness. Guy held his gun, and saw a single guard silhouetted in the front porch. The guard was smoking a cigarette and facing away from Guy, staring out to sea, likely bored to death.

"I'll go in front, you behind," signalled Tatyana as she ran forward with surprising agility. Like a panther she stole onto the short veranda and with a sudden movement felled the guard without a sound. "Come on," she hissed as she moved to the front door. It was locked, and she gestured to Guy to go around the back whilst she searched the fallen guard. Slowly she opened the door and moved in quietly, before seeing someone off to the left in the kitchen. A man walked in, cigarette in hand.

"You, you're back," he gasped, fumbling for his gun, but it was too late. Tatyana crashed her hand down on his neck and he fell to the floor with a thump. From the back she heard Guy moving forwards and they met up in the main hall.

"Follow me," she hissed as they made their way forwards, both armed with the guards' guns, small Mauser revolvers. There were rooms to both sides and a landing above them up the staira.

"The top rooms first, that's where the bosses are."

"Agreed," replied Tatyana, bounding up the stairs.

"I'll take the other side," said Guy, making his way to the main lounge area, where he saw a light in a large bedroom above the lounge area. He opened the door, taking a deep breath as a surprised Annalise leapt out of her bed half-naked and dived for her gun. Guy reacted fast and fired at the wall above her. "Freeze!" he yelled.

"What's the meaning of this?" cried Annaliese, pulling the bedclothes around her. "Who the hell are you?"

"Guy Tresanton," said Guy, coldly keeping the gun trained on her as he heard Tatyana approach behind him.

"Three men down, can't see anymore and the female wardens are locked in the next room."

"How many guards and girls?" asked Guy.

"I am not the leader, this is outrageous."

"Answer the question, Annalise;" replied Guy, "I know all about you and how my wife put paid to your uncle."

"Six guards and seven girls," said Annaliese, staring at the Russian girl.

"Call them here," shouted Guy as he quickly disarmed them and tied them to chairs, "a full set, Tatyana."

"The girls, now," said the Russian, and they were taken upstairs and into a room where they saw seven cowering girls, including the American journalist.

"Tatyana, you came back," smiled Zelda.

"Of course I did, told you I would," she smiled, hugging the American journalist as Guy helped the girls down the stairs, keeping his gun trained on a sullen Annalise.

"You have no idea what forces you are dealing with here," she said as they pushed into the main lounge.

"We are going to walk out of here once you have some clothes on."

"You won't get away with this."

"That's my problem," replied Guy coldly as the girls were brought in, some as young as eighteen, three pregnant. He looked across at Tatyana and came to a decision. "Get Lorna and Jem here to look after the girls, we have a journey to take with this one," he said, and nodded at Annaliese.

"Well done Guy, and my God it's Zelda," exclaimed Jem, smiling at the American. "I never thought I would see you again."

"Lots to tell," smiled Zelda

"I'll get the police over to clean this mess up," replied Jem.

"There are six guards in the storeroom and matrons," said Guy. "Can we leave you here to manage?"

"Best to, Lorna will stay also to help me, she needs careful handling," replied Jem.

Lorna smiled at Guy as they returned to the Hidalgo and he left her staring at him. They sailed immediately from the jetty as Padraig ran the engines at full revs to put some distance between them, and they headed towards Grenada. Guy and Tatyana relaxed in the main cabin and stared across at the sullen Annaliese.

"Need to know where we go on Grenada," said Tatyana as they looked at the Dutch girl exuding defiance.

"I'm in no mood to listen to lies, my wife's life is at stake here."

"There's only one way to find anything out from her, I need to torture her, that's the only way fanatics like that will talk."

"Not my style, Tatyana."

"It is mine," grinned the Russian girl, extracting her knife. "Leave me alone for half an hour, she will talk."

"I'll set the sails," replied Guy, leaving the Russian with her bound captor and shuddering at what would happen as he busied himself.

Half an hour later, Tatyana came up on deck, smiling. "She sang like a canary. It's the face, always is, too concerned about her looks, she told me that the headquarters is just above Fort George on Grenada, a White House."

"Did you hurt her?"

"Just a few bruises in private places," smiled Tatyana. "Don't worry, she will recover. I also found out Rose is in Europe, she's in no immediate danger though there's real hate between Annaliese and Rose, they had a bust up on the Lear Jet bringing her here and Rose won apparently."

"My God, so close, did she say where in Europe?"

"She claimed not to know but I've a feeling it's in a camp in the south of Spain."

"Okay, the head of the snake it is," said Guy looking out at the lightening sky, his own mind in turmoil. "Good work up there Tatyana, very professional."

Venice

Lucrezia looked around at the Doge Council as she finished her update. "The second rig will launch next week, the first rig is now fully operational."

"We have heard disturbing reports of problems in the first rig," said Hatari.

"There are no problems," said Lucrezia.

"Ten percent unoccupied spaces."

"Project Valkyrie, the citizens of the future, I will be interviewing them myself."

"I thought we were in charge of selection tests?"

"Not Project Valkyrie," repeated Lucrezia, becoming agitated. It had all seemed so easy before. She pulled herself together and spoke. "Ladies and gentlemen, Project Valkyrie is selective breeding run by computer programmes that ensures the best matches on millions of data points to produce the elite community that will lead our future world."

"You said we could select our own matches," said Benedict.

"First we must get the most genetically suitable breed."

"That wasn't my understanding; I thought if we paid we would get the chance to have our own offspring."

"Yes, but first the professionally selected ones are taken."

"Even if they don't want to be?"

"Yes: there can be no deviation, we have to have the best at whatever cost." It was the aspect of the project that she struggled with, but she knew she had to toe the line. "Providing we are happy with the standards we can entertain your own personal requests for breeding matches, as you can see this is a real game changer."

"Does this mean the linkages will be hidden?"

"Yes, there will be no awareness of who belongs to who as they all belong to all of us, that way we are one community."

"That's not what I thought we had signed up to."

"As you can see this is a real game changer that takes away the element of uncertainty, and we all like that in investments. Now, as for those returns I promised you, I think we will see a handsome increase on them."

"This resonates with some of those horrendous war films about the Nazis," said Contessa Gerhardt, "I'm not comfortable with this."

"Too late now, my dear, you are a fully signed up member and implicated whether you like it or not, now I will leave you with the explanatory video."

"Giuseppe, what is it?"

"We need to leave Lucrezia, I have a lead."

"The insurance policy?"

"Yes, it's come through, but we have a tight time window."

"We need to be on the next flight to the Americas."

"We need a day's delay, but I promise you it will be worthwhile."

Ypres (Leper)

They landed by private jet at Brussels airport and were chauffeured by S-Class Mercedes down to Ypres, a town that had been all but obliterated in the First World War. What now resulted after rebuilding was a new town with a new name to obliterate the horrors of the war, though an impressive Menem gate stood at the top of the main street as testimony to the British troops who had lost their lives.

Lucrezia looked around quizzically. She was here because Giuseppe said he had found what was needed and she trusted his judgement. The Quintet was at war and she needed ammunition. They were starting to become troublesome and interfering with her own plans. The Philosopher worried her, and the Composer was lethal; she had known this for some time, and had to prepare herself for the coming showdown. The reality was that she had come up with all the good ideas but not the cash, and questions would be asked, which was why she was so annoyed over the Spanish treasure debacle. Politics had reared its head and nothing could come between her and Mare Nostrum. Despite losing the treasure, she now had the Pope's Covenant and the Khans' Prophecy, both documents in a secret hideaway in Venice where they would carefully dissect them. Now her most pressing problem was the Philosopher, who was building an empire in the west, whilst the Composer was focusing on the east, which to her mind was a great balance of power, but the trouble was they all wanted everything. It was time to establish her own authority as the voice of Europe and she needed leverage. First the Philosopher and then Giuseppe had turned up an Achilles heel, a conspiracy that went back over a century. With her reservations over Valkyrie she had to fight the German extremists as she called them, and this was the way; there were people in the Quintet who were outright racists and she needed to build her case.

"Follow me," said Giuseppe as he walked into the Flanders Field museum.

"What have you found?"

"I got a call from someone in the Quintet hierarchy, I don't know who but not the Philosophers people, pointing me this way. My suspicions were aroused when I read the reports on the Philosopher's claims to be descended from Nietzsche himself, the man went mad towards the end of the nineteenth century but unknown to all he did father a son. The person on the quintet knows that happened but questioned the pedigree of the son."

"You're talking of the Composer."

"Guess so," admitted Giuseppe, "although no name was given. When I checked the story out there was indeed a son that not even Elisabeth Forster his sister knew about. Seems the son went off to war and ended up here fighting for the Germans, alongside Hitler of all people."

"Where are you going with this, Giuseppe, I don't have much time."

"Very well, to the point: Nietzsche's son died here and it was kept secret."

"Why?"

"Because he didn't die with honour, he was shot just outside this museum, then the town hall, for cowardice, then to preserve the family name it was arranged by the German high command to substitute him with another man, a soldier called Wittgenstein. All this was further hushed up when the Nazis took over, but the simple fact is the current philosopher is not from the Nietzsche bloodline, but rather that of Wittgenstein."

"Does anyone else know this?"

"No, and we are about to get the proof we need, as I said a Nietzsche certainly served in the Great War here in Ypres. We need to climb to the top of the bell tower."

From the top of the bell tower the views across the vale were stunning and Lucrezia couldn't help but be inspired. "To the north east there is the valley of Passchendaele where the last great Allied offensive took place, hundreds of thousands killed in a single offensive, the greatest single loss of life in the entire war."

"The facts, Giuseppe, please," said Lucrezia, panting as they went out onto a narrow rim around the top of the tower.

"There's a little enclave in the wall here," gasped Giuseppe as he lifted a large stone to reveal a leather satchel. "Nietzsche's so-called son returned to Germany claiming to be a war hero as did his sister, in reality he was a homosexual executed by firing squad."

"So the whole Philosopher thing is predicated on a lie, if she knows."

"She knows, when Elisabeth Forster went on to found the new colony of Germania she claimed Nietzsche's unknown son was a war hero, it underpins her whole story and how she is attracting zealous recruits from Germany even now."

"The basis of her power is fraudulent?"

"Exactly, and interestingly Frederick Nietzsche fell out with Forster before he died over this superman idea, he never did agree, even though he wrote about it, they were never in agreement about such things. Unfortunately for him, he died, and his sister Elisabeth took his work and misaligned it to the rise of the Nazis, she fell in with Hitler."

"So Germania is a fake?"

"There is no blood line, the Philosopher is a fraud, and don't you see Lucrezia we are in a very dangerous position. Mare Nostrum could be compromised; you have to distance yourself from these people."

"Excellent, it's enough to finish her claim whoever she is, so why here?"

"As I said, the successors of the Nietzsche name were lost at Ypres, Elisabeth died childless and her brother shot for either cowardice or homosexuality."

"Timely, as Sabine tells me that the Nazis are reborn in Germania and taking over the western organisation of Tutulus, we need to ensure the right people are in charge, now you have the necessary proof."

"What proof do we have?"

"The man wouldn't give it to me but will to you." Giuseppe signalled to the corner of the turret where a nervous looking old man emerged.

"My grandfather told me the story and gave me these documents, which are a photograph of the army record book and the real Nietzsche's son's passport," said the man in broken English. "He was told to shoot Nietzsche and to keep it quiet. They switched the army records with another solider who went on to presented to be Nietzsche's son when the real one was dead. They took Nietzsche's army record and identification tags, everything, this other man, the imposter, fathered a child called Nietzsche and no one ever suspected as he lay dying in Vienna that he was a fraud. The real message is this: Elisabeth Nietzsche, or the Philosopher as she calls herself, is a Jewess, here's your proof," smiled Giuseppe lifting the envelope from the man.

"Well done Giuseppe, this changes everything. Come on, we need to move fast."

Chapter 18

St George's, Grenada

Guy anchored Hidalgo in the commercial harbour away from the main cruiser docking area and well out of sight of prying eyes. They had arrived on the morning tide after a brisk overnight run and were anchored a mile out taking the opportunity to have a rest. As they tied up at the harbour a sullen Annaliese sat on deck, squinting in the direct sunlight.

"Tell us about this meeting," said Guy.

"Keep that Russian bitch away from me, worse than your dammed wife."

"You're in no position to demand anything, so tell me or you can enjoy her company."

"Behind the castle, there's a large white house in its own grounds."

"Good, then you shall show us the way in," replied Guy, looking across at the rest of St George's and thinking it looked peaceful in the sun. "Best to wait until early evening before we make our entrance, we'll keep them guessing and more importantly make sure all the big wigs are gathered there before we strike," he said as Annaliese looked nervously around at the arriving Tatyana. Not for the first time Guy wondered what Tatyana had done to her, but whatever it was it had worked as she had told them about the network of breeding camps led by the Philosopher. "So this Philosopher is actually a woman calling herself Elisabeth Nietzsche."

"Related to the real one?" asked Tatyana.

"I assume so," replied Guy thoughtfully, and he smiled as he saw a familiar face coming across the dockside.

"Good to see you again Monty, is Saba sorted?"

"Important stuff, yes, and there's no charges against Rose, it was deemed to be self-defence. The Dutch have sent over a small army unit, and even better I have convinced my superiors to support us, we're getting funding support."

"Brilliant," smiled Guy as the Inspector lit his pipe. "There's a major gathering this evening at the White House so we shall invite ourselves at the most inappropriate time."

"Good, and I've confirmed that Tutulus is formally registered here, I want to go and investigate," replied Monty.

"Tatyana checked it out earlier, it's no more than a registered office but it's their funding source so we will investigate."

"I'll get the police to gain a search warrant; it's time we took action, and fast."

It was dark at as they gathered on deck at six that evening, planning their next moves. Guy and Monty would take the lead, with Tatyana bringing Annaliese as a precaution. They made their way down to the hired Toyota truck car when suddenly powerful arc lights traced across the water.

"Stay where you are," boomed a voice.

"What on earth…" exclaimed Guy, turning to see a truck careering down the small road. "Padraig, get the engine started," he hissed as he ran back to the restraining ropes. Like lightning Padraig slammed the engine into reverse, creating a gap away from the dock as a truck roared to a halt.

"Let me handle this," said Tatyana, holding Annaliese as a shield in front of her.

"We've lost the element of surprise," cried Guy as five men on the truck raised their rifles. "We will need to anchor around the bay and come back later."

"Let me get the local police," said Monty angrily, "this is an outrage having vigilante groups roaming around. The police are coming down to chase them," he continued, closing his radio call, "seems they aren't corrupted like at St Bart's, they've also started a search of Tutulus."

"Well done Monty, we attack them in four hours," said Guy, dropping the anchor about fifty metres out on the bay in full view of the White House.

"Sabine, what is so urgent that we had to meet here? I have to be in the meeting," said Lucrezia, tired and irritated after the journey from Belgium and wondering why Sabine had called her urgently to the Castle.

"Simple really, you told me to look after your interests here in advance with the Quintet, I've done so specifically by saving your life through making alliances, in particular with a Spaniard called Aitor," replied Sabine, unfazed, "he has an interesting story."

"Go on."

"He can tell you himself," she said, opening the door to the ante room that they were in.

"Pleased to meet you at last, Architect," smiled Aitor. "I've heard a lot about you from the Composer."

"She's here?" asked Lucrezia, looking hard at the Spaniard, "I recall she had a partner, is that you?"

"Yes, despite some, shall we say, misunderstandings, I help her, in this case against the Philosopher."

"Why?"

"Because she's a dangerous fanatic and we need to work together. You are targeted as the Philosopher seeks to expand her control beyond America, they will strike you tonight when you are at your most vulnerable."

"And you are the one brought here as a child."

"Yes, part of the greater plan called Project Valkyrie; my natural father was Generalissimo Franco. I was brought here through the escape route to help establish the fourth Reich. There's a power battle in the Quintet between the hardliners and the more liberal over the next steps."

"That's the trouble with the Quintet, stuck in ideologies not pragmatic solution, a dangerous cocktail," replied Lucrezia, thinking hard. "If what you say is true then fortunately I have a Belgian insurance policy, but your help gives us a little more protection," she continued. "Very well Aitor, you and I have a deal. Sabine, thank you for the introduction, here's what we will do."

The main entrance hall to the White House was large and foreboding as she was met by Helmut to be guided through a number of doors.

"My dear fellow Quintet member," intoned a voice from the dark interior and Lucrezia recoiled. "It's good to meet first in private without any interference, we have to be so careful over security, and my men have already had to stop an unauthorised yacht from entering the harbour."

"What I have to say is private, Philosopher, it is my privilege to meet you."

"The privilege is mine," replied the voice, "it is a long overdue meeting."

"That's the way we were set up Philosopher, to work in separate regions," said Lucrezia meaningfully, "I don't recall the need to meet before and even now."

"There is always need for dialogue and much to discuss, particularly with fellow female leaders, we do make the best leaders, more tolerant of ambiguity," came the voice of Elisabeth Nietzsche. "We have much to discuss as Project Valkyrie and your own Mare Nostrum accelerate, however I am disturbed by reports."

"What sort of reports?"

"Moral issues."

"Project Valkyrie disturbs me," replied Lucrezia carefully. "I don't agree with the moral dimension of forced breeding, it's not why the Quintet was formed."

"Don't lecture me on our mission, that is our duty and I am the thought leader," said Elisabeth, "Project Valkyrie is my creation, criticise it and you criticise me, you are not part of the inner circle, just a vehicle to deliver. There can be no dissenter as to dissent is to be expelled, it was the Fuhrer's way."

"We are not living in the 1930's now," said Lucrezia, "your thinking is outdated and wrong, I never agreed with Valkyrie and you knew that."

"The Composer won't agree."

"Then I will discuss that directly with her, modifications must be made as we are on the brink of huge success but not with your outdated thinking."

"Modifications are a sign of weakness."

"You insult me," snapped Lucrezia. "The Doge and Mare Nostrum are tangible and work, not just words."

"Perhaps others will judge that."

"Aitor tells me you are overreaching yourself."

"He will toe the line and is out of favour with the Composer so what do I care, he never was one of us," said Elisabeth.

"You know about a town called Ypres in Belgium?"

"No, why should I?"

"Interesting things, war graves, they hold a lot of secrets, facts that some would rather weren't there, facts that don't lie, and one of those tells me that you are a fake, your blood line is false."

"How dare you, I am of the Nietzsche blood line."

"Could it be that you have Jewish heritage? I wonder how your fanatical supporters would react to such news."

"You are talking to the Philosopher," snapped Helmut as the door suddenly opened.

"So you had your henchmen listening all the time," said Lucrezia, "I should have guessed. It's just as well I took precautions also." She tapped her phone and Sabine entered, followed by Aitor.

"This is outrageous," said Elisabeth, "those accusations are unfounded and inflammatory."

"Where is the Composer?" asked Lucrezia coldly.

"How should I know, she never tells anyone where she is; now either you retract those accusations or I will have to take unfortunate action."

"I have proof here that the Nietzsche blood line stopped in the Great War and that you are an imposter," said Lucrezia. "The real Nietzsche was shot for cowardice and your father, a Jew, was brought in as an imposter to take his name. That's why you didn't come to Germania for some time and why your famous brother never supported this place, the whole thing is a sham and you are putting the Quintet at great risk and shame."

"You have no proof," snapped Elisabeth, red-faced with anger.

"For God's sake, it's time to stop the pretence," said Aitor. "We don't need to keep hiding, I am not ashamed and nor should you be but don't lie, you're not a descendant of Nietzsche."

"I refuse to listen to any more of these lies, you have betrayed the Quintet and will be reported before our meeting later, I cannot vouch for your safety," said Elisabeth, storming out, Helmut in tow.

"We are in great danger, Lucrezia, we need to get away before they strike, otherwise we won't leave here alive," said Sabine.

"I am protected by the Quintet and I have to meet the Composer first."

"She is threatened and the Composer is pulling the strings, perhaps with you dead they will work together and impose Project Valkyrie more quickly."

"You are seeing shadows where there are none."

"Sabine is right, Lucrezia, they are fanatical and know only one way, no one will leave here alive, the rigs and the Doge are to be put under Helmut's control," said Aitor.

"Who told you all this?"

"I have seen a document showing this."

"And you, Sabine," snapped Lucrezia.

"Gut instinct, which is what you pay me for."

"So what do we do?" asked Lucrezia wearily.

"Here's what we will do," replied Sabine carefully.

"I haven't brought the Prophecy or the Covenant," said Lucrezia as they sat down in formal session two hours later. A place was reserved for the absent Composer, along two places left empty for the departed Teacher and Professor, a symbolic act. For Lucrezia, the simple fact that the room had ten people in it and had a formal setting gave her confidence that nothing would happen yet, but she was on edge.

"I came here in good faith to plan the next stage of our great journey. We have much to be proud of as the Mare Nostrum rigs are working on target and the Doge Council has destroyed the interfering Elders."

"The breeding programme has been compromised," said Elisabeth darkly.

"They are working fine, now in order to succeed I will require full autonomy in Europe," continued Lucrezia, "we are equal partners and the Composer in not attending has allowed us to make the decision without her casting vote."

"That will not be possible under the movement, and you should know that your plans are counter to our core goal of building sustainable elites by whatever means necessary, Project Valkyrie is core to that and has been approved by the Composer."

"That's not practical and is morally wrong," said Lucrezia, realising Sabine was right, that they would never leave this place alive.

"Compromise is not an option," said Elisabeth. "The real movement was never about breeding, our great mission is all that matters. You are subject to that and the Quintet must have the Prophecy and the Covenant."

"I will judge when to pass them over," relied Lucrezia coldly, "and not to an imposter."

"Lack of trust is a deadly failing."

"There is no more to be said until I meet with the Composer," said Lucrezia rising.

"No one is above the mission."

"Is that a threat?"

"Just a fact, the Composer will join us in an hour, we will finalise this, just the three of us."

"There is no Composer here, she's getting her men ready. We have to act fast, they are going to attack," said Sabine, "Aitor has armed men positioned around the outside grounds of the White House."

"Why would he do that?"

"He wants out also, he will join us in Europe, and he agrees with you that Project Valkyrie is wrong. Guess as a Spaniard he doesn't exactly fit their ideal of blonde Nordic super race, and nor, I guess, do I."

"What do we do next?"

"Set them a trap, it's the only way. We need to be ready to move fast to a location we've found, and then arrange a separate meeting at a secret location tomorrow with the Composer, Aitor still has her ear. Get ready for a fast escape; they are heavily armed so we need to go soon. The Germans have the roads covered but not the river at the back, Aitor has his men guarding a powerboat."

"Very well, let me get ready," replied Lucrezia, heading to her room as her phone rang.

"Survival of the strongest is our credo, Lucrezia, the Teacher taught us that. You have done well so far, I will meet you tomorrow perhaps."

"Where are you Composer?"

"We will meet tomorrow."

"She's a fake, I assume you know that."

"I've had my suspicions."

"So why aren't you here?"

"That's my business."

"We agreed to meet, to work together for the common good, why do you encourage discord?"

"It seems to me that discord has arrived without my help, you have to work this through."

"Aitor says you betrayed him."

"The movement comes first, and you know that, the survival of the fittest."

"The deal was Asia for you, Europe for me and Elisabeth for America, why the discord?"

"You need to sort that, if she is a fake then you know the answer, destroy or be destroyed."

"Leave me alone in Europe, the rigs are working, Project Valkyrie is not part of the original agreement."

"The breeding programmes are essential, you know that."

"Then modify them to my requirements and you can have them in your region but not mine," said Lucrezia. The phone went dead and she heard a noise outside as the door was flung open by Sabine.

"We must go," she said as she hustled her forwards, grabbing the phone and stamping on it, "a trace, you are being betrayed, she was keeping you talking whilst the Germans got into position, fortunately we have stopped the first attack. Come on, there is no time to lose."

Lucrezia turned and ran behind Sabine, away from the long drive and down to the river behind the house. Gunshots sounded in the distance as she was escorted to a powerboat by Sabine. Aitor joined her and grabbed the main controls as she scrambled aboard. A blonde man broke cover, running across the small open ground between the boat and the jetty. Machine gun fire erupted on both sides and Lucrezia saw two blonde men fall as she ducked below deck.

"Can't get to the dammed controls," cried Sabine as cross fire slapped into the boat, which was now swaying dangerously.

"I have to get the craft moving or we will be overpowered," snapped Aitor, "they are about to storm the craft."

"Aitor, wait," shouted Sabine as he ran out to the wheel slashing at the holding ropes and revving the engines as bullets slammed into the decking. She gasped as she saw him stumble then regain his feet as the powerful engine started to bite in the water. Slowly they turned and started to pick up speed down the river, the fire storm intensifying. Sabine gasped as she saw Aitor slumped over the wheel and grasped the wheel engaging full throttle. "Aitor is dead but we are safe and that's all that counts," she gasped.

"Well done Sabine, a close run thing though, where now?"

"The airport and fast."

"One other job to do," replied Lucrezia thoughtfully, "besides, I don't run away."

It took some time for them to make their way up to the White House. There had been a great deal of shooting an hour earlier, or that's what they assumed it was. Guy wondered if it had been a firework display as they made their way carefully to the entrance to the estate. "We have to be careful," he hissed as Tatyana made her way slowly up the hillside towards the White House, along with Annaliese, who was handcuffed and gagged. Surprisingly there weren't any challenges as they made their way forwards, heading away from the main gates and down to the back of the house over the lawns. Finally, after some careful manoeuvring, they managed to get to the house and looked directly inside, amazed at the sight confronting them.

"Sabine with Lucrezia in the shadows there," hissed Tatyana. "Who else is there?" she asked Annalise, releasing the gag.

"Helmut and Manfred," replied Annaliese before the gag was replaced.

"Who is the woman in the corner?" asked Guy.

"The Philosopher," replied Annaliese slowly, "one of the Quintet."

"Great chance to catch them all unawares," said Tatyana surveying the scene.

"Perhaps it is a stroke of luck," replied Guy cautiously looking around. "Sabine always has a backup so we need to be careful. I'm surprised they don't have more guards around here."

"You don't stand a chance," jeered Annaliese, "best to give yourselves up now and plead for clemency."

"Gag her," ordered Guy, reaching for his new mobile as it beeped. "We do this the official way, Monty will be here in five minutes," he replied, signalling to them to sit down in the shadows. He concentrated on the developing scene in the main room ahead as the participants became increasingly agitated.

Suddenly, he saw one of the blonde men lift what looked like a gun, clearly suspecting that there were intruders, and Guy noticed masked figures appearing at the windows. Then all hell broke loose as he saw three machine guns spray bullets across the room, one of the figures laughing demonically, and he saw the red hair coming loose from the mask. He couldn't believe it and had to restrain Tatyana as the room then became filled with smoke. A loud bang followed, and all the lights went out. "Come on," yelled Guy "this time Sabine is not getting away. The bitch has excelled herself this time, that was a bloody massacre."

Pandemonium broke out as men fired indiscriminately from hidden positions, and Guy ran forwards with Tatyana. At the same time he saw flashing lights as the police stormed the front door and ran forwards to meet Monty. The main house lights were restored and the dead lay everywhere, mostly blonde men but an old lady in the centre, the Philosopher. Guy ran from room to room with his gun, desperately seeking Sabine and Lucrezia to no avail. "We need to stop them Monty, can we get the police to fan out, they can't have got far," he shouted in frustration.

"Where's Helmut?" wailed Annaliese as Tatyana held her.

"Where have they gone?" snapped Guy, looking at her.

"How should I know, they've killed the Philosopher and all her men."

"They can't be far, it's a small island," shouted Guy. "That was bloody Sabine; I would recognise the woman anywhere."

"We may be able to track them to the airport or the harbour," said Monty looking at the carnage, "must be over fifteen dead, what a mess."

"What's going on, Annaliese? They've all deserted you," asked Guy.

"You still don't understand, do you? They're ahead of you as always, the movement is bigger and will go on, that's what you don't understand, you and the rest of your small minded men. Helmut is part of the new order, Lucrezia has won, the Philosopher is dead, Lucrezia will be heading back to Venice, and you are both missing the most important thing."

"What's that?"

"The breeding camps are only the means to the end; the world will be led by our self-breeding elites."

"Thanks for your wisdom," replied Tatyana sarcastically. "As for me the old dictum that there is no honour amongst thieves says it all."

"What a mess," reflected Guy, looking down at the Philosopher.

"So what now, Guy?" asked Monty. "I have the police cleaning up here, we need to think ahead."

"The real evil is this Composer and we know nothing about her."

"The Germans' fourth Reich is dead though."

"Perhaps, but all this reminds me of a worm, cut off the head and it keeps reforming, Lucrezia will be greatly strengthened by all this but there are others, we have a long way to go."

"Perhaps, but they are suffering also. It takes time to build these movements and we have seen a major setback tonight."

"Or as Annaliese says merely a course correction, we have to get after them assuming that they have already left."

"A certainty, I would say, no doubt a private jet left the minute all this was over," reflected Monty, "I will do my best to track them down, and we need to concentrate on what we can change."

"We head to Europe," said Guy determinedly.

"I have to clean up here first, and Jem needs care," replied Monty.

"Look after Lorna, and I will take Tatyana," said Guy, as they surveyed what was left of the room. "I've a feeling the Dutch girl was right, if Lucrezia has the Prophecy and the Covenant then the rigs have to be stopped." He turned as Tatyana ran over ashen-faced. "What is it?"

"Annaliese has disappeared."

"Damn, then there is no time, we need to strike at the heart of Lucrezia's empire, the question is whether the Mare Nostrum rig or Venice is the right first step or indeed find my wife," continued Guy as Monty confirmed that the police had found no one.

"Difficult choice, "replied Monty thoughtfully listening. "What we do know is that Lucrezia has created these rigs and therefore has the confidence of her investors, if we can disable them it would hurt badly. There is a much bigger picture with this so called Quintet; we have to assume the Teacher and Professor are two then there is Lucrezia as the Architect and this Philosopher, which leaves this Composer as the other. I've a suspicion the rigs or Nostrum hold the real clues and that's where they are most vulnerable, not in Venice, the rigs need to be stopped," said Monty.

"I agree, Venice will be a rabbit warren;" replied Guy.

"Look on the bright side," said Tatyana. "We have effectively destroyed their American operations and a lot of girls have been saved from slavery and breeding."

Gibraltar

Rose looked around the dark cave and saw someone in the distance walking towards her.

"So at last you have woken," said El Hammill, looking down with distaste at Rose. "Never seen what you Chinese girls have, never fancied you myself, not enough meat on the bone."

"Disgusting slob," muttered Rose under her breath.

"We aren't going to kill you yet, much as you deserve it; the good news for you is that you are going to be part of Project Valkyrie. Seems we have clientele who like the Chinese experience, indeed one of our own investors in particular," he smiled.

"Go to hell," snapped Rose, sitting up with difficulty.

"Come and meet the other lucky girl."

Rose was dragged by two strong men into a closed off area and then through into a smaller room where nine girls lay in silence, and she was flung on the floor.

"Hello," Rose looked around at the girls. "I fully intend to get you all out of here."

"It's a harem," said one of the taller girls bitterly, "some girls are already pregnant."

"Same as what they are doing in the Caribbean," replied Rose, "well I've stopped them once and will do so again."

"Really, how did you do that?" asked the girl called Lisa.

"Enough, you won't be stopping us here," said El Hammill, indicating to three men to round the girls up. "We are leaving for the main Nostrum now and I expect impeccable behaviour. You will be meeting your selected partner tomorrow night after the grand opening and I fully expect you all to do as you have been trained, do I make myself clear?"

"No chance," said Rose, who was unceremoniously pulled aside and hit in the stomach.

"Unfortunately we have one who hasn't been trained yet," replied El Hammill, "but she is wanted so we will do our best." They were taken across to a large cargo plane sat on the short runway at Gibraltar, and within fifty minutes came in to land on the island of Malta, where a powerful jet boat stood waiting. Rose was barely able to appreciate the vast scale of the Mare Nostrum as she was pushed to the stairwell and into the heart of the rig. "I'm taking a special interest in you because we have a special partner who is interested in what you did to Kobus. The problem is that it might mean another journey, although just a short one."

"No one is going to rape me," said Rose, the fire returning to her eyes.

"Who said anything about rape?" smiled El Hammill as the door opened and a doctor came in. "We have special drugs we administer to you all to make you, shall we say, more pliable. You realise that it's not just about impregnation, that's when all the science takes over and the manipulation of the embryos."

"I'll kill you."

"Oh really?" said El Hammill making to leave. He went across to his command centre where the tall man waited for him. "Hello Benedict, Sabine will present your gift tomorrow."

"Not today, no one would know."

"I would know, Benedict, now if you will excuse me I have much to do to prepare for the grand opening. We have over three hundred on this rig, including half of the Doge Council, who as you can imagine are rather demanding, though not as bad as you, I still don't know what you see in Chinese girls. Now if you'll excuse me, we still appear to be having a few internal issues." El Hammill was seething inside with Waleed as the man had just told him the security system was down again.

Greater Antilles

"Very interesting how that panned out and a sad loss of one of our own but the subterfuge was disappointing. The involvement of the Elders was particularly concerning," said the Composer, making her way onto the bridge of her luxury super yacht. It was not quite as large as the super yachts of Russian billionaires, but it was ostentatious enough to suit her needs. She had used it as a base for nearly ten years as it was ideal in ensuring she was never traceable. "Your cousin Wolfgang died here, Helmut," she said, pointing to the island in the distance as the German followed her on to the bridge. "Good job you had the escape route planned."

"He died a hero, as did Manfred and Kurt last night," replied Helmut, his swarthy face reflecting his inner grief. "Lucrezia's getting too cocky and the redhead needs to be taught a lesson."

"All in good time, Helmut, there is much to do and we are all on the same side. Manage Annaliese now that you two managed to escape so well last night. She must feel indebted to you, it's all yours now, we need her to resurrect the last breeding camp, the one they haven't found."

"Already in process," replied Helmut, looking across to the Captain. "You have the coordinates?"

"Yes, she is one hour away."

"And you?"

"The Panama Canal and then Asia, I have much to do, incidentally the Hidalgo is unguarded heading towards St Lucia. Now if you'll excuse me, I need to talk to my colleague in Asia."

"Will you miss Aitor?"

"The man was getting ideas above his station."

Lesser Antilles

The Hidalgo was starting to gain speed and Padraig was humming to himself as he sorted out the sails, conscious that Lorna was ensconced below, relaxing after their ordeal. He frowned suddenly at a blip on the radar showing a fast moving craft approaching. They had guests. The speed boat came in fast, too fast for him to do anything, and he cursed as gunfire made him stop the engine.

"What the hell do you think you are doing?"

"Kidnapping, old man, believe you know my friend Annaliese who you may see on the other boat, she has a thing about Lorna so hand her over now."

"Go to hell," snapped Padraig, reaching for the pistol he kept by the wheel. He saw the familiar figure of Annaliese grinning on the other boat, and then a bullet hit him in the stomach and he crumpled to the deck. Helmut dashed below and dragged a screaming Lorna out by her hair, accompanied by a pleased looking Annalise. Struggling to raise his head, Padraig dimly watched them go, and gritted his teeth in determination.

Venice

"The end justifies the means, is that what you are saying?"

"Of course and where better to start the active breeding programme here in Europe than at the very top with one of the members of our illustrious Doge Council," smiled Sabine at Benedict. It had been a long flight home but she was in the ascendancy, having earned Lucrezia's trust and confidence after the Grenada experience.

"Really, how?"

"The particular partner we have in mind on her way here as we speak is an old acquaintance of mine and particularly good breeding stock."

"Very well, I will do my part," smiled Benedict. The tall South African was fully immersed in the Nostrum programme, and particularly pleased that it was already making a great deal of money.

"Mrs Benedict will never find out, of that you can be sure,"smiled Sabine, making a note to use the same as leverage in the future.

"She had better not," replied the South African as he was led through by a servant girl to a luxurious appointed bedroom. "Your companion will be here early tomorrow morning," smiled the girl.

She had no idea where she was, drugged again and moved with Zelda onto a small jet for the flight south. Her mind was reeling at all the different places and she felt queasy as the plane came into land. As she was helped from the plane she noticed the familiar looking floating city in the distance and realised where she was; she had to strike back, and quickly.

Chapter 19

Fortaleza - La Gomera

Victoria, deputising again for Guy, activated the encrypted connection to his phone. "Well done Guy, you've stopped the breeding camps, justified all the funding and avenged Charlotte's death, which has just been confirmed."

"There's a lot more to do, and it's a great shame about Charlotte," replied Guy, preparing to board a waiting powerboat on the Greek island of Santorini, the closest landfall to the newly moved Mare Nostrum One. "The Philosopher is dead but Lucrezia and Sabine escaped, worse than that we have an added dimension in a woman called the Composer who is pulling the strings."

"We must have them on the back foot."

"Possibly, but it's a many headed hydra, if that's the right word," replied Guy, looking across at Tatyana. "Can you check on the Hidalgo? I haven't heard from them for two days, which is contrary to what I agreed with Padraig, they missed their regular call."

"Will do, have you got directions from Santorini to the rig?"

"Yes, we have coordinates, but it's going to be difficult with their security systems."

"Was the Philosopher an expensive diversion?" asked Victoria, checking her notes.

"No, I believe it was a very real power struggle that she lost, otherwise we would be having a very different conversation. She certainly had a great deal of power, maybe we haven't seen the last of her but the three women all appear to have different agendas, unfortunately for us Lucrezia is a supremely well organised and this Composer is an enigma."

"We will have to do more checking," replied Victoria, puzzled that they had no leads on this Composer at all, "we will need help tracking this woman down as a priority, I've a horrible feeling she is the key to something far bigger going on. Do we have any pictures?"

"None at all, in fact Annalise doesn't even know, we have left Monty and Jem to do a search of the region with the police to track down any other activities."

"What happened with Charlotte?"

"Found dead on the Copacabana beach, her head almost hacked off."

"My God…"

"There's worse, I'm afraid," continued Victoria sombrely, "we've just had reports that the Hidalgo is drifting in the sea and has been boarded by coast guards, they found Padraig near death and Lorna gone."

"Oh no," replied Guy disconsolately his demons returning, "Lorna gone."

"Afraid so, you need help over there Guy, you can't take on this rig with just you and Tatyana."

"We need to strike now before they close ranks, they must be struggling at present after the recent events, I've every reason to believe that they have activated Project Valkyrie," continued Guy, shaken by the news and nodding to Tatyana as the large speedboat arrived.

"Wait for Monty."

"No time, we have reason to believe the first breeding centre is being established as we speak, any sign of Rose?"

"She's here in Europe but who knows where, we have achieved a great deal, Tutulus assets in Grenada have been frozen which will cause them problems though there has been a large fund transfer across to Asia."

"How large?" asked Guy?

"Tens of millions of dollars, impossible to say exactly as we can't access the details."

"So we've merely swapped one financial lead for another?"

"Perhaps. Are you aware that Lucrezia has the Khans' Prophecy?"

"That probably means Sergei must be dead," replied Guy, "he would never have let it get out of his hands, are we sure?"

"Pretty sure, along with a document called the Popes Covenant."

"What's the significance?"

"They're linked, and we have the monks trying to find connections in the vaults and the Chinese documents."

"So we need to strike."

"The Mare Nostrum for proof," replied Victoria, "the Venice activities are secondary; we need hard intelligence that Nostrum is used for the breeding centres and then can get Interpol involved."

"It's going to be tough with the two of us," said Guy as he ended the call.

"The two of us will do our best," smiled Tatyana, climbing onto the boat as a shadow loomed.

"Not just two of you," came a familiar voice.

"Rostov!" Tatyana smiled.

"God, I've been tracking you two since you hit the island."

"We thought you were dead," exclaimed Tatyana, hugging the tall Russian.

"Very nearly," replied the Russian, "spent a couple of days in the water, hypothermia nearly finished me but I survived with a good wash," he grinned. "Room for me?"

"Of course," smiled Guy, "your team?"

"The twins were killed but one other survived the Abu Dhabi attack, the bloody rig was well defended, Anton here," smiled Rostov as a small, bald Russian came forwards.

"What are your plans?"

"Impossible, too well defended as I found out."

"We have no choice, Rostov; they'll be taken by surprise as they're still having problems with the security systems, according to what Tatyana found out."

"The Turkish member of the Elders confirmed to us that the system has gone down again."

"Well that improves the odds from impossible to mad, we tried the clever way with the contracting company so can't think of a way except going straight in and counting on surprise."

"Is Sergei dead?" asked Guy.

"We have no proof, but they claim they have killed him and for that they will pay. Come on," shouted Rostov as he took charge of the powerboat and they set off out to sea.

Saba

Lorna experienced an all too familiar feeling of dread as she was hustled down the small aircraft steps and into the awaiting car. Annaliese glowered at her and rattled instructions into the mobile then drove to Kobus' old headquarters. Lorna was hustled into the main lounge area and the door was locked. She despaired that she was captured again, and that they had lost Padraig, and bitterly regretted their naivety in thinking they could just sail away. Lorna looked up as the door opened.

"Just a short flight and then a great chance for you to introduce me to your lovely cruiser," beamed Annaliese, rejuvenated after finding Helmut alive and now in charge under a better leader, the Composer.

"My cruiser, you will not be welcome there."

"It's not going to be like that, you see you are going to welcome me as your honoured guest and we are going to divest ourselves of your little guests before picking up some more mature girls."

"There's no way you are turning it into a breeding centre, it was used by my father for that, and I won't allow it."

"I'm afraid you will, you see I took a little precaution, your dear stepmother Diane, with whom I believe you have a certain attachment, is that correct? Here, have a look at my iPad screen."

"This is inhumane," gasped Lorna, seeing a picture of Diane strapped to a table with a man holding a large knife.

"Changed your mind, we will be there in an hour."

Aegean Sea (Twenty nautical miles east of Santorini)

The wind was howling at near gale force as they docked at the MN rig. Their message to the controlling tower had been that they were lost and in distress with a sick woman. It had probably only bought them a few minutes when they landed, but at least they had been able to attach to the extending hydraulic platform used for shipping. They would only have a few minutes before discovery, and Interpol wouldn't intervene in international waters. It took deft handling by Rostov to get them next to the lowered stairs before being greeted by glowering guards with machine guns, who frisked them before pushing them into a holding room.

"She doesn't look to be in distress," said the guard looking at Tatyana, "what's wrong with her?"

"Long term illness," replied Guy as the décor reminded him they were actually on an exclusive resort.

"Wait a minute, don't I know you?" said the guard, looking at Rostov, "you've got a nerve, guards alarm," he yelled to be felled by Rostov as Kirov expertly grabbed his gun.

"On the floor now," yelled Rostov, grabbing nylon handcuffs and trussing the two men. "Come on, we need to move fast," he said as they ran to the stairs, where Guy pointed to the control room. "That's

El Hammill at the window, Lucrezia's second in command, come on." They bounded up the steps as a shrill alarm went off in the distance. Tatyana reached the door first and slammed it open only to be confronted by El Hammill holding a revolver.

"Down on the floor, "he snapped, "did you really think I wouldn't see you coming from up here? I was expecting you an hour ago. Where's the other two?"

"Perhaps you thought I was dead," said Rostov, emerging from the shadows to knock El Hammill to the floor.

"You have no idea what you are messing with," snapped the Arab, stunned by the sudden attack but quickly recovering, "in fact, Tresanton, your dear wife is experiencing an intimate moment with one of the Doge members."

"Where is she?" screamed Guy. "Where have you taken her?"

"You will never know," said El Hammill, smiling coldly.

"Perhaps I can help," said Tatyana, kicking out and knocking the Arab backwards, causing him to bang his head on the metal door.

"He's out cold," said Rostov. "Come on up the stairs Kirov watch our backs, you and I need to get to the main control area," he added, and they bolted forwards as Guy and Tatyana entered the main conference room, where guards appeared out of nowhere. Guy and Tatyana ran down another corridor to their left, and then into a smaller room where Guy stopped and gasped. In front of him stood an exact replica of Bequia and Saba, a breeding centre, the proof they needed.

"Get photos and upload them fast," he shouted to Tatyana, "this will give Monty what he needs," he said, looking around wildly as they heard shouts. "Breeding centres so they can play at being God," he ran on through to the main control room.

"So you think you know it all? This is just the surface," snapped a groggy El Hammill, pressing a button as three men with machine guns charged in. "Throw down your weapons."

"Does Lucrezia know about this?"

"The rigs are totally my domain," snapped El Hammill, raising his gun, "and you two can join the fat man in hell."

"So you killed him?"

"Dead and in the stinking St Petersburg waters, I saw him die," replied the Arab gleefully.

"Your boss will kill you for this."

"I report to others not her."

"Think so, the Germans are finished if that's who you mean."

"You lie," said El Hammill, "I would have found out if that were true."

"She doesn't trust you that's why and this is the proof, you had your own plans all along didn't you that's why you kept a distance."

"Don't waste my time," said El Hammill gesturing to Waleed to come over. "Get the codes up we will need to reset them."

"Lucrezia is heading here with Sabine to destroy you, you're not one of the inner circles," continued Guy, "you are clutching at straws, it's over, and she has been tasked with disposing of you as surplus to requirement."

"She's the new top kid on the block and she hates you, it's the end of the road."

"I am the inventor of all this," screamed El Hammill, what gives you the right to question anything I do, anyone for that matter, he stared around wildly focusing on Tatyana as she smiled seductively. "The latest in electronic messaging and security the world can provide, nothing moves here without my knowing it, I am all seeing."

"Let me handle this I know his type," whispered Tatyana as she walked forwards and closed the door behind.

"You know El Hammill I've always had a thing for strong Arab men," her eyes widened in surprise at the banks of arrayed monitors in his private room.

"Nothing goes on without my seeing it," smiled the Arab still dazed by the assault but determined to do this his way.

"Lucrezia the Architect designed these?"

"No I did," bellowed the Arab angrily reaching across lustfully and not seeing the blur of movement until too late as Tatyana's foot hit him hard in the groin. He went down hard as Tatyana knocked him unconscious.

"What's happening in there?" asked Waleed, trying to see through the opaque glass.

"Were you in St Petersburg," asked Guy as he looked down the barrel of Waleed's gun and wondering where the hell Rostov and Kirov were.

"Yes but El Hammill shot the big man and threw him into the river, if the bullets didn't kill him the cold water would have done."

"You don't work for El Hammill, do you?" snapped Guy.

"Of course I do."

"You knew the security systems would malfunction, who are you working for?"

"You will never know."

"Ah now I understand," smiled Guy as the door opened and Tatyana emerged. "No honour amongst thieves is there."

"Since you are about to die you can know, you think you are so clever when you are totally in the wrong area, the Asian rig is the main one always was and I had to ensure El Hammill didn't do anything to compromise that, I wasn't Lucrezia's spy."

"You work for the Composer," guessed Guy.

"Correct," smiled Waleed, "you see, all your efforts have been wasted and now is the time to dispose of you."

"Seems like it," replied Guy as the Arab cocked the gun and tried to fire, staring in puzzlement at his chest as red blossomed there before crumpling to the floor, a six inch knife protruding from his chest.

"Rostov, thank God," gasped Guy.

"Come on, we're not out of this yet, there are over twenty security men buzzing around here, we need to do a thorough search of this place," said Guy, turning to the main stairwell.

Watch out," yelled Tatyana as El Hamill angrily slammed through the door, bleeding copiously. He rammed a knife into Kirov and the Russian groaned and spun around. Tatyana launched herself across the space but El Hammill managed to evade her, raising the gun again when two continuous shots rang out from Rostov and the Arab looked quizzically at his chest as red holes appeared.

"You in charge here," said Rostov as a small nervous looking man appeared at the door, shaking. "I want safe passage for myself and my three colleagues, otherwise I will kill your boss." Rostov looked around, there were too many guards on the rig, they couldn't take control and would do well to get away alive.

"Thank God, I have Monty on the line, the police are on the way, the photos did the trick," smiled Guy. El Hammill was dead.

Puerto Rico

Lorna groaned as she boarded her cruiser with Annaliese and Captain Jellico looked at her quizzically. "We need to move fast please, this is my good friend Annalise who is here to help with a new assignment, we have to cancel the pick up tomorrow I'm afraid," she said, barely noticing the old castle wall to their left as they slowly headed out into the estuary. She knew the island was technically part of the Americas but at the same time separate. She'd racked her brains but couldn't think of any way to stop the Dutch girl.

"Your stepmother will be so pleased. Head for Virgin Gouda, thanks to your disruptive efforts we've had to corral all our girls from the islands so there will be nearly a hundred coming aboard, and then we head to the south Caribbean, where we are going to have a nice little cruise until we meet a rig."

"A rig?"

"That's all you need to know," smiled the Dutch girl. The Composer was going to be very pleased with her: they were a match made in heaven.

Venice

Divert the flight," snapped Lucrezia angrily as she listened to Sabine's short report. It was unbelievable that the MN rig was now occupied by the police, who were claiming all sorts of things that she hadn't authorised. It was clear that El Hammill had been doing things his own way and she cursed inwardly. Despite her influence and protestations the police weren't moving yet and she was getting complaints from the clientele. It had taken all her strength and influence to calm the situation, particularly when a certain Inspector Columba had arrived and stated making accusations on the rig about her. Eventually they had agreed she was innocent for now and left, but the central mechanisms were all still in place, and they had another three rigs about to go operational.

She summoned Giuseppe. "Prepare for a jet to pick up the cargo, I want them all deposited in the safe area," she ordered, trying to relax after the escape from Grenada, and she looked up as Sabine entered.

"Bloody Tresanton is behind the rig attack, you really should have let me finish him before, I told you it was a mistake," said Sabine, emboldened by recent events.

"Not my way Sabine, and it's all recoverable, El Hammill was a rogue that has been filtered out so they have done us a favour, nothing has changed. With the Philosopher out of the way we have Europe to ourselves and influence now over the Americas so it's worked out fine thanks to Giuseppe and you protecting me, I owe you both."

"The Composer is the real power, Lucrezia, you know that," said Sabine, staring across at Giuseppe, who merely nodded his head.

"We are still the brains behind everything," snapped Lucrezia, "and don't forget that. We have the insurance of Tresanton's wife and Segovia, and Annalise has managed to take control of the Oleson Cruise ship."

"That is good news," acknowledged Sabine. "It's obvious though that the Composer has to be negotiated with and this Annaliese works for her now, she is well ahead of us managing remotely and playing you off against the Philosopher, now we've lost control of the first MN rig."

"We haven't lost control of the rig; the police are leaving as we speak, it's just a small blip, though it does mean I want you to manage them."

"All of them?"

"Yes, the overall programme; you are the obvious choice and have proven yourself a number of times."

"Thank you, but we have to negotiate with the Composer."

"That's my problem," replied Lucrezia, "you work with Giuseppe here, who is my foundation, always has been and always will be, so respect him." The old man looked uncomfortable and older than ever.

"Lucrezia, we have to go into the Doge meeting now, they are expecting you," said Giuseppe, trying to comprehend the events in Grenada even though he had stayed in Europe.

"What do you want me to do with Rose and Zelda after they have been seen to?" smiled Sabine.

"Put them in the same cell and bug it; it will be interesting to hear what they say, and put Sergovia in there also. Without your support, Sabine, we would have been in grave danger, but remember here in Venice we do things my way, the Nostrums must now be managed."

Lucrezia bustled into the meeting room and sat down at the head of the table. "I have good news that the Nostrum rigs are now all ready and have a full complement of attendees; in fact, it's oversubscribed."

"I believe there have been a few issues with Project Valkyrie, and some of the camps are compromised", said Benedict. "We have invested a great deal of money into this programme and I don't like to hear negative press, all these lurid stories of slavery and breeding camps."

"Yes, there have been a few issues in the Caribbean, particularly with a sensationalist American journalist, but that is all, we were relying on a partner in Latin America whose process was, shall we say, a little irregular."

"So no more bad press."

"As I said, teething problems, nothing more, your investments are perfectly safe and have already delivered as you will have seen they are making money. We will become the senior investor group and maintain our governance role," replied Lucrezia, "you will all hold governance roles; I now need your further support."

"In what way?"

"Phase two after the rigs is the institutionalisation of certain parts of the world, starting here at home with the future of Venice."

"Surely that is political."

"The opposite," replied Lucrezia, "it will involve you all in another lucrative venture as we detach the Venetian Republic into another Mare Nostrum, the ultimate Mare Nostrum, in fact."

"That wasn't part of the deal, that's part of a nation state," snapped Benedict, interested in getting to his next promised assignation.

"A state that doesn't want to be a nation state, I want Venice to return to its mercantile status as an independent nation unencumbered by the Italian state, which is led now by a puppet leader."

"Claudio Verdi reports to you," said Benedict in astonishment.

"And has done for years, now I want to make it more formal, so in return for making you all millions I need your tacit support."

"Won't this make you visible to the public?"

"Giuseppe will become President of the Republic; I shall be the guiding hand behind him after we dismiss Fabrizio Grete, who has become useless."

"So why is this necessary when we have so much else to do? Surely we need to keep away from such overtly political activities."

"Our beautiful city is sinking; it has been for centuries but it's getting worse, the technical reason is the Adriatic tectonic plate is slipping under the Eurasian plate but anyone can see the difference in water levels. In 1902 the tower of Campanile of St Mark's Church collapsed as its foundations shifted, and it's happening again. The whole of Venice is sat on ten million tree trunks, you can imagine their state after hundreds of years, it all needs decisive decision making and will become the Chief Mare Nostrum."

"I thought they were constructing a flood barrier," replied Benedict.

"It's taken nearly ten years and is inadequate. We need far more decisive action, major investments in infrastructure: the walls are crumbling."

"Makes sense I suppose," said Benedict, thinking of Rose.

"Can I have a vote then?" said Lucrezia, and was pleased at the show of hands. "Good, then I will take you through the plans," she said, then looked up in surprise as the door flew open.

"Ladies and gentlemen, can I suggest you all take a little break whilst we speak with the Doge," shouted Guy, flanked by Monty and Tatyana. "Lucrezia, it's good to meet you at last, after all the last time we saw each other you were about to disappear."

"This is monstrous and illegal," snapped Lucrezia angrily, wondering where on earth her guards were as she was stewarded next door. "You are trespassing and I have done nothing wrong."

"Illegal and immoral breeding camps, in effect modern slavery, young girls raped and murdered, that's what Project Valkyrie really is, am I right?"

"Stay where you are, all of you," shouted Monty from the back as some of the Council tried to slip away. He motioned to Guy to continue.

"Where's your friend Sabine?" said Guy as Benedict and Madam Ramping were brought into the room.

"I have no idea what or who you are talking about, I abhor violence, everyone knows that."

"This supposedly non-violent person was directly responsible for attacks on my home in La Gomera," said Guy coldly. "With her terrorist sidekick called Sabine, they systematically destroyed the monastery where I lived and killed two of my bodyguards."

"Is this true?" asked Benedict, looking coldly at Lucrezia.

"Rubbish," said Lucrezia, pressing a secret button, "you have no right to enter private property. The security police are coming."

"I can prove that breeding camps are on the rigs. And my own wife is still missing, probably sold into slavery," said Guy.

"Your own wife?" asked Benedict slowly.

"My Chinese wife," replied Guy slowly and meaningfully.

"Oh my God," muttered the big South African, looking in horror at Lucrezia.

"Enough!" shouted Lucrezia, "unless you both leave immediately you will be arrested. I am the law here, you forget that."

"I work for Interpol who have appropriate jurisdiction in cases like this," said Monty.

"So a very risky investment," continued Guy, looking at Monty.

"Police," shouted Monty as he saw the guards, "arrest this woman."

Four policemen swarmed in, and Monty called in his reserve men.

"This is an outrage," snarled Lucrezia, "Interpol has no jurisdiction here, this is a private meeting and no laws have been broken." She moved to the back of the desk, where suddenly she appeared to falter before there was a loud bang. Smoke filled the room as she disappeared behind a partition and pandemonium broke out as Monty and Guy ran forwards looking in puzzlement at the wall.

"Quick, there has to be a way through," said Monty, running to the side door and cursing as it was locked. "This group meeting is closed," he announced, "you will all be required to produce individual statements."

"This is unacceptable," snapped Benedict, "my government will hear about it."

"I'm sure they will, and the press will know about your involvement with breeding camps," said Guy. "The wall over there isn't solid, get a couple of men and we can break it down, there's got to be some sort of hidden passage behind it."

"You go with Tatyana, Guy, I need to cover your back here with the officials, it's touch and go whether they are going to believe us, there are a lot of angry people out here," said Monty.

"I'm with you," said Tatyana, running forwards and smashing her feet against the flimsy wall, which spun around to reveal a hidden corridor. Guy followed her through, and they ran down dimly lit corridors, gasping as they tried to keep their balance.

"There she is," shouted Tatyana as in the distance two figures were seen moving rapidly. One was Lucrezia and the other she immediately recognised as Sabine. They saw Sabine gesture to Lucrezia, urging her to move faster as another girl joined them.

"Segovia," moaned Tatyana disbelieving, "she must be coerced."

"This place is a labyrinth," gasped Guy. "I think we're gaining on them though," he shouted as they rounded a corner and ground to a halt in surprise as a familiar figure came across his path. "Stanton, what on earth are you doing here?"

"I need to talk to you."

"Later, she's getting away, come on," shouted Guy, gasping as the American hit him on the side of the head. He fell forwards and stumbled as Stanton slammed the door with surprising speed. Tatyana forced it open to be confronted by the American, who held them at gunpoint.

"That's far enough, both of you."

"It was you leaking information all the time, telling them about the prophecies and the Covenant, you traitor," gasped Guy.

"Lucrezia and the Doge are the future, you are out of your depth," replied Stanton, raising the gun. "I'm afraid it is the end of the road for you both."

"You were one of us."

"The dammed Elders are nothing more than a talking shop, I've achieved more in a month with the Doge than five years with you. It's all over, Guy: accept it."

"You got them access to La Gomera," snarled Guy, suddenly seeing how it fitted together. "God, you must have been laughing at us."

"Perhaps," smiled Stanton. To his astonishment, Tatyana then fell to the floor and in a blur hit him in the midriff with her foot. He fired, narrowly missing Guy, and then collapsed when Tatyana's foot caught him hard on the jaw.

"Well done, Tatyana," shouted Guy, leaping for the door when they heard an ear-shattering blast.

"The bridge has been blown, someone has cut us off from the Doge building," shouted Tatyana, trying to find another way out of the room as smoke permeated behind them. "We've got to get back out of here fast," gasped Guy, "it's a death trap; the place has been set alight."

"Lucrezia and Sabine," said Tatyana, "they have Segovia and the Covenants."

"The canal, it's the only way if we can get a boat to avoid the blaze," shouted Guy looking around desperately, "come on, there's still time," he yelled. He found a small boat and grabbed the oars, pulling with all his strength as they rounded the corner. In the distance Tatyana could see figures moving to the canal edge and a powerboat.

"A little closer and I can get a shot off," yelled Tatyana, when suddenly another boat sped across the small canal from a hidden recess and hit them in the side.

"Can't let you do that," said Giuseppe, positioning his boat square across the canal.

"We have no quarrel with you," said Tatyana, conscious of the silhouetted figures in the distance pulling away from them, "either move or we shoot."

"I thought you might take that view," replied Giuseppe resignedly, "take a look behind me."

"What do you mean?"

"I rescued her from the filthy hands of the South African and the breeding centres," said Giuseppe, pointing to the huddled figure in the bottom of his boat. "Never did agree with that programme, I rescued them all."

"Oh my God, Rose…" exclaimed Guy.

Chapter 20

Venice

The dark night was filled with foreboding for Guy as he struggled with a rush of emotions, cradling the drugged shape of Rose in his arms. Thomas Mann's Death in Venice and the haunting Mahler symphony from the film came into his head as he willed her to respond. "Rose, can you hear me?"

"Yes," she whispered, "don't worry, it will wear off, they brought me here yesterday, a flight with the journalist Zelda, held in the caves in Gibraltar."

"Gibraltar…"

"In the caves under the rock all heavily disguised, I have a signed statement from the girls which we can use in evidence, it's their centre of European operations for Project Valkyrie," she whispered as she held Guy tight, "it's been a long week since I left you at Almeria."

"You did marvellously in Saba fighting off Kobus, if anything that turned the tide, I'm proud of you."

"There's still time, Guy, I can see them getting ready in the distance," shouted Tatyana "we don't have long and Segovia's life is at stake."

"Go, Guy, I'm fine," replied Rose, standing up slowly.

"I've just heard from Rostov, he's attacking the palace from the other side though he's struggling to get through, he's trying to get around to us to cut them off."

"Very well, let's go."

"Sorry I can't let you," murmured Giuseppe, nervously holding up a small revolver. "Lucrezia asked me to hold you all here until she gave me the all clear, raise your hands and don't think I don't know how to use these things, I held off an entire brigade of American soldiers at Salerno."

"This isn't your fight, old man," snapped Guy. "Come on, you can see they are taking a young girl, another life ruined, you've proved you are a decent man."

"I am loyal to Lucrezia. If only she had taken my advice."

"Oh God," cursed Guy, desperately trying to find a way of disarming him. "If she gets away then this will go on, if she isn't involved in anything criminal then there is nothing to fear."

"I wouldn't let her get involved in anything illegal," retorted Giuseppe strongly. "She won't allow physical harm to befall anyone; all she wants is for her beloved Venice to return to its former glory."

"Really?"

"Come on Guy, we really have to go," shouted Tatyana, trying to manoeuvre the craft with a view to passing Giuseppe.

"Venice is her goal; the Mare Nostrums are to show meritocracy works, Venice will be a self-governing state within the Nostrum network."

"Giuseppe, for God's sake we have to go, this is misplaced loyalty."

"I'm just an old man, is that what you are thinking?"

"You are playing with fire, old man; this is far bigger than Lucrezia, bigger even than the Composer, it goes further. Even Lucrezia cannot and will not talk about it; you only know the tip of the iceberg."

"She is part of the Quintet, all have titles," replied Giuseppe. "This secret Composer…no one knows where she lives, and none know who she is or her background."

"Where is she based?"

"I've just told you we don't know, except I've heard Asia mentioned a number of times."

"Asia, as with the Teacher," said Guy, thinking furiously, "where is Lucrezia going now?"

"The secret rooms used for the Doge's personal security."

"So they are escaping, leaving you to face the music."

"She will be making her new plans," shouted Giuseppe, raising his voice as Tatyana moved closer. "I will shoot."

"No, you won't," replied Guy, "like your mistress you don't believe in violence, Giuseppe, I don't believe it's even loaded."

"Stop I said," shouted the old man, gasping as Rose kicked out, toppling him onto the water.

"Go, Guy, I will watch him," she shouted, stumbling ashore as Tatyana grabbed the motorboat and pulled them forwards.

"Stay put, Rose," shouted Guy as they fell into the motorised boat and surged forwards, seeing nothing ahead but clear water and then in the distance a glimmer of light. It seemed to go on forever, and Guy was beginning to despair that they would be too late when Tatyana gave a shout.

"They are boarding a powerboat, two of them."

"Great," said Guy, and he accelerated as he saw one of the figures turn their head towards them. It was Sabine, and he was suddenly conscious that they weren't armed. He saw a large black powerboat with darkened windows, looking more like a plane than a boat with its sleek lines. The figure ahead seemed to speed up; it was going to be close.

"Let me handle this," said Sabine, gesticulating to Lucrezia to get aboard. "The Russian bitch and Tresanton, this time it's my way."

"No killing, Sabine."

"Not this time, Lucrezia, Tresanton and I have old scores to settle so get ready to leave fast." She sprang along the dockside as Guy and Tatyana screeched to a halt, tumbling ashore and trying to get their breath back. Tatyana saw Sabine two metres away and gasped, trying to get out of the way and recoiling in shock as a blur of movement and blinding pain knocked her to the side. She saw blood pouring down her arm, then came the agony as the pain from the bullet reached her brain. Sabine stepped forwards raising a knife to kill her as Guy flung himself forwards to parry the knife thrust with his own knife. This unbalanced Sabine, and Tatyana scrambled up, kicking out and catching the redhead in the stomach. Sabine staggered back winded and tried to regain her balance, then gasped as Guy hit her hard and thrust his own knife into her abdomen. She looked in horror at the blood pouring from her stomach and fell slowly to the floor as Guy went to Tatyana's aide.

"I'll survive, make sure she's dead," stammered Tatyana as Guy saw a startled-looking Lucrezia departing. He turned in surprise as Sabine launched herself forwards, diving into the water and shouting for help. The powerboat turned around and Guy had to duck for cover as machine gun fire spluttered across the path. He dropped Tatyana behind a concrete pillar as he saw the powerboat spin around, stray hands reaching out for Sabine. An older man at the wheel looked coldly at them before opening the powerful throttles.

"They've got Segovia in there," gasped Tatyana, "I saw large metal tubes on deck, presumably the covenants; they've got away, dammit."

"A close shave, but you never learn, do you?" said Lucrezia as Sabine laid bleeding, receiving treatment from Danielle.

"She needs a hospital, I can't stop the bleeding."

"I'll be alright, they were lucky," gasped Sabine in great pain, "if the Russian hadn't got in the way I would have finished them off, I need to get to a hospital," she gasped as Lucrezia checked on the ropes holding the covenants.

"Pass my phone," said Lucrezia, turning as her mobile rang.

"I assume you have the Prophecy and the covenant aboard?"

"Of course I do, Composer," replied Lucrezia, puzzled, "where are you?"

"Close enough," purred the voice, "sacrifices are required for our ultimate success, and invisibility is fundamental."

"Where are you?" repeated Lucrezia, a cold feeling spreading across her stomach.

"Sacrifice for the cause is the ultimate reward," continued the cold voice, "you were always the one to keep a low profile."

"We are the Quintet," said Lucrezia, looking wildly around. She couldn't see anything.

"Collateral damage, Lucrezia."

"Where the hell are you?" yelled Lucrezia as the line went dead.

"The Composer?" asked Sabine, gritting her teeth at the indescribable pain as the boat smashed through the waves.

"Asking if we have the Covenants."

"Oh no," gasped Sabine, pulling herself desperately up to the boat's rail.

"What on earth are you doing?"

"Saving myself," she yelled as an explosion sent a ball of flame high into the night sky. The powerboat pitched violently and then erupted into a ball of fire.

"My God," exclaimed Guy as he watched the scene unfold.

"Segovia," shouted Tatyana.

"The metal tubes of the Prophecy and the Covenant," exclaimed Guy as the flames went higher, "I saw a flash over to the left that must have been a missile," he continued, "all dead, and the covenant gone."

"Not the Khans' Prophecy," murmured Tatyana, "we need to see if there are survivors."

"The police are there, Tatyana, we can't help. What did you mean 'not the Prophecy'?

"Lucrezia never had the Prophecy, the one she had was a fake."

"What?"

"We switched them when we first put them underwater, Sergei's uncle helped me hide the original in a cave, he had a duplicate which was the one El Hamill's goons were given, the real one is still in the cave in St Petersburg."

"Fantastic, are you certain?" asked Guy.

"Why do you think there has been no announcements from Lucrezia? The copy was good, an old scholar of mine transcribed the Mongolian texts into stories I made up, must have been an entertaining to have seen them try to decipher it. I didn't tell you earlier as I'd been worried for some time about a traitor in our ranks; unfortunately with Stanton I was correct."

"Brilliant," smiled Guy, as Rose came into view with a dejected Giuseppe.

The canal water was still lapping against the dockside as the explosion aftershock continued to pound. Guy checked once again trying to see if there were any other observers but the darkness defeated him. "We need to get back to the others," he said to Tatyana.

"What do you think caused the explosion?" asked Tatyana, who desperately wanted to contact Segovia.

"I saw a flash just before, a missile, I'm sure they would have had the power craft checked for bombs before they embarked, it was a missile of some sort."

"All under control, that was quite an explosion," said Monty as they re-joined him in the great hall with stunned members of the Doge Council. "Rose, my God, it's good to see you," he exclaimed.

"Give me a minute," replied Rose, walking across to where Benedict stood glowering at the proceedings. "You bastard," she snarled, and she hit him hard in the stomach. The South African collapsed in astonishment.

"What on earth was that about?" asked Guy

"Giuseppe saved me from being raped by that man as part of the breeding plans. He was all set to attack me when Giuseppe intervened."

"Interesting...so this Council were involved beyond financial investment, they are all declaring it was a business venture only and I had no proof of any wrong doing, apparently they did everything by the book and the Nostrum rigs are totally legal."

"So they can go free? I can't believe it," gasped Rose.

"Unless we can prove that the girls were kidnapped, it's circumstantial; we can charge Stanton and get him extradited."

"Surely we can prove the girls were kidnapped, we just have to ask them."

"Ask who? We only have Rose and Zelda but she's seen as having an angle," replied Monty, "the ones she travelled with have disappeared, including those we liberated in the Caribbean but Giuseppe is singing like a canary."

"Go on," said Guy, as he accepted a hot coffee.

"He hates Project Valkyrie; the breeding camp idea is totally alien to him. He told us that it started with Lorna's father and his idea of developing breeding camps in Norway, which the Germans in Germania copied. He warned Lucrezia not to get involved, but she developed the Mare Nostrum mobile rigs outside national jurisdiction, which ironically gave credence to the whole idea, so she was the main instigator of turning the concept into reality. They thought with the rigs they were free from morale constraint, and of course they were right."

"So the rigs are essentially breeding centres?"

"No, it was genuinely planned an elite gatherings and may still work that way but it had been side tracked because this El Hammill took his own slant on it. There are now four such rigs, all up and running and all fully subscribed."

"So they are all legal," exclaimed Guy with disgust.

"If we can get proof of coercion and violence or rape then it would be different, but we can't. Project Valkyrie at present is no more than a bad dream, a term or euphemism for the breeding camps but nothing else."

"But the coercion of Rose and Tatyana..."

"It's her word against the rest, they will also claim that we carried out an unprovoked attack on their rigs," continued Monty.

"But the island camps?"

"All cleaned up and closed down, the girls are gone."

"Come on Monty, you can't tell me you can't get anything out of this lot," said Guy in frustration.

"They say they are all honest businessmen who were misled, and unfortunately that's ultimately what they are; I will have to let them go in a couple of hours, they are powerful people."

"So unless we can find Lucrezia or Sabine…"

"Or anyone associated with Lucrezia, Giuseppe won't incriminate her, he is too loyal."

"But Tatyana's kidnap and journey…"

"No sign of the submarine, though I have tracked down the monastery in Galicia, they claim they never had any visitors on the night in question."

"Surely we can raid Germania?"

"Already done," replied Monty, "the place is locked up and abandoned, the rats have fled."

"And the White House, the base for the Quintet?" asked Guy.

"Closed up, they have cleaned up most effectively."

"No honour amongst thieves though, there must be something," spat Guy in frustration.

"But you need specifics and facts," said Rose.

"I have something," said Zelda, joining them. "Remember the poor girl murdered in Bequia? I know who did that, the girls at the house there told me one evening. The poor girl was called Jolene Taylor and was always resisting the overtures of the animals there. Finally she managed to escape, but the dammed dogs got her. She was dragged back and put in the same water tank as Tatyana, the difference was that animal Helmut then took a personal interest in her. Later he got drunk and wrote a long, grovelling letter to the dead girl's parents expressing remorse, and then he sobered up and couldn't find where it was."

"Who has it?" asked Tatyana.

"It's safe and sound with me," smiled Zelda, "It is my job, after all."

"He tried to rape me, too," said Tatyana, "after the tank treatment."

"But he escaped the White House," said Rose.

"Because he knew it was coming and rescued Annalise whilst we were occupied. Still this is factual evidence; we've just got to find him."

"I have something tangible, too," said Rose. "The girl in Gibraltar agreed to give me a written testimony."

"That sounds more promising," said Guy. "I'm sure it was this Helmut who warned me to back off. Still, none of it is hard factual evidence."

"I disagree," said Zelda. "I managed to get some other testimonials. I have enough to write an expose on the camps, hopefully enough to get a conviction on those managing the camps."

"If we can find them," said Guy

"That will all help," said Monty, "a public debate will draw attention and provide leads, and most of all it will start to undermine the elites living on the rigs."

"So what now, is this fourth Reich finished or is it still behind the Quintet?" asked Guy.

"This Composer must be linked in some way."

"So these modern day Nazis are behind the quintet?"

"No, Giuseppe told me that Lucrezia was distancing herself from the more extreme elements and I assume Project Valkyrie was that, my guess is that the Philosopher was their leader and with her death the pendulum swings."

"To Lucrezia, if she's still alive."

"She can't be alive, there are no survivors, not even Sabine, and there is a complication, again from Giuseppe, who let slip another name, one different to Tutulus."

"A new name."

"Yes, he saw a piece of paper on Lucrezia's desk with one word on it, she told him never to mention the word again, now he thinks she's dead he is telling us everything."

"What was the word?"

"Kappacca."

"Kappacca?" asked Guy.

"It's an acronym," said Rose, "an acronym for the convents, add A and you have the Khans' Prophecy, the Popes Covenant and then the Confucian Analects."

"The Confucian analects, where on earth did you get that from?" asked Guy.

"I did my research, and my parents were Confucian scholars, it's a well-known phrase and also Victoria mentioned it in the documents she is looking at. It provides legitimacy and indeed respect; my, you really are a long way behind in understanding," smiled Rose. "I did research some time ago into the Teacher, if you recall, and came across the Confucius Analects. Victoria and I talked and she told me she had discussed with you the significance of the unknown Chinese files in the monastery's archives."

"You never cease to amaze me," smiled Guy.

"Perhaps you underestimate me; after all, Chinese history is my specialist subject."

"The Chinese link again, all signs keep pointing back there," said Guy. "The work of the Teacher always predicted that, and Victoria mentioned the archives of a football match on La Gomera."

"A Chinese man who was the Teacher's grandfather and a German Count, both central tenants in bringing together the German and Chinese empires."

"Led by the Chinese."

"Could be," replied Monty thoughtfully.

"So where does this leave us with Mare Nostrum and Lucrezia's plans for Venice?"

"Not very far, I'm afraid," replied Monty. "The police here have been unable to find any survivors from the explosion; they say it was in a strong tidal area, so the bodies could have washed miles very quickly."

"No bodies also means that they could still be alive; Sabine is more than capable of surviving something like that."

"Here's something that should cheer you up," smiled Tatyana, seeing Rostov, Guy and Rose entering the breakfast room of the Hilton Hotel in Venice.

"We need some good news," smiled Guy, "you managed to fillet out the Doge Palace corridors?"

"Yes, all clean except in the cell they kept Sergei in," replied the Russian grinning, "finally, I hit gold."

"What do you mean?"

"In the corner was a little disturbance, and when I investigated I found a notebook with names and dates. Tatyana recognises the handwriting as Segovia's, she left us detailed accounts from Giuseppe's office of Mare Nostrum, including detailed accounts of payments to girls' families in Europe who went missing, it's proof."

"Fantastic, what a friend she was," said Tatyana sadly.

"And that's not all; the prisoner in that cell has arrived."

"What do you mean?" asked Guy, as the door opened and a wheelchair-bound man entered.

"Sergei, my God, you're still alive," exclaimed Guy, standing up and running across the room.

"It'll take more than a few bullets and freezing polluted Russian water to finish me off," smiled the Russian. "I've lost the use of my legs but apart from that I'm almost back to normal. I've only just arrived here, heard you were having problems with convictions and remembered Segovia's little insurance policy."

The next few days were spent combing the Doge Palace's grandiose rooms as Monty and Guy went diligently through Lucrezia's files trying to find clues. The Mare Nostrum Empire was thriving, but they struggled to get any further leads on Tutulus, apart from the discovery that it appeared to now be funded from Asia.

"This blueprint for the islands does show she was a talented architect," said Monty, admiring the drawings. "With the help of El Hammill, a match made in hell," replied Guy.

"Now that's interesting," exclaimed Tatyana, "there are many more notations against the Asian rig; it seems to have a special status, look."

"Now in position off Malaysia, what do the symbols mean?" asked Guy.

"No idea, but I'd bet money this is the lead rig and where we'll find this Composer, and possibly Sabine too," said Monty.

"They're dead, Monty," said Tatyana.

"I wouldn't bet on it," replied the Inspector. "It was built in a remote Indonesian shipyard under the highest secrecy of them all, and is now stationed out of national waters."

"It fits with what El Hammill said about centralised codes to control the communications empire; we need to get control of the dammed rigs."

"We can't touch them, "said Monty glumly, "we broke all the international laws when we attacked the Mare Nostrum in the Med, the elite there have complained to the highest authorities and by definition the people on those rigs are very influential. I've been officially pulled off the case, so retirement beckons again."

"So what can we do?" asked Tatyana in frustration.

"Attack them," said Guy, "but not until we are ready with proof. The Chinese archives on La Gomera are key, but first things first, we're going home. The answers lie in the east, it was always so," he said quietly.

Epilogue

Fortaleza La Gomera

Guy looked up and smiled as Rose walked across the lounge to peer out of the panoramic windows. They had been home for three days and were just starting to relax. "There was a point where I never thought we would see this place again," said Guy.

"It did get pretty grim, especially after Kobus' death; I thought I was finished," conceded Rose, taking a seat. "This is the same place we were sat when the invasion started," she smiled, as the door opened and a wheelchair glided in.

"Sergei, how are you?"

"Wheelchair bound from now on, I'll leave the robust stuff to you two."

"I have a huge favour to ask you," said Guy, "with the increase in the threat posed by Tutulus I need to be back out in the field. Will you take over as Chair?"

"You were chosen."

"It's not who I am, Sergei, and I do have a say in my successor, it lies in the gift of the current Chair. Victoria will support me."

"You have a deal, this place is certainly warmer than Russia, plus my beloved Khans' Prophecy is here now and I want to help translate the Chinese documents."

"On one condition," smiled Guy.

"What's that?"

"You loan me your assistant Tatyana, I need a partner in the field."

"What of Rose?"

"Those days are also over for me now," smiled Rose, "as of two days ago. Doctor's orders."

"You don't mean…"

"She does," smiled Guy, "I'm about to become a father."

"Congratulations," said Sergei.

"Tell me again how on earth you survived the attack in Russia," asked Rose.

"They shot me in the stomach but missed major arteries; I fell into the water and drifted for ages until my uncle fished me out, I was lucky he had decided to live on a small barge there after originally hiding the document, and he saw everything and saved my life after El Hammill had gone. From there it was a long period of recovery, mostly unconscious in a coma."

"And the Prophecy?"

"Here it is," he smiled, "it's a bit crumpled but intact."

"Has anyone opened it?"

"No, but now is the time."

"The monks here have language abilities; I hope we have someone who can speak Mongolian."

"It's in an old version of Chinese, actually," said Rose.

"Then we certainly have, I suggest we take a look and then put it into the deepest vaults you have as it will be a target. Hernandez, what do you think?"

"We do have Chinese monks here; a surprising number, actually," replied the ex-policeman, looking down at the document and calling across a Chinese man, who looked at the document with increasing astonishment.

"What is?" asked Guy, as Hernandez introduced them to Ronald Kwang.

"It talks of a great crusade, the Mongols and Catholics, with a common objective to control the known world. It mentions a solution to ensure their legacy that involves their common riches being pooled together in a place chosen by a trusted carrier."

"And that carrier?" asked Guy, knowing what the answer would be

"Admiral Zheng He was tasked by the Chinese Emperor with conquering the world for China, a secret agenda with his artefacts laying out the new order of the Elders."

"This is the common linkage," said Rose as Victoria entered, "between the two leading powers, the Mongols, and the Catholic Christians."

"And Zheng He, our own founding father," said Victoria.

"The Mongols were the supreme pragmatists and the Catholics probably became increasingly concerned by the rise of Islam and Buddhism," reflected Guy.

"It talks of creating a new world order only existing within the current boundaries of man's thinking, with two other documents, the possessor of all three having the key to Kappacca," said Kwang.

"The key?"

"The Papal Covenant, the Prophecy, and the Analects, all hidden by the smokescreen laid by Zheng to camouflage this real activity, I'm guessing," continued Guy.

"The formal joining of Mongol with Catholics," mused Monty.

"Shamanism, actually," said Kwang, looking up. "They had a value system of their own under the heading of Shamanism, with the Khan as God."

"It would have been seriously embarrassing for the Catholics if it got out that they had allied with the Mongols in this way," continued Guy.

"There are other things in here," continued Kwang.

"What?" asked Sergei.

"Predications of what would happen to those interfering, it needs a lot more work as it could easily be open to misinterpretation, and it will take a while."

"It can be worked on in the security of the vaults," replied Guy, looking out of the monastery window. "Confucius' Analects are the key; if we find that we will find the answers."

The next day was bright and sunny, and Guy made his way downstairs to the vaults, contemplating life as a father and how to handle his complex relationship with Rose. This was not helped by the total loss of contact with Lorna, who had made it clear in a strained call that she was taking the cruiser in a different direction and he wasn't welcome to come and see her. He was puzzled but also relieved that she had emerged safe from the kidnap attempt, apparently released by Annaliese, who had, of course, disappeared. The Hidalgo was safely back in St Lucia and Padraig was slowly recovering.

"What is it?" Guy asked as Fernandez confronted him ashen-faced.

"Kwang has gone, along with part of the Prophecy."

"What, how?"

"He left here two hours ago, must have had people outside waiting," replied Hernandez, "he had been here for nearly two years and was thought to be trustworthy."

"A sleeper," spat Sergei, joining them, "now we have lost the dammed secret."

"He might be a sole agent acting alone, we need to seal off the valley," said Guy.

"I fear it's too late for that, I heard a helicopter about an hour ago. I did wonder what it was doing but it came nowhere near the monastery so thought nothing of it," replied Hernandez.

Lesser Antilles

"Well done Lorna, can I complement you on how you handled Tresanton and your cruiser, and even good old Captain Jellico was convincing," smiled Annaliese. "Your help is much appreciated."

"My stepmother."

"Unfortunately, call me a cynic but I don't trust you not to go running to the police about this, she is my insurance policy."

"You promised me that she would be released."

"You know what you have to do," shrugged Annalise, climbing into the helicopter for the short ride back to the rig. She was in charge of the entire project now and revelling in her importance. She had even decided to move the rig near to Saba for old times' sake, so she could then look up at her uncle's Eagle's Nest, which should have been hers, except it had been confiscated by the Dutch. Still, she had something better, her own empire, only troubled occasionally by the visit of the Composer in her super cruiser. Now all she needed was to choose herself a husband, as the breeding programme was now far more female-friendly. She had received permission to choose her own partner and had Helmut lapping at her feet, which would make sure she kept control.

Lorna watched disconsolately as the helicopter rose into the sky, her beloved cruiser being used for the very same thing as her father Oleson had planned. It was almost unbearable, as unbearable indeed as the fact that she herself was pregnant.

Gibraltar

The rock looked down on the myriad of ships and boats passing by, and on board one particular boat the Composer smiled to herself. It was ironic that such an iconic rock should hold so many secrets known only to a few. One such secret was dear Sabine's diamonds, so carefully hidden here and now in her possession. It was a shame that Sabine had been killed, but she was collateral damage, a sad fact of war. Sabine had saved the redhead's life after the events of the Seychelles, but now she was no longer useful and was therefore expendable. The clash in Grenada had gone as predicted and now the Composer ruled supreme, with one caveat; there was another sixth and secret member of the Quintet, which was properly and more accurately called the Hexad, a member based in Asia who had been vital to the Composer's success.

She signalled to her colleague Jason Star and strode ashore, greeted and hailed by the many at the club. They drove in her luxurious Range Rover around to the other side of the rock, where she was taken through the hidden entrance into the cave. Inside, she was shown past where Sabine had been hidden a year ago and through to where a new batch of girls were being processed. She went past them and down to the most secret part, known only to her most trusted aide Dominic, an ex SAS man with impeccable credentials, who met her there.

"The tunnel is navigable."

"I've just been across and brought the latest contingent," smiled Dominic.

"Excellent, it's good to know we have our own inviolable link to Africa and onwards to Asia ready for the new phase of Mare Nostrum. A phase that will take the breeding programme to its logical conclusion, humans treated like horses; after all, why not breed and re-breed to get the highest possible pedigree? There was no law against it in her world of nations beyond boundaries."

"The Maestro will be pleased everything is ready, it's time to initiate the final phase; Zheng He would be turning in his grave if he knew what they had planned now. Incidentally, Dominic, you can call me by my Christian name, it is time."

"Thank you, Gudrun, it is a real honour," he smiled.

Alishan - Yushan National Park - Taiwan

The tall Asian man exuded authority and confidence as he surveyed the lush meadow below him. Not for nothing had the Portuguese explorers called Taiwan Formosa, the beautiful island, and he felt privileged to call it home, although he hadn't been born there. He went indoors and shook off the light raindrops before activating his console.

"You are safe and well, Gudrun."

"Very well."

"Good, we are on schedule despite the odd blips, the two strongest economies will underpin our next steps, are the facilities ready on the rigs?"

"Your headquartered rig in Malaysia is ready and I'm pleased to report that Annaliese has recovered the situation in the Caribbean."

"What of Kappacca?"

"The Confucius Analects are proving to be challenging but I can confirm we have possession now of the other two."

"Excellent, we are now ready for the final stages; first, though, take care of the Elders once and for all."

"Of course," replied Gudrun as she looked out across the Atlantic. "May I call you by your first name?"

"Of course, Jainyu it is from now on. It means the building of the universe; very appropriate, don't you think?"

"Very, one other point of curiosity, the word Tutulus means eight in life patterns, what's the relevance?"

"Eight is the lucky number in China, as you know with the Beijing Olympics, and eight life patterns mean specifically that there are two new members to be involved in our final push to glory."

Acknowledgements

HG Wells

The idea he championed the most vociferously was that of a World State, a global technocratic society without national boundaries. He was also clear that racial purity was a dangerous nonsense as 'all races are more or less mixed'.

I have taken liberties with the reputations of the Nietzsche's, Friedrich in particular, as he reportedly never had a son, and certainly not one who was involved in the First World War. The story of Germania, though, is very true, and is brilliantly told by Ben Macintyre in **'Forgotten Fatherland'**

About the Author

Driven by his deep interest in International History and Politics David wrote his first fictional book 'Bahamian Rhapsody' published in 2009. Written as part of a trilogy [The History Detective series] it featured his trademark deep research and multi layed story lines.

Working in a top international executive role that involved a great deal of global travel - to Asia in 
particular and America – he was to meet many types of businesses in developing countries that have been the inspiration for setting his books in the emerging industrial world and particularly in China.

"I have always wanted to write from my earliest days. Having exhausted the stocks of certain writers, I felt that I could do better and although my travels and background in History and Politics provide the fuel for my writing, I find that it's the characters themselves who drive the books to fruition – a process I enjoy immensely!"

Following the successful publication in China of the second book in the trilogy Chasing Columbus, the final part 'Khans Legacy' was published in 2013.

Sadly before completing the History Creator Series of which Beyond Nations is the first part David Died in February 2017 after a short illness.